Praise for author Michael B. Koep's
PART ONE OF THE NEWIRTH MYTHOLOGY

THE INVASION OF HEAVEN

"Must read for the summer! It's part adventure, part fantasy, a bit of mystery, and all fun."

—*Times Weekly*

"Sure to be on the shelves with Tolkien, Gaiman and others for a very long time."

—*Paper Safari Reviews*

"It is nice to have an author come up with a new concept when it comes to fiction. And Koep has done just that."
—*Reading Is A Way Of Life BLOG-USA*

"If *The Stand* and the *DaVinci Code* had a baby. Smart and the language is beautiful. 12 out of 10 stars!"

"Not only does Koep have a beautiful writing style and a flare for language—the book resurrects the imponderables of youth, bringing them yet again into the forefront of thought. That is a very good thing, indeed."

"The most unique book I've read all year--wholly original."

"Full of tricks, turns and slight of hand. A roller coaster ride right from the beginning."

—*Goodreads Reviews*

"Masterfully creative!"

—*Nspire Magazine*

"Wow, just WOW! This is the best novel in all the thrillers and paranormal romance novels I have read in a year!"

"I can honestly say that the ending shocked me. I have not seen a twist like the one in this book since the movie *The Sixth Sense*. That alone makes this a 5 Star book for me."

"I highly recommend this book to lovers of suspense, thrillers, and paranormal!"

"This book is totally WOW! A roller-coaster ride right from the beginning!"

"It's almost difficult to put into words how strongly this book affected me. It is filled with surprises, turns, twists and honestly, the end blew me away."

"Grabs you from page one, couldn't put it down!"

"If you enjoy a touch of the supernatural and art mysteries, then you will enjoy this book. Great Read."

"A remarkably inventive story told in an imaginative way. A story within a story. Looking forward to reading more in this series."

—*Netgalley Reviews*

FIVE STAR REVIEWS
from
Readers' Favorite

"The writing is powerful, filled with descriptions that immerse the reader in the action, it offers clear and sweeping visuals, and allow the reader to easily get into the beautiful setting."

"Trust me, you will want to get in on the ground floor of this series because people are going to be talking about it."

"This is the kind of book that one finishes and has to take a walk afterward, trying to feel the air, to touch things, to talk to the neighbor, just to ensure one isn't still in a dream."

"*The Invasion of Heaven* is the fruit of genius, of rich imagination, and sheer madness. Readers will love every page of this engaging story."

—*Readers' Favorite Reviews*

PART TWO

THE NEWIRTH MYTHOLOGY

LEAVES OF FIRE

MICHAEL B. KOEP

The Newirth Mythology, Part Two, Leaves of Fire
is a work of fiction. Names, characters, places and incidents are either used
fictitiously, are products of the author's imagination, or are brought on by an
ancient muse. Any resemblance to actual events, persons, living or dead, gods,
immortals or other is entirely coincidental.
~ *Tunow plecom cer* ~

www.WillDreamlyArts.com
www.MichaelBKoep.com

FIRST MASS MARKET PAPERBACK EDITION
Published by **Will Dreamly Arts**
Cover art, maps and text illustrations by Michael B. Koep
Back cover portrait by Brady Campbell
The Newirth Mythology, Part Two, Leaves of Fire
is also available in EBook and audio formats.

For information regarding special discounts for bulk purchases,
please call: 208-930-0114

ISBN:978-0-9976234-1-3

Library of Congress Cataloging-in-Publication Data has been applied for.

For Michael Scott

Ascott

Mother's
leaves

William's Map

My journey from home to London.
When I was a boy
1338

Strofford Manor
Waltham
North
gallows
London
Albion's House
Thames

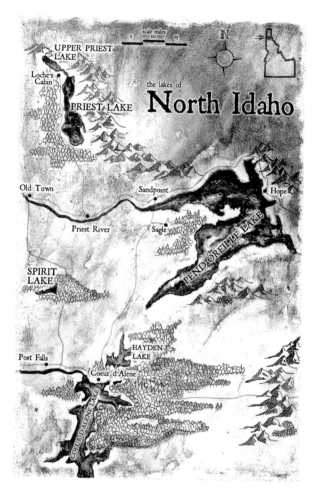

LAKE COMO

LAKE ISEO

LAKE GARDA

Venice

Milan

Verona

Padua

ADRIATIC SEA

N

scale miles
20   40   60

Northern Italy

Monterosso

La Spezia

LIGURIAN
SEA

Pisa

Florence

Synopsis

This is the second part of THE NEWIRTH MYTHOLOGY.

The first part, *The Invasion of Heaven,* tells of how Loche Newirth discovers that his mentor, criminal psychologist Marcus Rearden, is a murderer, and how Loche journals an imaginative and mythical story to capture him. It also tells of Loche's terrifying and supernatural incident writing the tale, and how his words have altered very fabric of existence. Throughout his narrative, Loche begs the question, *"This is really happening, isn't it?"*

In a desperate search to find Loche, Dr. Marcus Rearden is the first to discover and read the chronicle.

The journal portrays Loche, and painter Basil Fenn as brothers and artists with the ability, through their art, to open dangerous pathways between this life and the Hereafter. Basil's paintings and Loche's writings are of great interest to an ancient society of immortals called the *Orathom Wis,* whose mission is to guard the doors between this life and the next and prevent the crossing of divine spirits into our world. One of that order, William Greenhame, had been keeping a secret watch over the two and protecting them since they were children.

Another immortal, Albion Ravistelle, succeeds in abducting Loche, Loche's family and Basil to Italy and proposes that by sharing Basil's paintings with the world they could cure mental illness, and the darker elements of the human condition. The brothers discover that Albion's intention is instead to contaminate and destroy the afterlife with human fallibility, sin and imperfection.

At the intimation of Loche, Basil takes his own life to stop the invasion of Heaven and protect the natural order of existence. His death begins a war between the *Orathom*

Wis and Albion Ravistelle's forces. The journal ends with Loche's life falling further into the surreal when he learns that the immortal William Greenhame is his father. He also discovers that his wife, Helen, has betrayed him for the love of Albion Ravistelle.

Once Marcus Rearden completes reading the journal he tests the story's validity by contacting a character within the narrative, the love of Loche Newirth, Julia Iris. When she joins Rearden on a journey to find Loche, she also reads the incredible events depicted in the journal. Convinced the afterlife exists, that an immortal order of men and women protect it, and the fate of mankind hangs in the balance, both Rearden and Julia are enmeshed in Loche's snare. During the final confrontation between Rearden and Loche, Julia is mortally wounded, Rearden's crime is exposed and he is arrested. Soon after, Loche meets the real life characters from out of his imagination: William Greenhame, Samuel Lifeson and Corey Thomas, and he is forced to come to terms with the anomalous and supernatural quality of his writing. *The Invasion of Heaven* concludes with the discovery that Julia Iris is an immortal.

This second part, *Leaves of Fire,* now tells of how Loche's journal has inadvertently created lives, changed history and made myths and their characters, real.

And it grew both day and night.
Till it bore an apple bright.
And my foe beheld it shine,
And he knew that it was mine.
     WILLIAM BLAKE

The Newirth Mythology

part two of three

Leaves of Fire

Fated

November 3, this year.
Coeur d'Alene, Idaho, USA

Questions. Questions. Questions. Who is this man with all of the questions? There, on the other side of the glass. He is not from around here. An accent? Italian? Weird. The man's chocolate brown fedora sits upon the linoleum counter and the the red telephone is pressed to his ear. *"Did you really work with murderers? With all that you've seen and heard from these monsters, do you have nightmares? Do you sleep? What about art? Do you like art, Dr. Rearden?"*

Marcus Rearden answers. The visitor listens with focused and bedazzled interest. *What was his name again?* Each time Rearden is about to ask, another perfectly phrased question chants into his ear: *"How have you managed your fame? Your successes? What is it like to be Dr. Marcus Rearden?"*

What is it like to be Marcus Rearden?

The old psychologist stops the questions with an abrupt raising of his hand. "I am incarcerated you son of a bitch! *That* is what it is like to be me. And who in the hell are you again? What's your name?"

The visitor stares.

"I see. I get it. You must be the resident shrink," Marcus sneers. "You're the poor bastard that was sent here to learn if I'm crazy as a shit house rat? The local jailor's head doc, eh?"

"Not exactly," the man answers. "In fact, I would prefer if you were, *indeed*, as you say, *crazy*."

Rearden laughs and leans toward the glass, "Well *crazy* I'm not. And if there's one thing that I can't stand it's some young, fifty-something shrink trying to analyze *my* mental state. Mine, of all people. Do you have any idea who I am?" Marcus waits for a response that does not come. "Listen, I know your job here is a piece of shit —here in this little town. Oh I've dealt with your pithy type on many occasions." He settles back into the metal chair and relaxes a bit. "The thing I can't seem to understand about your position is how you can stomach this level of our practice. How do you keep coming in to work each day? To the city jail house? How can that be an uplifting profession? Aren't your usual customers meth users, and wife abusers? Backward baseball cap, tattooed, Blue Ribbon drinking drunk drivers that like to wrestle with each other? My god man, that must get terribly tedious. Bottom feeders, day in, day out. How do you keep going?"

The visitor grins.

Rearden feels a weird sensation, as if the grin is malevolent. During his career he had seen such twisted, leering smiles before. The psychologist narrows his eyes and he begins to scrutinize this person—this visitor suddenly seeming to be something more than a local correctional psychologist. Rearden keeps eye contact. His professional experience makes the subtle confrontation easy for him. *What is it lurking behind that smile? That weird smile.* Rearden knew weird. He knew to trust his gut when weird happened along.

"You impress me," the visitor says finally, his grin fading, then reappearing in his eyes. "I was told that you were quite potent in your vocation. It is easy to see why you've found success. And so, too, how you have become what you have longed to cure."

"Who the fuck are you?"

"What if I were to tell you that I have found a way to rectify the horrors of the human condition. Fear. Pain. Crazy. What if I were to share that remedy with you?"

Rearden's eyes widen. The words are familiar as if from out of Loche Newirth's journal. He feels himself blanch—an anxious release of adrenaline. He marks his tone with apathy. "Let's just say that I have a former colleague that would love to know of it."

The weird grin appears again. "Ah, yes. I would very much like to know more about this colleague of yours. I presume you're speaking of Dr. Loche Newirth?" Rearden's eyes flit slightly at Loche's naming. He knows the staring match has been won by his opponent.

"Dr. Rearden, I am Ravistelle. Albion Ravistelle. I am the Director of the European Mental Health League. I would very much like to learn more about your former student."

And it comes to Marcus Rearden in a flash—the journal—as if he, himself, was standing before the artist Basil Fenn at the Uffizi—when Basil Fenn blew his brains out—the way the journal described the event. Rearden's recent past screeches through his soul: the journal, Julia Iris and the treacherous drive through the snow to find Loche. Rearden sees his wife's pale face—terror is frozen there. Vengeance. Yes. It was his former student, Loche Newirth that had caused it all—all this fear—this pain—this crazy. Rearden feels a grin ooze onto his face. He imagines the smile must look—weird. *Fate has not forgotten me*, Rearden thought. *Vengeance is fated.*

He brings his face near to the glass. The heat of his words fog on the pane, "What do you want to know?"

William of Leaves

April, 1338
the village of Ascott-under-Wychwood, England

Young William watched as his mother's fingers transformed to long wisps of green stems. They grew from her hands like yarn flung from a loom. Tiny purple and gold flowers burst from the vines filling the hovel with a moist, sweet scent. The slender shoots weaved across the floor, along the walls and over the small bed where Simon the Thatcher, his wife Margaret and their two daughters lay in a deadly fever. Their faces were bloodless, thin and hollowed by days without food.

Geraldine of Leaves stood in the center of the small room, her arms outstretched and her face raised to the thatched ceiling. Her eyes were closed, and she chanted a soft, rhyming spell. William watched tendrils climb and tangle. The room became a forest glade with his mother as the axis.

She had told William that she learned how to do this when she was a little girl—William's age, perhaps—six-summers. It was her mother that taught her about the one Mother. The Earth Mother was where all love, hope and healing came from. There was only one seedling—one seed that brought all green, and healing and goodness to the earth—and if it died, so too would its fruits and the works of its healing.

Both the seed and his mother were the same thing, at least that was how William understood it. And he loved it when she would begin to speak the words—words he found difficult to catch for they somehow sounded like water rushing over stones, or wind in the tall, bowing grass. And he loved it even more when she would use the

Craft—when her fingers would grow and sprout like ivy. He felt the air tingle all around him—and a delightful chill ran along his skin as he watched her.

His little fingers pinched at a single thin stem spiraling around his foot, and he broke it off. It was not quite as long as his forearm. He coiled it and tucked it into his tunic.

It was when Simon the Thatcher stirred that Geraldine's words fell away. The man labored his head from the pillow and saw his bed, and his seemingly dead family beside covered in moving vines and bursting flowers. He marveled. His heavy eyes blinked at the sight. "Have I gone?" he asked. Loose stones rattled in his lungs. "Am I in the grave, below the ground? Does the earth take me in?"

Geraldine began to chant again.

The man asked softly, "Geraldine? Is that you? What is happening, Geraldine?" Simon then lowered his head back and stared at the ceiling. "I am either dead or the sweating sickness is leaving me, for the pain departs. I feel—I feel the winter is passing."

Geraldine's voice silenced. Her arms dropped to her sides. The vines, the lush leaves and blossoms vanished. There was still sweetness in the air, like after a spring rain. William watched the sleeping family. One by one they opened their eyes. Simon sat up again, turned himself out of the blankets and placed his bare feet on the dirt floor. His face was coloring. He reached over and touched the foreheads of his wife and daughters. Joy and tears filled his eyes.

He looked up at Geraldine. She stood smiling at him. "I had the strangest dream," he said to her. "I dreamt that the earth was pulling me to its bosom. Burying me, and at the same time, lifting me skyward. The room was a forest of roots and vines."

"Fevers will make one see things, it is true," Geraldine replied. "Sometimes the plants and herbs can bring a strange reverie—from out of darkness they seek light. That is the path to life. All we need is here, soil and seed, sun and rain—fire and smoke, laughter, pain. We do not die, we dream. We only dream." She lifted a small wood cup from a steaming pot of water. "Let this cool, then drink. Make sure each of you drink it until it is gone. Heed no more thoughts of the grave."

Helen

Los Angeles, June 26, 1972
The Hyatt Continental House, Sunset Strip

I have arrived.

Helen Craven considered the statement with a giddy, champagne-buzzed smile. She was not yet too drunk to walk, luckily, and the quick fingernail scoop of blow whiffed with a droplet of 1966 Dom Perignon and a light cherry snuff that some giddy English woman had gracefully administered on the elevator ride up gave her feet the confidence she needed—as well as increasing her smile to climactic, euphoric proportions. She felt elegant. Everything was bright. Colors were lush. And the raging echoes of the band's performance at the LA Forum were still singing in her ears—ringing as if the very air surrounding her chimed and tingled with joy, electric youth and godlike beauty.

Top floor.

"Here we are darling," the man said. His name was Richard. He was English, too. A good looking guy, maybe ten or fifteen years older.

She had met Richard just a few hours ago, backstage with the band's manager, dark eyed, goateed, Peter, a massive hulk of a man. At their introduction, she held out her hand, and Peter's smile flashed. She noted something sinister. Something powerful. As it should be, she thought, for if he was indeed the caretaker of the gods she had witnessed on stage tonight, the man must have a mighty swing, with a power that could outweigh any hammer of heaven. And the man had weight, without a doubt. Helen Craven looked at how tiny her hand was in his—her bare, rail-thin braceleted arms reaching into

Peter's well-fed heft and meaty grasp. He, too, used the word, "*Darling*," and nodded to Richard. Again, that smile laced with cherry powder.

Helen Craven, or as she was known on the Strip, *Helen Storm*, was not new to the reality and language behind such smiles. After all, she was fourteen. She wasn't really, but for some reason, fourteen was a number Richard liked.

She'd had some backstage experiences. Seven that she could recall. But the last time she was at the Hyatt Continental on the Sunset Strip was with the drummer for Green Apple—a B-level British band that was warming up for T-Rex a couple of months ago—his name was Terry, and he was beautiful. Glitter and silk and sex. Her first time. And Miss Storm learned quickly the code that came with the lifestyle—most of its elaborate constitution communicated with a simple *smile*.

And Helen Storm was ear to ear. Her thin ivory chiffon tightly crisscrossed over her heart and tiny breasts, her black hair dancing along pale shoulders, and the sparkling of glitter hazed eyes, she strode beside Richard like a sacrificial bride, arrayed for the hands of a god—a god that waited for her in the penthouse suite, room number 1400. He was a guitar player. She heard Richard call him Pagey. His real name was Jimmy.

"Now do us all a favor, will you, love?" Richard said quietly as they approached the door, "as I said before, he's expecting someone else, and we can't seem to find her just now, but we will, so until then, please spend a little time with Jim. And do enjoy yourself, yeah?" Helen nodded, suddenly nervous. She couldn't think of what to say. She just smiled at him. "I knew you would be perfect for this. And have fun. Jim is truly a lovely man." With that he knocked on the door, waited a moment and then opened it for her to enter.

The door shut behind her and she stood with her back pressed to it. The large room was lit with several candles. The windows were open and the soft hush of the Strip traffic wafted through the suite. Back in the dark, in the far corner, Helen could make out a seated form—silhouetted—a fedora on his head and his hand atop a long cane. She could not see an expression, but she imagined that his eyes sparked faintly like jewels in the shadows. Helen would never forget the sight, the moment, the high. *I have arrived.* Quietly, almost in harmony with her ringing thoughts, with a quality of calm and welcome came the man's voice. Though it wasn't exactly what Helen wanted to hear:

"Hello, *Lori.* What took you so long?"

Helen held her breath. Despite all of the smiles, and her incredible fortune (standing in Jimmy Page's hotel suite, for God's sake), she knew that her response to the question would either invite an extended stay, or a cold dismissal.

Richard had explained it plainly enough: "Jimmy has a fancy for a model named Lori and we've been working on arranging a meeting, but she is delayed. So until she arrives, please keep him occupied. You and she look alike, and that should appease him. Well, not really, *alike.* But you're the same age, at least." *Alike enough from a distance or from across a candle lit room,* Helen mused. She had seen pictures of Lori, and thought that she may have even met her once at the Rainbow. Either way, Helen believed herself to be much prettier and certainly luckier (again, she was standing in Jimmy Page's hotel suite for God's sake), and the model Lori was not. But none of that helped her come up with a response to Jim's lingering question: *what took you so long?* Then she heard words coming out of her mouth:

"*I have arrived.*" She felt a rush when the sound of the statement lilted in her voice. It sounded sexy and real. She trained her eyes on the seated form across the room. She sensed him smile.

"And so you have. Since I saw your face, I've thought of nothing else," he said leaning slightly forward. "I've waited for you."

Again, Helen suspended her breathing. What now? She lowered her gaze and looked at her long legs, her ice-blue wrap of a skirt and her bare stomach. How did she get here? What did she want? Just hours ago she was let in backstage—and that was a dream come true—admission into the mysterious and hypnotic world of *Led Zeppelin*—but now to be within reach of Jimmy Page's bed, his touch, his magic, was all too much suddenly. To think that her beauty and her need to be needed brought her here, and the power of that yearning could actually bring a god to his knees. The scent of cherry snuff was fading. But replacing its sweetness was her confidence made up of things wholly pure and simple: her eyes, her petite body, the curved line of her hips and the earnest hope in her eyes. Her heart. The way she could make him feel like a god, and how he could do the same for her—if only to say the right thing. The right prayer.

I've waited for you, he had said.

Helen took three strides forward into the candlelit room. She stopped and rooted her feet firmly, feeling a sudden invincible wave crash through her. She assured him quietly, "Yes—and now I am here. My name is Helen Storm. I am all yours," she said.

Loche, Julia and William

November 3, this year: Verona, Italy

Julia Iris' quiet voice begins to recite a poem. Loche Newirth stares at her—his five-year-old son Edwin is asleep in her lap.

Now, find the single star
And watch it blink,
Until the mountains fade
And you to sleep.

Above the deep blue sea?
Just watch it sink.
When sky and water join,
Sail off to sleep.

It hides sometimes in trees
Like owl eyes wink,
It soon will fly away
Take wing, you. Sleep.

High over desert sands
Right where you think.
Through snow and rain and skies
Of clouds, so sleep.

If there's no sky above
If all is black as ink,
   There's light—
   Oh yes, there's light indeed.
   Just blink and see it
   In my eyes,
   Where I will always keep you bright
   My single star,
   It's time to sleep. It's time to sleep.

The room is silent now save the sound of traffic below.

"Why does that poem sound familiar to me?" Loche asks.

Julia smiles at him, her fingers threading through Edwin's hair. "I wonder if it was *you* that wrote it," she said. "As you've written me. Just as you've written William, Helen. . . *history*."

"I don't remember writing it," Loche says.

Across the room, William Greenhame sighs, "It is no matter."

Julia drops her gaze to Edwin, now deep in dreams. Loche stares at the two of them. Edwin is breathing low. They are holding hands. Julia's face is lit with the gold of the day's end. Her eyes are weary, red and sad. On the table beside her is the glass of wine that she had been given when she arrived, two hours ago, and she has not yet finished it. The crushing realities of the last few days have been hard on her. Sleep has been impossible. Loche understands.

He can see her mouthing the rhyme again, attempting her usual trick for sleep, her father's poem: *Find the single star and watch it blink, until the mountain fades and you to sleep.* Her father used to whisper it into her ear —when she could not drift off—or would not. It had always seemed to work.

How do I know this? Loche wonders suddenly, *did she share this story of her father with me?* He cannot answer himself with certainty. *She knows the stars. The constellations—all because of her father's rhyme—so she could find her way home.* "Just see the star and think of nothing else," her father had said. "Let everything fall away and sigh. The mountain below will turn from blue to purple and finally to sky. All the mountains eventually fade into the sky. It's okay. It's okay," he would say.

Julia smiles. And Loche sees it—and he is better for it.

"You alright?" Loche asks.

Julia turns to him. "I don't know," she says. "Did you write the poem? My father's poem?"

"Wondrous strange," William Greenhame says.

"No," Loche says, "I mean, I don't think so. But it is familiar to me somehow. All I know is that I wrote about you for the first time at my cabin at Priest Lake. Though, I've dreamt of you my whole life. I seem to remember new things about you each moment. It is hard to explain."

"Like what?"

"Like your father's rhyme. The little song to help you sleep?"

Julia is transfixed. "I've never shared that with you," she says.

"No," Loche answers. "But I know of it, somehow. It just came to me, just now."

"Can you read my mind, or something?"

Loche shakes his head, "No. Not that I know of."

"Perhaps," William interjects, "as the Author, the Poet, you have meditated long on the very essence of Julia whilst you wrote her. Whilst you created her. Oh, how the mind wanders when we are in the throes of making. We uncover subtlety and potent substance with the penning of a single heart crossing word."

Loche closes his eyes and attempts to return his memory to his desk at Priest Lake. The pooling ink, the cramp in his hand, and the whirling rage within him. When he conceived of Julia, did he know her past? Did he write it in his thoughts to help with her rendering?

"I can't—I can't," Julia begins to rub her eyes and shake her head in frustration. "I don't get it. How can any of this be real?"

Loche reaches to her. She senses him and pulls away. "And I," she forces a whisper, "I'm like William—I am like Samuel and George? I can't die? Is that it?"

From across the room William Greenhame chants in answer, and to himself: *"Ithic veli agtig."*

Without moving his eyes from Julia, Loche translates the Elliqui phrase: "Why does my death delay?"

He sees her fingers brush across her stomach. Three days ago, Dr. Marcus Rearden's gun went off during a struggle and a bullet struck her in the abdomen. She woke at Loche's cabin—there was a ring of white foam around the fatal wound, and then, nothing. Healed. Since the terrible event—miracle—she must have checked and rechecked her stomach every few minutes. Searching for a scar she would never find, save in memory.

She struggles to conjure her father's eyes. The star glinting there.

Leonaie

November 3, this year,
Coeur d'Alene, Idaho, USA

Moonladder

Half way up the ladder,
Ladder to the moon,
She turns to me and says:
> *"Here I am.*
> *Do not be afraid."*
>> *Do my eyes*
>> *Give away my hiding place,*
>> *These shadows in my face?*
>> *Here beneath the mirror moonlight,*
>> *Can you see into my shell?*
>> *Here upon this rung*
>> *Where my grip is slipping?*

She wraps her arms around me,
Presses her fingers to my skin.
And there below,
Is the sea. The sea skimmed with stars.
Oh the sea.
>> *How did we raise this ladder*
>> *From under that heavy husk*
>> *Of water, waves and still, empty space?*
>> *And where are we off to now,*
>> *Climbing together*
>> *Out of the grave deep,*
>> *Upon this wooden, swaying ladder?*
>> *Up and up.*

> *"Here I am.*
> *Do not be afraid."*
>> *What are the chances of one more step?*
>> *Of five or ten?*
>> *Can you climb, my darling?*
>> *The ladder will reach.*

Leonaie Echelle, eyes green, gold and grey
Pulls me in closer and I hear her say:

"It is not the moon that I am climbing to
Nor the stars pinned to the sky.
Not back down to those black waves
Speckled with the hovering face of heaven.
No,
I will be the moon.
I will be the stars.
I am no longer an empty shell,
Come from the sea filled with the sound of the void.
    If it is the moon you are climbing to
    Or the stars you are trying to reach,
    Here I am.
    Here I am."

—Samuel Lifeson, 1953

Leonaie Echelle folds the poem back into its envelope and holds it upon her lap. She stares at it for a few moments and considers just how the paper has yellowed over the years. The address scrawled across its face is still crisp and legible, as is the return address—all in Samuel Lifeson's distinct hand writing: little hooked loops, and winged fringes on the *S* and the *L*. She places the envelope beside the lamp. Leonaie takes her reading glasses off, and lets them hang by the cord around her neck. She smiles at how decorative the envelope looks combined with the gilded framed portrait of her and her husband, Charles (twenty-eight years ago), an antique pen upon its olive velvet box that her mother had given her (forty years ago), a pair of baby shoes (her son's, who is now 63, or 64?), and the lamp she bought when she was just a girl in France. Green, gold and grey glass beads hung from thin iron arms—a stained glass shade—a black base.

Then, curiously, there is a small sticky note on the table before the picture frame. She hadn't noticed it before, or perhaps she did, she isn't sure. She pulls it from the table top and lifts her glasses to read it. It is written in her handwriting. It reads:

November 3, Samuel is coming at 3.

Don't forget.
3pm

Her heart leaps. *What day is it?* She stands up from the bed, as quickly as her body allows, and grasping her cane she hobbles over to her small kitchenette to get her cell phone. *Damn things*, she thinks. Her son bought it for her, and she can rarely remember how to use it. But she loves it as a time piece. One press of a button and it appears, the true reminder—the real date—the real time:

2:47pm
November 3

Another leap of the heart. Setting the phone down her hands rise immediately to her hair. *Up or down*, she wonders. She has always been fickle about her hair. Leonaie moves a couple of steps to the mirror beside the door and studies her face. Her hair is long and silver white, still thick. The wrinkles along her cheeks and forehead are bothersome and infuriating. She is surprised every time the mirror reveals them to her. Were these new wrinkles around her eyes there yesterday? Not that she can recall. And the pink pouches of skin below her eyes— where did those come from, for God's sake? *Am I really ninety-four?* Leonaie rubs gently, but the pockets remain, and she sighs. Then, she catches a spark of light. Her eyes are gold today, more gold than green, and that is a good sign. Leonaie's eyes are hazel: green, gold and grey, and the colors would shift back and forth from time to time. There is one thing that never changed about her eyes, they are always lit as if from behind, illuminated and piercing, like the face of the sun on a forest stream.

She knows the person behind those eyes, and quickly forgets the imperfections, forgets the pain in her right hip, forgets the wrinkles and the long years that put them there. She feels better and gives herself a little wink. The reflection in the mirror smiles her devious little smile right back.

Leonaie turns, limps back to the bedside and notices the picture frame of her and her husband, Charles, again, and the yellowed envelope that contains a letter. Or was it a poem? *That shouldn't be out on the table*, she thinks and reaches over to the envelope, slides her fingers inside and pulls out a worn piece of parchment. Unfolding it, a sticky note catches her attention, in the direct center of the bedside table. Something is scrawled on it. She plucks it up, places her glasses on her nose and reads:

November 3, Samuel is coming at 3.

Don't forget.

3pm

Her heart leaps. She rises toward her cell phone upon the kitchen counter. *Damn thing.* She presses her favorite button on the phone and there appears what she needs:

2:53pm

November 3

That's today. She leans over to the mirror and wonders if she should wear her hair up or down.

"Leonaie?" comes a voice and a light knocking at the door.

Leonaie doesn't answer but instead stares deeper into the glass and those damned wrinkles.

"Leonaie?" says Olivia Langley. Her bright smile, Irish green eyes and deep red hair are all peeking in from the door way. "Do you remember what today is, Leonaie?"

"How did I get this old so quickly?" Leonaie asks, her gaze still points into the grooves and lines along her cheeks and brow. "And look at the suitcases under my eyes, for God's sake. What's become of me?"

Olivia steps into the room and joins Leonaie in the mirror. Olivia watches the old woman struggle to erase the lines—press the weary years away—the envelope still in her hand. "We should put that away, don't you think?"

Leonaie stops and stares at the envelope and the sticky note. "You're right," she agrees. "Would you put it back in the book? Oh and close the door, won't you dear?"

"Sure," Olivia says. She closes the door. Taking the envelope she crosses the room and places it back inside

Leonaie's worn copy of The Complete Works of William Shakespeare—at page 713, at *All's Well That Ends Well.* The sticky note she crumples and tosses into the waste basket.

"Hair up or down?" Olivia asks.

"I don't know. What do you think?"

Gathering the thick hair in her hands, Olivia lifts it up over Leonaie's head and lets dangle a few locks. The spirals shine beside Leonaie's cheeks. "Oh, I like that," The old woman says. "Let's do that." Olivia pulls a thin stick from out of drawer, threads and twists it into the coil letting fall a funneling stream, spilling down like silver water from a fountain.

"At least my eyes look the same."

"That they do," Olivia agrees. "You look beautiful."

"Oh dear, that's sweet of you. Sweet dear."

"It's almost three, Leonaie."

"Yes," she replies, "I almost forgot. It's a good thing I wrote that note—otherwise, I may have."

"I wouldn't have let you forget. Now do I get to meet him this time?"

Leonaie wrinkles her nose, "Have you not met him yet?"

Olivia shakes her head. "No. I know that he comes every week, but. . ." She pauses. "But hopefully I will today." Leonaie smiles. She knows that Olivia is lying. Playing along. She knew Olivia was told to entertain the old lady's notion of the mysterious Samuel. Leonaie's imaginative promptings—it helped Leonaie, and she loved Olivia for that. But, for what it is worth, Leonaie thought Olivia loved the story—a poet writing to his beloved—the handsome Samuel is still alive and holding on to some kind of unrequited love—was never letting go —was always just one visit away.

"And Mr. Lifeson and I would love to have coffee in the courtyard, if you can manage it. We met in a courtyard, you know."

Olivia nods. She'd heard the story a hundred plus times, ever since Leonaie was admitted to the

Greenhavens Community, some three years ago. "And I know this sounds ridiculous, but there was this ladder leaning against a tree—an apple tree—and when I first saw him I was so nervous I climbed up that ladder and pretended to pick apples."

"And when he saw you," Olivia picks up the story, "he stopped at the base of the ladder and asked you, now what was it, 'Are you picking apples for a pie?'"

"That's right," Leonaie cuts in, "and I took one look at him and my God, I knew he was the one. Then I looked down over my arm, arched my back a little bit—let my little butt stick out just a tickle, and I said to him: 'My apple pie would make you want to marry me.'" Leonaie laughed a pure, singing laugh. "Can you believe that? Oh dear. . . so naughty."

Olivia laughs. Leonaie always made her laugh. "You're bad."

"In the best way," Leonaie adds.

The two women's faces are both framed in the mirror —both are smiling. Then slowly, as if some regret crosses Leonaie's thought, her smile fades and her eyes squint slightly. "But," Leonaie sighs, "I was already married." Olivia's expression falls away, too, watching her. They are both searching their reflections. Leonaie seeking some way to return to that time, to do it all again, only this time, the right way. Olivia trying to imprint the old woman's longing upon her own spirit—as a lesson—as a warning. "Live your life, darling, like there's no tomorrow," Leonaie says, her eyes flitting to Olivia's, "because there isn't a tomorrow. Have no fear, look here." Leonaie fixes her eyes to Olivia's—the old woman struggling to feed her young friend food that only she can taste.

Smoke

April, 1338,
the village of Ascott-under-Wychwood, England

"Are we to church, Mama?" William asked. Geraldine closed the door to the Thatcher's house and turned toward the lane leading to the village abbey. She took William's hand in hers.

"Yes, to see Father," she said.

"Then we go home, Mama?"

"Then we go home."

"And to work, then?"

"Yes."

The two walked along in silence. It was cold. Geraldine stopped suddenly and looked at the sky. William looked, too. Light was fading, though it couldn't be much past midday. Certainly well before Vespers. Then William could smell smoke. His mother's grasp tightened upon his hand as she began to walk again. This time a bit quicker.

Before entering into the nave, William cried, "Look, Mama, snow." He turned his palm out to catch some of the falling flakes. Its descent was slow, hanging, almost weightless. When it touched William's hand and his upraised face, it was not cold. Instead, it was like dust, and it smeared black and grey across his skin.

"That's not snow. It is ash," his mother said. "Come, get you inside." Black clouds of smoke billowed over the sun.

Once inside, Geraldine crossed herself, William did the same, and they both called out, "Father! Father! Are you here?"

"Yes, my dears, I am," came Father Radulphus Grenehamer's voice. William ran up the aisle and into the arms of the priest. "Hello, my little one. And hello, Geraldine," he said.

"Good afternoon, Father," she replied. "I see an empty church."

"Yes, it is true. I pray in solitary."

"Will you take my confession?"

The priest studied her carefully, and nodded, "I will. Come."

William sat on his mother's lap inside the dark confessional box. Through the lattice he could see the priest's profile. A crucifix hung on the grid between them. William studied the suffering Christ, his punctured, bleeding hands, the crown of thorns dripping blood into his eyes.

"Forgive me Father for I have sinned," Geraldine said.

"Go on, my child," Father Grenehamer replied.

"I have had," she paused, glancing down at the young boy in her lap, then back to the priest, "I have had— *thoughts*."

"What kind of thoughts?"

"Wonderful, loving, dear, *exciting*, thoughts, Father." She cleared her throat. William studied the deep brown wood panels. Carved crosses and clouds. "Thoughts of closeness, of kissing, of desire. Thoughts that can be seen as impure, by some."

"By *some*, do you mean the Church?" Father Grenehamer asked.

"I do."

"I see," the priest said.

"Would you like to *see?*" Geraldine grinned at the wooden grid. The priest didn't answer. "These thoughts rarely have clothing, you know" she added.

The priest coughed suddenly. "Is your husband aware of these, thoughts, as you call them?"

"Oh, he is indeed."

"Then, my child, the desire for your husband is not sin. It is only natural to long for the one you love."

"I do not see it as sin, either. Father, my sin is much larger, though, only my husband, and his Church see it as sin."

The priest shifted in his booth.

"My husband has not been to my bed in a week's time," she said, her voice charged with slight anger.

"Perhaps, his duties are divided," the priest said.

"That is all too true, Father," she replied.

"Perhaps he struggles each day from keeping both his soul and his heart from breaking."

Geraldine lowered her face into her son's hair. William began to trace the crosses on the back of the door with his finger.

"Perhaps, dear Geraldine, your husband is hearing a different call than yours. A voice that is not of just this earth, but of the moon and sun, the celestial spheres—the voice that brought all into being from nothingness. A voice that calls each of us to join in a life beyond this."

The two fell silent. William was growing restless. Little of this conversation mattered to him. He wanted to go down to the church's undercroft to where the wooden toy horses were. One was broken. He wanted to fix it.

Geraldine peered into the lattice. "As I said, my sin is not that I desire my husband, but rather, it is that I *do not* desire his Church. I detest it, father. I *loathe* it. I will accept his choice of god, but *not* his Church. And I am angry that he chooses *it* over me." She again lowered her face into William's light brown hair, "Over us."

Father Radulphus Grenehamer sighed. "Do you choose *your* Crafts over your husband?" he asked. "Your gifts, your healings, your powers? Would you forsake them at his asking? No. No you would not. And he would not ask that of you. What you can do, I have witnessed. You bring light, healing and love into this world. And though much of my Church is fearful of powers like yours, I must believe that my God had your kind conceived in his design. For if there are countless stars there must be countless powers."

"Father," William said when he sensed a lull in the exchange, "Can we go down to the toys now?"

"Wife," Radulphus said without heeding his son, "do not ask me to forsake my God, for he holds my undying soul. You possess my heart and all that is good in this life."

"Ralph, I won't ask that of you," she replied, "but it is your Church that vexes me. It keeps you from my bed. And these thoughts I have, are *torture*." Geraldine smiled at the priest. "Husband, when will you come home?"

His response was a whisper, "Wife, quiet now. I had hoped to come tomorrow after Vespers. I will spend the next two nights with you. But, I'm afraid, we must be more careful."

"Do not say that, Ralph," Geraldine said. "*Do not* be *afraid*. Everyone knows you have a wife and son, anyway."

Father Radulphus Grenehamer took his wife by the hand and with William in his arms and straddling his hip, he led them back to the night stairs down to the undercroft below the altar.

Once they stood enclosed within the small stone chamber, Father Radulphus set William on his feet.

The priest asked, "Have you tended your work at home? Tended the chickens? Mended the fence? Stacked the wood?"

William nodded. "I carried the black soil from the stream that Mama wanted, too." He smiled.

"Very well then, you know where they are."

The boy dashed to the corner of the room and opened a large cabinet. From it he pulled four carved wooden horses, one green, one black, one grey and one blue. The blue horse had a broken leg. He set them on the floor and looked up at the couple. Their fingers were enlaced.

William turned his attention to the toys, specifically, the blue horse. From his pocket he pulled out the thin vine he had plucked from the Thatcher's house. It was now brown, withered and without leaves. He wrapped the horse's broken leg with it.

He whispered to the horse, "I am sorry our last adventure hurt you, mate. I borrowed a magic vine to bind you."

"He looks more and more like you everyday," Geraldine said.

"And it appears he's a healer." Radulphus said.

Geraldine smiled, pulling the priest close. He leaned down and touched his nose to hers.

"How are you today, Wife?"

"I am missing my husband. You don't visit as often as you should. We are only a short walk away, you know."

"The Lord's task list is long and has kept me from being idle, I'm afraid."

Geraldine raised her fingers and laid them across his lips. "*Afraid.* Again, do not say that. *Do not* be *afraid.*"

"I know, my sweet wife. I am sorry."

Radulphus kissed her forehead. He crossed the room and returned with two goblets of wine. They sat watching William play on the floor.

William had now tied a short stick onto the blue horse's knee. He set the toy on its feet and tested its stability. He looked up at his parents.

"And how is Simon and his family?" Radulphus asked.

"They will be well by evening. Weak, but well."

"Did they witness your Craft?"

"Simon claimed that he felt the earth pulling him in— that he saw leaves and vines. I assured him that it was the fever."

The priest nodded. "And was William with you?"

She did not answer, but took a long pull from her wine.

"Geraldine, you must shield him. We spoke of this. The Craft will be dangerous for him—dangerous for all of us."

"I know," she said. "But husband, he must know the truth about me. He knows to keep these things to himself. He knows the dangers."

"I know the dangers, Father." William said suddenly. "Mama made the Thatcher's family a drink with herbs in it. It made them get well. That is all." The boy nodded with a sure, brow wrinkled expression. "Look," he said raising the toy. The blue horse's leg was firmly wrapped with the stem—healed.

The Priest smiled. "Very good, William."

When the three ascended back into the nave, William could smell the smoke again. His father took no notice. Smoke drifting through the village was not unusual, and often it would sneak its way into the abbey.

They stood before the door and embraced. William watched his father kiss his mother's lips for a long moment. When they parted they stared at each other smiling. "Tomorrow evening, look for me after dark," he said.

She grinned at him, "I will have a fire in the hearth and bread on the board."

Opening the door and stepping outside, William sensed something was wrong, though he could not verbalize it. It was still well before Vespers, and the spring sun should be high. A cloud of deep ashen smoke choked the light. Both his mother and father gazed up into the fume and wondered at it.

William said, holding his hand out, "These aren't snow flakes. It is ash. See?"

"So it is," the priest agreed.

Across the abbey courtyard was a gathering of a dozen people. There was panic in their voices. The priest reached back inside the church door and laid hold of his walking staff.

"Father! Father! You must help us. Father!" they cried hurrying to the priest.

"What? What is it? What is this smoke? You there, Robert, Robert Emory, pray, what is this fearful disquiet?"

"Father!" Robert said, coming forward. "Father, you must come to the village square. They are *burning*—" his words broke off. Fury and tears stained his expression. He placed his face into his hands. "They are burning. . . Rioters have come from London, they carry the banner of Christ, and they are righteous in their madness. They are killing those they believe to be *witches*. They've burned seven already. They are scouring the village for more."

William saw his father's countenance shadow.

Robert looked over the priest's shoulder to Geraldine. "They seek you, my lady. They seek *you*."

"She is a Christian woman," Father Radulphus shouted.

"It will make no difference," Robert cried. "They are incensed and without restraint. They bear the device of the Almighty. They claim that resisting them is to renounce God himself. They are driven on by Gravesend, the Bishop of London."

William felt tears. Sudden. Stinging. He looked to his mother and clung to her leg. He hid his face.

Radulphus's instinct forced him to take a step, shielding Geraldine. William heard his father's booming voice, as he'd heard it in mass, controlled, focused and clear. It always brought a chill. "Come, all. Let the bells toll. You are called to God's house, all! Bring them, Robert. Bring God's people to His house."

"I will," Robert said. He and his followers took to the path, running.

Geraldine said, "Ralph, you will bring the riotous host. We must flee."

"There will be no greater protection than God's house."

"This has nothing to do with *God*," Geraldine cried.

The priest turned to her. "Trust in the One that created us, my darling wife—let his power protect us. His design does not favor the misguided."

Before Geraldine could respond, a high pitched call like a cat's wail drifted across the abbey courtyard. A line of torches had entered the lane from out of the wood.

"Jerrrreeee. Jerrrreee."

William pushed his hands against his ears. "Mama," he cried, "Mama."

Geraldine pulled him close.

"Jerrrreeee. Jerrrreee," came the howling summons in chorus. Others in the crowd were crying out, "Witch! Bring the witch to God! Fire! Bring fire!"

Robert Emery and those with him froze before the advancing host and stepped a few paces backward before fleeing across the churchyard to the trees.

There were fifty or more. A small army. Held high were several crude crosses draped with red sashes. They carried long poles, axes, sickles and billhooks. "Jerrrreeee!" William went cold all over. He felt his mother's fingernails on the back of his neck.

Arrival

Los Angeles, June 26, 1972
The Continental Hyatt House, Sunset Strip

"My name is Helen Storm. I am all yours."

Helen saw by Jimmy's expression that she had conjured some effect, but not what she wanted—his face told Helen, *you are not Lori. Not even close.* But she waited—bathed in golden candlelight. She did not waver. She seemed to float in midair within a ring of twinkling points of fire. They stared at each other, he from the shadows, and Helen from within a candlelit star. Neither of them smiled.

"My name is Jim, Helen. I'm pleased to meet you," he said finally. Oxygen returned to Helen's lungs and she allowed her chest to slowly heave the relief in. "Won't you join me for a glass of wine?" Jimmy entered the circle and offered her his arm, and she took it. His long dark curls dangled in his eyes and he laid his hand over hers as he escorted her to the open balcony. She looked up at him as they walked. She was strangely comfortable— safe.

What was it about this band? About this man?

Jimmy wore an open deep-blue satin blouse with cream-silk piping, and shining pearl snaps like wet forget-me-nots. Tiny red poppies were embroidered into the loose fitting sleeves. Flaring at the knee, his bluish-black pant-legs resembled a flowing skirt. Jimmy was beautiful. Beautiful in a way that was familiar, like a friend. Like a girlfriend.

"Please," he offered, pulling a chair out for her to sit, "table for two." She moved to the chair and sat down. The view was perfect. Surrounding them was the Hollywood, California skyline: block clusters of homes etched into the surrounding hills, the hazy high-rises outlined by the distant twinkle of lit windows and the orange Sunset Strip snaking west into Beverly Hills. Then, a glass of candlelit red wine being filled before her eyes—Jimmy filling his own glass and seating himself.

"Richard brought you here, yes?" Helen nodded, and stared. She reached for her wine and took a gentle pull. "So I'm sure you're aware that I am expecting someone else."

"Lori" Helen said. "Yes, he told me. He wanted me to keep you company until they found her." Helen set the glass down nervously, then added with as much confidence as she could, "But it was really *me* that you have dreamt of."

Jimmy squinted at her and nodded slightly. "Ah, I see. So fate has intervened? And here I am thinking that I knew what I wanted—but you apparently have other ideas. Is that it?"

His tone was kind, but it was laced with something that she was not familiar with, sardonic wit, clever rhetoric. She was suddenly aware that she was out of her depth. Jimmy Page's interests in such things, the occult, philosophy, art, and certainly fate and self determination, were well known. And she flushed at the thought of entering into a discussion with *those* themes—*with him*. But she started it. She was the challenger. In an attempt to disguise her hesitation she reached into her purse and lifted a cigarette to her lips. Before she could pull out a lighter, Jimmy extended his long, thin arm and lit it for her.

"So I take it by your silence that you are here for a reason?" he asked.

"Yes," she replied. *I have arrived.* She wanted to share it all with him—to be wanted, coveted, adored by the sweet and beautiful guitarist for Led Zeppelin. She had ached for him ever since she had heard him play in 1968 —a record given to her by her neighbor. Posters of the band on her walls, Jimmy Page's eyes staring at her naked body, her fingers between her legs as the turntable churned out his grinding riffs—her father shouting and pounding on the door, *"Turn that shit down, goddamn it!"*

"And what reason is that, pray?" he asked swirling the wine in his glass. She couldn't help but let a subtle smile curl to her lips. He did not mirror it—instead he lowered his eyes down into his wine as if troubled. This was the first tremor of failure. The first time in this glorious dream that waking was near. *Turn that shit down!*

She leaned toward him and said, "I believe in dreams, and that I am supposed to be here, with you" a little too childishly. "I mean, I believe in fate. And for me to even be here, is *crazy.*" He did not respond. His gaze falling deeper into the red, glowing wine. *Slow down,* she thought, but her words gained momentum. "Richard saw me, just as I was calling him—like in a dream, he heard me. You know? And it was the first step toward you. The first step of my arrival, and I. . ." *Slow down.*

Helen Storm stopped. She saw that Jimmy was not looking at her anymore. Instead he seemed apathetic, bored—not the magical creature of her reverie, worshiping her. She reached for her glass and tilted it to her mouth as sensually as she could. She then drained it and set it back upon the table. Jimmy was miles away. Had she blown it? How many times had Jimmy Page encountered a giddy fan rambling on about crushes, serendipitous meetings—meant-to-be scenarios? But, of the thousands of girls at the Forum that evening, it was *her* sitting across from him. *Didn't that count for something?* Self conscious and feeling inadequate, intellectually at least, she remained silent. She fired her wide eyes into the guitarist, filling her mind with the kind of manifestations that she believed brought her to the attention of Richard—that brought her to this seat overlooking the Sunset Strip, the Hollywood Hills, the land of dreams. *Love me,* she commanded him, *love me.*

It was time, she thought.

Helen shook her head lazily and her long black locks draped down. With one hand, she reached up to the tight fitting chiffon stringing along her shoulder and nudged it over her bare arm. Her eyes clung to Jimmy, pleading with him as if she were falling from a great height. Jimmy watched and traced the line of her cheek to her shoulder to her hand pulling—the edge of the crossed fabric tugged at the tip of her breast. She bit her lip and stood—her chair tumbled over backward. She lowered the other side of her top and peeled it down around her middle. Tucking her thumbs deep into the waistline of her skirt, she hooked downward.

The Rest Is Silence

Verona, Italy, November 3, this year
Orathom Wis safe house

Julia Iris turns her eyes to the star above the mountain, so far away—wishing she could sleep. She asks, "So, Helen, William, Samuel Lifeson, George Eversman, we're all the same? We're all immortal?"

Loche turns to Greenhame and motions for him to answer. William stands and crosses the small living room, and lowers himself beside Julia. He takes her hand. "No one is the same as another. You are now part of a family that is suspended from many of this world's absolutes, it is true. But just as those that are doomed to die are as unique and powerful as the stars in the sky, so too are you, my dear, Julia. Yet, you are now an enduring power. And you will find that your sameness with others will be defined by how you *use* that power." Julia stares at him. Her expression is a mixture of wonder and fright—half of her face is lit by the yellow dawn, the other in shadow. "Sounds a little too make believe? I'm sure. All of this might appear archetypal in nature—such things are present in life—though they may be marginalized to our entertainments. To be clearer, the choice of light and darkness is one in the same many times. And not always easy to determine."

Loche interrupts, "William, now is not the time for your philosophical rant. She is still coming to terms with all of this. And so am I!"

"I know well enough, son. But now is the time to determine a course, and set out—*unwaveringly*, mind you." Greenhame points his finger at Loche's heart with an urging, almost mocking gesture. "For we know all too well how *you* managed to internalize a reality you thought myth."

Loche winces. Words on a page or was it a real experience? Is it a memory, or a story he made up? The pistol angled below the chin—the stutter—the canvass that stretched out behind—the Uffizi—his brother Basil Fenn? A chill skitters along Loche's spine, and he feels tears rushing to his eyes. He turns away as Greenhame stands. The warmth of his father's hand upon his shoulder is healing, and strangely absolving. But it is uncomfortable, too. These new revelations, these vexing truths are not limited to only Julia's paradigm.

"Son?" Greenhame's voice is low.

But it is not just a story. Not now. These things *really* happened. And he must accept it, or go mad.

Loche remembers when he wrote of Basil's eyes internalizing the gift of the firearm—his own unspoken suggestion—it was as if Loche told his brother, "*You must take your own life to save us all.*" Did he think that? Or just write it? Of course Loche delivered that message to Basil through metaphor and insinuation, back in Venice, not two weeks ago (or in Priest Lake, when he wrote of the event). But it was the gun he had placed beside his brother's hand that had finalized the conversation. And despite his intention, Loche remembers a fleeting feeling that Basil would not go through with it, or hoped that he would not. Yet, the terrible truth remained: there is only one way to stop the invasion of Heaven, and that is to eliminate the doors. Basil was now dead—one was now closed. Loche Newirth was still wide open.

"What of the assembly at the Uffizi? What happened to all of those important people?"

Greenhame scowls, "We are awaiting official reports."

"What of Howard Fenn? Is he alright?"

"We have returned him to Sandpoint, Idaho. He is getting along."

"And the paintings?"

"We, The *Orathom Wis,* have captured a great many. Albion Ravistelle has a goodly amount as well."

"What have I done?"

"Son, no more. There is much to discuss. But not now." Loche nods at his father. William returns to his chair. Loche sits down on the couch and lays his hand over the joined hands of Julia and Edwin. He watches her stare out at the drained colors of the Verona skyline. Her face is expressionless and statue-like.

She says, "It seems strange to think that I've never been badly injured—my whole life. I've always thought that was weird. How could such a thing be real?"

"Why, yes. Yes indeed," Greenhame agrees. "There are qualities that our kind possess—subtle and simple qualities. Call it a second kind of focus. We call it *Rathinalya* or your life circle. Tell me, have you always been coordinated?"

"What do you mean?" Julia asks.

"I mean just that. Have you noticed a certain strength of dexterity?"

Looking at her hands, Julia shrugs. "I guess so."

Greenhame frowns slightly and leans in closer to her. "Okay. Let me ask you this, when you have a knife in your hand and, say, you're slicing vegetables for a salad —have you ever cut yourself?"

Julia thinks for a moment. "No. Not that I remember."

"Very good. When you are faced with some activity that poses *any* risk of injury—cutting tomatoes, playing sports, picking up broken glass—you are unknowingly protected by your *Rathinalya*. We have an innate awareness, albeit subtle, but enough to see one, maybe two steps ahead of our mortal counterparts—and that awareness keeps us from simple injury—sometimes *lethal* injury. For example, when picking up broken glass, our hands will perform the task with the utmost precision and forethought. Our eyes will map out the careful process without fail, and our hands follow. Simple as that really." Greenhame drains his wine into his mouth.

Loche flinches as Greenhame flings his wine glass from his hand at Julia's face. There is a ring, like wind through a chime and then a click. Julia's free hand is before her eyes, and tangled within her fingers is the stem of the glass. Her eyes are wide.

Greenhame smiles. "Nice reflexes. You see, your *Rathinalya* is always circling your body. But it is not armor, nor is it perfect, as you've recently learned." He gestures to her stomach. "Sometimes there are dangers that are beyond our instinctive skills to prevent. But those are usually things that are out of our control—accidents, if you will. A car accident for example. And so, too, is the occasional danger that is inflicted upon us, like the wound from a firearm," William points to his temple and glances at Loche. Loche recalls writing the grisly head wound that William received during the siege on Basil's flat in Sandpoint, Idaho. William then points to Julia's abdomen. "Our *Rathinalya* is good, but it is not a shield against chaos."

"You said there can be a *lethal* injury. What does that mean?"

"We may not die by any *natural* occurrence—but we can be slain, though, not easily." By her squinting eyes William sees that he must explain further. "We can be vanquished if our bodies are destroyed. If we've the chance to heal from a terrible injury, say a bullet wound or a stabbing, or a terrible fall—which may take some hours, depending upon the severity, we can return anew. But if we are not allowed time to heal, or if our bodies are hacked apart and limbs are hewn away, and our head and body become estranged, or if we are burned and incinerated, we will cease to be." His voice is again low, "And there is pain. We feel every pain just as mortals, only ours is more profound and enduring. Our memory of pain is everlasting. Once you find yourself at the threshold of some lethal harm, the pain is indescribable and terrible. Not because of the injury itself, but rather the agony of being barred from the *Orathom*. The agony of returning to the Life, the *Alya*. There is no pain that can compare." Greenhame lowers his head into his hands and shudders.

"But if we are indeed vanquished, a few of us believe that we can then enter into the Dream—the *Orathom*." Greenhame shifts in his seat uneasily and adds, "Though, it is only a belief. A longing, I suppose. For it has been said since our very beginnings, we immortals will have no Dream to enter into. Our myths, our ancient stories—the mighty *Thi*, the maker of all. Our tomes say our lives are limited to the here and now, of this world only, and that if and when we die, we become—*nothing*. We fade into oblivion. The gift and curse of *Thi*. It is a terrible irony— immortal only here in this life, to protect this world, the mortals and their stories upon *Endale*. Nothing after. We were never meant to sleep. Never meant to dream. Rest is a gift reserved for those that want it not. *Ithic veli agtig.* The rest is silence."

The last of the sunset sparks and dies. Loche notes a darker patch of rain clouds forming in the west, like a shroud over the stars. He sees Julia close her eyes, and imagines that behind her lids her sight scours for some trace of a skyline—any single point of light—a star to comfort her. A single star that would, in time, begin to blink as the deep night approached, and the heavy mountains rooting her dreams to the earth would vanish into the night air. But there will be no stars out tonight, and sleep is far, far away.

Julia leans into Loche as he pulls her close. "I love you," she says. He opens his mouth to answer, but no words come.

The Ladder In The Courtyard

November 3, this year, Coeur d'Alene, Idaho
Greenhavens Retirement Community

"Can I come in, for God's sake? Why is this door closed?" It is a man's voice. It is Leonaie's husband, Charles.

Leonaie's face darkens. Then, as if by habit, a forced smile pushes the cover back. She senses Olivia tense. "Don't worry," she says, motioning for the young woman to open the door, "It's okay. It's okay. It will all work out."

"But Samuel will be here any minute," Olivia whispers.

Leonaie grins at her. A kind of thankful expression—appreciating Olivia's play acting skills. A grin that says, *Charles can't see Samuel, you silly girl, he's in my head.*

Another knock. Louder this time. "Leonaie?"

"Yes, dear," Leonaie calls turning back toward the bedside.

Olivia opens the door and in walks Charles Echelle. A man of seventy-four years, tall, thin and athletic for his age. His wiry frame still has a fair amount of lean muscle, and he is well aware of it. He wears a close fitting yellow shirt with a collar and grey slacks. His grey hair is thinning and in his eyes is a kind of inconvenienced distain for the environment around him. "Leonaie, why can't those bastards out there remember who the hell I am?"

"Visit more often, dear, and they might. Goodness, I just might remember you, too."

Olivia laughs.

Charles huffs.

Leonaie lowers herself down to sit. "Dear, did you know, in the afternoon, someone brings me a glass of wine. Delivers it to my room. And it is always a delicious, cold chardonnay. Did you ask them to do that?"

Charles steps further into the room and looks around scowling—"Not me," he says quickly. "If there's one thing you shouldn't be having is wine—with your memory being the way it's been." He shoots a muted glare at Olivia.

"Don't you be mean to her," Leonaie says sharply.

"It's alright, Leonaie," Olivia joins. "The doctor said she could have a glass of wine every afternoon, Mister Eschelle—he didn't seem to think it would be a problem. In fact, he thought it was a great idea."

"Well, keeping my wife boozed up doesn't seem like practical medicine to me." Charles stands next to his seated wife and presses his hand on her shoulder. Olivia notes how awkward the gesture appears.

Leonaie sighs and says, "Charles, it is so nice of you to visit. That always makes me feel a little better somehow." Leonaie glances at Olivia and then up to her husband's face—he is still scanning their surroundings with distaste.

"And what is that smell, for God's sake?" he growls.

"That's pee, dear," Leonaie says flatly. "Some of these old folks here can't seem to pee in the designated pee-pee spots."

Olivia laughs suddenly and then covers her mouth with her hand. Leonaie always makes her laugh.

"Well someone should open a window," he says gruffly.

Then from the door comes a voice in chorus, "I agree. Smells like piss."

Charles and Olivia turn to see Doctor Victor Živojinović, or as many of the residents call him, *Doc Victor.*

"And why doesn't someone do something about it Doc Victor? It's terrible."

"I agree, Charles, but I'm afraid we've not found the right ingredients for pleasant smelling urine. Nor have we been able to develop a better method than diapers. Things could be worse. Take it easy."

"And I see that I've come when you have an examination scheduled?" Charles says to Leonaie.

"Impeccable timing, dear," Leonaie said. "But we won't be long. Can't you stay? I'll be having tea with a friend today, won't you join us?"

Charles shifts in his stance and considers his wife's words. *She's delusional again*, his expression says, and he suddenly flashes a pleading look to Doc Victor. The doctor nods knowingly and points his pen into his clipboard.

"No dear," Charles says, "I have plans with our old friends the Gramms a little later today. But I'll come back to see you tomorrow, or the next day."

Leonaie continues to stare out the window. "Very well, sweetheart. Have a great time. Tell them I said hello." She has no idea who the Gramms are.

Another awkward gesture, a kiss this time, on the top of his wife's head. He turns toward the door and collides with the doctor as he exits.

Doc Victor sighs. Leonaie watches Olivia finish up tidying the room. The woman pauses a moment to catch a look at the doctor, his pen still scribbling. Doctor Živojinović looks younger than Oliva. He looks to be in his early to mid-thirties. Leonaie had overheard Olivia and several other of the Greenhavens Community female residents often place him into the center of what Leonaie calls, *saucy talk*. The man is quiet, intelligent, gentle and (Leonaie suddenly suppresses a giggle), wildly fuckable. His physical appearance is not stunning, though it is attractive despite the weird mustache and wire rimmed glasses. He is tall, with finely sculpted features, dark hair, dark skin, but what twitterpates Olivia, her friends and even Leonaie is the rare occurrence of coming under his gaze. His eyes are in some way similar to Leonaie's, but they are greener and filled with a compelling depth, as if he can see through one's thoughts—as if he can read one's mind—and the rest of his face shines out a genuine like for what he reads there.

With his head still bent down into his clipboard, his eyes shift up to Olivia. She is caught staring. Her face flushes with red suddenly and she spins toward Leonaie. Her voice wavers, "Leonaie, is there anything else that I can—you need?"

"No dear," Leonaie says, looking at her, a slight smile on her lips. "Just set a place for my meeting today in the courtyard, won't you?"

"I will. And doctor?"

"No, thank you Olivia. I'll take it from here."

The door closes behind her. Doc Victor continues to scribble on his clipboard.

"We'll have to make this quick, Doctor," Leonaie says, still her gaze points to some place well beyond the parking lot outside, the Denny's sign above the freeway, the mountains in the haze. "I have a friend that's about to visit."

"A friend? I thought he was much more than a friend."

"Fair enough. He is my very *best* friend."

"That sounds more like it." Doc Victor stands between Leonaie and the window. He stoops over and looks carefully at her face and her color. He cradles her chin in his hand and then slowly reaches to her neck. "Any more pain?" Leonaie doesn't answer. His fingers continue the examination, moving to the glands along her throat.

"I hate that fucking mustache," she says quickly. Doc Victor pauses, his hand now behind her neck, feeling the tightened muscles along her cervical spine. "Please tell me that *you* don't think it looks good."

He barely smiles. "Maybe I do think it looks good. I've had beards in the past, but never a mustache." His hands glide to her shoulders.

"You look like a pimp's bookkeeper," she says, eyes still tracing nothing. "Of course, a cute bookkeeper with those little wiry glasses. Are those new?"

"No, I've had them a long while," he replies, his hands now unbuttoning her blouse. Her green-gold lit eyes shoot to the glasses and study them a moment. They look old. Very old.

"How long have you had them?"

Victor watches his hands unfastening each button as if he is stepping slowly down a ladder, then he raises his eyes to meet hers.

"I found these glasses in London—1813 was the year, I think, so yes, a long time. I didn't need glasses, of course. My eyesight is perfect. It always has been."

"There must have been a *woman* that first said you looked good wearing them?" Leonaie asks.

Victor nudges Leonaie's blouse off of her shoulders and it drapes down across her back. Her arms are thin, white and wrinkled. Her chest is now bare. Victor lowers his face into hers and waits. "You were the first to say that I looked cute wearing them," he says. Leonaie lets a smile curve into her eyes and lips. She leans and kisses him softly. When she pulls away, Victor's eyes are closed, reveling in some memory, some distant pleasure—an expression she has seen on his face many times.

She wonders what consumes him. Is it the taste of her? Or the memory of her when she was younger, standing upon a ladder, her little butt poked out just a tickle—or perhaps he is recalling her shape framed in a hotel window with the Parisian skyline lit behind her. A smile slowly spreads across his face. The smile is so large that one side of his mustache comes loose and begins to sag—the glue giving out.

Leonaie reaches her hand up to press it back down. "Ridiculous," she says shaking her head. "You don't have to wear a disguise all the time, you know. Besides, it doesn't make kissing you an easy thing with that fucking porcupine on your lip. How about the next time you visit, you fake *shave*?"

"As you wish, dear," he agrees.

"And if you don't mind," Leonaie shrugs, "these babies are getting a tad nipply out here, and they're not what they used to be," she nodded to her topless torso. "So if you have some examining to do, have at it." She then flashes him her mischievous grin, "And thanks for the seduction bit. Very sexy."

"I wasn't sure if I had you," he said continuing his examination of her breasts, her stomach and abdomen.

"Oh, you had me. You've always had me."

The doctor raises her blouse back up over her shoulders, buttons it and lets his hand rest upon her cheek. "You are more beautiful than anything I have ever seen."

Leonaie laughs sadly, "Then I think your *perfect vision* has some serious issues, *Samuel Lifeson*."

We Only Dream

April, 1338,
the village of Ascott-under-Wychwood, England

They were robbers, drifters, beggars. They wore no uniforms save a single swathe of dirty red slung across their chests like a wound. At the rear of the throng were nine horsemen. Four were English soldiers in the livery of the new King, Edward III. Four others looked to be monks, dressed in simple habits, but at their sides they bore long, jeweled swords. At the center rode Stephen Gravesend, Bishop of London. His cloak and the high minter upon his head glowed red through the haze.

The host poured into the abbey courtyard.

Geraldine pulled both the priest and their boy back, "We must go, now!" she hissed.

Father Grenehamer replied calmly, "There is naught to fear. The Lord will protect us from evil."

"Ralph!" She cried. "*The Lord* is far from this place."

"Stay. Believe," he said.

Father Grenehamer strode a few paces into the lane before the church and lifted his arms, as if to embrace a long awaited friend. His staff held high, "My lords, you come to God's House. Come, for all who enter these grounds are sheltered by his love. His peace."

The jeering host encircled the priest, mother and boy. As the horses drew near, Radulphus called to the Bishop. "Welcome, your Excellency. Welcome. What is your errand here, pray?"

Bishop Gravesend halted his horse. The four monks positioned themselves like barriers. The largest of the four rose in his stirrups and surveyed the grounds. His horse stopped beside the bishop. The angry crowd fell silent. Gravesend stared at Father Radulphus for a moment—a slow scan from head to toe. He looked to the larger monk, and the monk nodded to him. Gravesend's eyes then ticked to Geraldine and then to William. William felt the gaze as if a cold wind had breathed through his tunic. A horrible chill raked at his entire body, "Mama," he whispered, "Mama."

"Geraldine of Leaves?" he said.

William looked up to his mother's face. What he saw was unexpected. She was calm. Firm defiance was seated there. And if William was not mistaken, the hint of a smile.

"Geraldine of Ascott?" he shouted again.

"I am," she answered.

"You are hereby charged with witchcraft, sorcery and heresy. By the powers vested in me by His Holiness, Pope Benedict and his Majesty, King Edward III, for sins against God and His people, you will be purged of Satan by the trial of fire."

"Mama," William cried. Her hands clasped his shoulders and held him tight.

Geraldine lowered her face to William. Her smile was taut as wire. She touched his cheeks with her fingers. They were soft, like the petals of spring daisies. "Do not be afraid, my dear son. Soil and seed, sun and rain, fire and smoke, laughter, pain."

"Take her to the village square," The bishop said, turning his horse.

"Your Excellency," Father Grenehamer cried out. "There is no evidence for this claim! She is a child of God. A Christian woman. You cannot do this, my lord. This is *not* God's way."

"As Bishop of London, Father Radulphus, I speak for God. If you resist, perhaps you are in league with Lucifer, protecting his spawn on Earth. Take her," Gravesend said.

William watched his father's staff spin from the gesture of welcome into a menacing angle of wrath. Before he could blink, there were two resounding cracks and two red sashed men lay unconscious in the lane. The priest paced backward while the staff spun like a windmill in a gale. One end then crashed through the teeth of an advancing foe. Another step back, the staff whirled again, this time splitting a man's chin. Blood spewed from his nose.

William felt hands yanking him from his mother. He bit at the fingers. He tasted blood. He tore free. More rioters fell to the ground from his father's vicious defense.

"Geraldine! Boy! Get you inside!" Radulphus shouted. His voice, like he'd heard it at mass, was filled with the boom of a thunder god. Geraldine lifted William into her arms and turned toward the abbey door. But a sudden jolt sent them both to the ground. Rolling over onto his stomach, the boy saw his mother lying face up in the grass. Blood was streaming from a cut below her right eye. She reached for him. Then he heard his father's voice again, only this time it was a cry of pain and rage. The mob had pulled him to the ground and they were striking him with fist, foot and club.

"Enough!" Gravesend shouted. His horse was now towering over them. The violent blows stopped. They dragged William's father to his knees. "Enough, priest! Foolish choice. You are under arrest for treason against his Majesty and God Almighty. Take him inside, for now. We will send a contingent to dispatch him to the Tower. Keep him here until they come." With a sidelong glance at the large monk at his side, the Bishop gestured to Geraldine now being hauled to her feet, "Take this witch to her stake. God's will be done."

"And what of the boy?" one of the red sashed men asked.

The Bishop peered down his nose at young William. He shook his head and sighed mournfully. He held up his right hand as if he were blessing the boy. William memorized his face, his red vestments, the cross upon his headdress. The man was pale, as if ill. An elliptical blister upon his cheek.

"Thou shalt not suffer a witch to live. Nor should we suffer a witch's offspring to foul God's people." With another look to his Sentinel monks, Gravesend said, "Kill him."

The howling voices of his father and mother together split the ears of those near. "Mercy! No! No!"

William heard a knife drawn from behind. The arms that held him in place bore down with strangling force. But as they squeezed, William's body somehow shrunk inward and he wriggled free, back and down. He rolled forward onto his knees and pushed with his feet, vaulting his body at Gravesend's horse. From the ground he caught hold of a short billhook and swung it at the first man that reached to seize him. The sharp blade connected and severed a finger. Two more men rushed in. William managed to stab the weapon into the thigh of one as the other wrestled him down.

William was roughly turned to his parents. Mother and father struggled toward him but were both forced to their knees, restrained by too many hands.

"Mama," William cried.

The gaze of his mother lit into the boy's eyes. Her smile glistened. "We do not die, sweet boy. We only dream. Seek for light in the dark."

A silver blade gleamed before him then dropped below his chin. He felt it rest there, cold and sharp.

"Dream."

The searing sting was quick. His head jerked slightly to the right. The bitter of blood. The flavor of steel. Air coughed out from his lungs. William, son of Geraldine, dropped onto the green grass beside the lane that led to the House of God.

Time To Go

Los Angeles, June 26, 1972
The Continental Hyatt House, Sunset Strip

The knock on the door went unnoticed—Jimmy Page did not move. He sat gazing at Helen with both desire and boredom. She could not tell which. When the door opened, Richard marched into the room, glanced at the topless Helen, and then leaned down and whispered quietly to Jimmy. Helen heard every word, "We have Lori. Should I bring her up?"

Jimmy nodded. Richard stood up straight, again let his eyes brush over Helen's chest and tight skirt and he smiled at her. He sighed, "Well my lovely dear, it is time. Time to wake, I'm afraid."

Helen's eyes shot to Jimmy—now finishing his wine and standing—then back to Richard, smiling and scanning her—back to Jimmy, turning away toward the dark corner where she had discovered him.

"Jimmy?" she cried, "Jimmy, can't I stay for awhile? This can't be over. Please don't leave. Please stay!"

From over his shoulder Jimmy attempted kindness, "I'm sorry love, tonight I've had long standing plans. Maybe another time. Won't you give your number to Richard. Next time we're in town I'll—"

"No, Jimmy," she sobbed. "Let me stay. My whole life I've dreamt of being here, with you. And I've finally arrived. Please, please, let me stay tonight. We had a moment, didn't we Jimmy?"

She watched Richard's face twist to worry, as if this was all a mistake, and he would certainly hear of it tomorrow on the plane. Somehow she could hear him thinking, *fans were one thing—crazy, freak-show, fanatical chicks were another*. His eyes rose angrily from her chest to her teary eyes. "Time to go." He took a step toward her, but Helen eluded his grasp and stumbled out of reach—toward the balcony edge. And then it came to her. Feeling the concrete ledge beneath her hands, she hurled her body up and stood—wavering on her platform shoes. "Jimmy!" she cried.

The guitarist's back was turned. "Jimmy," she cried again, this time making sure the terror in her voice would whirl him around. Jimmy's face paled. Helen Storm stood on the ledge, fourteen stories above the neon lit pavement, her top was around her waist, her arms stretched out wide and her thin legs teetering.

"Helen," Jimmy sprang forward, carefully. "Helen, dear, what are you doing? Please don't—"

"I want to stay for awhile, Jimmy," she cried. "You can't understand what it is like to always be ignored—you are *Jimmy Page*. I have loved you since I first saw you—heard you. I'm here, and now I want my dream to come true." *Turn that shit down, god damn it!*

"Alright love," Richard said softening, "You can stay, just come down and we'll—"

"I want *you* to leave," she hissed at him. "I want to be alone with Jimmy."

Richard's palms were faced out. He turned his head to Jimmy looking for some answer to his fuck-up. Jimmy didn't look at him but rather trained his eyes on Helen.

"Helen," he said, stepping nearer, his voice soft and sincere, "I don't think this is the best way to get my attention, you know. Yes, please, come down and we will talk awhile longer. You're scaring me. I don't want you to hurt yourself. Won't you please come down?" He held out his long, finely pointed fingers, reaching for her.

There it was again. That comfort. Like the *Rain Song*. Like the chorus of Tangerine, *Tangerine, living reflection from a dream*. Helen felt him. She felt his compassion, his goodness, his magic. She lowered her right hand and gestured for him to come closer, in awe of him as if he were an angel from out of the shadows of her dark childhood. She only made it through because of him. His music. His face.

Jimmy continued to move closer, his arm outstretched to her. But just as their fingertips touched, Richard lunged forward, grabbing for her legs.

"Stop, Richard!" Jimmy shouted as Helen kicked at the man. Richard managed to lay hold of her left ankle— but her other foot was in midair, and he caught a crushing blow from the right platform shoe. His head jerked to the side as his grip slipped. Jimmy lunged for her wrist, but too late.

The June night was warm. Up here she thought she could smell the brine of the ocean from a far off summer wind—the fingertips of a storm—rushing ever faster— from across the world, probably. Arriving here after a terrible journey—arriving here and cradling Helen Storm as she tumbled backward and down, head over foot to the land of dreams that waited below.

What It Means To Be Made of Stars

November 3, this year
Verona, Italy.

Julia's abdomen aches. Or at least she imagines that it does. *Apparently an immortal can have aches and pains?* It has been said that pain exists only in the mind. With all that was now troubling her—the ache, pain and utter discomfort of her new life, her new reality is very real. She rubs along her navel. Her pace is slow upon the slick, gray cobbles.

She slipped out of the safe house unnoticed, nearly an hour ago. Her mind grapples for some anchor, some solid point between what she had come to know or expect of this life, we're born, we age, we love, we work, we raise a family, we travel, we save our money, we retire, and hopefully, we die in our sleep. That, and this unbelievable truth, this inconceivable reality, this undying body. *I cannot die.* Or more accurately, I cannot die *naturally.* Again, these thoughts start an anxious series of deep breaths as she meanders listlessly through the upper streets above Verona's Piazza Bra. The sounds of traffic and tourists fade away, and she focuses on the click of her boots on the cobbles, the cold dusk rain tapping on her hat. Little gold rectangles of light blur out of weathered facades and curve up and away like a candlelit hallway.

The sky is a quarry of grey clouds. Heavy, jagged bones of mist slog across the last smear of sun. Shadows in the alleys and cross streets trap reflections of light and mash them down to single dots, specks of white on black puddles—hedged smudges of silver on wet stone-paths. She keeps on. Very soon she will not be able to distinguish the rising hilltop from the sky. They are merging. Somehow it is a comfort to think that there just might be a kind of bridge, a ladder that can connect earth and the heavens. She wonders if she just keeps going through these darkened, antique streets, ever rising up, she just might find a way out of this impossible to believe circumstance. Perhaps there is a route through this labyrinth of houses to the hilltop, then an unnoticed step onto an airy plateau, through the boulders of rolling cumulous and eventually out of the blankets of grey mist, up to where those mythic immortals are sketched in starlight—those beings that she had read about when she was a girl—those gods that appear before us still today in films, on holidays, in greeting cards, as statues in ancient cities, in religions, in language—they are in our very DNA.

Her father had taught her about the constellations when he would help her to sleep. A simple rhyme: *Find the single star / And watch it blink, / Until the mountains fade / And we to sleep.* To think that there above is her ancestral fabric and that she is woven into it brings on another series of deep breaths. It has been said that we are all made of stars, but few of us share that same, unending light.

Julia rubs her stomach. She walks on. Her eyes take turns lifting to the dull dark above and then to the glistening stones beneath her plodding feet. She is lost. She doesn't care.

The new phone that William had given to her vibrates. She looks at the screen. It is Loche. The third time he's called. There are also texts from him:

Where are you?
Julia come back- it is not safe
Call me!

She smiles at the letters of his name. She imagines his face, the feel of his arms around her, the taste of his skin. Her fingers touch the key hanging from the necklace at her throat. The phone vibrates again. Her thumb hovers over the answer button, but she declines, shakes her head and tucks the phone back into her pant pocket.

Out of professional habit, her mind drifts to the restaurant she owns, *The Floating Hope*, on the lake north of Sandpoint, Idaho. The administrative tasks that occupied most of her time are nagging at her: personnel scheduling, food and alcohol orders, the wine tasting group on Thursdays, the remodel of the back board room, the accounting, et cetera. Somehow, this newly discovered immortality does not completely eclipse all that she has accomplished in her short life. *It seems that it should*, she thinks. *How can anything mean what it did? What of business, networking, clientele? Of family, friends and love? What of love? What of Loche Newirth?*

Deep breath.

She shudders. She will outlive him. She will watch him age and wither away while she remains unchanged. The years will pass and she will linger. She will remain. Alone.

Her feet halt and she peers up to the sky pouring over the hilltop like a black, cresting wave. She feels tears.

Behind her she hears the faint tap of footsteps. She spins toward the sound and squints into the dark. A single figure comes to a stop some twenty yards behind her.

"Who's there?" Julia gasps, suddenly aware that she is long overdue to return—that Loche and William are indeed worried—that she has wandered too far and is lost. Then, the fear fades as quickly as it has risen. A confidence. A resolve. An untapped strength. "Who's there?" she calls again, only this time with a tone of command.

The figure makes no answer. After a moment it begins to move toward her with slow precision. Without looking away from the approaching stranger, Julia's mind quickly accesses several things at once. Two possible escape routes. The first, and nearest, is an alleyway ten paces to the left, and the second is ahead of her where the path branches into three separate directions. She does not take the time to consider just how these possible scenarios formed from out of her subconscious, nor did she give the possible routes any notice when she had scanned across them earlier. A rapid inventory is next. Did she have anything she could use as a weapon? *No.* Then lastly, she feels the muscles in her legs and torso tense. She feels vigor and a warm rush of energy charge through her. Her focus sharpens and she begins to make out details. The figure is her size, arms to the sides, graceful stride, long hair—it is a woman, still in silhouette—long overcoat, scarf, gloves. Steadily the woman moves closer. The heels of her boots tapping and scraping the cobbles. At about ten feet Julia calls again, "Who are you? What do you want?"

Her pursuer stops. Though she is still draped in shadow, Julia can detect attractive features, shapely eyes and the line of a slight smile.

"I should kill you right now, Julia Iris," the woman says. The word *kill* bounces into Julia's ears and reverberates there for a moment.

"Good luck with that," Julia replies, quite uncertain just where such a response came from. But despite the sudden rush of courage, Julia takes a defensive step back —her thoughts rifling through the escape routes. "How do you know my name?"

"A good wife should always know who her husband is fucking."

A tinge of pain visits Julia's mid section, the memory of the bullet wound—then the recall of that long snowy drive from the lake to Beth Winship's funeral, and the reading of Loche's journal. Loche's wife had inscribed the inside cover. She had betrayed him. She, too, is an immortal. "Helen?"

"Clever girl," Helen remarks.

Julia now allows her eyes to quickly sweep the darkness surrounding them. The gloom has deepened. She takes another step backward.

"I'd like to teach you a couple of things," Helen says opening her coat and pulling from it a thin, lightweight blade, "about what it means to join the family." The steel glints like a spark.

The Ladder

November 3, this year, Coeur d'Alene, Idaho
Greenhavens Retirement Community

Samuel Lifeson shakes his head and sits down beside Leonaie. She puts her arm around him. "Samuel," she says, "you should be moving on, you know. My time is running out. Remember? We said a day would come when it would be time for both of us to move on? I'm nearly done here—and you should be heading out to another lifetime."

"You've been saying that for years," Samuel replies.

She lowers her head and rests it upon his shoulder.

There is the buzz of a vibrating phone. It is muffled and apparently buried in his doctor bag. Samuel does not move to answer it.

"How's the memory?" Samuel asks.

Leonaie sighs, "*I don't recall.*"

"Really, Leonaie," Samuel presses, "still forgetting short term things?"

The old woman nods and moves to stand up. Samuel reaches for her wrists in support. "Yes, I'm forgetting things sometimes, but that's natural at my age isn't it? I mean, it's not bad or anything." Leonaie looks at him with a flash of anger in her eyes. "There are some things that I wish I could forget."

Samuel nods.

"But no matter how I try, you always come back to me. The poems you've written. . ." She pointed to the large Shakespeare book at her bedside.

"I've written another for you," Samuel says. "It is about our first trip to Europe in 1964." Leonaie closes her eyes and breathes deep—a sigh of euphoric memory.

"Oh dear," she grins, "tell me that it is about France—our hotel near the Louvre—three days and we didn't leave our room—"

"Room service, the views, the wine, and us," he joins. "And the damned Louvre right there—"

"The Louvre," she says sarcastically, "waste of time—you had *me* to look at. Louvre had nothing on me—at the time, at least."

"It still has nothing on you," Samuel says.

"Maybe."

Samuel places his hands on her shoulders and turns her toward him. "Do you remember where we are going next week?"

"I seem to recall something. What was it? Are we off to France again?"

Samuel waits.

"Let me see," Leonaie says. "I remember."

"Well?" Samuel presses. "What are we doing next week?"

"Are you testing my memory?" Leonaie tries to hide the fear tugging at her expression—"We're going to Italy for my treatments," she says.

"I will be with you. I will not leave your side. They've done it, my love. They've found the missing strand. The ladder can now reach. You *will* become the moon." The old woman falls into Samuel's embrace and hides her tears. "Do you still want this, Leonaie?"

"Of course I do," she answers. "But how can they be sure it will work. It has gone wrong so many times now."

Samuel holds her closer, "They have it this time. I've seen it with my own eyes. They are calling it the *Melgia*, the Moonchild Gene. It has been cultivated from the soil of the earth—from the very Tree of Life. You will be one of the first."

"They named it *that*?" She asks, "*Leonaie* would have been a better name."

Samuel laughs. "Moonchild has a better ring, don't you think? Though this fountain of youth has been sought after since the dawn of time, if it wasn't for you, I would have never pursued it to this end—or beginning, if you will."

The doctor's bag vibrates again. Samuel sighs. Again, he lets the phone go to voicemail.

Leonaie then breathes out, "I'm afraid."

"I would not lead you down a road that was not safe, nor would I bring you into a life that you do not want. You have the chance to become like me, immortal. Your age will reverse, youth will come upon you and we can return to our lives as man and wife again. Death will not part us."

Leonaie steps out of his embrace. "You have said many times that death would be a blessing. You have said over and over that the pain of life is never ending, and if only sleep could come, you would be at peace. Do you wish these things on me?"

"There is a price, Leonaie. The price we've spoken of many times. I do not wish upon you the realities that come with this choice, but I also do not wish for you to fade into illness and death. I told you when we met that I am selfish, and I want you to stay with me. And I believe, Leonaie, that you can handle the ills of the eternal path. You of all people might save me from madness. For when you are gone, madness will be all that is left to me." He pauses, searching her face, "Have you changed your mind?"

"No," she says without hesitation. "I am scared. That's all. Everything is fading—my body, my mind—and it feels natural. To think that I can cheat death seems, well, *un*natural. It seems wrong, somehow."

Samuel smiles at her and touches her cheek again. "Don't see it as being wrong, my love. See it without fear. We've climbed from the sea to the sky. We've reached for the stars, and now, right now, we've managed to touch one."

"And you will place me among them?" Leonaie asks.

Samuel pulls her close to him. She fits perfectly within his embrace.

He whispers, "The ladder *will* reach."

Closing her eyes she sees him at the base of that ladder, all those years ago. His face pointed up to hers. A light is there. It grows brighter as he begins to climb. Apples dangle heavy around her. She is nervous. She thinks of pies. Apple pies. Delicious and sweet. Her grandmother's recipe—passed down to her, so long ago. So long ago. As he rises to her she wonders briefly if the ladder can hold them both. The thought vanishes as she leans her face into his. Their lips meet.

The branch above cracks.

Two muted pops then the sound of glass crackling.

Leonaie's eyes flash open, the weight of the ladder slumps upon her. *But, that didn't happen, when we held each other there, high up in that tree.*

Her memory vaults her back—back into his embrace —in her room at Greenhaven's Community. But something is wrong. His body is weakening. Then a spray of glass shards—a burst of dust in the air.

"Samuel?" she cries. "Samuel!"

She tastes blood.

She feels his arms loosen and drop away to his sides. Leonaie struggles to balance him as he sways like an axed tree. Looking up, Samuel's face is blank, eyes wide and distant.

As Samuel's body begins its heavy decent to the floor, Leonaie is trapped between. She does not have the time to understand what has just happened. He falls as if dead, crushing Leonaie Eschell beneath.

Returning Color

April, 1338,
the village of Ascott-under-Wychwood, England

"How is it, my dear son, that your skin is still warm? That here, crimson still stains your cheeks? My dear, William. My sweet boy, William. Oh Heavenly Father, mercy upon me!"

The voice was familiar. He knew that it was his father calling to him. He had never heard that voice cry. There was a sprinkle of water on his cheeks. Gentle drops tapped upon his forehead and upon his closed eyes. Then, William could see.

His head was lying upon his father's lap. He felt crying breath warming his skin. Radulphus' face was crimped in sobbing throes of despair, bowing nose to nose with the boy. Shifting his focus around, William could see the ceiling of the abbey and the dimming colors of the stained glass windows. There was a wet cloth bound tight around his throat. It was uncomfortable and he lifted his arm to discern why it was there. When his fingers touched it, his father's breathing stopped. Their eyes met.

"Papa?" William whispered. His throat was raw and sore, but better than it was a short while ago. "Papa, why are you crying?"

Radulphus froze. William could see the color of his father's eyes quite clearly, for they were opened so wide that they were surrounded by white. The irises were like full moons, and blue as the river on a bright winter's day.

"Papa?"

His father did not speak. Instead, his eyes, face and hands began to examine William's little body with ferocious speed. His breathing was a combination of sobbing and laughter. When the bandage was torn away from his throat, Radulphus gasped in a hushed whisper,

"Oh sweet God. My sweet boy. My sweet, dear boy." His eyes flooded. Tears again dropped heavily upon William's cheeks. "There is no cut—there is no wound—oh my sweet William, you are alive. You are—you are—"

William stared at him. He recalled the bitter flavor, the gushing of air, the sting. And now, he was here. And he was fine.

Then, from some deep place within, William heard his own voice whisper, "Mama?"

Radulphus' arms coiled around the boy, hugged the child to his chest and wailed. "Shhh," he said through his weeping, "Shhh."

"He's dead, priest!" A voice of jagged stone. The coarse yell came from the other side of the abbey near the entrance. Two of the armed rioters sat drinking wine. "Best you bury the little rat!" he said over his shoulder. He wore a hood.

"Aye," the other said turning. William could see his sallow complexion and squat face. "You'll have a little time before the Bishop comes—then you're to the Tower." He turned back toward the fading light from the open door. He tipped his cup into his mouth, swallowed and added, "Cryin' won't help you, and prayin' won't do you no good, Priest."

"And after that, you're to the pits of Hell for trying to save a witch."

"Aye," the thickset one agreed, "God's will be done."

"God's will."

"Mama," William whispered.

"God's will, indeed, brothers," another voice entered the conversation. William strained to see but could only make out a looming silhouette of a man framed in the doorway.

The two guards stood, "And who may you be?" the hooded one asked.

"By order of Bishop Gravesend, I have come to escort the priest to the Tower," the man replied. His tone was carved in royalty and command.

"Do you bear the seal from his Excellency? We were ordered to release the priest only with such token."

"Knave!" the man shouted. "Look you upon these vestments. Tell me what you see?" The shadowed figure unsheathed his sword and held it point up before them. "The gold upon this hilt? Does it not shine like the summer sun? And do you not see that I carry the ensign of King Edward the Third engraved upon the pommel? Bring the priest to me. Now!"

The two guards did not hesitate. They placed their mugs upon the floor and marched down the aisle toward the priest. William squeezed his eyes shut.

"Come, Priest. Your escort commands."

As they drew near, Father Grenehamer struggled to replace the red stained bandage. He whispered to his son, "They think you dead, William. Pretend to sleep, boy. Pretend to sleep."

William's body went limp. The priest stood, cradling his son, his face still stained with tears and blood.

"You can't take the boy with you!" The stocky guard huffed, "Drop him or I'll drop you."

"I will bury him," Radulphus said. "He must be given his rite to Heaven."

"No time for that now. Drop him."

"My Lord," the priest called to the King's escort. "Surely, you will see this boy laid to rest under the eyes of God?"

"Drop him or I'll pay you with this," the hooded guard raised a billhook and wriggled it before Radulphus' eyes. William felt his hands cluster into fists.

"Nay!" the escort shouted. "Let the boy have a proper burial. Come, *you two* can dig the grave. Priest, bring him. This shall be the last mercy you receive—remember it well."

Buzzing Lights

Los Angeles, June 26, 1972
The Continental Hyatt House, Sunset Strip

"Can you fucking explain what happened? Because I surely can't make any sense of it! Christ! I'm not losing me fucking mind am I? You saw her. We both saw her. She fell fourteen fucking stories, Jim! Fourteen fucking stories—hit the pavement—sounded like a fucking sack of watermelons. It should have—it should have ended her!" A line of saliva hung from Richard's lower lip. "By the time I got down there to figure out what to do next, she's sitting on a bench staring into space. What the fuck, Jimmy?"

Helen saw Jimmy Page's eyes slide from Richard to the two huge Zeppelin body guards that stood beside him and then back through the square window in the swinging door to Helen. Helen was seated on a plastic chair in the hotel's main floor kitchen. Florescent lights sterilized the room: bright, stark and unforgiving. The band's on-the-road physician was examining her for injuries. He seemed to move in slow motion.

The guitarist turned his attention back to Richard. The man's face was pale with shock and disbelief.

"And *you* shouldn't be down here," she heard Richard saying as he took both of Jimmy's wrists and pulled him toward the elevator. "She'll be in a cab to who-knows-where in a few minutes. This is the last place *you* should be." Jim resisted. Richard let him go. "Jim, please."

"No one saw anything, right?" Jim asked. "Like you said, you got her out of there without being noticed?"

"I think so," Richard nodded, "but we shouldn't take any chances of getting you involved in—in—whatever the fuck this is." He shook his head. "So let's go. And besides, you've got a date. Remember? Lori is waiting." He motioned to the body guards to escort Jim back upstairs.

Jim held up his hands. "Both of you, back off. Richard, stop it. I won't stay long, but I want to learn more about this."

"Oh Christ," Richard sighed, "this isn't some of your *magical mystery* research, is it? Hey, buying haunted mansions and witchy books are all fine, but a badly bleeding fourteen-year-old in the back kitchen of a Los Angeles hotel with two brutes and the Satanic guitar player from Zep—this is another thing entirely. Let's go."

Richard again moved to take hold of Jim, but this time he stopped. Jimmy's eyes were intent, angry and communicated a clear and concise message. All Richard could do was sigh, let his head sink and his hands drop to his sides. "This is bad. This is really fucking bad."

"It would be worse if she were dead," Jimmy said.

"You saw it. Right?" Richard looked up quickly as his mind replayed the event. "The chick fell from the top of the building and got up, walked to a bench and sat down to think it over. What the fuck? Things are getting weirder and weirder out here on the road." Richard covered his eyes with his hands and sighed. He then repeated, "What the fuck?"

Again Jimmy's eyes strayed to the young girl through the window. Her face was smeared with blood, black clouds of mascara streaked down her cheeks, and her eyes were as wide as the moment he met her—still hopeful, still glittered, but there was something else lurking there. A question was screaming out, though she struggled to secure it behind a mask.

Run

November 3, this year
Verona, Italy

"Don't," says Helen Newirth.

Before she can recognize the decision, Julia pivots and runs—escape route number two—the lane ahead that breaks into three different alleyways. Attaining the fork, she takes the left path leading up to Verona's Roman Theater. Turning a sharp corner she sees two men in long coats blocking the way. They carry unsheathed blades. Her mind flashes two alternate routes. She whirls to the right and down through a narrow fissure between two buildings. As she does this she hazards a quick look behind her. Helen is there, dangerously close. She hears her boots rapping on the stones.

A gleam of wet pavement is the only light ahead. She topples two trash cans as she passes, crashing them into Helen's path. The cadence of Helen's boots does not lose rhythm, save a momentary pause, as if she had hurdled over the obstacles with ease.

Julia reaches the opening and tacks to the right, heading uphill again. From an adjoining street, a black vehicle screeches out into the lane. The headlights blind her. Without thinking, she jumps into the air just as the car clips her at the thigh. A crushing wave of pain jolts through her body. There is the sound of crackling glass. Julia rolls limp from the smashed windshield to the wet pavement. The car slides to a stop beside her. Two men get out. They wear long, dark coats.

She can still hear Helen's boots clicking. Still running toward her. Then another thick stab of pain, this time to the side of her head. Helen's right boot, midair, kicking at her face. Julia raises her arms to block, but all is blurring.

"I said, don't," Helen says. Her tone is calm, punitive, "I *said*, don't." Helen then places her knees down upon Julia's biceps and begins a series of harsh punches to the face. Helen speaks to her between each blow. "I want—" strike, "you to understand," strike, "that pain," strike, "can be," strike, "never-ending."

Julia Iris passes out.

Sons and Fathers

November 3, this year
Verona, Italy

"She's been gone too long," Loche says.

William Greenhame nods. "This is true. Have you tried to call again?"

"Four times now. She isn't answering."

"Seems to be a pattern," Greenhame agrees. "Samuel, in America, has not been answering, nor have several others of our people."

"I don't like this," Loche says.

"Nor do I," William says, his fingers typing a message on his phone. "I'm sending a group to seek for Julia."

"How did she slip away?" Loche asks.

William shrugs, "Clever girl. And yet, careless. She is not yet aware of the danger at hand. Don't be too troubled. She is, after all, rather dangerous herself."

Edwin bounds into the room and climbs into Greenhame's lap. A wooden sword is in his hand. "Can we fight now, *Greenum*?"

William looks into Edwin's face, beaming. Loche notes how the man's eyes suddenly glisten.

Before William answers Edwin, he hesitates, glances at Loche, back to Edwin, and then again at the boy's father. Holding Loche's stare he says, with a sprawling grin, "Call me, *Granddad*."

Loche shakes his head, "William, I don't think that I'm ready for that."

Edwin cries, "Granddad?"

"That's right, little one. I am your *Granddad*."

"You're *my* Granddad?"

"Correct. I am your father's father."

"But you don't look like a Granddad. Not old."

William smiles, "Ah, well that may be true. But I'm afraid that *I am* quite old, ancient, elderly—over six hundred years old."

"You are not."

"I am, too."

"No you're not."

"If you don't believe me, ask your dad, little one."

"I'm not so *little,* you know," Edwin says with slight defiance.

"Oh, yes you are," William says. "Just look at these little mitts." Edwin holds his palm up and spreads his fingers. He lays it into William's hand. "You see, this is a wee, little claw."

"Excuse me, Greenhame," Loche says.

William, still speaks to Edwin, "But you see, this wee clamper can still wield a sword."

"Wield?" Edwin says. "What's *wield?*"

"That, my dear little fellow, means to employ, use, brandish, swing."

"William—" Loche says.

"Swing!" Edwin cries, "I know how to swing a sword." He climbs down and whips the toy sword through the air.

"That is good," William laughs, clapping his hands.

Loche, "You two, please!"

William stands. From beside his chair he lifts his umbrella and taps it against Edwin's sword. Edwin retaliates with a series of chest high crosscuts that pushes the laughing William back a few steps.

Loche watches the exchange. He tries to accept that what he is seeing is his son and, truly, *his own father*—having a play sword fight—a Granddad and a grandson. He wrote Greenhame into his life—as his father—and it came to be. Again, he tries to work it all out, like he has so many times in the last couple of days. Then their laughter together, the tapping of their imagined weapons, Edwin's earnest attempts at besting his tall adversary, and their genuine camaraderie sweeps the surreal aside—presses the fear back—reminds him that somehow, this was all supposed to happen—that there is a reason for this. His boy and his father, playing together—something he never thought he would see.

Edwin's attack is fierce and he drives William back into his chair. The boy then drops his sword and rushes in to tackle. William gathers him into his arms. They are both laughing.

"Why did you drop your sword, my little leaf?" Greenhame asks.

"I'm done *wielding*, for now, Granddad."

William turns to Loche. Loche nods at him. "Granddad, huh?"

"Well," William says, "I've waited long enough—for you—and him. So, yes, *Granddad* will work nicely."

"Very well," Loche says.

"Now," William says to Edwin, "why don't you go into the kitchen. I put some cake and milk on the table in there for you."

Without a word, Edwin dashes from William's lap to the hall leading to the kitchen.

Loche watches him disappear around the corner. He reaches to his phone and checks it again. "Nothing. Where is she?"

"Loche," William says, "understand that the young woman is dealing with something you can only begin to imagine." He lifts his fingers to his chin and turns his gaze away in thought. "Now, isn't that something?"

"What?"

"Well, it seems that you did *imagine* it, yes?" Greenhame says. "But let's just say that you cannot fully empathize. Not yet anyway. It would take you at least a lifetime. Julia will be fine. She's intuitive, thoughtful and disciplined. Whatever steps into her fate, I believe that she will either dance with it or crush it underfoot." Loche sighs. William eyes him carefully. "And, as I'm sure you've begun to consider, to love an immortal carries with it its own perils. A curse."

"You mean, the dangers surrounding *Orathom Wis*?" Loche asks.

"No, I am not speaking of our defending of Humanity against the intervention of the Divinities. Though, it is a twisted, tricky, deathly business, indeed. No. I am speaking of the danger to your heart and soul, son. There are no perils like that of lost love."

Again, it hits like a wave. He had thought of it. He will age and die, she will live on. "I will prepare for it," Loche says quietly. "Whatever time we have together will be enough for me."

William's face shadows, "That is noble of you. But again, shortsighted. You may have written we *deathless beings* into existence, but for all your imaginings, you know naught of what you've done—what you've made— what it is to be, *we*." William stands and crosses the room. "It is not of the danger to *your* heart that I speak, but of Julia's. The time you have will be enough for you. For you will end and leave this world. To the *Orathom*." He turns and glares at Loche, "But not her. Her love for you will go on, here, unrequited, alone. She will watch you wither. She will watch you forget her. That is how our kind dies, Loche. We are driven into madness by watching those we love, leave. *Ithic veli agtig.*" William turns toward the window. "You will be her *curse*." He forces a smile, nudging the curtain to the side. The tone of his voice lightens. "But it is no matter. I will not question the ruling powers of love, *damn them*. Too long have I thought such thoughts, worried such worries, *cursed such curses*. You know that well about me, do you not, Doctor?"

Loche senses his wonted therapeutic process, discerning each of William's words, considering his body language, his facial expressions—seeking ways in which he can ease pain.

There is a knock on the door.

"Fear me not, Loche," William says, moving to answer, "for I may have been mad once—but that was well before you made me *immortal*." He pauses and stares into the dark grained wood of the door. "Now I'm both, it seems. Alas. *The big deep heavy.*"

William turns the latch and swings the door open. He bows with reverence. *"Anfogal,"* he says.

Loche stands to see the visitor in the doorway. Tall, gangly, long-limbed—a slight wavering as he stands there —slow, almost undetectable swaying from side to side. Loche is struck with a sense that he has met this person before. His hair is shoulder length, orange-brown, framing an awkward, long lipped smile, and two eyes lit like tea in the sunshine.

"Anfogal," William says again as the two shake hands.

"Stupid crazy, eh?" the man says.

Loche's heart rate jumps. He whispers to himself, "George Eversman."

George takes a long arching step into the room and places his hands on Loche's shoulders. "The Poet. The Poet. You been writing? Look like you find the gift, no?"

Loche stares at the man.

George laughs. The sound is bright and cheerful. Loche's shock of meeting a character that he has written is eased by the sound. "No worry, Poet. We meet before, only you were not a Poet then."

William says, "Loche, this is the leader of the *Orathom Wis*, George Eversman."

"Yes," Loche replies, in awe—in shock, shaking his head, "yes, I know. I can't tell you how I know, nor begin to explain what my mind is attempting to sort out—the crisscross of reality—reality and—"

"Stupid crazy," George adds.

All Loche can do is nod.

William's phone rings. "Excuse me," he says and steps outside.

"Well, work we have to do," George says, "and work we must begin now."

He gestures for Loche to sit.

"The news is reporting about the battle at the Uffizi," George says.

"My God," Loche breaths out. "What are they saying?"

"Not good," George waves his hand toward some vague place. "Not good. Many are gone. Most everyone is out of their mind. Ravistelle's security did well to keep witnesses away. Only a few can tell what they saw. Barely." George places his long fingered hand upon Loche's shoulder. "News says that it was a kind of chemical attack—some terrorist plot."

Loche shakes his head. The nightmare of his writing reaches further. The story devours each coming day.

"I've killed—" his voice falters.

"Don't worry, you," George comforts. "Dis was all to happen. Dis was all supposed to be."

"But I—"

"Stop, now." George scowls. Loche wonders if there will be an end to what he's created. His mind ticks through the plot points—the dire consequences of his imagined worst case scenario. What if Albion Ravistelle succeeds?

"We leave soon," George says, "Your work as Poet is just begin. But you no write now. Not now. Now, you living in your poems, right? You understand? You living in your work, now."

Loche leans forward and listens.

"But your work no happen here," George raises his spindly fingers and grabs at the air. His peculiar grin stretches out. "Not dis place. No, you go to the other place, where the gods are. Your job is there."

"What does that mean?" Loche asks, finally.

George answers, "You go with me. I take you to see your brother's pictures. Your job is *in there*." He laid a flap-like hand upon Loche's shoulder, "You go and find Basil. You find Basil. Help him close the door on the gods, for good."

William enters quickly placing his phone into his vest pocket. He is holding Edwin's hand. Edwin's mouth is smeared with dark chocolate. The little boy looks sleepy. William leads him to the couch and lays a blanket over him. The boy immediately begins to doze. Loche, too, suddenly feels the fatigue of travel.

"Are you going to tell me a story, Dad?" he says.

"Not tonight. It's too late," Loche tells him, pulling the blanket up.

"Are you done with your book yet?"

"Not yet," Loche answers.

"Are we writing the good stories, Dad?"

Loche grins. "That's all we can do."

The boy closes his eyes. Loche watches him drift off.

"*Anfogal*," William says, turning to George. He bows again. "Corey Thomas has called and confirmed—*it* has begun."

"How many?" George asks.

"Three are gone, so far."

George sighs. He drops his gaze to the floor. William continues, "The attacks are widespread. The *Orathom Wis* is at war." William is calm, but Loche detects some inner rage being held back.

"What has begun? What attacks?" Loche asks, pulling his son into his arms.

"Albion Ravistelle," William replies, "has ordered the assassination and vanquishment of the *Orathom Wis*. He moves to destroy our Order on Earth."

"We must go," George says. "Ready your people, William."

"I will as you say," William replies.

"We retreat to *Mel Tiris*. Send the summons."

"I will as you say."

"*Mel Tiris*?" Loche asks.

"A castle along the Rhine River. North. It is our last stronghold. Reminiscent, they say, of the majesty of *Wyn Avuqua* in *deli aun*."

"You mean the civilization above Priest Lake?"

"Correct."

"Samuel," George interjects. "Where, where is Samuel?"

"In America, *Anfogal*," William answers. "He has not called in. We have attempted to contact him—"

"Why is he not here?" George says. After a moment, George snaps his fingers, "Leonaie. Try phone Leonaie?"

"Of course," William says shaking his head. "He's with Leonaie at *Greenhaven's* in Coeur d'Alene."

"What?" Loche says.

"*Greenhaven's Retirement Community*," William answers, dialing. "I own the franchise. My dearest friends are often near the end of their lives. They are really the only ones with some sense of life's meaning. I've a fascination with the elderly, you know. I've used much of my fortune to ease their passage from here to there."

"Leonaie?" Loche asks.

William waits as his call rings through. "Samuel's love," he answers, "*His* curse."

Julia.

As if in answer to his thought, Loche's phone rings. But it is not Julia's name that appears—instead, a number. The Idaho 208 area code does not immediately register. It isn't until he presses *answer* that the number suddenly makes sense to him. He holds the phone to his ear and waits. His eyes slowly drift to Edwin.

The boy is asleep. His little chest rising and falling— deep in dreams. His mother is calling.

The Assassin

November 3, this year, Coeur d'Alene, Idaho
Greenhavens Retirement Community

Leonaie Echelle straddled Samuel's naked body, her thighs gripping his pelvis and her fingers clasped behind his neck. She covets his face—a face haunted with the sight of her, lit with awe and joy. She could see him watching her as the arc of her body slowed to a stop. The only movement she now felt was her breathing, her rib cage rising and falling, and the surge of blood coursing beneath her skin.

"Leonaie."

There was nothing that would pull her eyes from his. She felt her body relax and her weight gently drop pulling him deeper inside.

"Leonaie, my darling."

Then she rolled off and laid beside him. She touched her nose to his. "Let's not visit the city. Paris will not miss you today. Let's stay in, eat, drink and make love," she had said.

"Leonaie. You must wake."

"What do you mean?"

"Leonaie! Wake!"

Leonaie's eyes bat. Hard particles of what she guesses is glass plink down her cheeks. In her sight is Samuel, lying on his side, staring at her. She nuzzles her nose to his again. "Hello," she sighs.

"Leonaie," Samuel says, "are you with me? Are you hurt?"

The question is strange. *Why would I be hurt? I am in bed in a Paris hotel*, she thinks. As if in answer to her question, a throbbing ache and sting visits her senses from several points in her body. The pain rouses her to the present.

"Don't panic, my darling," Samuel says in a voice straining for grace. "But in about thirty seconds, men are going to enter through the door. They will cut me apart. And, I'm afraid, I can't move."

Leonaie gapes. Samuel's smile is grim.

"What? Why? What has happened?"

"Seems they have quite a good marksman outside. I've been sniped. A well aimed bullet has severed my cervical spine, at least, this seems evident. I can't—well, let's see, I can't move from my—my shoulders, no, wait, my neck down. Nope. Quite paralyzed. Alas."

"Samuel, my darling—"

"There is no pain, my sweet dear, however, I won't be able to defend myself, so I will need your help. Listen closely. Can you move?"

Leonaie feels a surge of adrenaline, each of her limbs flex and she sits up. "Yes," she says. *Barely,* she thinks.

Samuel continues, quick but calm. "Inside my bag, beside the bed, is a syringe of Demerol. You will also find a square velvet bag—it is black. Shrouded in the bag is a five by seven painting on canvas by none other than Mr. Basil Pirrip Fenn." A chill ripples through Leonaie at the recognition of Basil's name.

She starts, "You warned me to never look—"

"That is correct," he says, "do not look at it. But you will need our visitors to look. Hold the syringe in one hand and force the painting into their line of sight. Raise it to their faces, Leonaie. Once the Center takes them in, you must sedate them." Samuel shrugs his shoulders suddenly, "Ah," he cries, "yes, I am coming back—but still not quite there—it will take a few minutes for my body to recover. You must succeed or we will both die here today. Can you manage it, my love?"

"I don't—I don't know if I can—"

"You can do this. Hurry, Leonaie. Hurry."

The old woman struggles to stand. Her lower back and right leg shoot with a ferocious pain. She moans as she straightens and takes hold of Samuel's *Doctor Victor* bag. She immediately spots the syringe. It is oversized, full of the drug with a long needle capped with a plastic tip. She tears it off and tosses it away.

Samuel's phone is within. It begins to vibrate.

There are footsteps in the hall.

"Did you find the demerol?" Samuel calls from the floor. He is faced away from the door. "Leonaie, I can't see you. Did you—"

"Yes," she answers. "I've got it."

"The painting, Leonaie. You will need the—"

"I have it." Leonaie feels the velvet bag and lifts it out. Its top is rimmed in elastic. She recalls the dangerous nature of Basil Fenn's paintings.

"How will I know which side has the Center?"

"You will know," Samuel says.

Leonaie's finger runs along the edge of the wood frame. She determines the correct way to hold it.

The door handle begins to turn.

Samuel whispers, "Courage, my love. Courage."

Leonaie limps her feeble legs before the entrance. The knob rotates without sound, then the door pushes toward her. It moves slow. But Leonaie is too close, and as it opens into the room it presses her slippered feet quietly back until she is pinned between the wall and the open door.

She cannot see who has come. She feels faint.

"Ah," she hears a voice say. "Send word."

Another voice, quietly: "Target achieved. Preparing to cut. We're on our way out."

Leonaie thinks that she hears a nearly inaudible voice say, "Copy," as if from an earpiece.

She lets her lids fall and listens. Her breathing is low. Her pulse is thick, sluggish. There is the sound of footsteps entering the room. Two? Three sets of feet? *When they are in, they will close the door. They will close the door. Right now, they will close the door. They will see me.*

Then from the floor she hears Samuel, mocking a woman's voice in shrill surprise, "Excuse me! I'm not decent!"

The door pulls away from Leonaie's face as her hands grip the painting and the syringe. To her amazement, she is not discovered. She shrinks back and sees one man to her left, his back to her, taking one last look into the hallway before closing the door. Another man, very tall is looking down upon her poor Samuel. Both men are dressed in casual attire. *Golf shirts*, Leonaie thinks. They both look as if they could have elderly parents residing here. The man to Leonaie's left turns out and away, again failing to see the old woman three feet from him. He unslings a backpack and lays it on the bed.

Samuel's tone is jovial, "Really, you two, who's the shooter? Hell of a shot. I've not been hit like this in. . . well. . . come to think of it, I've never been hit like this."

"This will be easier if you don't speak, Samuel," the tall man says without tone.

"I assume that you would call such a target, the sweet spot, yes?"

The tall man does not answer.

"Perfect shot—base of the skull—severing the spinal cord—that satisfying puff of pink mist—resulting in, of course, paralysis."

The shorter man unzips the backpack and pulls from it a roll of plastic sheeting and a blue satchel made of what looks to be tarp material.

"Paralysis, at least, for a short while, considering fellows like me. Just enough time to, well—"

The man sets the sheeting on the floor, steps on the edge and kicks the roll away. It unravels a long swath. He then lifts from the bag, one by one, varying steel implements: a bone saw, a thick cutting blade and a sheathed dagger.

"Enough time for," Samuel continues, "some practice at meat cutting."

"Truly, Mr. Lifeson, your silence is best."

"I'm a little disappointed at your lack of courage, however. Guns are bullshit. Quite dishonorable."

"You will see a blade momentarily, Mr. Lifeson."

"It appears that you know my name, but, I'm afraid, I can't quite place you." Samuel says.

"It doesn't matter," the tall man replies.

"Oh, but it does indeed, matter, my boy, for if you are to do what you're about to do, I believe that it is only proper that you introduce yourself to me. Might you roll me toward you? I think a nine-hundred and seventy-two-year-old man deserves to meet the children that have the balls to end him."

The tall man does not hesitate. He crouches down and lays hold of Samuel's shoulder rotating him onto his back. The man then rolls him again. Harder this time. His shoulder blades crack on the tile. With one more pull Samuel's body is framed on the plastic sheeting. Samuel's head lolls to the right.

Leonaie sees his eyes scan the room in quick darts. He does not pause on any one spot, but Leonaie knows that he's seen her, cowering against the wall, behind the two assassins.

Samuel then trains his focus on the two men. "And you are?" he asks.

"The name is Wishfeill. Emil Wishfeill. "

"Wishfiell. Wishfeill. Hmm. Why do I know that name? I knew a Felix Wishfeill." Samuel stops. "Wait a moment. This is quite out of character for Albion Ravistelle. Please tell me that he didn't send Felix Wishfeill's son on a quest for vengeance."

Emil Wishfeill is silent. He flings his open hand through the air and slaps Samuel across the face. The crack causes Leonaie to nearly lose her balance.

"Aye," Emil says. "You cut him up in Venice—tossed his head into the sea."

Samuel winces at the blow. "That I did. Your father was a misled tool. I do formally apologize that his actions have caused you and your family grief, but had he remained in service to Ravistelle, he would have been an accomplice to the end of humanity as we know it—quite simply. Such business makes for a bad reputation. Though I see the apple hasn't fallen far from the tree."

Emil reaches into his coat and produces a pair of long plastic gloves. He pulls them on, keeping eye contact with Samuel. The shorter man, holding the bone saw rounds the side of the bed. "Here." He hands it to Emil. The saw blade is thick and serrated. Emil examines it.

"This is going to hurt," he says to Samuel. "A lot."

Leonaie's tears rise. She lifts the painting up as if it is a gun. Her grip is tight though she is trembling. The painting shakes at the end of her outstretched arm.

"Do you think that this is the first time I've been dismembered?" Samuel asks. "I know this pain. I know it well. That is more than you can say, young Wishfeill. How old are you? What, thirty? Thirty five?"

"Old enough to take you down. My father taught me the weaknesses of your kind, and your darkest fear."

"Did he?" Samuel asks.

"No more talk," the shorter man growls. "He's stalling you. Begin before he has the chance to heal."

Samuel continued, "So instead of injuring me to unconsciousness, you intend to cut me apart while I watch? Is that it?"

"You will feel the pain and you will watch your life force divide and fade. The greatest fear of your kind, watching the light die."

"Ah," Samuel says, "vengeance should have no bounds."

Emil lays Samuel's lifeless arm out onto the tile and rests the serrated edge at the center of the bicep. He stops, shakes his head and grins. "No," he whispers, "I'll get to that." He then moves the saw down the arm to the bare wrist. "Let's start at the extremities." He smiles. "Ouchie."

"*I* will watch," Samuel says, now eyeing the blade closely. "*You* will watch, your douche bag *friend* here, will watch. But I do not think your father, even with all of his ill chosen malefactions and untrained wit would want *her* to watch." Samuel's eyes tick up and over Emil's shoulder. The two men turn.

Leonaie feels their shock at the sight of her and it forces her to stagger back. As she thrusts the painting out in an attempt to remove their eyes from hers, to capture them, her grip fails. The canvass falls to the floor, face down. Leonaie drops to her knees to retrieve it. Emil's companion steps toward the old woman and places a foot upon the painting as Leonaie's attempts to claw it from the floor. "And what have we here?" he says. The man bends, takes hold of her thin arms, lifts her to her feet and presses her against the wall. He notes the syringe and easily pulls it from her hand.

Emil, still kneeling beside Samuel, sighs and laughs. "Oh my," he says. "This day just got better. So, the mighty immortal, Samuel Lifeson, calls to his defense his," he pauses, searching for the right words, "his, *old lady*. This is too good to be true."

The other holds up the syringe. "It seems their weapon of choice is—what is this? Something to sedate us?" Leonaie begins to cry, staring at Samuel. She sees his face struggling with rage and helplessness.

"Did you really think this old bitch could move fast enough? Really, Samuel? You could have sent her away. Instead, you've given me a sweet, sweet gift. A sweeter revenge. More than I could ask for." He looks up to her. "Leonaie is the name, right?" Leonaie does not answer. She looks down at the painting still under the shorter man's foot.

"Leonaie." Emil's voice is gentle. "Watch this."

Who's Grave Is This?

April, 1338,
the village of Ascott-under-Wychwood, England

William took hesitant peeks.

Outside the sun was setting. The smoke was still thick, hanging on the air like dirty lace over a window. All above was a lurid scarlet.

The two guards drove their shovels into the earth. Soon, they were waist deep in the tiny grave. Radulphus had chosen a place behind the church out of sight of the lane and the courtyard wall. William's eyes were shut. He could hear the shovels, the heavy shifting feet of a horse nearby, and he could feel his father's hand upon his chest. With great care he cracked his lids open slightly. His father was on his knees beside him, looking around as if searching for something. He then noticed the tiny glint of light in William's eyes. He covered them with his hand.

"Deeper. And make haste," the escort said.

The sound of the digging sped up.

"Priest," the escort asked, "you knew the witch?"

"I did," Radulphus replied. He moved his hand to William's forehead and caressed it.

"Did you know of her *Craft?*"

"I knew that she brought light and healing to many."

The escort sighed. "Yes, I have heard tell of that. *Simon the Thatcher*. The plague has been purged from their house—from their blood. I have heard tell that she was a master of herb lore."

Radulphus did not respond. William peeked one eye open His father's head was turning this way and that, as if searching for some sign—some path to take. The two guards were now chest deep in the ground. William chanced a look in the direction of the escort. He could see his high boots and richly fashioned garments. A long sword with a gold hilt was sheathed at his side. His face was proud. William was fascinated by the noble expression and attractive features. Then, with a sudden burst of fear, William realized that the escort was looking at him—straight into his peeping eye. William let his lids relax and all went black again. His heart pounded in his chest.

"Well bless my soul," the escort muttered. After a moment he asked, "Was the boy the witch's son?"

"He was," Radulphus answered.

"Troubling. Had he a name?"

"William."

"I wonder if he carries with him any of her *charm*?"

"He carried only what a son should—the beauty of her eyes, and the warmth of her love. He was too young to carry more."

"Ah, so he does not possess traces of her Craft?"

"He now possesses nothing. Not even breath." William heard his father's voice break into weeping.

The escort's tone became stern, "Which of you drew the knife across the lad's throat?"

The digging stopped. The coarse voice of the squat-faced guard replied, "God's will, my Lord, 'twas I. I put an end to the murderous tyke, on Bishop Gravesend's word."

"I see," the escort said. "And did he bleed?"

"Aye, the little devil did. Like a coney on the board."

"I would very much like to see the wound. Where did you slice him?"

"Across the throat, my Lord," the man said.

"Priest, remove the cloth from his throat. Show me this knave's handiwork."

"Leave the dead in peace," William's father said—his voice booming. William felt a raking heat across his skin.

William heard the escort shift in his stance and cough. suddenly. "Priest, I think I know what lay behind that bandage. And if I am correct, I am overjoyed. But, do show these gravediggers that things are not always as they seem. Do but peel it away."

William felt the air still. He dared not open his eyes. Yet, some strange confidence quelled his fear. An unexpected comfort. It was something about the way the escort spoke. A kind of caring and sympathy. Empathy. Behind his closed lids, William imagined his father and the escort staring at each other—the escort gesturing that all will be well.

William felt his father's fingers pulling at the bandage. Flakes of dried blood skittered down the sides of his neck. The cool of the spring night chilled the skin on his bare throat.

The boy heard the two shovels drop into the dirt. One of the guards gasped and began whispering a sacrament. The other cried out, "This cannot be—there is some evil afoot. The Devil! He's the Devil I tell you!"

"William?" the escort said. "Bring terror to these riotous knaves." There was a ring of a blade unsheathing. "Do open your eyes, boy. Open your eyes to a life never-ending."

William saw the two guards. Their heads and chests rising a little above the ground. Like faces of sculpted shock and fear, they gaped at the boy. The smaller of the two raised his shovel and climbed toward him. "You shall not live. By God, you shall not!"

Then a flash of silver metal streaked across William's vision as the escort's sword sliced the man's head from his body. It lolled to the side and dropped into the grave. The rest of him followed.

Radulphus pulled William back and away.

The escort remained still and held his ground. "Come, come, tool," he said to the other guard, "if you must kill the boy, you must kill me first."

The squat-faced guard rolled his body out of the grave. He plucked up his sword from the grass and unsheathed it. "You devil!" he spat. "I'll gut you."

"I would expect nothing less."

The guard rushed forward and threw his blade in a round sweep toward the escort's throat. The escort simply took a single step back. "You see, William," he said, adjusting his stance, "the best defense, always, is to stay out of the way." Again the guard swung, this time in a cleaving motion, aimed at his opponent's shoulder. The escort stepped to the right. "Another perfect example," he continued, "there is no sense in parrying this knave's sword just yet, for he does not have the skill of a master." Another poorly aimed swing and another dodge. "As a swordsman, you will learn that the first few moments of a duel are paramount to understanding your enemy and his abilities." The guard roared with fury and frustration. With a slight pivot, he stabbed forward. Finally, the two swords connected, the escort easily deflecting his attacker away. "You'll also find that words are a much better weapon than the sword. You see, this poor fellow is easily angered. Ah pride. What weakness."

The guard paused, heaving and enraged. Fear tugged at his eyes. He glanced quickly at the body and the severed head piled in the grave and then back to the escort.

"Something to keep in mind, William," the escort said, "when faced with a wild, uneducated man with a sword, is that they can be evermore dangerous than a master, for one cannot anticipate their movements. There is no poetry in them. No strategy. His only concern is survival—and when faced with death, a desperate man will do nearly anything to live. He will become savage."

The guard narrowed his eyes at the escort. He gripped his sword with two hands and held it up in defense and waited. The escort smiled. "And here, the knave has learned. You see, William, words can be deadly. If the prideful cannot master what he hears, he has no armor."

The escort stepped forward and dealt a series of blows. Slow and precise, each swing was given with intention so that the guard could defend with ease.

"And now," the escort said, taking a defensive step back, "is the end of the lesson. Watch carefully, for this is something even he won't expect. Remember, every duel should have surprises, a story, poetry and meaning. There's nothing worse than two brutes swinging wildly trying to break the other's limbs. I prefer dance and elegance before the end. Now watch carefully." The escort lowered his sword and sniffed the air. He then said to the guard, "Come now, sir. Bring your best violence."

Before the escort could finish his invitation, the guard pressed. The escort batted the blade aside twice. "Yes, very well, you're in earnest," the escort said. The third thrust met with its target and slid deep into the escort's belly.

The escort let out a wheezing groan and fell to his knees. His hands covered the wound as he collapsed onto his back.

William turned his head into his father's chest and clung to his robes.

"Who's the knave now?" the guard spat.

Radulphus climbed to his feet and lifted William into his arms.

"Bring the devil rat here!"

The priest backed away but was halted by the touch of the guard's blade upon his cheek.

"God's will, Priest. Drop the tyke."

"I won't," Radulphus said.

"Then I'll kill him in your arms."

Then the voice of the escort, "I'm not dead yet."

William saw the guard turn. In the air, whirling toward them, was a silver gleam of light followed by the sound of a snap, like a branch cracked against the trunk of a tree. The guard sunk to his knees and fell back onto the ground. A dagger from the escort's hand was impaled in his forehead.

Why and How—The Gift

Los Angeles, June 27, 1972
The Continental Hyatt House, Sunset Strip

The doctor finally took a step back from Helen and turned. He looked through the window with an expression that was crimped and bewildered. He exited the kitchen and joined Jimmy and Richard.

Helen could see him through the window, his head in his hands. She heard him say, "Well first of all, mates, I think you can let me in on the joke now."

Richard took a step forward, "What do you mean?"

"I mean, she's fine—and there's no way she could have made that fall without some kind of cut, or worse. I mean really, what are you two smoking? What's the joke? Where did the blood come from?"

Richard jerked his head to Jimmy and his mouth opened to protest.

"I don't get it," the doctor said.

"Neither do I," Jimmy agreed as he pushed the door open and walked through. Helen's eyes shot to him. A wave of relief washed over her—and the same kind of excitement that she felt earlier in the evening. Only now, the sharp light erased the mysterious glitter, the haze of a candlelit buzz and the plushy excess of rock riffs and red crushed velvet shoes. *This was the real backstage to this lifestyle*, Helen thought suddenly. The blood on white tiled floors in a bright hotel kitchen—a bloodied, young female fan, and a guitarist. She scowled. *I hope he doesn't think he caused all of this.*

There was blood on her face, bare legs and hands. Her chiffon top was splattered with red. One of her velvet platforms was cracked and broken. The hair on the left side of her head was matted and caked with dried blood.

But there was not a single trace of a laceration, no scars, punctures or tears in her skin. Jimmy moved toward her and picked up the wet washcloth that was wadded up on a stainless steel prep table. He took it to the sink, rinsed the blood out. Kneeling before her he softly pressed the cloth against her forehead and scanned for something that would explain why she was still breathing.

Helen stared at him. She was frightened, but her heart raced on the edge of bliss—for the man of her dreams held worry in his eyes—worry for her.

"Helen," Jimmy asked almost in a whisper, "can you tell me what is happening? We watched you fall from the top of the hotel. You are not hurt, and for that I am grateful and elated. But, I don't understand. Can you tell me what you remember?"

Helen felt the memory of pain. It was a flash in her mind, brief but shocking—and she winced. Her tiny frame quivered as if from a sudden chill. Then she was still again. She opened her mouth to speak, but no words came. Confusion drifted across her face and she looked down at the dried blood smeared along her bare arms. She lightly brushed at her left forearm with trembling fingers as if trying to uncover what was beneath the skin.

"Both of my arms broke. The pain was awful. My wrist bones were poking out. That's where the blood came from," her voice was quavering. "I saw the bones. My right leg too, both my thigh and ankle. And I could feel something wet on the side of my head." Her hand rose to her matted hair. "Really wet. It must have been my head. It was a lot of blood. When I saw pools of it around me, I passed out."

The face of Jimmy Page was unflinching. She looked at him, "And when I woke up, I was on my feet, walking to the bench. I felt sort of, well, tired and foggy. Like I just woke up in the middle of the night to get a drink of water—but I wasn't really quite awake. Maybe like sleepwalking or something. Then, Richard was standing beside me and he was trying to pick me up. I was so tired that I let him." Helen glanced over Jimmy's shoulder to the window in the door. "Then I woke up a little more, and I'm here."

Richard entered the room and stood beside the door. He was still pale. "Still feeling alright, love?" he asked Helen. She nodded without looking at him—a hint of disgust crossed her face. "Right," Richard carried on, "well it is again, time to go."

She read confusion in Jimmy's face. What did this mean? How did she survive the fall? Why was he a witness to this? She could see his fascination.

Why and how—two of Jimmy Page's most used words. Jimmy was a seeker, she knew that. Hell, the whole world knew that, and the media was getting an enormous amount of mileage when it came to the mysterious guitarist from Led Zeppelin and his dealings with the occult. Of course, most of their so called facts were imagined and misunderstood, but it was a great story, after all. And for whatever it was worth, the devilish image sold records, fascinated fans and best of all, scared the hell out of the God fearing Christians. They had painted a picture of a man searching for answers to life's biggest questions in evil places—places that had been demonized—rituals that were medieval and dark. They called him a worshiper of Lucifer, a student of black magic and he may have even taken part in human sacrifice. *Whatever.* She could imagine Richard telling him, "Fuck it. If stories of Old Nick make us a few extra quid—where do I sign my soul over? Collect your books, Jimmy, I need a new car." But fans knew that Jimmy Page was indifferent to the media's depiction of his pursuits. Despite the dark prince image, he was purely curious. *Why? How?* It was true that last year, 1971, he had purchased Allister Crowley's Boleskine House—and it was indeed filled with a sinister mood, pagan artifacts and a multitude of books about gods long vanquished by the so called One God. He had also opened his own occult bookshop and publishing house in London. Conventional folk considered his inquiries into the nature of things as dangerous, but Jimmy would shrug and say, "You don't quite get it." He had been quoted as saying that his interests were liberating and uniting once you eliminated the stigmas that had been bred by the Church. The basic principle of Crowley's, *do what thy wilt*, had been taken out of context so many times that he finally gave up trying to explain to the media. Instead he merely played the mystic, studied deeper into his fasciation and remained open to a wider view of humanity, and whatever else.

And sitting before him now was a kind of gift—a kind of answer to the speculative texts, the mythic tales, the wonted leap of faith—here before him was a person that was impervious to injury, that could heal at miraculous speed—and had no conception of how or why.

Richard's voice was louder this time, "Now, Jimmy. We shouldn't waste anymore time." Then to Helen, "It's time to go, love."

"She can't leave looking like this, Richard," Jimmy said blankly, still studying the young girl. "We should get her a room so she can clean up—and a change of clothes."

One of the hulking bodyguards stepped into the room and relayed a message. "The police are on their way again —I don't think it's about this," he nodded to Helen, "but there's been some complaints about the festivities upstairs."

"That does it," Richard blurted. "Bring the robe. Is the cab waiting?"

"Yeah, it's outside. He's waiting at the service entrance," he said. The bodyguard leaned out of the door and received a plastic wrapped bathrobe from the other massive bodyguard. He handed it to Richard.

Richard tore the plastic off, shook the fabric out and held it up by the shoulders for Helen to thread into. "Alright, my sweet—it is time. Jimmy, help me here."

Jimmy bowed his head. She could see him struggling. His curiosity was completely engaged. *Why did they meet? What is her purpose?* "I think she should stay," he said finally.

"Cops are here," came the muffled voice of the bodyguard outside the room.

"Fuck this!" Richard cried as he nodded to the bodyguard. The huge man moved quickly over to Helen and stood her on her feet, whirled her around and backed her into the waiting bathrobe. Jimmy stood up and laid hold of her wrist. Richard, said, "Damn it, Jimmy. Let go. Let me do my job. If you want jail tonight, a reputation darker than what you have already and federal charges, by all means, drag this out! If you want to keep playing guitar and writing songs, let me get her out of here!"

After the guard had tied the robe tightly around her waist he lifted her up in his arms and moved toward the door. Helen didn't resist. She trained her eyes on Jimmy hoping he would stop them.

"Wait," Jimmy said. "How can we get in touch with you, Helen? Do you have a telephone number?" Helen shook her head. At Richard's prompting, the guard stepped through the door and started down the service hall with haste. Jimmy started after them but Richard and the other guard blocked his pursuit, and held him forcibly back. "Richard, let me go!" he yelled, struggling to break through.

"Let me do my job. Let me do my job."

Jimmy stood still. Richard's hands were still pressing the guitarist's shoulders.

"Sorry, mate," Richard said as easily as he could manage. His sweaty, wide-eyed face hovering uncomfortably close. "But you must understand—of course you understand—it would be this kind of thing that would end us in the States."

Jimmy shoved Richard back and glared at him. "Fine," he said flatly. "This may not be the place—but you find out where she's been dropped. I will meet with her again. You arrange that. Do you hear me?"

The car door slammed shut. Helen pressed her hand to the window and spread her fingers. Jimmy waved at her. As red and blue lights flashed against the white brick of the alley, the cab screeched away. Helen's eyes stayed on Jimmy until the turn onto Sunset.

Ransom

November 4, this year
Verona, Italy

Julia's eyes flip open. She feels the cold of a window against her forehead. There is the flavor of blood. Outside are streaming lights of passing cars, neon signs tracing in long smears, and a blurring landscape speeding by. She flinches—the memory of the beating—Loche Newirth's wife looming over her—then gripping fingers turn her chin from the window to the seat beside. Helen Newirth lets go and caresses Julia's cheek.

"It appears I lost my temper," Helen says. The light of a street lamp angles across Helen's eyes. Two sparkling lights stare into Julia's face. Julia jerks away. Helen's hand pulls back for an instant. Once the initial shock recedes, Julia feels the woman's long fingers again touching her, an airy fragrance of flowers, the soft skin of her fingers—tipped with finely polished nails. "Take it easy, take it easy," Helen offers.

There is no color in the eyes piercing her—grey and deep as the stone sky overhead. There is age somehow, Julia thinks. Age that does not match the attractive shape of her mouth, smoothness of her skin, or the sincerity of her expression. No, it is seated deep within the woman's gaze, behind her eyes, perhaps. Julia suddenly feels young. Like a child beside an elderly lady—an elderly, thirty-looking-gorgeous-something.

"Let's call my husband, shall we?" Helen says, holding up Julia's cell phone. "I think he's worried about where you are."

Julia does not answer. She continues to stare at Helen.

"I see that you're healing just fine. The bruises are going away." Her tone is motherly as she gently paws at the last traces of Julia's disappearing cuts. "I suppose you've never been beaten like that? Probably not," she says. "Not yet used to the pain, are you? Not used to the thrill of being hurt and healing so quick. Not used to *wanting* more." Helen lowers her hand and places it upon Julia's thigh. She squeezes it, "Would you like more, darling?"

Julia is silent.

"Because our kind must learn to live with pain, you know. The reality of torture has a very different meaning. You see, regular folks that deal with pain, beatings, torture, will eventually pass away. Die. For example, if I were to, say, carve into your tummy with my knife, dawdle around in there for a couple of hours—get fucking medieval with you—" Helen inhales with a wincing hiss, "Ouchie."

Julia feels her hands begin to shake.

"The next day?" Helen says, raising her eyebrows. "All better." She shrugs. "Then we start all over again. And again. And again."

Julia hears her voice and is surprised that it does not quaver, "No such thing as *all better* after something like that, Helen."

"Oh," Helen smiles, "you'll survive. And you'll be sorry you did—" She shifts her body, scoots close and lifts Julia's cell phone so that they can both see it. Loche's latest text:

I love you, Julia. Please come back. William has sent some of his people to look for you. Call me.

"It is nice to be loved," Helen mocks. She swipes the screen with her thumb to Loche's contact information. "Ah, he has a new number, *and he didn't share it with his wife*—the *mother* of his child. How irresponsible." Helen taps Loche's number into her own phone.

She then leans her lips to Julia's ear. Her breath is warm and as she whispers it brings a terrible, prickling chill, "I can do anything I want to you. I will tear the skin from your face—pull handfuls of hair from your head—

slice your tits off. You're mine now." Julia feels Helen's tongue gently glide into her ear, hot and wet. The woman then turns Julia's eyes to hers. "We can prevent torture, Julia. We can prevent a lot of things, that is, if you'll do as I ask."

"What do you want?"

Helen's phone lights up. Julia sees Loche's number. Helen presses send. "I want my son back."

Look Here

November 3, this year, Coeur d'Alene, Idaho
Greenhavens Retirement Community

Emil leans into the saw and the blade tears through the tendons with the first push. Samuel Lifeson's face infuses with red heat and tears. Leonaie struggles to turn away but the man grabs hold of her head and forces her to look. Samuel cries in a fury-filled whisper, "Look in my eyes darling. Look in my eyes. Oh sweet *Alya* mine, look in my eyes." Leonaie obeys.

The second push with the saw digs deep into the wrist bones. Blood gushes onto the plastic and runs into the tile troughs. "Eyes here," Samuel whispers again. "It does not hurt. It only hurts seeing. Only when you let yourself see it."

Leonaie's vision mists at the edges. Her legs weaken. Her captor tightens his hold and keeps her flat to the wall.

Emil's last two thrusts with the bone saw sever the hand from the arm. He lifts the hand up, dangles it before Samuel's face and then forms it into a fist. Flipping the index finger out he points it to the ceiling. "We'll use this to keep track, shall we?" Emil hisses. "The hand says, *number one*. Cut *one* is complete."

"Fuck you," Samuel spits.

"No," Emil replies, "*that* looks like this." He flicks up the middle finger of the bloody hand. "The long bone. That is what we used to call it." Emil dashes the hand heavily down onto Samuel's chest and aligns the bone saw at the bicep.

"Why not go for the throat and end this," Samuel says. "I can't feel a thing with my spine severed. Makes for a rather comfortable cutting, I should say. I'm not feeling the pain you had so badly wanted. Why prolong this?"

Emil waits upon the notion. He looks from the saw to the motionless body before him to Samuel's face. "True," he says. "True." He lifts the saw. "Bring her to me," he says over his shoulder.

Leonaie's body tenses. She tries to pull away. The man is too strong. She sees the painting still beneath his foot.

"You won't do that. You won't do that," Samuel says.

"Yes, in fact, I will. She's not far from the end anyway. Tell me, would it hurt you to see her hand cut from her arm?"

"You son of a bitch."

"No. Thanks to you, just a fatherless son. Bring her. Lay her wrist over his throat. I think by watching *that* pain, Samuel, you'll cry out. You'll feel that, yes? That will make you wail for your actions. For your loss." Leonaie hears triumph in Emil's voice as if he has finally gained the initiative. "Don't worry, Samuel, after that, the rest is silence."

"Emil," the shorter man says, "just finish him. We are out of time. We are here to take him—she is of no concern of ours."

"Do as I say!" Emil commands.

Leonaie can feel that the man will obey. He easily lifts her away from the wall and pushes her down onto the blood slicked floor. He takes a step to the side. His foot lifts off of the canvas. On her knees, she falls forward and stretches out on her stomach to seize it.

The man watches her. Leonaie's fingers find the wood frame. She slides the small piece into her hand.

"You want this, I see," the man says.

"What is she doing?" Emil asks. "What is that she's reaching for?"

She rolls over onto her back and thrusts the face of the painting before the man's eyes. Leonaie's voice is coarse, "Look here."

The painting's weight is like a large stone. She raises her other arm up to support it. She thinks the light in the room changes—some kind of glitter or strobing pulse sparkles just outside of her focus.

There is a low thud to her right. She turns her head to see Emil's head locked in between Samuel's knees. Emil is tearing at the stump of Samuel's arm. She jerks her focus back to the man above her, scooting her body so that she can see his face. What she sees there she never forgets. Pulled like clay from the chin and forehead, his visage warps and lengthens. His eyes, like swollen black pools filling ever wider with dread and defeat, begin to tear with blood. A strange, thin string of light from the painting touches the center of each inky hole, as if lightning could linger and dance upon a midnight lake. A low, mournful moan issues from his chest as his strength gives out. Unconscious, he drops vertically onto his knees and topples forward, pinning Leonaie.

Emil wheezes struggling for breath. Samuel then begins a gruesome series of blows to the assassin's head with both his fist and the stump of his other arm. Blood and a white foam splatter with each strike. She sees Samuel's expression. He is calm, focused and without emotion.

"Samuel," Leonaie breaths out. "Samuel." Her right rib and hip begin to throb with sharp pains. The dead weight of the man is crushing the air from her lungs. "Samuel."

Samuel then sees her and halts. Fear shadows his face. The hesitation gives Emil the chance he had been waiting for, and he twists free and rolls with clawing effort a few feet away toward the window. His fingers wiping at his bloodied eyes.

Samuel crawls to Leonaie and hefts the unconscious man to the side. He casts a brief appraising glance across Leonaie's face and body. "Breathe darling," he nods. He then reaches up to the bed and pulls the dagger into his remaining hand.

Emil is now staggering to his feet. He kicks at the lower portion of the shattered window. The jagged glass breaks and falls out. He hurls one leg over and maneuvers the rest of his body through. Before he drops out of view he glares back and raises Samuel's severed hand. He waves the mutilated appendage like a child would wave goodbye to a father. "Until we meet again, Mr. Lifeson. I'll hang on to this for you." He then falls away. Samuel staggers in pursuit. But at the window he stops, drops to his knees and stares after him.

Leonaie sits up. She manages to roll over and slowly stand. With a few delicate steps she joins Samuel at the window. Emil pauses beside a waiting vehicle. Its door is open. He peers back at Samuel and Leonaie before climbing in.

"Are you alright, darling?" Samuel asks.

Leonaie looks at his maimed arm, still dripping with a white foam. "Oh this?" he says, hiding the sight of it. "I will be fine. It is not the first time I've had to deal with a missing hand. Not easy, but I'm fine. But are you okay?"

"I think so," Leonaie replies. "I'll be sore."

"I'm afraid that our departure time has just moved up to today. We must leave now."

The door behind them opens suddenly and Olivia enters. Along with her are two large male residents. All three are armed with long, steel blades. Olivia holds a cell phone out to Samuel. "I wish I'd known you were Samuel Lifeson," she says. "I could have provided better security."

"I doubt that I would have been able to visit for the last few years, Olivia, had you known. But thank you," Samuel replies.

"It is the owner of the Greenhavens Community on the line. He said that you've not been answering, so he called *me* to get you on the phone. He'd like a word."

"*Word*? You mean *words*. He's not one on short discourse," Samuel places the phone to his ear, and with a grin at Leonaie he says, "Well now, William Greenhame, I told you to leave me be for a few hours while I play doctor with my lovely gal." Then he begins to inspect the stump of his wrist, "I am afraid that I'm still in surgery. Can I call you back?"

The Mandate

April, 1338
the village of Ascott-under-Wychwood, England

William pushed against his father to be let down. Once on his feet he ran over to the escort. The man was now sitting up with one hand over his stomach. Blood was sloshing out onto his knees. The boy scrabbles at the grass and grips two handfuls. He looks into the escort's face and then down to the wound. His mother would have done something like this, he thinks, and he cautiously presses the handfuls of grass against the escort's stomach.

The escort lets out a slight laugh and a sigh, "Why William, you've got your mother's care, I see."

Radulphus knelt down beside his son.

"Foolish fear mongers," the escort said. "The fearful and ignorant are the worst of all humanity. They breed pain. And how the gods adore them."

Father Grenehamer crossed himself as he stared at the blood.

"Priest, my apologies for the violence. It was unavoidable. Had these two lived, they would have brought the mob upon us and prevented our escape."

"Escape?" Radulphus asked.

"Yes," the escort said, "you two will come with me. There is much to discuss. We haven't much time. A contingent is coming to take you to the Tower."

"But," the priest said, "you're hurt. What can we do to ease you?"

William raised his head and looked at both men. The escort smiled. "Oh this? It's nothing."

"My lord," Radulphus said, "I've seen hurts before—and this is—" He broke off.

"Nay," he said. "For I think the kindness of your son has healed me." He removed his hand from the wound. It had stopped bleeding. He lifted his tunic and showed them where the guard's sword had penetrated. "You see?"

He wiped at the wound, but there was nothing there save a trace of white foam.

The boy and priest stared in wonder. "Who are you?" Radulphus asked.

The man smiled. "It is a pleasure to share with you my name—my *real* name—for there are few that will ever know it." William heard a change in the man's voice. It suddenly had a thick accent from some far away country. "Our kind must have many names as the centuries pass. Many faces. Many disguises." he touched William's cheek with his fingertips. "But our childhood name—it never fades. It is always there. It helps us to remember who we are—to remember a time when we were not cursed." He held his hand out to the little boy. "How I wish I had known you were of the *Itonalya*, before. . . Hello William son of Geraldine, son of Radulphus. My name is Albion Ravistelle."

William watched the firelight. It warmed his face as he stared into its deep caverns of orange coal. His father and Albion sat with him. An iron pot hung from a chain over the flames. It simmered. Nearby was a small pavilion with striped panels of deep green and yellow. Albion's horse drank from the stream a few paces from the encampment.

William's tears surged and disappeared in throes. He felt sleep was close. He missed his mother's voice and her touch.

Radulphus put his arm around the boy.

"What's to become of us?"

Albion looked at the two and sighed. Their bowls were still full of the stew he had prepared, and neither had lifted a spoon to taste. "Eat. Gather your strength."

"You saw Geraldine? She—she's no longer?"

Albion shook his head. "Father, *she* is gone. William, your mother has departed."

William did not stir. The fire was a comfort. Something about the heat. The way it devoured the wood with such beauty and light.

"You're sure?" Radulphus asked.

"I am, Father. I am. If there is one thing about *the fearful* when they are incensed—they are thorough. She is gone. I was too late. But even had I arrived in time, at my best, I could not have overcome the mob." Albion leaned closer to the fire, "And even still, saving her would have been *against* my mandate, for I was sent not to save your wife, but to eliminate her."

Radulphus glared at him, "To *eliminate* my wife?"

Albion nodded, "Yes—two assassinations on this journey. One with pleasure. The other, your wife, with much discord."

"I do not understand. You were sent? Sent by whom?"

"I pray thee, rest easy, Father," Albion comforted. "All will be known in time. But what of your remarkable son? Are you not astounded at his swift restoration? What a gift. What joy to have him here at your side, alive."

"In truth, my lord, I know not how to feel or to conceive," Radulphus looked down at his son. "I have never seen a miracle such as this. It must be the hand of God. Praise him."

"And *that* it is," Albion agreed, "the hand of God. Or so I am instructed to say."

"What is your meaning?"

"When the mob had done my job for me, my visit to the church was merely to offer *you* a fate outside of the Tower. I also have a keen interest in the woman's herb lore—but we will get to that. But, it was when I saw this boy stirring, peeking, beside his grave—still living—I realized that here was one of *my* kind. He is of the *Itonalya*. Within his veins is the blood of immortals."

William pushes his gaze deeper into the fire. Faces appear in the coals. He imagines his mother staring back at him. She is smiling.

"It was easy to see by your care and watch over the boy that Geraldine was more to you than a mere lamb of your flock. You are the boy's father, and the woman's husband. A simple riddle to solve, though, unexpected. I commend you. Love and desire should not be held prisoner to ideology." Albion gestures to the stew. "Eat. It will strengthen you."

"But why do you speak of saving her when you were sent here to eliminate her?"

He paused and thought before answering. "I was sent here to eliminate two. Your wife was one. Yes. In spite of her healings, her peace—her light, she brought joy—hope. These kinds of spirits we will let flourish, though in the end, it is against our ways and our laws. Eventually, she would have been eliminated. Either by me or another of my Order. No spirits cross into the *Alya*—good or bad. Other spirits, however, are not like Geraldine. I take great joy undertaking *their* vanquishment."

"Of whom do you speak?"

Albion looked at the small boy. William was still mesmerized by the crackling fire. A sparkle of light glittered in his eyes. "The Bishop of London. Stephen Gravesend. He is not a man—he is a spirit of malice. A spirit that brings sorrow, fear and terror in the guise of God. My favorite kind of prey."

"Still, I do not follow," Radulphus said.

"Father, spirits from beyond this life, godlike powers, cross into our world. They grow within this weak flesh and exist as a man, as a woman—as a murderous bishop, as a healing witch. These spirits ache for what they themselves cannot possess: our delicate, limited, human condition. The passion of our existence—our pain and joy they themselves can only feel when they are among us, living through us—as one of us. Their desire is a story long written in legend and lore. Their crossing is an occurrence as ancient as the belief in the gods themselves.

"But such crossings are forbidden—forbidden by a power beyond all powers."

"The Almighty God?" Radulphus said.

Albion nods, "If you wish to call *It* that. Though, 'tis nothing near to the reality—but if it helps you to understand, then, yes. So much more, beyond faculty, beyond hope of sight. And yet, *It* sees all." Albion bows his head. "*It* forbid all deity intervention with mankind.

Time and again, a spirit will break through. And we are here to hunt them down and send them back.

"I am of an ancient order that has been given the task of eliminating those that cross. The *Orathom Wis*, the Guardians of the Dream. I am Albion Ravistelle of the *Orathom Wis*. I am immortal. We hold the doors. Spirits of light, those like your wife, though against our mandate, we will afford them a lifetime, perhaps—but Gravesend— he that tried to kill your son—I will take great joy sending him back from whence he came."

"Father?" William said suddenly. Both men turned to him. The boy's focus was deep within the fire's core. "Is it wrong to kill men?"

Radulphus placed his hand upon his boy's back. "Yes."

William said, "But if the Bishop is not a *man*, is it wrong to kill him?"

The priest looked at Albion. Albion answered, "This is true, William. He is not of this earth."

"Then it is not wrong, Papa?"

Radulphus stared at his little boy.

"He killed Mama," William said, "but he could not kill me."

"No, my boy, he could not," Albion agreed.

"I will kill him," the boy said. His eyes rose from the fire. A reflection of flame danced upon the tears rising there. William's quavering voice said again. "I will kill him."

Albion studied the child—not yet seven springs. Innocence was gone from his visage. Lurking there now was charged anger and longing.

Albion said quietly, "So be it." He then rose and motioned toward the tent, "But first, eat. And then, to sleep."

Higher Learning

Los Angeles, July 1, 1972
Helen Storm's apartment near Hollywood.

Helen Storm felt self conscious as they studied her. Her Led Zeppelin t-shirt hugged tightly to her torso. She was pale and thin—delicate in every way. Her expression, glued to Jimmy Page's face, was a mix between shock and delight.

"Helen," Jimmy said gently, "this is my friend, Albion Ravistelle."

The man sitting beside Jimmy wore a tweed suit and tie. A brown fedora rested upon his knee. Helen took little notice of him. She still could not believe that Jimmy Page was sitting in her tiny apartment in Hollywood. She pulled her longing gaze away from the guitarist to acknowledge the introduction. She nodded at Albion then swung her attention back to Jimmy.

"At first I didn't believe that it was really you on the telephone," Helen said. "I told my roommate, Tracy, and she didn't believe me." Helen gestured to the girl behind her. Tracy, stood beside the sink with one hand gripping the counter and the other behind her back. Her eyes, like Helen's, were whirlpools of wonder. Tracy didn't seem to notice Albion either. Jimmy sighed and looked at Albion.

"My dear," Albion said to Helen, "Mr. Page tells me that you had quite a fall."

"I don't remember much about that," Helen replied. "I was pretty high. I think I just blacked out."

"Well *something* weird happened," Tracy said suddenly, "'cause when she got home that night she had blood all over."

"Yes, that was weird," Helen agreed. "I must have—I must have cut myself or something."

"But you didn't have a cut," Tracy said to her.

Helen turned and glared at Tracy. Tracy pressed her lips tightly together and obeyed some silent command. Albion watched the two with interest and reached to his water glass. The glass was cloudy and smudged. He took a sip anyway.

"That is why we've come, Helen. We want to talk with you about what happened that night. My friend Albion here, well, he and I have spent a lot of time thinking about such strange and out of the ordinary things. He tells me that he has some experience with what you may be going through." Albion listened and observed the young girl. Helen watched Jimmy's lips.

"I'm not *going through* anything," Helen said quietly.

"My dear," Albion began again, "I believe you to be a very special young lady. If what Mr. Page tells me is true, you have a wonderful, dare I say, magical gift. Something that will serve you for the rest of your life. And it is a very lucky chance that my acquaintance with Mr. Page has brought our paths together." Albion leaned toward her and with a kind, sonorous tone asked, "Tell me, Helen, what do you really think happened when you fell fourteen stories? What do you think is going on within your body?"

Helen was now intrigued by this strange man. His accent was European, but she didn't know what country. His face was creased with fatherly care. His eyes were gentle. And as she stared at him she felt as if he knew more about her than she could offer up. There was a magnetic pull, as if her innermost thoughts were drawn out by his comforting, empathetic glance.

Since the fall from that high balcony, Helen began the difficult tracing of her past. Something she hated—and at one time vowed that she would never look back. She tried to block out the numbing winters in Salt Lake City, her stepfather's booze-blurred face, the steel clasp of his belt whistling through the air, the locked bedroom doors, voices screaming at each other in the adjacent room. *Fear*. The first time he beat her, she was ten. She could still feel the searing burn of the leather. Echoes of his slurring voice yelling things like, *shut up, worthless, stupid.* Her mother apologized for him, pleading for her to understand his position. "He's had a hard time and work is hard to come by," she would say, we need to support him. But her mother was never there, and she never witnessed the abuse. Helen was forced to keep silent, keep the secret—threatened that if she told he would hurt her mother. So Helen quit speaking altogether. The beatings continued.

She remembered the terrible bruises, purple and black welts swollen and hard to the touch. Her stepfather seemed pleased when he saw her pale skin blemish into lesions. She would watch his face, his eyes reddened with fury and wonder, his cheeks jiggling at each blow, his expressionless mouth open, breathing in her cries, wheezing out grunts of exertion—sharp boozy fumes. He would leave her on the floor of her bedroom when he finished. The door would slam shut and Helen would tremblingly trace her fingertips over the burning lumps. She would watch them swell up and tighten. Their surfaces would fill with a blackish stain and quickly fade to pink like a sunrise beneath a storm. Minutes later, the pain would fade, the pink blot would wash out and her wounds would vanish.

Even if Helen were to appeal to her mother for help, she had no physical evidence. And her stepfather, either too enveloped in his drunken fog to notice or freakishly delighted that his handiwork disappeared so quickly, he would never remark about the anomaly. Helen was trapped.

The final beating from her stepfather was last December, The pounding rhythms of Led Zeppelin blaring out of her stereo speakers drew him to her bedroom. As each savage blow landed, she could hear Jimmy Page's guitar weeping and calling for her. Robert Plant's voice seemed to herald her next move. *Cryin' won't help you, prayin' won't do you no good. When the levee breaks, mama, you got to move.* When the door slammed behind him, she rolled over and stood. She paid little heed to the injuries that were already healing. She stared at her grey eyes in the mirror, checking her courage, then she pulled a suitcase out of the closet, opened the window, thrust one leg out and rested it upon the fire escape. She paused and looked back into the room. The needle on the record crackled against the center label. She climbed back in, raised the needle and gently rested it back down on the third track. She turned the volume all the way to the right and snapped the knob off the silver stereo face. The tender drone of Jimmy Page's acoustic guitar vibrated through the walls and her spirit. She left the window open. Before she stepped onto the bus, two blocks away, she could hear Robert singing from her window. *Made up my mind, gonna make a new start. / Goin' to California with an aching in my heart.*

And Helen would not fully consider her body's swift ability to heal as unusual until a day or so after she met Jimmy Page. Along with the rest of her past, she had blocked out this special gift. And Albion's question— *what do you think is going on within your body?* Helen could only shrug. But she now knew that she was different. And she wished her heart and soul could mend in the same way.

Albion said, "I have spent my life studying ways in which I might ease severe injury, cure disease, stop the body from aging. Long ago, I planted a seed with my fellow scientists to solve the riddle of mortality. Every year we are getting closer to an answer. But you—you are one of us. You are one of us. Tell me, have you ever been on an airplane?" Helen shook her head. "What would you think about joining Mr. Page and myself, to Italy? To Venezia? To Venice? I'd like to offer you a job, Helen. And an education."

Custody

November 4, this year
Verona, Italy

"Aren't you going to say, hello?" Helen says to her husband.

"Hello, Helen," Loche says. His grip on the phone tightens.

At Helen's naming, William ends his call to Samuel in the United States. His expression is filled with concern.

"Oh how I've missed you, dear."

Loche clenches his jaw.

"Shouldn't we talk?" she asks. Her tone is sugared.

Loche shivers. Another jolt of bewilderment as he weighs his writing's verisimilitude. In the journal, he left his wife in Italy. She had betrayed him. She was never really his wife—she was a weapon that Albion Ravistelle was using to spy. To manipulate Loche's gift—to be his muse. Helen had also been with Basil Fenn for a short time—for the same purpose. To inspire, to exasperate, to delight—to draw out the best and the worst of the artist—to be the catalyst behind it all.

Loche scowls. Why did he write her character into this fate? Why did he turn her into an adulteress? Was she always deceitful? Had she always loved Albion Ravistelle? And now, this woman, his wife, the mother of his child is on the phone, and he struggles to allow the truth of his words to flow over him. He lets the fiction of the journal mix with the evidence around him. Slowly, he begins to trust the planks that he has laid out over the abyss, and he takes a step.

"Helen," he says, "I am sorry that this has happened. I don't know why or how it has come to this. Somehow our lives were strained from the very beginning. It was never my intention for you to be unhappy. To feel trapped. I just thought that people choose eventually to compromise to be together. I may not have been everything you wanted as a husband, but for my part, I loved you. I will always love you. I don't know why I turned you into—into what you now are."

Loche waits. No sound. He stands and motions for George and William to follow. The three enter the hallway and close the door.

Loche hears Helen sigh. He taps the speaker control on the phone so George and William can listen in.

"Dear," she says, "you didn't *make* me into anything. It is me that should be apologizing. And I love you, too. But, Loche, not in a way that will last. My heart has always belonged to someone else. I am sorry." There is a long pause. Loche squints—lowers his head into his hand. "But there is one thing that will always connect us, and that is our son. I want him, Loche. I want him with me."

Loche nudges the door open and looks at his sleeping boy. "Helen," Loche says, carefully, "I don't know how to answer you."

"Simply, Loche," Helen replies, "tell me that you will give me what I want."

"I think we need to talk about this, Helen," Loche says. He adjusts his tone—control—calm—care—familiar techniques when speaking with Helen, he thinks.

"Yes," she says, "let's talk about this."

"I am now thinking of Edwin's safety. We have found ourselves on different sides of a dangerous situation and —"

"Loche, you are clearly out of your league. Don't start with me! Don't put on that calm, psychologist bullshit—you know damn well what is at stake here—all of this has been going on for longer than you can believe—a very long story—and you must know by now that the *Orathom Wis* are nearing extinction. They are nearly destroyed according to our reports—and if you are with them, you are putting Edwin in danger. You are not safe where you are. I am holding off an attack at your location as we speak—because of my son."

"Helen, I don't trust you or your state of mind. And what you're asking me to do is beyond my control anyway. But more importantly, I will not send my son into the hands of killers. And it appears that you have chosen them over us."

"I thought you might respond this way. So *fucking* rational. As usual. So *Mr. Fix-it*. That's fine. Since we're talking about choices, I have one for you. But I don't think you'll like it. Your choice is a kind of lose-lose situation."

"What is it, Helen?"

"Simple, really. I have *Julia.*"

Julia's voice floods into Loche's ears. "Loche, I'm sorry. I am so sorry. I never meant to—" The room circles in a dizzying spin.

Helen interrupts, "She never meant to get involved with a family man. Well, she's certainly gotten her young, immortal little self into quite a pickle. Where should I start, Loche? Should I torture her, beat her, cut her? What do you think?" Helen stops. Her air veers toward a kind of restrained lunacy. "You must understand, Loche—a mother should not be separated from her child—and a mother will do *anything* to get her child back. I must sound crazy, scary—but you've stolen my baby. Bring him to me, Loche. Bring him to me."

"What choice, Helen?"

"Julia is dead anyway, Loche," Helen answers. "Julia can either be killed quickly, or we can take our time. That choice is up to you. I will insure that she will not suffer if you bring my boy to me. I promise. I promise, Loche."

From the background, Julia cries out, "Loche, get Edwin away! Don't give her—" then a snapping sound, loud and sharp. Loche thinks that he hears Julia choking. A rustling overwhelms the phone's speaker. Scraping static. Silence.

"You can prevent *more* pain," Helen says.

"Let me speak to Julia," Loche demands.

"Sorry, dear. Seems she's passed out. She won't be able to talk for at least fifteen minutes. And that is only if I decide to pull my knife out of her mouth."

Abrupt burning tears blind him. William places a steadying hand upon Loche's upper arm. "Helen, what are you doing? What have you done?"

"Loche, this awful situation is just a small part to a very long, long story. I'm sure it seems unbelievable—but now with what you've seen with your own eyes, use that writer's imagination of yours and consider the kinds of things I'll do to Julia if you keep Edwin from me."

"Tell me what you want me to do, Helen."

"Bring him to Venice. You know the place—you have two days. After that, Julia goes into a box and underground—alive of course, and I will figure out a different way to get Edwin."

"Helen," Loche pleads, "don't do this. Don't do this."

"I want my son. Bring him to me."

The call ends.

The Leaves of Fire

April, 1338,
outside the village of Ascott-under-Wychwood, England

William had seen dead bodies before. Many, in fact. The first he could remember was just as he was able to walk—on one of his mother's healing visits. A blurry image in his mind. A family of three, huddled together in the dark.

When Geraldine had opened the door and stepped into the room, William could tell immediately that something was wrong. Perhaps it was the sour smell. It made him cough. The family was seated on the floor together beside a table leaning against the wall. Welts of purple and pink stained their skin. Their open eyes were large and black at the centers—and they stared away beyond the walls of the cottage. Beyond even the trees and the sky.

"We're too late," he remembers his mother saying. "Too late. Come away, William." She pulled him back and closed the door.

It was not long after that William began noticing death all around him. He watched his father slaughter chickens. One autumn, his father snared five coneys and showed William how to dress them for a stew. William had found dead rats at the riverside. A year ago, he and his mother saw several bodies drifting down the river. The smell was awful. They were men, women and children. No one ever told him who they were or why they were floating there. A little girl, not much older than William, her hair splayed out on the water like gold weeds—her eyes stared up at the grey sky—still, black pupils. Geraldine lifted him up and carried him all the way home.

She said to him, over and over, "They dream, and they are gone from here—far, far away, little one."

"Can't you save them, Mama?" he had said.

"No."

"Can you teach me to heal them?"

"No. It is too late for them. They are dead."

"Too late?"

"Yes."

"What's *dead*, Mama?"

"It means that their bodies are gone."

"No, Mama. They were floating on the water. I saw them."

"I mean, their bodies are broken—their bodies are dead. They now dream."

"Where?

"Far from here," she said.

"How far?"

"Very far. Too far away to reach."

William shakes his head. He lifts his hands and places them just next to his ears. He remembers his latest experience with death: Albion's sword cleaving the guard's head from his body. Then they buried both bodies. *Their bed*. Their bed where they will dream.

William turned onto his side and peered up at the pavilion ceiling. It was still dark. He could make out the wheel spokes above and the center pole rising up into black. Beside him he could hear his father's breathing. A few feet away, Albion was lying on his side facing him. His eyes were closed. With a gentle twist William turned himself out of the blanket and stood. He looked down and felt a crushing wave of loss. His mother was gone.

Before he could understand what he was doing, William was running along the stream toward the road that led back to the village. *Maybe*, he thought, *his mother was not dead—not burned. Maybe she got away. Maybe she waited for him in the village square.* His feet scrambled up onto the road and he ran as fast as he could. The night air was cold. With each footfall his confidence increased. *She* would *be there. She would be waiting.*

Crossing the bridge, he passed the first of the small houses that defined the outer boundary of the village.

There were no lights. He crawled beneath a fence and hurried across a narrow field—a shortcut to the village square. A lingering bitter smoke hung in the dark.

Something snapped in the distance behind him. *A branch maybe*, he thought. William dropped to the ground and struggled to listen. His panting and booming heart made it impossible to hear. He held his breath. Aside from the thud of his blood coursing through him, he heard nothing but the quiet sigh of the night—the line of trees ahead combing an April breeze. He rose and darted ahead, aiming for the cover of those trees. They bordered the square. As he moved closer, his eyes searched for his mother. He imagined her beneath the boughs, crouched down. Hiding. Waiting. *She will be hard to see*, he thought, *for she can make herself look like leaves, like a tree. But she can see me.*

"Mama?" he whispered, calling. "Mama? Where are you, Mama?"

But she was not waiting there. He weaved a quiet course through the grove but found nothing. He then lowered himself to his knees and turned his eyes to the square.

The plot of land was no larger than the Abbey courtyard, which William could run across and back before his father could finish reciting the ten lines of The Lord's Prayer. Surrounding it were several small structures. A pole fence jutted out from the tree line marking the south end. Opposite were a collection of open stalls that were used on market days. William recalls the times he and his mother would come here to buy vegetables, cloth and, most importantly, wooden toy horses. But there were no vendors here, now. He had never been to this place at night. And he had never seen it without people bustling about. He shuddered at the lonely gloom.

I'm not alone, he thought suddenly, *for somewhere near, my mother waits. I can feel her eyes on me.*

William remained in the trees until he felt the courage to walk out into the open square. His first steps were careful. He called, whispering again, "Mama? Mama?"

The smell of stale, heated soot caught his attention as he edged further in. And then he saw the mound of ash.

It was as high as his chest, conical and whitish grey, and as wide as the trunk of an old oak tree. A sour fume rose from its tip, and at its base was a nearly imperceptible, incandescent orange, buried deep within. William crouched down and leaned his face closer, relishing the radiant heat upon his cold brow and cheeks. He had not noticed the bitter bite of the night air until he felt the unexpected warmth. The unexpected fire.

He then scurried backward in terror—in question. *What was burning here?* He rose to his feet and began to circle around the mound. As he stepped to the right, the answer became clear. There was not just one grey cone of smoldering ash. There were nine neatly raked piles in a row. Stabbed into the ground in the middle of the row, no longer hidden now by the night's shadow, was a tall crucifix hewn out of tree limbs. A long length of tattered cloth, like a wide ribbon, hung from the crossbar. It was too dark to see a color, but William knew that it was red, like the sashes Bishop Gravesend's followers wore. Like blood.

The bitterness on the air now made sense. The empty square was suddenly colder than before. A chill raked across his shoulders. Searing tears rose. His stomach lurched and he vomited.

"Mama," he croaked between throes. "Mama."

He took a deep breath and wiped his chin. Slowly, he climbed to his feet and looked up at the cross again. "No, Mama, no," he said.

He began to walk along the row, his eyes scouring the piles and the surrounding ground for anything that might disprove his fear. The dark made it difficult. At the fifth mound William saw a torn piece of fabric—quite likely from a garment. He picked it up and examined it. It was not his mother's. He tossed it onto the pile.

A long, black smear stained the ground near the seventh mound. It stretched from the ash pile away into the darkness, toward the square's entrance. William sensed the smear had a reddish hue, like the hanging sash upon the cross. He knew it was blood. His face crimped as he fought back his imagination. He spat and moved further down the row.

When he arrived at the last mound, his eyes were blurred with tears. He turned in a circle for a last look around. A last desperate wish for his mother to appear. She was not here. She was gone.

There were no more questions.

He dropped to his knees at the base of the last mound and pushed the tears out of his eyes. He thought of his father and how he must be worried. Then, sudden anger and fear stabbed at his heart. The face of Bishop Gravesend flashed into his memory, the tall crimson headdress, the cross upon his chest, the long nose and arrogant glance.

Why did he burn her? Why? She only loved. Only loved. Why did he kill her? She was light in the dark. William's hands squeezed to fists and his eyes narrowed at the glowing base of ash.

But the glow was not orange.

There, like new buds on a bough, young leaves—a circle of living vines and ivy shoots had whorled out. There, at the base of smoldering ash and buried coals was a wreath of bright green. William's eyes squeezed shut then opened wider at the sight. He reached down and pushed his hand into the leaves. His mother's fingertips— soft as rose petals, strong as forest vines. He could hear her voice. He caught the scent of her sleeping, and the taste of her kisses.

Another hand then appeared beside his in the leaves. Startled, William looked up to see his father kneeling beside him.

"Papa?" William said.

The Priest did not answer.

William watched his father's head bow down.

"Father?"

"This rage," Radulphus said, "this rage possesses me, boy. We must not allow it to rule us. No eye for eye, evil for evil. It is not the will of God. Your mother would not have it."

William began to cry.

"She would bid me turn away. Run far and keep you from harm. She would bid me to love. She would bid me to love."

William listened. He wanted to lie down in the leaves and sleep.

"What am I to do, boy?" His father asked. "My wife and my God show me the path to forgiveness. The path to healing." His voice lowered to a near silent prayer.

Healing.

There were only three things William wanted at this moment. Sleep was foremost in his mind. Sleeping in his mother's arms was next; and in the strangest way, he seemed to have found a way to do just that—here at this base of ash. But most of all, William sought healing. His entire body ached of loss and need. Though just yesterday his throat was cut and he was left to die in his father's arms, he awoke. He healed. But not fully.

There was still pain. Too much for his heart to manage.

But the word *healing* had rung in his ears, and he heard his voice say, "Mama knows how to heal. . ."

The priest halted his prayer and stared into the coils of green. "Aye, *that* she did."

"These leaves are Mama's leaves?"

"I believe they are."

"Me, too."

"I wish I could die, Papa," William said.

Radulphus found William's hand.

"I wish I could make the pain go away, Papa. If I die, will it go away?"

The Priest pulled a small leather pouch from out of his tunic and he laid it down beside the pile. "Let's take Mama with us, shall we?"

William gently lifted a handful of ash and soil, and funneled it into the pouch. He then pinched three leaves up by the root and planted them on top. He tightened the drawstring. The glowing leaves drooped from out of the bag's mouth. He held it up. Radulphus smiled.

As they stood the priest gasped. William looked down to the wreath around the pyre. It was withering and burning away in flames of emerald green and gold. The boy turned his attention to the three leaves in the pouch. It seemed that they moved, pointing their fine tips to the flames below. As if saying goodbye.

"What does this mean?" William asked.

"I am uncertain," he replied. "She often talked of the seedling leaves, if they perish, all they've created will die. Perhaps you carry with you the final seedlings of her Craft. Guard it well. We must go now."

They crossed back to the line of trees at the square's edge. As soon as they stepped beneath the boughs, William caught sight of Albion Ravistelle leaning against one of the trunks.   "Hello, William. Your father was worried," he whispered. "But I had the feeling that you needed to see for yourself."

William lifted the leather pouch crowned with green. Albion smiled. "Ah, life from fire," he says. "Another reason I would have spared your mother's life, for as long as I would be allowed, that is. She had a way, it seems, of bringing beauty out of man's violence and destructive habit."

William hugged the bag to his chest and stepped nearer to his father.

"We should get back," Albion said eyeing the surrounding fields. "Dawn is in the air, and your father is still wanted at the Tower. Come."

The Less You Care

September 3, 1972
Venice, Italy

A pearl grey sky. Helen sat beside the railing overlooking the canal. She imagined Albion sitting there with her. Sharing a bottle of wine. Watching the boats. Holding hands as the Venetian traffic floated by.

But he was away on business. And they had not held hands before. Not yet.

The air was warm—a light September breeze from off of the Adriatic. She would have never known about the Adriatic Sea to the East if it had not been for Albion. She'd never known about a lot of things—Italy, fine food and wine, clothes—celebrities, too. Dinner and parties and laughter. And more time with Jimmy Page. One night she danced with Albion on the veranda while Jimmy played a piece he had been working on called *The Rain Song*. The moon was a white thorn in the black sky. Venice was sparkling. The champagne was sweet and dizzying. Helen smiled.

Across the waterway were the basilica domes of Santa Maria Della Salute, or what Albion called simply, *The Salute*. Something about how he had a hand in seeing it built. *What year was it? Sixteen something?* Helen shakes her head. It is crazy to even imagine. After the city survived a terrible outbreak of the plague in medieval Venice, Albion worked with artists and architects to construct a kind of monument to the city's deliverance. The pestilence took hundreds of thousands of lives, and Albion wanted to show the world (this one and the next) that the plague could be overcome, and hope could be restored. But there was more to it, for Albion claimed that the Black Death was not a *natural* occurrence. Certainly,

Helen could remember a thing or two about The Plague—infected rats, and fleas, and how the disease spread, and Albion agreed with all that. But then he went on and on about a crossing spirit or deity that engineered the death of millions by introducing what later became known as the Black Death. Albion said that he and his old friend George hunted, caught and eliminated the perpetrator. *The monster*, Albion called him.

And for Albion, *The Salute*, was the gravestone. At least, it was supposed to be. Originally, the structure was to be twin spikes, like stone spearheads aimed at Heaven. A kind of warning to the gods. "One spear was mine, the other, George's." But it did not turn out that way. Albion explained that it became impossible to build anything monumental during those times without the assistance of the Church, and when they got involved, the project became wrapped in Roman Catholicism. What's more, the *Orathom Wis* had always been hidden from the eyes of mortal men, so it was foolish to attract attention. The spears turned to domes. It didn't matter much to Albion in the end, he had told her. "Things you believe in, your hopes—often fade." He offered, "You'll learn that the longer you last, the more your heart breaks, the less you care." Sometime later, when they were talking about another of life's vagaries, Albion added to the maxim, "The less you care, the longer you last." Helen could see the phrase made a circle, and she could sense its sad beauty.

She could smell the sea. It was better here near the bay than the stinky cloistered canals further west. Here, the eastern silver sky and sea were separated by a thin line of land, a ribbon of green. The gentle gusts from out there were like everything else she had experienced in the two months living with Albion, new and needed. *I have arrived,* no longer held the same meaning. "There is no *arriving*, Helen," Albion said. "And if there was, how boring. For once you've arrived, you're through. And no, by the way, it is not *the journey* either. Journeys are tedious and tiresome things. Why would we yield to endless travel and difficulty? No—arrivals, journeys! For us, life is only life. It is all we have, and all we'll know. Keep it. Use it. Protect it. Such metaphors are not for us, they are for those that will one day die—that will one day age, face illness, decay. They need such trifles to appreciate the life they'll lose. We live on and on."

She closed her eyes. The two months had passed with incredible speed. Each day had been filled with life lessons, most of which contained a seeming counter-intuition. What might be acceptable for a normal human being would be completely offensive to Albion and those like him. Littering and pollution, for example, were an outrage. He told her about the first time he watched a pipe spewing sewage into the Thames, or the first time he watched black smoke billow from a coal chimney, or the tragic and foul contaminations of the Industrial Revolution. He knew that there was something inherently wrong with humanity to allow such poisonings. Throughout his long life, he had been an advocate for the preservation of the environment. Large sums of money he had pushed around to lobbyists, ad agencies, artists and politicians to help educate the world as to the dangers of unchecked waste and pollution. Though many of his efforts were now becoming a part of the 1972 media vocabulary, he was still extremely concerned about the damage that had already been done.

Helen did not mind him rambling on about such things. She hadn't given much thought to any of it. It was no big deal for her to toss a soda can into the canal, drop her cigarette butt into the street—yet, to Albion, these acts were intolerable. "Because you'll still be here when the sun is blacked out and the flowers won't bloom—you'll be here when all the water is sour and the food is gone. You'll *still* be here. Humanity does nothing to care for their children, leaving them a future smeared with filth and darkness. Death prevents them from truly seeing the mark they leave behind, and the suffering of their offspring. Selfish, shortsighted idiots! And they speak of *the journey.*" Helen smiled at how animated he had become on that particular tirade.

"More wine?" a voice said.

Turning, Helen saw Corey Thomas holding a bottle. "Hi Corey, I would, yes. Thank you."

Corey poured and sat down opposite her.

"I was told that Albion was away on business so I thought I would join you for awhile. I have tasks I must attend to shortly, but a few minutes near the water would do me well."

"Right on," Helen said.

"So, how are you faring? I understand that since you've joined us you've been learning much."

"Yeah," she replied. "But my head is spinning, you know. There's so much. It's really hard to believe sometimes."

Corey nodded and sipped.

"Like, all of this stuff that Albion says can only really make sense if you are like us—oh, and you, too. Like, *Itonalya,* and all that."

"Yes," Corey agrees.

"I don't remember if you told me, but how old are you?"

Corey shifts in his seat. "I am well over four-hundred-years-old, Helen."

"How long have you known Albion?"

"A goodly amount of time. I met him after I became a part of the *Orathom Wis*. Our first meeting was sometime around 1850. I forget exactly." He laughed lightly, "One thing you might consider, Helen, is to pay attention to your day to day dealings. It would serve you well to place memory exercises into your routine."

"Yeah, probably, right?"

"Very probably. I have trouble sometimes recalling all that I've seen, all that I've done, the age I've lost and won."

"Me too," Helen giggled.

"Well, it's best to start when you are young."

Helen turned to the Grand Canal again and sighed. "So, both of you were a part of this, *Orathom Wis*?"

"We were," Corey said.

"And why did you leave it?"

Corey paused a moment. "Albion must have shared that story with you—given the lectures you've had to endure."

"Yes. He told me that he split because of his friend William and his kids—what were their names? *Basil, and Alexander or Loche*? Something? I dunno. That he wanted to help save them—that they were crossing spirits and the *Orathom Wis* was supposed to eliminate crossing spirits. Right? And he and William saved them. Right?"

"Yes, that is fairly accurate," Corey said, "and all fairly recent. Loche and Basil were thought to be crossing spirits, so naturally, the *Orathom Wis* were to eliminate them. George Eversman ordered it. But William Greenhame, the boys' father disobeyed and with the help of Albion, they managed to save them. The boys are in hiding now. Even Albion doesn't know where they are."

"Won't this George person come looking for Albion?"

"Very probably."

"And where is his friend? What was it? William?"

"He, too, has disappeared. He'll turn up again, eventually. Eventually, we all come back."

Helen shook her head. "Sounds like a movie."

Corey nodded, "I think it would make a very good movie."

"So when all that went down, you joined up with Albion?"

"That's right," Corey said. "William is my friend—and Albion and myself, along with a few others, believe that his sons might very well be the two prophesied—to change the pathways between this life and the next."

"Yes," Helen sat up straight, "yes, Albion told me about that. Like, an omen or something."

"Correct."

"Like something out of the Bible?"

"Vaguely, yes."

"From some ancient civilization, like Egypt,"

"Correct."

"He told me the name of where your—our kind first lived—what was it?"

"*Wyn Avuqua.*"

"Yeah, yeah! *Wyn Avuqua.* But it's gone now?"

"Yes."

"There was a huge war—a really, really, *really* long time ago."

"Correct."

"And since then you all have been waiting on this *omen thing* from that place."

"Correct."

"And *Wyn Avuqua* was in Idaho? Idaho. Weird."

"Correct."

"Is that next to Pennsylvania?"

"No. It sits between Washington, Montana and Canada."

"Right. Right."

Corey smiled. "You learn quickly."

Helen grinned. "Yes," she said. "It's funny that you were talking about memory exercises. I've been thinking the same thing since I met Albion, because if I want to be with him—" Helen stopped and reached for her glass. She looked into it. "If we are going to be together, I'd better get a move on learning as much as I can. He's really smart —and really worldly. And if I—" her words fell off. She felt her cheeks flush. "I dunno."

Corey watched her. "You're in love with Albion?" he asked, simply.

Helen's eyes flashed and she looked away. "Am I stupid? I mean, would he really even think about me that way? I'm so young."

"*Ithic veli agtig,*" Corey said. It came out like a mournful sigh. "Love for us is a quite a tricky thing, Helen. We have all loved. Loved desperately. Deeply. And we have all lost. Terrible heartbreak. As with all things, and like our human counterparts, we must weigh what is worth bearing and what is not. Albion was married once

—centuries ago. Her passing was something he almost did not recover from. Such loss for our kind is something we must learn to endure. The less you care, the longer you last."

Helen thought a moment. Her gaze reached out to sea again, out over that ribbon of green between the sea and the sky. "But first your heart must break, right? So that means that no matter what, you risk it. Even as we last. Even as the time goes by—a hundred years, we still care, don't we? Well, I'm young enough to risk it. I will love no matter what. No matter what. I will try. I won't wish for my death to come soon. This *ithic veli agtig* stuff. If I can do almost anything, I will. I will."

Corey didn't answer. He, too, looked out to the shining sea and the darker clouds brooding further out—distant lightning flashed.

The Prestige

November 4, this year
Somewhere over the Swiss Alps

Loche Newirth stares out the window of a private DC-3 commuter plane. Below, the Alps lay crumpled like a white bed sheet. The morning sun is rising steadily and glaring into Loche's face. He lowers the window shade and looks down at Edwin, his head resting upon his thigh. His eyes are open.

"Dad?"

"Yes, Edwin?"

"Where's Mom?"

"Mom is visiting some people right now."

"What people?"

Loche recalls what he had written in the journal, and the compound of Albion Ravistelle. "Do you remember when we went to Venice? Where they had the black boats? The black boats on the water?"

"I remember that place. Yes. I remember."

Loche shakes his head. His only memory of the Bauer Hotel, Albion's stronghold, is in his imagination; the recollection of a story. "Well, that's where Mom is."

"When are we going home, Dad?"

"I don't know."

"Are we still the storytellers?"

"Yes, we're writing the good stories—painting the beautiful pictures."

"We will always do that?"

"That's all we can do."

"I want to go home. Do you want to go home?"

"Yes, I want to go home, too."

"Will Mom be home when we get home?"

"No. She will be staying in Venice for a while longer."

"I miss her, Dad."

"I know. I know. Things are going to be a little different from now on. We need to fix some things. It's time for some changes, and we shouldn't be afraid."

"Like what, Dad?"

"Well," Loche pauses.

William Greenhame sits down beside them. "*Mutantur omnia nos et mutamur in illis.*"

Edwin twists over, sits up and scowls at the words. "Huh?"

"All things change, and we change with them," William says. Edwin's scowl deepens as he climbs into William's lap.

"I've never seen him be so comfortable with anyone but Helen and me—and Julia."

William does not appear to hear Loche. Instead, he holds up a coin in front of the little boy's eyes and performs a sleight of hand magic trick. The coin disappears. Edwin's eyes sparkle with wonder. "*Abracadabra,*" William says. The coin appears again from out of Edwin's ear.

"Do it again!" Edwin cries. "Again!"

"I remember when my father had that kind of power. He taught me this trick, you know. Simple, isn't it?" William says.

"What's that?" Loche asks.

"The trick is simple. But it isn't the trick at all, it is Edwin's simple lack of understanding that can make a disc of metal vanish and then fall out of one's ear. Make the impossible, possible. I just created a new reality for him."

"Do it again!"

"*Abracadabra*," William says. This time, he pulls the coin from Loche's ear. The boy takes the coin and examines it closely. He laughs.

"A new reality until he figures out that it is just a lie. *A trick,*" Loche says.

"True," William agrees. "But until then, he thinks we can have money fall from our ears. When he does finally *get it*, he'll have another *new* reality."

"A much more difficult one." Loche takes a deep breath and exhales. "So this is going somewhere, right? You're moving toward a point?"

"I am, indeed. Don't I always arrive at one, sooner or later? Stay, I will be faithful," William replies. He looks away, at some seeming distance, "Did you know that the word *abracadabra* is all about change and making?"

"I don't know the etymology, if that's what you're asking."

"It's Aramaic. There are many ways to translate it, though, where you're concerned, I prefer this meaning: *I create like the word*. Now, isn't that remarkable?" Loche turns and lifts the shade. He squints at the division of stunning clear blue and the white range of ice below. "Words. Words. Words. They are made of magic. The arrangement of little characters—vowels, consonants. Language. Amazing isn't it? You know, that is why they call the construction of words spelling."

"Spelling?" Loche asks.

"Yes, my boy. Spelling. Spells. Wonderful, yes? And the use of spells—words bring about change. And you must now deal with the changes that you have created. You must live within your words and seek a way to close the doors between us and what comes after."

"I cannot let Julia suffer," Loche says. "I will not let that happen."

"When we arrive at *Mel Tiris*, you will be led to the high tower. You will be placed within a stone room that is filled with hundreds of your brother Basil's paintings—the very windows that look upon *Elysium*. You will remain within until you have found a way to stop our existence from colliding with theirs."

"William, I don't know if I can—"

"My son, you can. You are the only living being that can enter those doors and return unharmed. You *must* succeed."

Loche's mind returns again to his hand scrawled pages. The impossibility of Basil's art—the ice-blue Eye beyond—the sight and envelopment of omniscience. The madness.

"And I," William takes Loche's hand. "I will take my grandson to his mother."

"What?"

William closes his eyes and nods sympathetically. "I know, I know. Please listen. I will take my grandson to his mother. And I promise you, he will return to you, safe, and with Julia. And, quite possibly, with Helen."

"Mom?" Edwin says.

"William, I cannot—I will not allow you to—"

"Loche, this is the only way to save Julia. And if *you* fail, it won't matter what happens to Julia, Edwin or any of us. As you've said, *it is time for some changes, and we shouldn't be afraid.* And so it is. You will roam about in the astral plane. Edwin and I will have an adventure. I will create a new reality for Helen, and bring Julia home. I will make the impossible, possible. Something that even Helen will not expect."

"How will you do that?" Loche asks. His eyes pleading.

William sets a warm glance upon his grandson. "I still possess some of the same magic my mother gave to me, all those years ago, when I was Edwin's age. It resembles every mother's love for her children. It is healing. It is magic." Loche shakes his head.

William grins, "*Abracadabra.*"

Vengeance Is Fated

April, 1338,
outside the village of Ascott-under-Wychwood, England

Through the tent opening William could see the dim light of morning. Albion was packing a small cart hitched to his horse. He moved at a brisk, efficient pace. Within a short time he had tied down the last of the camp's gear. The final task was to break down and pack the tent. He was singing a quiet lament. William could not understand the language, but as each word lilted and fell, pictures appeared in his mind—a great walled city—ancient and silver in the sunlight—anger, sorrow, then finally flames as its high towers crumbled to dust.

Nye thi so zjoy goshem
Thi nugosht bensis ensis
Mel hamtik, del hamtik, enthu
Sisg ag
Orathom ethe
Lithion talgeth
   Thi fafe wis
   Thi fafe wis
A Wyn Avuqua
Endale che
Thi col orathom
Tiris liflarin thi avusht
Lithion nuk te lirych
   Orathom thi geth
   Fethe thi geth
     Ithic veli agtig
     Ithic veli agtig

William rose. He picked up the leather pouch crowned with leaves and stepped through the tent door. The air outside was cold. A bitter fog clung to the trees.

"Good morning, William," Albion said. "I hope your rest was deep and pleasant. I am sorry if my song woke you."

William stared at the man.

"Here," Albion said, handing him a small wooden bowl of dried fruit and salted meat. William wasted no time. "Slowly, boy. You may be immortal, but you can still choke—and that is terribly uncomfortable—no matter what."

Albion watched him while the last morsel went down.

"That's better," he said. "Now then, don't you want to know where we're off to today?"

William nodded.

"We're to London, my lad."

"London?" William asked. "I've never been to London."

"Never to London?" Albion laughed, "What a wonder it will be for you. Your first city visit. And *I* will escort you. It shan't be the last—for you will visit the greatest cities of the world in your long, long lifetime, my dear William. You will one day see my city--the heart of the earth, Rome. You will see its greatness, its towers, its riches, its art. But so too will you see a cities filth, and its destruction of the green earth. Alas, man's art cannot be made without some pain left behind. Take a deep breath of these sweet woods. You'll long for them once we enter the city."

William still stared.

"How I wish we could both see the city of our ancestors, *Wyn Avuqua*, the pearl of Earth." Albion paused. "Ah, I am sorry. Perhaps you are not ready for my philosophies and fears. You are young, my lad. Yet, not too young to begin—for if we are to eliminate the darkness that is Bishop Gravesend, you will need to be sure—you will need to believe in your heart that it *must* be done."

Albion grinned. He eyed the boy toe to top. "But before we get to all of that, a bath would do you well, a clipping to that tuft of hair and some decent clothes—if you're to be my ward. We'll then arrive at the matter of vengeance. Something that will require great deal of wit rather than brute strength. The deed which you will need to perform is something beyond your size, I'm afraid. 'Tis nothing to do with your muscles, your arms, or even your sword. It is all in here, my boy." Albion laid his index finger to his temple. "Your mind must be made up that this life consists of two things, the spirits that belong here, and the spirits that do not. Gravesend's spirit cannot be harmed, but his body can be eliminated. This may look like killing, but it is in fact, far from it. It is simply the closing of a door."

"My mama is dreaming."

Albion's face shadows. "Yes," he said, turning toward the cart. His hand pulled at a strap. "Yes, she dreams. Or so it is said. . ."

"My mama said—"

"Aye," Albion said, his tone became stern. "And she was right. She was right. And this evil Bishop—we will send him to the *Orathom*—to the dream." Albion then spat, "Even the evil are allowed the dream."

"But will he find Mama again?"

Albion laughed, "I think not. The gods do battle *here,* William. In our hearts and minds. On our very doorsteps —our green battlefields—our swollen market places. No, little one, whatever ancient grudge Gravesend has endured through the eons of stardust, only his kind will know of it. We, here, often pay the price. Perhaps your mother gave birth to you to win the final match. All happens for a reason, they say. It has all been written before."

"And when I dream, will I get to be with Mama?"

Albion lifted his gaze from the cart to the fog in the trees. He leaned on his elbows and sighed. "Well, there is the tragedy, William. The *Orathom* is not open to our kind. Our gift is long life. Immortality. And no other gift. We are now. And beyond, we are nothing."

"No Mama?" William began to cry.

"No, William. I am sorry."

"William," Radulphus said, stepping out of the tent. The boy turned to his father. "Hold your tears, son. Do not believe everything this man says. If there are countless stars, there must be countless powers—and countless possibilities. What is a man to do caught amid Heaven, Earth and the fires that rage below?"

"A good question, Priest," Albion said turning around. His accent shifted. William now understood that Albion's home was in Italy. "What is a man to do? *Accept reality.* Believing in what we want is quite different than what is. The sooner the boy discovers this, the better."

"You do not know the truth," the Priest said.

"Nor do you," Albion replied. "Yet, let us quell this argument with this fact—I am over four hundred years old, and I've a rather profound and unusual perspective upon the misgivings and tragedies that belief brings."

"As do I, and I still say that—"

Albion raised his hand. "Stop. This bickering is pointless." He sighed. He sounded like a normal Englishman again. "Though it tears my heart that we *Itonalya* are barred from the Dream, I accept my charge— my duty I embrace. And you will learn to do the same, young William." Albion smiles at the Priest, "It appears that your tutelage will be of two minds, for I don't believe your father will allow me to teach you the finer points of actual truth."

"On the contrary," Radulphus said, "truth is my aim."

"Mama," William cried, suddenly. He was staring at the smoldering coals in the circle of stones.

Albion looked at the priest and then back to William. "They burned her. She is dead. Now, we must move on."

"Have you no pity?" Radulpus said. He knelt down to his son. "William. . ."

"Pity?" Albion asked. "It is the truth—and it is time for him to harden his heart for the task ahead. There is no greater teacher than tragedy."

"His mother believed love was the ruler of our experience."

Albion turned back toward the cart and adjusted the ropes, "Tell that to the hundreds of families that cry out for their daughters, wives and mothers this morning. Love will not end Gravesend's need for suffering. He desires to feel the human experience and he is now drinking deep upon the anguish, torment and grief of others. He is drunk on the blood in his cup. We must end him. I would have ended Geraldine had she shared *his* cravings—but she did not. Her elimination would have been inevitable by our hand, eventually—but Gravesend did my work for me. So, let us take that pain and use it.

"Gather up your things—London is three days away, if we don't run into difficulties. And Gravesend is a day or more ahead of us. But who knows? We just might catch him on the road."

"And if we catch him?" Radulphus said. "Then what?"

"You and your son may exact your revenge."

Radulphus pulled his son away and stood. "We cannot repay evil with evil."

Albion laughed. "Really? Evil? You cross bearing folk. Goodness me. The only evil you will do in this case, Priest, is allow Gravesend to continue his destructive path through your idleness. Oh, and rob your child the satisfaction of seeing justice done. I'm uncertain as to which sin of yours is worse—offering your other cheek to a murderer, or letting your son watch you do it?" Albion's tone softened and he turned to them. "As I've told you, Gravesend is not a man. He is something altogether different. I know it is hard for you to conceive. Understand that God's work is a mysterious list of tasks.

"These things you do, Priest, love, guide, give, teach—all noble pursuits, and most needed in these times. Indeed, they might very well be accounted as God's work. Certainly, fighting evil with evil is insane—fighting fire with fire. Take some comfort that there is some truth in your scriptures. Recall this one—*Vengeance is mine, I will repay, says the Lord?*" He turned back to the tent and lowered it to the ground. "I do God's work, too. *I* am *Its* vengeance."

They spoke no more.

Radulphus joined Albion in disassembling the tent. William watched the two for a short time until the purling of the stream caught his ear. He walked to its edge and sat upon the tiny smooth stones. The small inlet was laced with lush leaves and thick, bright green vines. He thought of his mother and her peculiar Craft—her magic—her leafy hands, vine-like fingers, her hair wreathed with stem and berry. The rush of the water over the rocks reminded him of her voice. When she'd chant he always thought he heard a rustle of wind, or the whisper of a stream. He set the leather pouch of leaves on the stones and leaned his ear to the water. Was she speaking to him? Was her voice mingled with the stream's swishing murmur? He closed his eyes and imagined her smiling face. He imagined her lips whispering into his ear. He could not catch the words.

Basil Fenn's Collection of Answers

November 5, this year
Mel Tiris, France

A circular stone room—Loche feels comfortable. He smells the old dust and the stain-trodden planks beneath him. He closes his eyes and imagines his home, that he is hidden in his own fashioned castle tower surrounded by his locked cabinets. He drifts through his old life, wishing that none of this had happened. But he is not home, and turning in a wide gyre, he sees that the size of the room is three or four times larger than his study. There are no cases of books, no desk or portraits of his family. Instead, the room is filled with hundreds of covered paintings leaning against the brick walls. Many are secured within wood crates. Some ten easels are positioned in a circle. Upon each is a rectangular shape draped with a thick black shroud. In the center is a padded leather swivel chair.

"Good, no?" George Eversman says.

Loche considers his words.

"No good."

George slaps Loche on the back. "Don't worry, you. You can do dis. I know you can do dis. You must do dis."

"George," Loche says, "I've only written about Basil's paintings. I've written them to be something that can wipe out rational thought. That they can literally destroy the human mind, leaving the observer in hellish madness."

"Right," George says. "You want some water while you work?"

"George, I've never looked at one of these before. I've only written that I have."

George scratches his chin at Loche. "You must live within your writing, you. Silly man. When will you get it? Yes you have been in there before," he points into the blackness of one of the fabric covers. "You have. You have. You just don't remember."

Loche scowls at the scene. "No, George, I wrote about it and I—"

"Stupid crazy, you. You have done it before. You must go again. Find a way to stop them visiting. Block the path forever."

Loche sighs heavily.

A man enters the chamber, large limbed and tall. He bows, "*Anfogal*," he says to George, "the last have arrived."

"Ah," George says to him. "Good, good. Meet in Great Hall. We come right away."

"I will say so," he replies. Before he turns the man extends his huge hand to Loche. "We have not met yet, Dr. Newirth. We have crossed paths—though only briefly. I saw you during the battle at the Uffizi." Loche studies the man's size again and remembers writing of the two *Orathom Wis* that defended him when he reached his brother's body upon the Uffizi stage. The word *mountain* came to his mind, suddenly. "I am Justinian Pierce. It is an honor to meet you." He bows again.

"Pleased to meet you," Loche replies.

Justinian again addresses George, "*Anfogal*," and turns toward the long spiral stair to the lower chambers.

"Good fella, Justinian," George says.

"They call you, *Anfogal*. What does that mean?"

"You don't know your *Elliqui*? Hmm, another thing to learn for you, eh? It mean much. Too much to say in words. Maybe closest is *God Leader*. I am he who leads gods back home. So are we all, we *Orathom Wis*. We send them back. Maybe *Anfogal* might be *Master*, too. So many things when we speak *Elliqui*."

"Arrived? Who has arrived?"

"The last of the Order. The last of us in the wide world. In the wide, wide, wide world. You meet them, come."

George moves out of the room. As Loche follows he stops in the doorway. He imagines the shrouded paintings behind reaching for him with arms of shadow.

To Kill A God

April, 1338
On the road to London, England

When it started to rain, Radulphus said, "You cannot expect this boy of no more than six springs to kill a man."

William pulled his hood up and turned to Albion. The man's stride was long and tireless. He strode beside the wagon with his hand resting upon the rail.

Radulphus rode on the seat beside William. He said again, "You cannot expect that, Albion. Do you?"

"A boy of any age that has seen what he's seen, can do anything. When I was young, I knew enough to stab a man," Albion said. "He can know it, too."

"I forbid it," Radulphus said.

"I can learn," William said.

Albion laughed. "You *will* learn, William. But your father is right, I believe. I do not think that you will be up to the task for a number of years, at least."

"I do not like this," Radulphus said.

"What's to like?" Albion said.

Water began to drip from William's hood brim. He lowered his head and watched it puddle between his feet. From out of his cloak he pulled the leather pouch and let the rain tap upon the leaves.

Listening to his father and Albion discuss what he would do or not do over the last day was becoming of greater interest. Days ago, his life was one of watching, listening and waiting. Mostly working and reciting the prayers his father had taught him. Beyond that, life was simple. Now he was off to London. A journey to take a life—the life of a Bishop. To avenge his mother, or to kill a god. Or both.

Simple.

The road ahead curved right into a cluster of trees. Overhead, deep grey clouds pressed down and in between the new spring leaves.

"I will kill Gravesend, Priest," Albion said finally. "I will need your help, but the killing will be my doing."

William's father did not respond.

"Gravesend's treacherous and wicked past is a long tale of woe. We have only just discovered his divinity in the last year."

"A year?" Radulphus said, astonished. "You've known about this for a year? Sounds as if you are taking your time."

"Please," Albion said, his tone a little irritated. "You do not know of what you say. It may seem like a long while, but it is nothing to the permanence of death. Before we take a life, it must be determined the life's origin is indeed that of the divine. We are not murderers. We remove deities from this world, not men and women."

"And how do you determine that?"

Albion laughed, "Not without difficulty. And, I'm afraid, it takes time. There are many clues—for example, your wife was easy to see—healing a hurt that cannot be healed. A power of earth and sky and root was present in Geraldine's very essence. I, myself, know a thing or two of herb lore. She was, in truth, a witch. Though she was careful to keep her power and deeds on the perimeter of her community's gossip. When curing horrible pestilence becomes the topic of conversation, Geraldine's name was often whispered—sometimes sung. We've known of her for years. Again, with a blind eye.

"But not all bridging spirits are as easy to see, simple to know. There is a great deal of wonder in the natural world. Things impossible to explain—things that are not driven by divine intervention. And there are a great many evil people in the world. Many that may, indeed, deserve death, though I am no judge in such matters—and I was not born to administer punishment. Such extremes are, here beneath the spheres and the stars, sometimes simply human." He spat. "Shortsighted, ignorant and intolerable."

He navigated another wide puddle. "Then there are telltale signs.

"Bishop Gravesend has been clever to conceal his divinity beneath the mantle of the Church. Ironic. His power is in manipulation and the ability to persuade the common man to do his bidding. The trouble is, Churchmen have been doing that for centuries, be they evil or no. Those that claim a connection to a god, and a punishment for nonbelievers, have a particularly powerful influence upon the weak. Not really a godlike trait for a man, but a rather diabolical place for a god to hide, if you ask me. Gravesend has found the perfect outlet for his bloodlust. He is protected by the very people his word can condemn. He is protected by fear."

Radulphus said: "You bring God low. You reduce his word speaking like this. This is blasphemous!"

Albion laughed.

"Do not mock me," Radulphus said.

"I do not mock," Albion replied. "And yes, it is blasphemous—to you, at least. And to half the world that believes as you do. I do not attack your precious faith, Priest. I attack your fear. Now, let it be. In your words, *If there are countless stars there must be countless possibilities*. I dare say, with such thoughts, there just may be some hope for you. You've seen your son killed and resurrected—a wife with the gift of healing—and I am an immortal—according to your ways, you are surrounded with sacrilege. Take heart, there is more to the story. There is always more to the story."

The two men fell silent. William listened to the creaking wagon. The rain was falling harder now. He pulled his cloak tighter around his shoulders. He imagined the roots in the leather bag drinking deeply.

Radulphus asked, "So how was it that you learned Bishop Gravesend was not of this world?"

Albion's head turned and looked up at William. William felt the glance. "There are two signs: *deed and sense*. Their deeds are sometimes difficult to discern, especially in Gravesend's case. The easiest is the sense. We can sense it."

William's father shook his head, "What do you mean?"

"William knows the sensation well, though he does not know its importance yet. We of the *Itonalya* possess a kind of forward thought—an inherent grace. There is no magic here, I assure you. We call it *Rathinalya*. That is, we are deft. Extreme dexterity in physical movement. We learn quickly and we are not prone to accidents. Along with that, we can sense when we are in the presence of divinity."

William shivered.

Radulphus asked, "Sense?"

Albion did not answer immediately. He reached up and placed his hand upon Williams forearm. "Do you remember, William, when Gravesend was near to you? Do you remember a faint, far-off quivering, like a chill?"

The boy nodded. He recalled the subtle sensation of a thousand pin pricks tingling across his entire body. When Gravesend and his sentinel monks approached, the feeling was unmistakeable. "I felt a chill," William said. "I was scared."

Radulphus pulled the boy to him, "I was chilled to the bone, and scared, too. Such a sense seems natural given the circumstances."

"Yes, yes," Albion growled. "It can be understated. It can also feel like a million bee stings." Then he said to William, "You felt the *Rathinalya* with your mother, too? Faint, yes?"

William nodded again. This time the memory was like his mother's fingernails gently grazing the back of his neck or his cheek. His heart warmed at the thought. He longed for her.

"It is another aspect of the *Rathinalya*. This sensation will visit your skin when you are in the presence of a bridging spirit." Albion dropped his gaze to the muddied ruts and dodged another deep hole.

"Deeds," he said a moment later. "Geraldine's works were that of leaf and root. She healed using the green earth. Some have claimed that she could shape her form into a tree-like goddess—and others say that she's a penchant for mixing herbs and weeds into a restoring tea. A curing brew. Something that I have great interest in."

"I have watched her gather roots and leaves for such teas," Radulphus said. "Remedies passed down to her from her own mother. The Craft has helped many."

"I am sure it did," Albion agreed.

William glanced up at his father. *Did he never see Geraldine's fingers shape into vines, her hair flutter into leaves, her eyes glisten to green jewels?* He then turned to Albion. Albion's eyes were upon him.

"Which brings us to Gravesend," Albion said, "and our challenge."

"Yes, what of his chilling deeds?"

"One might think that the murdering of hundreds of innocent women, men and children, too, would be enough to prove Gravesend's special power—or better still, his ability to rally the powers of the church to condone the killings. Trouble is, as I've said, it doesn't always take a god to make a fool of man. Man is quite capable and willing to do that to himself. Abuses of power are in your blood. Gravesend might very well be an astute manipulator, but I have seen with my own eyes his real magic—if magic is the right word. And it brings us to the task at hand, and my delay in achieving Gravesend's demise.

"I do not think we will catch Bishop Gravesend on the road," Albion said. "For such a large host, they move with good speed. He is well protected."

"I recall, indeed. There must have been over a hundred—and four of the King's Guard, as well," Radulphus said.

"My last count was eighty-seven. And yes, four of King Edward's pawns, but *they* are not my chief concern. Nor is his rabble of red-sashed followers with pitchforks and clubs. If you remember, there were also four *other* horsemen accompanying him—long swords, simple habits. They wore the cloth of monks."

"I do remember," Radulphus said.

"Me, too," William said.

Albion leapt up and over a wide puddle. His feet splashed. "They," he said without a pause, "are his trained protectors. Considerably more dangerous than mere King's men. And if you think that Gravesend is merciless and cruel—" He broke off.

"Who are they?"

"They are of Gravesend's house. They are, Father, of Gravesend's making."

The priest cast a sidelong glance. "His making? You don't expect me to believe that he *made* them? Like God made man."

"No," Radulphus said. "Don't be a fool. Rather, he has manifested something within them that is unnatural. He has placed a kind of possession upon them. He claims them as part of his clergy. Monks, he calls them. They are indeed disciplined, studied, devoted to their faith and to the Bishop—they pray unceasingly, sworn to a vow of silence. And they worship Gravesend. I have never seen Gravesend without them present."

William shuddered. He reached beneath his cloak and let his hand touch the cool pouch of leaves. He imagined his mother's fingers squeezing his hand.

"Like Geraldine's works of green, Gravesend has focused his powers into four men. They are human, but they carry a portion of Gravesend's power. I do not know their strength, yet."

"And it is they that have prevented you from your mandate?" Radulphus asked.

"Yes, among other complexities. Taking a life is never an easy task. Taking the life of the Bishop of London is, well, complicated. He is seldom alone, he is known and famous, he is protected by his own arts—his own sworn protectors—and, his home is a fortress. I had hoped for a bow shot on the road. As I pursued the host from London to your village, I once had him poised at the tip of an arrow. The opportunity was not certain. I did not risk it."

"So now, what is your plan?" Radulphus asked.

Albion reached up to the horse's reign and pulled back. The wagon came to a halt.

"We will not engage him on the road—we will not exercise the bravery of being out of range with bow or dart—we will not confront him with sword and call for a duel, nor gather an army and lay siege. No.

"I think," he said thoughtfully, "we will enter into his life as pilgrims. As men of God. I will figure a way to gain an invitation to his table; we shall break bread and drink his wine. Once we are in his company, within his chamber, coddled beneath his shepherding arm, we will then decide how to best return him back across the threshold."

"You will use us," Radulphus said. "You will use us as a disguise for your goal?"

"I admit, yes. What better cloak than a humble priest," he pointed at Radulphus, and then to William, "a young, motherless boy." Then he paused and pointed at himself, "and the boy's *father.*"

"*You* will play his father?"

William looked from one man to the other.

"I believe it will work," Albion said. "I will figure a way through my vocation to gain audience."

Radulphus shook his head. "This is too dangerous."

"Think of it this way," Albion pursued. "Consider what will be hidden—a true priest, dangerous with not only God's word but a whirling staff, a boy of six springs that cannot die, and one of the *Orathom Wis*—an immortal god-killer. We three are not to be trifled with."

Albion climbed up onto the wagon. He took the reins and snapped the leather on the horse's hind. The wagon lurched forward.

"I have means to get us close to him. Our disguise will disarm him. I will place us at Gravesend's table. And *he* will be upon the plate. You will have the chance to avenge the woman you both loved."

The Respect

November, 1976
Prince Rupert, Canada

Be quick. Kill quickly. Do not hesitate.
   Reduce suffering.
   Kill quickly.
Have no contrition.
   You are of an ancient order. The Orathom Wis.
   You are a finger on the hand of Thi,
     The One.
Take no pity.
   They do not know that they are gods.
If you seek to avenge their wrong doing, don't.
   You are no judge.
You are a door warden.
   Keep the doors.
Protect the innocence of Man.
   They cannot know of us.
A god on Earth will destroy the fate of man.
   Return gods to the Orathom
Always, always cut them to pieces.
   No sense in taking chances.
For the love of Man do we serve
   And those beyond this world.
Deviate from these laws
   You become the hunted.

These are the fundamental dictums of the *Orathom Wis*, the Guardians of the Dream. *The Law*, as Albion called it. But now, Albion and many others had left the Order a couple of years ago. He had explained that his friend William went against the Order to protect his two sons from being assassinated. The boys were believed to be deities. Together, Albion and William saved them from certain death.

Helen felt a tug of righteousness.

November smothered the sun early. Ice cold mud caked Helen's boots, all the way up her thighs. Crouching beneath a massive blue spruce, she lifted her eyes up to the darkness filling the branches. Soon she could move. But not yet.

She closed her eyes and imagined Albion's lips whispering the instructions into her ear. *For the love of man. . .* The wet of his mouth sending chills. But he had instead lectured her on these items over and over from across a table, during trainings of all sorts—and now, on her tenth time out, of course, she had it all memorized. And there was more, but she was too cold to labor through it.

"But the Order has its job, and it is undeniably important," Albion had said, "and there is no better way to prepare you for the *Itonalya* than to train you as a Guardian, as one of the *Orathom Wis*. Perhaps we will win the Order's favor by doing our part. And one day we shall repair our disloyalty."

She leaned back and sat, laying her gloved hand upon the canvas duffle bag. It was no larger than her gym bag back in her hotel room in Seattle that carried her running shoes, towel and toiletries.

Of all places, *Canada.* She shakes her head thankful snow had not yet clasped the coast. She was prepared for it, though. High boots, fur lined parka, thermal underwear. She had even bought ear muffs at a small gas and grocery stop just before crossing the border from the United States. They were warm, furry and purple. *They would have made Albion laugh*, she thought.

She smiled. If there was anything that thrilled her these days, it was the ability to make the older than the hills, holier than thou, Albion, laugh. Not an easy thing to do. Maybe it was because she had decided that no matter what, she would try to hang on to her youthful self even with all of this immortality heaviness. *What's to worry about? What's to stop us from laughing all the way to eternity? Laughing. Loving.* Leave the *heavy* behind.

Love had not yet kindled between her and Albion. She wrinkled her nose at the thought, and the cold breeze vaulting up through the valley.

On a couple of occasions, she felt the time was ripe, but she waited. The chances of connection seemed to be cultivated from a physical attraction alone—and not the respect that Helen so badly wanted from this strange and powerful man. One day she would share her body with him—and that would be something that he would not forget—but she wanted him to bow to her. She wanted her entire being to be coveted. That meant that she must learn all she could of his ways, his mandate and his past. But she must also expand her view of her new world, her new life.

And right now I'm at school.

Blackness. Helen stood up and stepped out of the cover of the tree. Squinting she could make out the cascade of falling hills pouring down to the ocean a few miles away and the city of Prince Rupert below. She rotated around the tree and looked back. A splatter of tiny lights glittered against the horizon a football field away. A small elementary school.

It's time.

Helen yanked the small canvas bag up and slung it over her shoulder. It was heavy. She then pulled her umbrella out from under the boughs and began her descent.

She wondered if all elementary schools smelled the same. It was true that she had not been in an elementary school for a few years, but today, when she entered, she was transported back to her own school days. Glue, wet coats, Fritos and banana. Windows were plastered with gold stars—tiny scissored mobiles hanging from doorways. Helen loved elementary school, and she

recalled how she would often be the last to leave class—
the last to get on the bus—the last to want to go home.

The way was dark, muddy and in places, steep, but
she moved easily along, making sure to step upon large
stones as often as she could, careful to move like a breeze
and minimize the breaking of a branch or the bending of
grass. She also tried to cross diagonally, zigzagging to
hide her trail. There would be no erasing her presence, of
course, that was sure, but the added effort would buy her
a few hours, at least. Her breath was a ghostly vapor. She
thought of herself as a ghost. A moving spirit of mist.

As she crossed downward her thoughts lingered on the
small faces she'd seen this afternoon. Tiny eyes filled
with innocence and rainbows.

Helen stopped. Rain began tapping at her umbrella.

*Would she ever be a mother? Would she bring a child
into this world? Take him to school? Brush his hair?
Teach him the alphabet? Sway to Led Zeppelin with him?*

Pack a lunch with Fritos, a banana and a PBJ?

Helen knelt and set the heavy bag down. She listened
to the rain pockmarking the mud. Somewhere out there in
the dark a rivulet was spilling over stones. She thought it
sounded like unanswered questions.

*Will I be a mom? Is that the answer? Is that why I'm
alive?*

The gush of runoff strengthened.

She stood and hurried further down.

The land flattened. Helen crept to the edge of a
clearing and strained to see if her ride was still waiting.
She was certain that she'd made the right turns, even in
the pitch black. From her belt she lifted a small flashlight
and shined two brief winks into the dark. The answer was
like an echo—one tiny blink of light, then two, then black
again.

Helen dashed out into the clearing, the bag thudding at
her side as the rotors began to whine to life. A metal door
slid open and two arms reached down to assist her aboard.

Moments later the helicopter was far out over the Pacific ocean veering South.

Will Albion be the father?

Could we be the parents of a child?

What a father he would be to a little boy. . . the things he could teach him. . . that we could teach him.

She pulled off her purple earmuffs and strapped a headset on. The cans were cold.

A static hiss and a voice, "*Ansisg?*" he asked. "*Ansisg?*" It was *Elliqui* for *god end*—a way to confirm the mission of ending the life of a bridging spirit had been a success.

Helen nodded.

The pilot raised his thumb.

The language of *Elliqui* had come fairly easy. A number of words shot through her mind:

child: *gia*
mother: *afa*
love: *thia*
parent: *shaf*
joy: *ad*
tomorrow:_____

The *Elliqui* word eluded her.

Outside was nothing. Cold, black, blindness. She knew the icy Pacific churned below. To the east rose the ragged coast. Above and beyond the empty sky and clouds pregnant with rain, ice and snow. She shivered feeling the lonely chill of flight—the solitary ache of this new education.

The goosebumps suddenly reminded her of the *Rathinalya* that she had felt when she slid her umbrella sword through the neck of the *Bridger,* as she was wont to call them. It was powerful. Pinpricks and shortness of breath. It was always a relief when a *Bridger's* heart stopped beating and the menace of the *Rathinalya* faded away.

She reached to the canvas bag and pulled it between her feet.

"Far enough out? This good?" her voice crackled in the headset.

The pilot raised his thumb.

Helen thought about little boy names: *James, River, Raine, Hunter. . . there were so many.*

Edwin? Edwin is nice.

She raised her arm and lowered the side door window. A whipping gale swirled into the compartment. She unzipped the bag, reached in and tangled her fingers into a thick tuft of hair, gripped and lifted.

Always, always cut them to pieces.
No sense in taking chances.

It was either the wind or a trace *Rathinalya* that dragged like icicles over her scalp.

The head was smaller and lighter than ones before. She had not killed a child *Bridger* before. The eleven-year-old boy's head appeared strangely peaceful. She stared at the little face. He had no idea it was coming.

Kill quickly.

He only cried for a moment when he saw the sword.

Take no pity.
They do not know that they are diviners.

Helen pushed the severed head out the window and let go. It spun out into the darkness.

Have no guilt.
You are of an ancient order. The Orathom Wis.
You are a finger on the hand of Thi.

Helen closed the window, sat back and pulled a blanket around her shoulders. She could see her dim reflection in the black glass of the window. She wondered if Edwin would look like her. If he would understand.

The Muster of the Itonalya

November 5, this year
Mel Tiris, France

Another stone room—massive—brick and mortar rising some fifty feet to thick ebony beams above. A roaring hearth lights the room from one end. Long tables, wood plank chairs, iron railings and couches make up the furnishings. Loche's mind returns home again. This was the kind of Grand Hall he had envisioned all of his life. On the walls hang long banners of rich gold and green bearing the device of a single eye. Flaming torches light the chamber with a warm, welcoming glow.

A hundred or so men and women are gathered in the hall. Their ages appear to vary between twenty and fifty. Loche knows, however, that he is in a room full of immortals. He wonders at their different manners of dress and ethnicity. Asian, African, American, European, Middle Eastern—*delegates of the world,* Loche thinks.

There are two notable anomalies amid the gathering. The first is young Edwin, the only child in the room. He is sitting upon William Greenhame's lap. The second is seated beside him. She is an elderly woman. Her hair is silver-grey and white. Though she appears to be carrying on a pleasant conversation with William and Edwin, Loche cannot help but notice an air of discomfort, as if the room is too cold, or the wooden chair is too hard for her. But despite her years, which Loche guesses to be ninety, at least, there is still a spark in her eye, and a natural, ageless beauty. Loche then considers the reality that she might be, after himself and Edwin, the third youngest in the room.

As George and Loche approach, Edwin leaps from Greenhame's lap, runs and crashes hard into Loche's thighs. Loche lifts him into his arms and kisses the boy. "Are you okay, Edwin?"

"I like this castle, Dad. Kinda like our castle. Can we make a room like this at our castle?"

"That's just what I was thinking," Loche tells him.

"In a way," Samuel Lifeson says, rising from beside the old woman, "you have a Grand Hall already. Though, not quite as large."

"And underground," William adds.

"Aye, that it is," Samuel agrees. "That is, if you remember the Hall beneath your home." Loche recalls writing about the underground chambers below his house in Sagle, Idaho—a surveillance bunker. He extends his arm in a gesture to shake hands and stops suddenly. Loche notices that Samuel's hand is gone. Quickly, Samuel extends his left, "In some cultures, this might be seen as an insult, a handshake with the left—please know I mean nothing of the sort. Nice to see you again." Loche shakes his hand, "What—what happened to your—"

Samuel smiles, "Never mind. Don't you worry about it. A rather short story I will save for another time." Samuel nods at Loche, "You've been out of sorts since we've met. This is the first time I've seen you—calm."

"Perhaps it's being here in a castle. Reminds me of home, I guess," Loche says.

"Ah, well, for me, I cannot abide castles. Bad memories, you see. I only enter them these days when I have to. And regrettably, now is one of those times." Samuel winks at Edwin, "Hello, little one. How do *you* like the castle?"

"I want to live here, but at home," Edwin says.

Samuel then turns to the woman sitting beside William, "Loche, this is my dearest, Leonaie."

The old woman's eyes sparkle. The two shake hands as she nods to Edwin, "What a strong little boy you've got there," she says.

"I'm five," Edwin says flushing red as Leonaie stares at him.

Justinian Pierce steps before George again, "*Anfogal*, they are ready to begin."

"Good," George says, "let us start."

Justinian motions to a group of three men and one woman standing at the end of the hall. They are raised upon a stage and appear to be wearing a kind of livery. Their garments remind Loche of a medieval surcoat—a long draping tunic rich in green and gold, belted at the waist with decorative swords on hangers. On the floor astride both sides of the stage are two helmed pikemen. Their long spears held point up—the tips gleaming in the firelight. To the right and left of the pikemen are two more coated and helmed soldiers, each bearing a drum slung before them.

One raises his mallets high and strikes. A thunderous boom reverberates through the hall. Edwin's little arms latch tighter around Loche's shoulders. The sound decays slowly into the ancient stones. Then silence, save the crackling fire. Then, another massive boom. The other drummer begins a series of echo strokes, matching the initial beat and then fading in increments. His mallets falling softer at each fall. The fire then takes its turn snapping out random pops, like a needle on a record.

The drummers repeat this echo cadence several times. At every first stroke a rush of adrenaline starts through Loche's body, and as the echo drum fades his heart eases and calms. A kind of relaxed focus builds within him. A clarity of body and mind—hypnotic and wide awake. Loche feels as if he could both fall asleep and run miles without tiring.

"*Verceress willo gos ~ Ithic veli agtig,*" The surcoated woman from the stage shouts out.

The congregation answers in solemn unison, "*Ithic veli agtig.*"

The fire hisses and snaps.

"*Anfogal*, with your leave," she calls out to George.

George shouts out, "Say on!"

The woman steps back to stage left and one of the men steps forward. He looks at the assembly.

"It has begun. Our enemy has shown himself. He is known to us all. He has betrayed us. Albion Ravistelle. He and his followers have forsaken us. In the language of old, they are the *Endale Gen*. He has set the *Endale Gen* to eliminate us. This shall not be!"

"*En dal ay jen?*" Leonaie whispers to Samuel.

"New Earth," he replies.

Another boom, but not from the drums this time. In percussive chorus the group shouts out, "*Hoy!*" Again, Edwin is startled and his limbs cling tighter to Loche.

"We are all that remains of the *Orathom Wis* of the great realm *Wyn Avuqua* of old. We are the door wardens, we hold the way between the gulf of Kingdom Come and the Kingdoms of Clay. We serve the One Law. We serve *Thi*. We serve humankind. We keep the fire from the fingers of gods."

Loche watches as many of the assembly mouth the words along with the speaker. He wonders if this was some kind of mantra or prayer.

The room shudders again, "*Hoy!*"

The man steps back as another moves to the head of the stage. "Welcome all," he says. His tone less formal. "As you know by now, many of the *Wis* have been slain. Please, let us *Iyuv Talgeth*."

Like a wave, the congregation lowers themselves to one knee. Loche looks around, sets Edwin down on the floor and they too, take a knee. "What's this?" Loche whispers to William.

"It is still uncanny, that you do not know." He leans close, a tear rolling down his cheek, "You should know— you made all of this. *Iyuv Talgeth* is a prayer for the slain. Our slain. It means *to pine for what is forbidden to us*—a hereafter. We have nothing after this life. Our prayer is to those that have left us, and we lament and long for their place to remain somewhere in existence. Alas, all we have is here—and yet, what joy, *all we have is here.*"

One by one the assembly rise to their feet. It is not until George Eversman, the last to stand, his lips curved downward and his eyes teary, that the man begins to speak again. "*Ithic veli agtig*," he says from the stage.

"*Ithic veli agtig*," the group replies.

"Our intelligence tells us that Albion Ravistelle has targeted *Orathom Wis* across the globe, and has murdered at least eighty. There are still many unconfirmed reports. Latest intel from inside the *Endale Gen* is that Ravistelle will strike us here, at *Mel Tiris*. A siege is expected in the coming days."

Loche hears Samuel groan, "I knew it. I knew it. I loathe castles."

"You have been gathered here to repel this attack. We believe that the *Endale Gen* is intent on retrieving the remaining paintings of Basil Pirrip Fenn. We have close to half of Mr. Fenn's work secured here at *Mel Tiris*, and we must protect it. All of you are aware of the power of these pieces of art—and you are also aware that in some ways, these paintings are in direct opposition with our mission on Earth. Basil's paintings are the doors—the largest doors between the *Alya* and the *Orathom* that have been experienced. *Anfogal* and our top advisors believe that we have the chance to not only close the pathways to the *Orathom* by using these paintings, but there is a chance that through the paintings, we can end all deity intervention forever. That, my dear guardians, means mission complete for us."

"*Hoy!*" reverberates through the hall.

"However, this feat will not be led by any of us in the *Orathom Wis*. It will be done by none other than Basil Fenn's brother, the Poet, Dr. Loche Newirth. It is he and he alone that can traverse the astral plane unscathed. We must protect Basil's paintings and defend Loche Newirth. We must provide him the time to end the invasion of Heaven.

"You know your places. Marshals, proceed to the weapon take. Squad leaders, report to Tower West for briefings. All others, please prepare to defend against the Enemy. Are there questions?"

A woman calls out, "Can we expect deity intervention in this fight?"

"I would expect anything," the man from the stage replies.

"What of Cythe?" another in the congregation asks, "*It* was seen at the Battle of the Uffizi. What if *It* comes? Has Albion Ravistelle truly joined with—with *It*?"

Loche's skin crawls. Fear stops his breath. Cythe. Nicholas Cythe. Loche had written the character as the Devil himself—*It*. The evil manifestation in every myth known. *It* is now somewhere in the world.

George Eversman steps up onto a tabletop. "*Wis*!" he yells.

"*Hoy*!"   the gathering booms.

"If *It* comes, I will deal with *It*. Do not fear. If you fear It, *It* wins. We are in dis. Yes? Tell me!"

"*Hoy*!" A fueled, powerful resound.

"Defend the keep. Let no one ascend the towers. If they come, they do not leave alive. We are the *Orathom Wis*! Be they man, immortal or god, if they come here, they do not leave alive. Go and be ready!"

A final, "Hoy!" nearly shatters Loche's ears.

A Wider View

November 5, this year
Venice, Italy

There is the strange sensation of movement, as if a boat is carrying her across water.

"I think she's waking, darling."

Julia Iris knows the voice. There is a hiss laced within it. It belongs to Helen Newirth, and the last time Julia saw Helen's face, heard her voice—*there was—pain—the knife was in her mouth—the blade cut through the back of her throat—*

Julia begins to cough. Her eyes flip open. A bright, grey light stabs into her vision and she raises her hands, covering her face. She feels the wetness of tears and saliva.

A comforting hand caresses her upper arm. Through the blur she sees that it is Helen. Julia recoils. Then two large gripping hands seize her.

"Don't," Helen's voice says again. The tone is kind, but firm. "Don't. Everything is okay. Everything is okay, dear. If you stop struggling he will let you go."

Julia turns. Beside her is a massive, bald headed man. His arm is wrapped around behind her shoulders and he squeezes with frightening strength. There is no expression on his face.

She heeds Helen's words and goes limp.

"Are you okay?" Helen asks. "Can you relax?" Julia nods, still studying the brute beside. His eyebrows raise at her as if he is double-checking her affirmation. Julia nods again. With emphasis this time.

"Carlo, let her be." Carlo lifts his arm away and rests easy.

Julia then looks around.

Lounging across from her is Helen Newirth. She is leaning against a man that looks to be in his mid fifties. He is wearing a crisp, chocolate brown suit, white shirt and muted orange tie. Both are pinching the stems of full glasses of wine. There is a blanket over their legs. "Would you care for a glass of wine, dear?" Helen asks.

Above them and just behind another man is standing. His long tunic is striped black and white, and he wears a hat with a wide, round brim. He is pressing a long wooden pole down to his side. Old buildings pass slowly by beneath grey clouds. The movement suddenly makes sense. She is reminded of little Edwin's words from the Priest Lake journal, *Black boats! Black boats on the water!*

"A glass of wine on a Venetian gondola is something not to deny yourself, Miss Iris." The man says. His Italian accent is thick. Helen passes her glass to Julia.

"I am sorry, dear, for the violence," Helen says, "but I knew you would be all right, after all. It is really the effect I was going for, you know. No real damage done. I hope you can forgive me." Helen smiles. It is a lovely smile. The woman looks nothing like she did on the street in Verona. The hard, sharpened features, the killer instinct, the cruel, pitiless, unforgiving spirit—these aspects have vanished from Helen's person. Across from Julia sits a flower—light and supple, soft and desperately gorgeous.

Julia stares at Helen as her hand rises to her throat—to the memory of her latest injury. How many times must she endure this uncanny and impossible mental scarring of physical pain. Pain that is quick and quickly gone?

"Oh don't worry, Julia. It's all gone, like I said it would be. We've even cleaned you up. We changed you out of those nasty, bloody clothes. You should see yourself. You look beautiful. Doesn't she, darling?"

"That she does."

"You know who this is, don't you, Julia? This is Albion Ravistelle. This is my *real* husband."

His eyes glint under the grey as the boat turns into a wider canal. He looks nothing like she had imagined from

Loche's writings. His face shines out a genuine benevolence. A caring from a deep seated resolve. He looks fatherly, and yet alluring and sensual. Julia shifts her eyes back and forth between them, and it somehow adds up. The two appear to be made for one another, as if they were both cut from some ancient cloth—as if the names of Albion and Helen could be included among the fateful marriages of classical antiquity.

Then, perhaps, it is merely the Venetian air. Maybe the gondola ride. The wine. . .

Julia sits up and looks at the wineglass in her hand. "Cheers," she says. She tips it back and drains it into her mouth. Four large gulps and it is gone. "Nice," she says. She sets the glass down on the floor between her feet.

"That it is," Albion agrees. "It is only a Rüdesheimer Apostelwein, bottled, 1727. But never mind. It was made to be drunk."

Julia looks over the side of the boat. She searches the possible escape routes—over the side to the dock ten feet away and through the narrow alley, jump from the boat to the passing window ledge—

"Don't," Helen says, almost as a whisper. "Julia, don't run. Just wait? There is a lot to talk about." Julia senses Carlo tensing at her side. She doesn't hesitate.

Her feet push and she springs toward the water. Carlo is too fast and just as she rises, her body is slammed back into the padded seat. She struggles a moment longer until noticing Carlo's expressionless face again. *While he is near*, she thinks, *I'm going nowhere.* She stops and waits. Carlo eases his hold. She reaches gingerly down to her wineglass and lifts it before Julia and Albion. She wiggles it, gesturing to be refilled. Her focus is trained on the massive Carlo.

Albion leans forward with the bottle and pours. "Very well," he says. "Let's slow down, shall we? You'll learn what it means to slow down, Julia. Let's start with how to enjoy a vintage with grace." She sips from the glass and looks at the two cuddling before her.

"What you must think of us. What you must think of me. The things you've been told. The stories. Ah, the stories," Albion says, "Odd, isn't it? The three of us here? The way things appear. The way we interpret another's actions, words and deeds. How quickly we can pass judgement without knowing the whole story. There is of course, your side of the story. There is mine. There is also a version called the truth. Yet, as these many centuries have crawled by, I've learned that even truth has its own sides, its own agenda. Truth, for mankind is a limited resource."

Julia watches him speak. She takes another sip.

"Truth. Let's speak of truth, shall we, Julia Iris, immortal? The truth is, I should have had you cut into pieces and incinerated. Such a swift act would have saved me and our cause some trouble. I know that sounds inhuman. But, we are not really human, after all, are we? No. We must live by a different set of standards, we undying people. We *Itonalya*. And because we strive for a higher excellence, I give pause in mandating your execution.

"Let's alleviate the suspense, shall we? I want three things from you, Julia. Very simple things the first of which may appear medieval in its process. You will serve as ransom for my wife's son, Edwin. We are holding you to see his safe return to his mother. I am sure you can understand this.

"Second, I want you to be open-minded, behaved and a good listener. I want very much to share with you, my side of this long, long tale. A wider view. Oh the stories they must have told you. Again, it pains me to entertain what you must believe about me—my intentions, my mission, my hopes. I think you'll find reason behind my method. Reason, sweet Julia, that will lend to your new found reality.

"And finally, once you have heard and seen, once you have measured the depth of my plight versus what you know already, once you have listened to your heart, I want you to join my cause. Only then can I pass judgement on your survival. I have given every known immortal this choice. Most have found the wisdom and have joined with me. George Eversman and the remaining *Orathom Wis* have chosen oblivion. They can, and will, have it. You, Julia, are one of us—you deserve your chance to choose. And you shall have that chance."

The boat exits the narrow water streets into a wider, busier canal. Julia turns toward the bow. Ahead of them is a yellowing stone structure, looming up against the overcast sky like an armored knight. Gothic windows reflect the churning waters and traffic of the venetian boats. The lower floor is hemmed in crimson balconies. Below is a waterside dining area. Julia recalls Loche's descriptions of this place in the Priest Lake journal. She imagines Basil Pirrip Fenn sitting at a table with his cigarettes and his coffee—his dark eyes tracking boats as they pass.

Julia feels the wine. Its effect is calming, and strangely energizing—a sensation unlike she's ever felt before.

At the landing, a man wearing a suit and tie waits. Small, wire rimmed glasses sit low on his nose. He waves. "Dr. Angelo Catena," Julia whispers. Then, stepping out from the dining area another man, similarly dressed, joins Catena. It is Corey Thomas. She had met him just days ago at Loche's cabin, with William and Samuel. The surprise and joy at seeing him nearly causes her to raise her arm to wave. She refrains, and turns back around reaching for her wine. Albion watches her as she drains another full glass into her mouth.

"Nectar of the gods?" Helen says, raising the bottle to pour more. Julia holds her glass out.

The Window

April, 1338
The House of Albion Ravistelle, London

"Now, not all monks are bad," Albion had told William, "especially those that brew." The beer was delicious. It made him dizzy. At the word *monk*, William shivered. The thought of the larger of Gravesend's sentinels came to his mind.

"One of the monks with the bishop," William said, "he was big. Very big."

"Father Cyrus," Albion said. "Yes, a large man. Frightening to behold. He is Gravesend's right hand. I know little of him save his allegiance to the Church and to the Bishop—and the tales of his cruelty. Horrible. Horrible."

William turned away. His stomach tightened and the pace of his breathing increased.

Albion had three foaming mugs brought to their chamber just a few minutes after they arrived. Two filled and one half full for the boy. William and his father sat staring through a large pane of glass. They sipped the beer and marveled at the view of the Thames, not a stone's throw away. William pushed his fingers to the glass.

"You've not seen a window before?" Albion asked.

William shook his head.

"Nor has he had beer," Radulphus said. "And I have never had beer this good." He took a long swig.

"Yes," Albion said. "One of the first things you learn, when faced with the condition of long, long life, is that money must be had, and much of it. You learn to grow your fortune. And that, of course, brings good beer." He laughed lightly. "I would have windows in every room of my house," he added, "if it did not draw too much attention. One day, every house will have them. But now they are limited to nobility and the rich. I felt that a single window in this room, to see the mighty Thames on cold mornings was worth the whisperings of my neighbors."

William traced the river as he took another sip from his mug. Sitting upon the window sill was the leather bag. The leaves appeared to be reaching for the sun.

William felt a sudden ease from the beer's effects. It somehow cushioned the thoughts of Father Cyrus. Slowly, his thoughts drifted to all he had seen on this day.

They got their first view of London before noon. Albion had led the wagon out of a thick grove. The bright sky was like cold silver. His eyes stung coming under it. "Take a breath now, you two, and smell the last of the free air," Albion said pointing down, "for the sweetness of the country is soon to be replaced."

They were perched on a high hill. Below, like a crosshatched drawing were the lines, roads and crossings of London. Chimneys belched woodsmoke and other fumes that William could not guess. Little grey roof peaks appeared like small toys on a board. Through the city center slithered the Thames River. Tiny boats appeared motionless on its surface.

"Ah," Albion whiffed. "The legacy of man. You can smell him for miles. But, the city is cleaner than some. At least they've begun to understand their footprint."

William stared.

London.

Houses were packed together with more houses. The smells became sharper. More profound. William was often forced to pull his cloak up to cover his nose and mouth. There were times that his eyes would water from some hidden stench as they rolled in.

But the people were busy. The buildings, some of them two, three and even four stories, were structures beyond his imaginings. More horses than he had ever seen. Men and women of nobility passed—bejeweled and wrapped in velvet and fine leathers, hats with colorful plumes of blue and crimson. Soldiers with their silver tipped pikes and proud stares, helmed in iron—vendors calling out at market—exotic fruits, baskets of bright red apples (William's mouth began to water), a skinned boar on a spit. A line of clergymen. A passing old man. A woman and her small son—the boy carried a toy horse.

William looked up at his father. He reached for his large hand and gripped it. Radulphus looked down at him. "Did you see the apples? How I would love to have an apple," he said.

Albion stopped the wagon. "Just a moment." He turned and walked a few paces back.

The warm scent of baking bread wafted across the father and son. The two turned toward it, their noses both lifted in thankfulness. Just beyond the corner of the street they could see a small fire dancing within a domed, clay oven. A long wood table was crowded with loaves, golden brown.

"As you wish," they heard Albion's voice. When they turned he was holding three shining apples. He bit into one, held it in his teeth and handed the other two to both Radulphus and William. William held it in his hand and stared. It was cool to the touch.

"Come now," Albion said, a chunk of apple falling from his mouth as he spoke. "It's only an apple. Just wait until you taste the cakes at my home." He smiled. He sniffed the air and added, "And the bread."

Not twenty paces from their wagon, at the entrance to a chapel, William caught sight that made him shiver. Clawing itself out of stone cornice on the chapel facade was a demonic face. Its sneering lips and watchful eye glowered down at the boy. Looking away William saw, in seeming opposition, a tall figure carved in stone. It was in the shape of a woman in flowing robes. One of her arms was upraised and in her other she cradled a small child. Elegant angelic wings rose up at her back. William thought he caught the likeness of his mother in the cold features of the stone face. He would not forget the expression the sculpture wore. It was staring at something beyond William's sight.

William took a bite of the apple. It was crisp and sweet. He could not help but smile.

The Mirror

June, 1975
Venice, Italy

Helen stared at herself in the mirror. She wore a work of art. It sparkled in the candlelight. The piece was her favorite of Albion's collection, and it nestled against her cheeks and lips as if it were made for her face alone. Of the many Venetian masquerade masks he possessed, this was by far the oldest. Mid-sixteenth century, encrusted with tiny rubies around the eyes, plumes of carved deep green leaves rising up at the forehead, and light as a feather, its lines were as sensual as the gliding silk curve from her smooth breasts to the slope of her thigh.

"We wear masks to be equals, Helen," Albion said. He sat behind, his legs crossed and his gaze absorbed her.

She pivoted back and smiled at him, her fingers feeling the cold gems of the mask beneath her fingertips. "It's beautiful," she said.

"You are beautiful," came Albion's echo.

She loved the feel of the leather against her cheeks. With it on, she was no longer Helen Craven. Her past did not matter, her deadly deeds of late were nothing, and what was to come was as hidden as her identity.

"Equals?" Helen asked.

"Yes," he said. "The Venetians took to wearing masks to hide their social status. Politicians, the rich, nobility, the clergy and the everyman—the fish monger, the mason and the beggar—all were without identity, without rank and most of all, without culpability. Wearing the mask at Carnival enabled the priest and the miscreant to come together and experience human pleasure without consequence." He laughed quietly and added, "Well, for the most part."

Helen felt her abdomen tighten. "So, if you put a mask on, you and I would be equal?"

"If I noticed you at Carnival, and you did not know me, and I did not know you, yes, we would be equal. We would be free to tease and trifle."

"I think you're flirting with me now, Albion."

"That may be so," Albion agreed. He stood and moved close behind her. She looked at him in the mirror, his eyes glinting from over her shoulder. "You have made me very proud."

Helen beamed. "I have?"

"You have. You have exceeded my expectations. Of the many *Itonalya* I have trained through the centuries, you have shown an unrelenting focus—promise, spirit and skill rivaling the most powerful of your immortal family. I am proud—and you should be proud of yourself."

A bead of tear glistened. She watched it swell and drop, threading itself down into the maze of rubies below her eye. She removed the mask and noted that the expression on her face was filled with gratitude. Albion laid his hand upon her cheek and chin, and grinned.

"There, now," he said, comfort in his voice. "You're not used to such compliments. The torture of your youth is a mere blink in time, Helen. I am sorry for the abuse you were made to suffer. But you survived. And it is over now. Look, now, at this woman in the mirror. This is a face gods envy. The woman angels fear."

Helen spun and pressed her mouth to his. She heard herself let out a quiet sough of yearning as she felt him pull her in, his hands falling to the small of her back.

How many gods had she killed? Twenty? Thirty? And in how many countries? She had followed his instruction without fail. Studied. Learned. All to be closer to him. She would give all to be his possession.

When he pulled away, Helen remained frozen. Her eyes still closed, her chin upraised and her lips swollen and empty.

"This cannot be," Albion said, retreating to the other side of the room. "There are too many things yet to be determined. Too much at stake."

Helen relaxed and let her hands fall to her sides. "Will I ever be yours? What must I do?"

Albion did not answer. With his back to her, he said, "Look into that mirror, Helen, and tell me if you can carry on with your training. If you can be two people. One with a mask, one without. Can you change your identity and become another person?"

"Why? What do you mean?"

"Turn," he said.

Helen turned back to the mirror. She was startled to see anger in her eyes.

"Our kind must possess this skill—the ability to change our lives and forge a new name, perception—position. We must do this to survive. We cannot simply carry on through the centuries and not be noticed."

"I am not yet twenty."

"True," came his voice from the darkness. "But now is the time to begin—"

"So how do I start?" She squinted into the mirror trying to locate him in the room behind. "For you, I will do anything."

Albion's dark eyes then rose over her shoulder, the rest of his face hidden behind the black of a leather mask. He lifted her hands up and pressed them flat against the mirror, then she felt the silk skirt being drawn into a ball and raised up. When he entered her, his heat was the first thing she noticed. Then, her legs spasmed as he pulled her pelvis back. Again she let out a moan of triumph. She narrowed her eyes at him in the mirror and noticed his lips smiling below his mask.

As he pulsed within her, she pressed back, taking him fully inside. It was painful and gorgeous.

"Equals?" she whispered. "You can try. You can try."

A Little Waker Upper

November 5, this year
Venice, Italy

Corey Thomas' face had remained expressionless when they were introduced. Julia struggled to reflect the same, but she couldn't keep her eyes from lingering a little longer upon him. They had met at Loche's cabin—briefly. How he had managed to keep his loyalties to William and the *Orathom Wis* out of Albion's mind is beyond her. He fought against Albion at the Battle of the Uffizi—how was he able to hide that fact? Regardless, it is a relief to know he is a friend.

Dr. Angelo Catena's eyes were troubled, and darkened a bit further when Albion suggested the first stop on the tour of the compound would be The Sun Room. At its mention, Julia too, felt her anxiety rise.

Now Julia stands before a black curtain. At her feet, carved into the white marble is the number nine.

"Eyes forward," Albion commands.

She obeys.

"Mr. Ravistelle," Angelo says, "I believe it would be safer to begin her initiation on two or three. Nine has been proven quite powerful and—"

"Dr. Catena, please. Julia is of our blood. She is quite capable of returning."

"There have been damaging effects reported by even those of the *Itonalya*—"

"We will not allow her to remain within long enough for anything permanent. We need only expose her to the truth. Though it will burn, it will surely teach. And Julia needs an accelerated education."

"Let it be said, then," Catena says, "that I opposed this viewing."

"Noted," Helen sneers.

"Catena," Albion says, "I understand your concern. And I appreciate it."

Julia risks a look around. The room is circular and massive. It was several floors underground—underwater. The walls of white glare so brightly that she was forced to squint when she first entered. Around the perimeter are numbered viewing stations before black shrouded stages. This is the very Sun Room Loche described in his journal.

"Julia, yet another lesson for *Itonalya*," Albion said. "I guarantee that after this viewing, you will consider my invitation to join our cause. You are about to look upon infinity, the godhead, ever-last and beyond. The majority of mankind cannot withstand such a sight. These works of art pull from mankind their sin, their imperfection and their humanity and hurl these attributes into the *Orathom* —it will, in time, destroy the afterlife. For those that are the sickest at heart, the most disturbed, the maligned, the paintings can bring them to perfect health—but so far, such cases are few and far between. You, Julia, will return alive, but the memory will forever stain your thoughts. Once you behold what is beyond, we will be able to converse about what is now before us."

"Corey," Albion says, "please have them open number nine."

Corey steps between Julia and the black curtain. He grips both of her shoulders as if to position her at the proper angle. He steals a quick look into her eyes—a brief flash of warning and comfort. *You'll be okay*, the expression seems to say, *I'll be right here*. He steps behind her, "Open nine."

Julia braces herself and scowls into the splitting black curtain.

She expected a fine, silky line of light to appear. A kind of spider's thread that would reach from the surface of the canvas to her eyes. And then, as it had been described in Loche Newirth's journal, a maddening journey to some inexplicable vision of the afterlife—a sight beyond what the human mind can fathom—an experience that could kill the viewer. This was the artwork of Basil Pirrip Fenn, Loche's brother. Paintings not meant for the eyes of human beings. Basil's work was for *them*. For the gods. The paintings, as she understood it, were a kind of peep hole for them to look in upon us—to feel what we feel.

Gods. An infinite population of divine, celestial beings existing along the astral plane. Dwelling in a place reserved for us after death. Heaven? Afterlife? Elysium? Valhalla? Nirvana?

She thinks of her father's rhyme to steady her. *Find the single star / And watch it blink.*

She squints as the curtain moves, and recalls the three words Loche used in the journal to describe what comes next:

Silence.

Flash.

Gone.

But there is no burst of light.

She sees a pair of shoes first. Black. Grey slacks. A man standing there upon the stage. There was no painting. No gilded frame. Instead a man of seventy or so. Greying hair. Gaunt.

"A little waker-upper?" he says. A long, thin smile.

"Oh God," Julia whispers.

"Not exactly," Dr. Marcus Rearden replies. "But I knew that I wasn't crazy. Or, at least, not completely."

Behind Rearden, heavy upon an easel, is a black shrouded rectangle—much like the one he had propped up beside Bethany Winship's coffin, the last time she saw him.

He casually pulls the cloth down and it cascades to the floor revealing a painting that Julia knew. She flinches at the memory. The lurid reds and blacks, Rearden's murderous eyes bearing down upon his beloved Beth. The very painting that she and Rearden transported from

Priest Lake to Beth Winship's funeral. It was Loche that had painted it. He had done it to capture his mentor.

Rearden watches her face and then leans to the side to take sight of the painting.

"Isn't this something?" Rearden says. "Tormenting, to be sure. I've not thought of much else since the moment I saw it. It haunts me more than the act of holding Beth's head underwater—the quaking of her shoulders."

A sudden wave of nausea. Julia raises her hand to her stomach.

"The thing is," Rearden continues, turning his eyes back to Julia, smiling, "I loved her. Isn't that something? I loved her."

The Timeless Pie

November 5, this year
Mel Tiris, France

George Eversman's eyes dart back and forth from the page in front of his face to Leonaie. *What an odd looking man*, Leonaie thinks. She has always thought that. From the first time she met him in the late sixties. Of course, she cannot seem to recall where that was. Through the years she'd known George as Samuel's boss. Though, she was aware he was much more than that. Older than any of their kind. She squints, searching for his age. She was told before, that is sure. *Was he over one thousand years old? Goodness, that's a long while.* She watches him. *What an odd looking man—deep set eyes, long, thin lips—now what does that remind me of,* she thinks. *Who was that rock singer? Stephen Tyler? My goodness, yes. Strange to remember that. He looks a lot like* that *fellow.*

George lays the documents down upon the table. Leonaie looks at the paper, trying to recall why he was reading it.

"I know about dis already, Samuel," George says. "But I need you here."

"I know, *Anfogal*. I know."

George stares at him.

"*Anfogal*," Samuel says, "you've always known that this day would come. I must now choose between duty and love."

"But what you are planning—dangerous. Dangerous. You must wait until we have defeated Albion's advance. Then, I help you. *I* help you."

"We do not have the time. She is slipping—her memory." He points at the documents, "Ravistelle has developed the science. He can reverse age to one's prime and graft the missing rung to the ladder. He can make a mortal, immortal. Since my youth, I have given my soul and duty to the *Orathom Wis* and to you. I must now depart on an errand of my own. I go to save my love from death."

That's *what the documents were about*, Leonaie recalls suddenly. She reaches to the pages and slides them around to remind herself.

Samuel wrote this for her.

Moonchild.

The Melgia.

The successful genetic experiments that Albion Ravistelle's team has been working on over the last ten years.

The Fountain of Youth.

The Fruit of Life.

Dearest Leonaie, here is a little about the science behind it all. They've found a way to keep telomeres, the lids on the end of the DNA chain, from deteriorating. As these telomeres shorten, we age. So, by introducing the ribonucleoprotein, Telomerase, which is a reverse transcriptase (a kind of enzyme that regenerates DNA production), voilà, you've got infinite cell regeneration, and immortal cells, and thus, biological immortality. And better still, age reversal, to what Ravistelle's team calls, Prime—the biological age inscribed upon an individual's DNA in which the organism is at its strongest, both mentally and physically. The point that cell and metabolic structure reaches full maturity in tandem with mental function. Brilliantly simple, really. Like making an apple pie (you know how to make those). The first keys to the science have been around since the middle of the twentieth century. The following decades brought huge technological strides, of course, but as with most controversial advances, the powers that be held their findings close. The science was solid, but there was no single organization authorized for human trials. This didn't stop Albion. No. He kept on.

Many did not survive the early trials—but finally, Albion introduced a secret gene—he managed to unlock a

MICHAEL B. KOEP 🌿 181

*science that had long been a mystery. Combined with the
very experiments that grew organs, kept rats going strong
—well, he found it. It worked. It worked on humans. It
will make mortals immortal.*

Leonaie shakes her head and blinks. George is staring
at her. She feels Samuel's gentle scratching between her
shoulder blades, "Darling," he says, "did you hear me?"

Where am I, she thinks. "I was just thinking about
making an apple pie," she says. "You know, dear, when I
was a little girl, my father would whistle and we girls
would dance? I had three sisters. For some reason, I
remember Mother making apple pies when we would
dance. I always put those two things together. Oh, and
you, too." She winks at him, "You know what I'm talking
about."

"Leonaie," Samuel said. His face is concerned, but he
is smiling. "George asked you a question."

"He did?" she laughs. "I'm sorry, I was thinking about
pies and telomeres." She turns to George and leans
forward, "I'm sorry, George. Getting old ain't for sissies.
What did you say?"

George smiles at her. Whenever they had met in the
past, he was always kind. She likes his face despite its
weird shape. "Do you want dis? You want to be like us?"
he asks.

"I want him," she says pulling Samuel closer. "I want
to stay with him."

George laces his fingers before his chin. "What plan?"
he asks Samuel. "How will you do dis? You tell me.
How?"

"Corey Thomas will get us in. He has scheduled
Leonaie for the procedure already. He's put in order all of
the official clearances through Ravistelle's security. We
need only arrive and check-in, have the procedure, and
get out. Corey has already outlined our escape. Leonaie
and I will return, hopefully, before the siege upon *Mel
Tiris* begins."

"You will be recognized when you arrive at
Ravistelle's door."

"I will disguise myself. He will not know me. Nor will any in his charge."

George nods to Samuel's missing hand, "Hard to hide dat."

Writing the Good Stories

November 5, this year
Mel Tiris, France

"What's wrong, Dad?" Edwin asks.

Loche wipes at his tears. "Nothing. Nothing. It's just the dust in this old room. It makes me sneeze, too." Loche fakes a high pitched *ach-hoo*. Edwin echoes it and laughs.

"So you're okay to go with Granddad? He's going to take you on a plane—to see Mom."

"Yes. I'm okay. It will be fun. How long will it take?"

"Oh, about the same amount of time it took to fly here. A few hours, I expect. Not long at all. You'll get to see the black boats on the water again."

"I remember that place, Dad. I remember."

"And if you ask Granddad, he'll take you on one of those boats."

"I will ask him."

"Good."

"Good."

Loche shivers at the impossible situation before him. How could he ever make sense of it? He cannot believe that he is about to send his son off with his own newly found father, to his wife that has deceived him their entire marriage, to a militant group, this *Endale Gen*, intent on a kind of genocide—while he must uncover the shrouded paintings in this room and cross the threshold of death to find a way to save both humankind and divinities alike. To save existence. He presses his forehead against his son's and breathes in the smell of him. *This is really happening.*

"We're writing the good stories—painting the beautiful pictures, right, Dad?"

"Yes. Yes we are."

"And I get to go and see Mom?"

"Yes."

"And you can't come?"

"No. I have to work here."

Edwin gives a solemn nod. "You need to write your book some more?"

"Kind of," Loche says.

"When are you going to be done with your book, Dad?"

"When I know the end of the story."

"Will the ending be good?"

Loche stares at his son. "Yes. It has to be."

"When you're done writing, can we go to Disneyland?"

"Of course we can."

"Can we take Granddad, too?"

"Yes."

"Good." Edwin gives Loche a squeeze and stands up. "I need to get my wood sword before I go. Bye, Dad."

"You do as William—as Granddad says, okay?"

"Okay."

"I love you, boy. I love you with all of my heart."

"I love you, Dad."

William Greenhame peeks his head into the room from the door. "Get your sword, good squire Edwin. The plane awaits."

Edwin runs out laughing.

Loche watches William's eyes follow the boy down the circular stone steps to the chamber below.

"He gets around this place quite well," William says. "It must remind him of the castle you built for him in Idaho."

"Yes, I suppose so."

"I have spoken to your mother, Diana. She wishes you hope, love and courage."

"Where is she?" Loche asks.

"She is safe. I will not tell you where, for now anyway. Just know that she sends her love to us both. I will one day soon tell you all there is to know of my beautiful bride, your mother." William places his hand upon the door. "I am not coming in to ease your concerns, son," he says. "There is nothing I can say that will take your fears away. I know. Believe me, I know." He tilts his head slightly, "But, Doctor, you have the tools to deal with all of this, I think.

"I have watched you grow up, and I've trembled at every step you've taken since you were born. I had accepted that you would never know me—like a father, I mean. Too dangerous, of course. It is unfortunate that you only know me as a manic madman seeking therapy. Warranted, I grant, but the maladies you've diagnosed me with are rooted in the despair and helplessness of not being able to, well, to read to you—to teach you about the sky and the stars and the sea. To show how to fight with a wooden sword through the living room and into the kitchen and out the back door into the trees. But I have always been near. And there is no father prouder than I am of you."

"Thank you, William," Loche says. "But I—it's still a little difficult for me to completely empathize—"

"No, no," William replies, "don't try. Don't try. Our relationship will always be—a little odd, surely. We will become what we become." He laughs, "Imagine what it will look like thirty years from now—you will wrinkle and I will look like *your* son, I'm afraid. For now, we might appear as brothers, but that will change. Alas. The wheels turn ever.

"But it seems that fate has provided me a joy that I'd not dared to dream of, Loche. Little Edwin has captured my heart. And he will receive the care and tutelage that I have longed to devote to you. All that is mine, is his. Your fears for him I cannot quell—but if we believe in the power of words, place *these* into your story, Loche, know that with every sinew of my being, all of the love I possess, I shall be to both you and he, a *granddad*. He shall return to you, I swear it."

Loche's eyes flood with tears. "Bring him home, William," Loche breaks. "Bring him back to me."

"I will, and more," William answers. "*You* had better be here for us when we return."

Loche feels the looming weight of Basil's shrouded gallery behind him, and he turns toward the chasm that awaits. "Go," he says over his shoulder. "Go."

The Bath

April, 1338
The House of Albion Ravistelle, London

The beer was nearly gone and William's eyes were heavy.

"You will both sleep in this room tonight," Albion said. He then chuckled looking at them. "The friars that make this ale know their business well, yes? I would think that you are both ready to drift off now. But not yet." He stood and moved to the door. A long, thin chain hung from a hole in the ceiling. He gave it a gentle pull. Somewhere below a distant bell rung. "First you will bathe—and we shall see what we can do to dress you in the appropriate clothing for our venture. After that, we will sup. And then," he smiled at William, "*then* you can sleep."

A light knock on the door startled William. "My lord, Albion? How can I be of service?" A woman's voice called from outside the closed door.

"Ah, Alice," Albion said. He opened the door.

Alice wore a long grey smock with a green mantle. Her hair was silver grey and eyes clear blue—like sky. Taking one look at William she said, "Goodness me, what have we here, a little boy or a drowned rat?" William looked down at his muddied cloak, and his hands, soiled and stained. He imagined that the rest of him matched. Alice shook her head, "And a Holy Father?" She bowed reverently and crossed herself, "God save you, Father."

A sudden expression of shock drifted across her face when she met with the priest's eyes. With an abrupt glance at Albion and then back to the Radulphus, she squinted and smiled. Albion placed his hand on Alice's shoulder, "This is Father Radulphus Grenehamer of Ascott."

The woman shook her head as if in anger and glared at Albion, "Oh dear, Father, did my lord Albion bring you both through a storm of mud? We must get you both cleaned up!"

Albion sighed and nodded, "Thank you, Alice. Please have prepared hot baths and fresh clothes—and supper for —"

"Yes, yes," she broke in, waving a hand. Her tone was flustered, "I'll see to it. We'll have to find some clothes to fit the lad—I'll burn the clothes he's in—goodness me." She fired another dagger at Albion, "You didn't drag this Holy Father and young boy through London looking like this, did you, Albion?"

"Alice, I—" Albion began.

She waved her hand and smiled at the two visitors. "Ah, me." She walked into the chamber, laid hold of William's cloak and pulled it over his head. Pinching it between two fingers, she held it away from her as if it was something long dead and slimy. She took a look at the boy, "My word," her voice was astonished, "have you eaten? Ever? This boy is thin as a sunbeam."

Again, William looked down at himself. His body was rail thin. The clothes he wore were overlarge and hung loose over his shoulders. Alice made a careful survey, scanned the priest's condition as well, then turned to Albion.

"My lord," she said with a tone straining for patience. "I have noted that there are still unused provisions on the wagon, along with some extra clothing—or did you forget? These two could have certainly used what you yourself did not need."

Albion smiled, "Alice, I—"

Another wave. This time with a single finger waggling between them. "I pack extra things for you to use when you are upon the road. Need and want is not hidden in this dark country, my lord, Albion. And we can provide. You need only look away from your blinding pursuit to see it, and so much more."

"Alice, I—"

"What is this boy's name?" she said, turning away from Albion.

Radulphus answered, "His name is William."

Her smile comforted William and she reached to shake his hand. "Pleased to meet you, William—Father. I am Mrs. Eloise Smith, you can call me Alice. I run this house for my lord, Albion Ravistelle. Welcome."

Albion tried again, "Alice, I—"

"What is your will, my lord?" Alice asked, exasperated.

He smiled at her. "If I may? A few items concerning our guests? William is the priest's son."

Alice circled back and eyed Radulphus. Her face was expressionless. Radulphus placed his hand on the boy's head.

"And the boy," Albion continued, "is *Itonalya*. He is of the undying."

The woman's eyes ticked to William. He liked her face. It was broad and plump, and it looked capable of endless laughter. But now it was solemn and thoughtful. Motherly.

She gave a subtle nod and said, "Oh, my sweet, sweet boy—so new to the world—so new."

William was surprised to hear his own voice, "Are you like us, too?"

And there was the laugh and the joyous grin he had imagined. She howled, "Oh my!" She then knelt down and held William's eyes, "Such curiosity. I like that. Let's say that I know a thing or two about what it means to live —and good living starts with a hot bath, a hot supper and a soft pillow."

She whirled around and faced Albion again. "*Your* bath waits for you in your chamber." Then back to William and the priest. "You two shall come with me."

"What is this place?" Radulphus asked.

A hot vapor hung before William's eyes. Moisture dripped from the stone walls and ceiling.

Alice stood before a shut wood planked door. "This is the house bath chamber. There are not many like it in London. None that I know of, come to think of it. My lord

Albion, had this room built after he visited a friend with one like it. In Rome, I believe it was. Or was it Japan? Or was it on the coast? All of Albion's houses, from here to the East have a room like this. But this is the only one I've seen."

Opening the door, a plume of steam burst into the hall. The heat was a delight. William closed his eyes, and inhaled deeply.

A fire roared in a thigh high square of rust colored brick. Its light was blurred by the steam. The ceiling, floor and walls were of mortar and rock—large rocks like those William had seen along the stream beds near to his home. They were round and smooth. A huge, copper cauldron full of boiling water hung by iron chains over the flames. One narrow cedar chute was angled from the cauldron down to a basin on the floor. The tub was big enough for William's father to lie down inside. Another chute ran from the tub up to a small square door above. A green, woven mat of thick yarn hung upon a rail near the door and soft, white towels were draped on a bar just opposite. Four torches lit the room.

Alice moved to the nearest cauldron and twisted a small, wood handle. It poured hot water down into the chute and into the basin. She then pulled an iron chain and a tiny door at the top of the wall slid open. From it issued cold water. It, too, ran down into the filling tub. The woman dipped her hand into the bath checking the temperature and made adjustments so that the water was, "Not too hot, not too cold."

While the water rose, she opened a cabinet and from it she took a cake of soap and a long handled brush. She handed them to William. "For your backside," she instructed. Opening the door she said, "Wash now, you two. I'll see to supper."

The Apple Upon the Book

June 1975,
Venice, Italy

They had slept tangled together. For a brief moment, she had possessed him. A fading belief.

Helen watched the curtain flutter. Outside the morning air was a rush of waterway traffic. The breeze from the ocean was sweet. Her legs searched the cool sheets again for his body beside her, but he was gone. She partly expected to wake alone. Then, she heard the distinct sound of a tea cup and saucer.

Albion was seated across the sun-washed room, a newspaper open upon a table and a breakfast covered in chrome domes. He was dressed in a tie, his suit jacket hung over his chair.

"Good morning," he said.

Helen sat up, pulled the sheets aside and stood. She waited for him to look. When he did, she strode toward him. Albion's lips curved slightly as her naked body approached. Her hair draped in thick dark curls over her shoulders and breasts. She leaned down and kissed him. "Good morning," she said. In a basket her fingers found a yellow apple. She plopped down in the opposite seat with one leg draped over the armchair. She leaned back and bit.

Albion stared at her.

"Off to work?" she asked, then added playfully, "so soon?"

"I am," he said. She watched his face. It was a mix of obsession and study. She felt as if she were the subject of a painting. "And I won't be home for dinner." He looked back to his paper.

On the table was a large, hardbound book. Old by the looks of it. Helen gestured at it with the apple, "Why do I think that's for me?"

"It is, indeed," he replied, lowering the paper and folding it.

"What is it about?"

Albion smiled, his hand caressing the cover. "It is a history. A tale of a race that have lived a long, long while. It is, Helen, about the creation of our world through the mind of *Thi.* It is the story of our ancestors and the gods. It is filled with terror and triumph, tragedy and harmony —it is about how a people, chosen to protect an afterlife at the quiet limit of the world—our reward is now. We receive nothing ever-after."

"Is there fucking?"

"Much," Albion laughed.

He pushed the book across the table. "It is called the *Toele.*" Helen took another bite from her apple and placed it upon the cover.

"I am leaving, Helen. It will be quite some time before we see each other again."

Helen sat up. "Where are you going?" She heard shock in her voice. Fear.

"I have business around the world," he replied. "And I will explain it all to you when I see you again."

"When will that be?" There was now a pleading in her tone.

"It will be several years, my sweet Helen."

"Years?" she cried. "But I thought—I thought we were —"

Albion stood and pulled his suit jacket on.

"But I love you. You can't go. Not now. Now is all we have."

"And I love you, too," he said. The words were like a gale. "If we are to be together through these empty courts of earth, I must prepare our place—our home for forever."

"Albion," she said, "take me with you."

"I cannot. Your training is not yet complete. And upon my return, you will face your final trial. If you succeed, we will not part again."

He rounded the table and knelt beside her. His fingers weaved through her hair and he pulled her close. His other hand tangled in hers. He was inhaling her, breathing her in, and she became air. She rose above the two kissing forms and looked down. Below, within a room of velvet, candles, wood and lace was a man in formal dress and a woman, winding her flesh into a coil around him.

Moments later, Albion stood and walked out of the chamber.

Before she let her body slide to the floor, she reached for the apple upon the book.

Memory

November 5, this year
Mel Tiris, France

All Loche Newirth can think of are black holes. He is in a castle chamber surrounded by hundreds of them. He hasn't the faintest idea of what a black hole is save that it has something to do with a gravity so intense that even light cannot escape. Maybe in school he learned something about space-time and quantum theory. Maybe he has some inkling about general relativity. Maybe there is a vague recollection of what an event horizon is, but other than a few key ideas, he is at a loss. Way back in his childhood he recalls the Walt Disney movie, *The Black Hole*, and the terrifying pupil-black spiral upon the theater screen. A tiny starship eddying on the outer edge of doom.

His own smile surprises him. He shakes his head and surveys the shrouded paintings. Each contains an inescapable vortex, a crushing and maddening Center. A direct vein to the eye of a god.

These were Basil Fenn's paintings. Not for the eyes of man, but for the gods themselves. Once they were completed, they served as windows upon the human condition where gods could feel the pleasures, the sorrows and the fear of humanity. It was believed that the works were in some way secret passages for the celestial host. An alternative to the dangers and pains of entering the forbidden home of humanity as a bridging spirit.

The smile fades.

But if man looks in, his fallibility, his imperfection, his sin, his fear and all that he is, is drawn into the hereafter like disease.

A knock startles him. "Yes?" he says.

The door creaks open and stepping in is a man that appears to be in his mid to late forties. His hair is very long. It reaches to his waist. He wears the livery of the *Orathom Wis.*

"I am Athelstan," he says, simply. "It is a great honor to meet you, Doctor. I am sent to guard your door and to assist you."

"I thank you," Loche says, "But I believe it would be safer to be alone—"

Athelstan nods. "True. True. Though, *Anfogal* insists that I remain in the chamber and help in any way I can. I will move paintings, lift shrouds from paintings, cover paintings, ease your hurts, bring food, water. . . I am your servant. And if the siege rises to this door, I will be your shield."

"Very well," Loche says.

Athelstan moves to the door and locks it. He unsheathes his sword and leans it against the wall. "How might I serve?"

Loche wonders, *where to start?* "Is there a way to know the subject matter of these paintings without lifting the shrouds?"

"There is, indeed," Athelstan says. "Upon the backs of each painting, in the lower right corner is Basil Fenn's signature, but also there is often another name below it. We believe those names are the subjects of the portraits."

"Very good," Loche says.

"Is there a name you would like to begin with?"

"Yes," Loche says, "Mine. I feel as if I should look into the first painting that I wrote about. Basil's portrait of me."

Athelstan walks around the perimeter of easels and inspects beneath the shrouded backs. "Here," he says. "Here."

Loche enters the circle and sits in the chair. He rotates and stares at the still covered work. Athelstan is positioned behind the easel, one hand gripping the shroud.

"At your command," Athelstan says.

"Do you know what a black hole is?" Loche asks him.

"It is what remains after a star dies," Athelstan answers.

"Okay," Loche says. "But *what* remains?"

Athelstan shakes his head. "Memory. Only memory."

"Remove the shroud."

Just Stories

November 5, this year
Venice, Italy

"You see," Albion says, "the story is the most important thing. Stories are traps by their nature. Paragraphs assembled to confound current perception, delineate altered states and offer plausible alternatives. They suspend disbelief, of course. Make us forget our surroundings and change our very behavior."

Julia cannot keep eye contact with him. Every few words out of his mouth, she looks away. Perhaps to another escape route. To the cruel beauty of Helen's face watching Albion pontificate. To the fading light in the windows—the crystal goblets, red velvet bed curtains, the paintings on the walls—to Rearden just off to her left and behind—likely his head tipped back and his legs crossed, like Loche had described him in the—

"The journal," Albion continues, "Loche's journal— the story is everything. Paramount. I would very much like to see it for myself."

Julia looked at her hands laying upon her lap. Marcus Rearden had already shared his firsthand experiences with Albion about Loche Newirth and his poetical gift. Loche was the named *Poet*. The one fulfilling a long known augury among the *Orathom Wis*. If Basil Fenn's paintings were the doorway for the intermingling of Heaven and Earth, Loche was foretold to be the wordsmith.

"Let us make this simple, shall we?" Albion said.

Julia looked up at him.

"Let's begin with a biggie. Loche Newirth, in the journal to ensnare Dr. Rearden, wrote of a woman named Julia." Albion points at her. "That's you. And because of this epic work of fiction—you came to life. Better still, he created you."

"I don't know," Julia replies.

"Very well. How's this, Loche's tale has changed the very fabric of reality?"

"Sure." Julia says.

"His writing was guided by some force greater than all of the divinities together to spin a yarn that can alter existence? The very mind of *Thi*, Itself. If these things are so, then I wonder if he has considered any rewrites. I wonder how we might improve upon his first draft?"

Julia looks away.

"Perhaps pen a new system of belief, and of gods? A new fate for our abandoned kin, doomed to nihility." Albion leans toward Julia, "Do you believe in what he has done? Created me? Created you? Restructured reality and all that is—and has unwittingly placed himself at the center of it all?"

Julia shrugged and twisted around. Rearden met her eyes. She replied, "You'd have to read the book."

Click

November 6, this year
Somewhere over Italy

Both William Greenhame and Edwin are asleep. The little boy is slobbering on William's shoulder. He had climbed into his granddad's lap an hour or so ago, just after takeoff, and quickly went out. Greenhame followed.

How cute, Leonaie thinks. *And, amazing to think that they are related. William doesn't look to be thirty five. A thirty-five-year-old granddad. Samuel said that he was over six-hundred-years-old? Is that right?*

Leonaie studies the two sleeping forms. She pictures her own children when they were Edwin's age. She would scoop them up in her arms, sit on the davenport and whisper to them until they fell asleep. The quiet of their breathing. The afternoon amber on the window.

The compartment shudders.

"Just a little turbulence," a voice says.

There is a hand in hers. She looks down. It is a strong, long-fingered hand. She follows the interlaced fingers up to the wrist, to the cuff of a white shirt, suit coat, up the arm to the shoulder, a solid jaw line, a faint smile, and arriving at two, keen bluish-grey eyes, she flinches meeting them.

"Not long now," he says.

Leonaie nods. *What a handsome face. What a highly kissable face.* She stares. She notes that his expression tangles into concern.

"Leonaie?" he prods.

"Yes?" she says.

"Are you alright?"

Glancing back to the sleeping William and Edwin she lets out a sigh and breathes in. Sweet oxygen. *That is*

William, that is Edwin, she turns to the man whose hand she is gripping, *and that is—that is—*

"You know," she hears her voice say, "when my sisters and I were little girls, Dad would whistle and we would dance beside the stove. He could whistle a pretty tune. And we would ice skate on the lake in the winter. . ." She smiles at him. A click, as if the gears of a lock had been keyed. *He's heard me tell this story before. Of course he has. Sweet Samuel. My dear, sweet Samuel. Samuel is his name. Goodness me.*

"Oh Samuel, I'm fine, dearest," she says, suddenly clear. It all floods back. "Will the treatments hurt?"

Relief rises into Samuel's face. "I wouldn't think so," he replies. "Though, we can expect some discomfort. Your body will go through some metabolic changes, surely. We'll know more when we arrive."

"Where is Charles?" she asks.

Samuel nods and assures, "He is fine. Greenhaven's has informed him that you have joined several other residents on a week long retreat to Priest Lake. He was thrilled."

She raises his hand to her lips and kisses it.

"Can't stand that control freak," she chuckles. She turns again to the young boy adrift in dreams upon his granddad's chest. "Look at that little fellow. So peaceful."

A few minutes later, she is asleep. Her grey curls, like a scarf of spun silver, drape over Samuel's shoulder and chest. Her own weight cannot be much more than little Edwin's. How similar they are, she and he. Like beginnings and endings. The young and the old—their dreams in the embrace of immortals.

The Pharmakiea

April, 1338
The House of Albion Ravistelle, London

Cut into thin slices and garnished with apples and onions was a plate of beef. William's eyes were wide at the sight.

"You are blessed, Father," Albion said to Radulphus as he stabbed his knife into the meat and began to fill his plate. "For lent has ended. Please, partake."

Radulphus smiled and looked at William. The boy was mesmerized. Not only by the beautiful plate of cooked meat, but the cakes, the bowl of figs, and another plate filled with something he did not recognize. But best of all there was a warm loaf of golden brown bread upon a board. Albion noticed him staring. "Here," he said, "you be the first to break bread here at my house."

William received the loaf and admired its perfection, its color and its heft. It smelled of unknown spices. His fingers squeezed and tore the crust. He set his portion on his plate and passed the rest to his father.

He had never known food like this. His mother had prepared him many good meals in his short life, but nothing with these seasonings. Albion spoke of mustard, clove, coriander, and a type of ginger called the *grains of paradise* from places like Sri Lanka, India and Byzantium. The flavors and the descriptions of their origin filled William's heart with a longing to see those far away places.

A goblet of sweet water and a half goblet of wine were set before William. "The water is good, so have your fill," Albion told them—then with a grin to Radulphus, "But the wine is better."

William looked at his father and could hardly recognize him. His face was clean shaven, his hair was neatly trimmed and there was no trace of the stain of travel upon his brow. Radulphus bowed his head and gave thanks to God for the feast before them.

After their bath, Alice had brought both visitors new garments. For Radulphus, a new ivory colored alb that dropped well below his ankle. The long garment was tied at the waist with a cincture and around his neck was draped the linen stola. The embroidered crosses were green and gold.

William's new clothes, he was told, once belonged to Alice's son that had passed away some years ago. They were of a rich green and brown linen and elegantly made. They fitted him well, and it was similar to Albion's mode of dress, rich, but not gaudy—it proclaimed nobility.

William looked down at his tunic and noted how unstained it was—how clean. He looked at his scrubbed fingernails and spotless hands. His hair had also been trimmed. He frowned, feeling how much had been sheared off.

Albion lifted his wine, "I drink to my own dear Alice. She has transformed you both. Clean, smelling of flowers and sage, and dressed as if we're off to mass at Saint Paul's." He brought the goblet to his mouth and gulped.

William felt a heavy drowse upon him. He yawned.

"Nay, Gravesend will never recognize your faces."

"Can you be sure?" Radulphus asked.

"I can," Albion said, his words slurring. "For I've journeyed with you for three days, and even now, as you sit at my table, I can scarcely place you. Have no fear." He shoved a cut of beef into his mouth.

"And how shall we gain an audience with his Excellency?" Radulphus asked.

Albion nodded at the question while chewing. "Simply," he said, his mouth still full. "I have been in his company before. You see, I am no common man struggling for a scrap from his table. I am a respected business man here in London. I have made my reputation through apothecary and *materia medica*—I have a hand in creating, and I supply, many of the latest medicines to the city of London. This food's spice, these flavors that you are both finding great delight? The delicious beer and wine? These are from the same monastery gardens that cultivate the herbs and oils for my remedies. For the last one hundred years, I have endeavored to learn all that I can about the human body, its ills, its failings and how it can be improved."

"Like Mama," William said.

Albion smiled at William, "Yes, my boy, like your mother. Geraldine knew herb lore, and she practiced it with much success. We, also, have healed and cured a great many maladies. But too often we find contradiction in our effort—and too few consistencies. What will aid one might hinder another, or do nothing at all. Still, we labor on to find answers, and most importantly, we strive to change the fears of medicine and its use."

"The very fears that brought Gravesend to our village? The very fears of my wife's Craft?" Radulphus asked.

"Yes," Albion said. "Using a plant to heal is *not* the Devil's work. If wood is used for fire, to warm our bodies in winter, using aloe to treat a wound and heal it has nothing to do with the shadow of the Underworld. Whipping one's self and begging the Lord to forgive you for your illness won't do much either, other than give you more pain and include your name in the long list of man's idiocy.

"And blood letting? What insanity! Cutting a man to allow a sickness to escape? Dear me. A man needs all of his blood. Spilling it is messy, painful and does no more good than asking God to intervene. God will not. And also, wearing donkey skin will not eliminate rheumatism, gulping down a young frog will not take away asthma, and washing your hair in a man's piss will not remedy ringworm."

"Prayer to God will cure—"

"Father," Albion interrupted, "the next time you are cold and without a fire, will you pray for God to set one alight, or will you light it yourself?"

Radulphus did not respond.

"Forgive me." He sighed. "It is true that words can be powerful in the healing of our woes. Words themselves are made of thoughts—made up of letters. Their formation are a kind of magic—of course, that is why we call their combining, spelling. Proclaiming our desires is like casting a spell out into the void. Whatever powers that are out there do, indeed, listen. Though, their listening, and our crying out are not enough to combat man's madness, man's sickness. Perhaps one day, I will find the answer to cure us all." Albion took a thoughtful pull from his wine, "Perhaps one day." He looked at William. William stared back.

"So you are an apothecary?" Radulphus asked.

"No," Albion said, "I am an herbalist, a *pharmakiea*, a student and a supplier of medicines to those in need. I have been called an apothecary, but I do not practice as they do. Though, I do endeavor to understand and create cures."

"And this will gain us audience with Bishop Gravesend? Doesn't he view your efforts as inspired by the Devil himself?"

"You're beginning to understand," Albion said. "Indeed, he does. He has publicly denounced my practices. Though no official Church order has been issued to interfere with my business. We are doing some good, mind you, and we have some political power. Herbs from one of my monasteries cured King Edward's niece just this past winter. The Crown will support us as long as we hold Christ's Cross aloft, and we practice beneath it. If we do not, we are heretics, witches and fodder for Gravesend." Albion sipped, chewed and sipped again, "Though I'm but a fly to Gravesend, he knows of me and my pursuits. He wants me finished and would gladly have my head on a pike if he could."

"And you want an invitation to his table? This plan of yours isn't sounding promising."

"Ah, still don't understand, Priest? Truly, what better company to invite to dinner than the one you intend to eat?"

Alice entered. In her hand was a square folded parchment sealed with wax. She smiled at William as she handed the note to Albion. "A letter to you, my lord. Addressed to Mr. Aloysius Stell. From his Excellency, the Bishop."

"So, he has answered my request," Albion said, setting his goblet down.

"I think not," Alice said. "For your missive left late last night. It could not yet have made it to him."

Albion smiled. "Then what chance is this, I wonder?"

"Aloysius Stell?" Radulphus asked. "Is that you?"

Albion took the note and broke the seal. "As I said, you know my real name, Albion—I have been Aloysius Stell of London some five and thirty years. In ten or more years I will need to fashion a new name. A new person." He looked at William, "To appear natural to this world, our kind must change place, name, family and home—for if we remain, man's fear will seek us out."

"I must say," Alice broke in, speaking to William, "you look much better now than the drowned rat I met this morning." William looked down at his clean clothes and full plate. "And I see that you are enjoying the food. Eat. We'll put some meat on those bones yet."

Suddenly, Albion began to laugh. He slapped his hand down upon the table and rose. "Irony," he said, "and what happy chance!"

"What does the letter say?" Radulphus asked.

Albion pressed both palms down upon the table and bowed his head. He was still laughing. "It is as if he were here with us." He lifted his head and said to Alice, "Please have prepared my large wagon for a two day journey."

"I assume you are to be traveling north to Stortford?" she said.

Albion nodded, smiling at her.

"And you've been invited?" she asked.

He nodded again. His smile widening further.

"Please, say on," she said.

"He's ill," Albion said, simply. "Bishop Stephen Gravesend is ill. He did not return to London after his crusade. Instead, he has retired to his manor at Stortford. This invitation was written yesterday morning, signed in his hand. Aloysius Stell is summoned to bring what remedies he has for what his scribe calls the sweating sickness."

"The plague?" Radulphus cried.

"I think not," Albion comforted. "There is a chance, but I think it more likely that he suffers from a corzya or lagrippe. Coming away from Ascott and the reports of illness there, I am guessing he is taking precautions—and bending his ideology to save his own skin."

"What is corzya and lagrippe?" William asked.

"Maladies not to be taken lightly, I can tell you that. Fever, coughing, plugged nose and filled ears—often the head hurts and the body is weak."

"Mama could heal that," William stated.

"Perhaps this illness will take his life," Radulphus said.

"It will not matter," Albion was quick to say. "For his life will be taken. Either by illness, or by our hand."

Alice led William and Radulphus back to their chamber by candlelight. Once they entered she turned their bed down and lit a small candle near the window. "Sleep deeply," she said before going out.

William pulled off his tunic and stood beside the bed. From his satchel he lifted out the leather pouch—the three leaves were bright and sharp. His mother's gaze in the shadow.

Then he noted yet another experience that was to be unique: a mattress of feathers, clean linen sheets, heavy woolen blankets and two big feather pillows. Quite different from his straw mattress in his mother's house. The boy looked at his father and said, "It is soft."

"Aye, that it is," the priest agreed. "I expect we will sleep deeply, as Alice commanded."

William slid himself into the sheets. Radulphus blew out the candle and laid beside him. After a few moments, William scooted his little body nearer to his father and nudged his head into the crook of his arm. The air was cool and the bed was warm. He could still see the green leaves in the dark.

"I wish Mama was here."

"So do I," he said.

"Is she with God?"

"Yes."

"How do you know?"

"I know."

"How?"

"Because that is where God's children go after they die. God wanted her in Heaven"

"Where is Heaven?"

"It is above, in the sky. It is God's Kingdom."

"Why did He put us here and He stays there?"

Radulphus didn't answer immediately. After a moment he said, "We must show Him that we love Him before he will let us come to his house."

"Mama didn't love Him, why did He take her?"

"God has a plan."

"Mama didn't love—"

"God has a plan."

"Is she in God's house?"

"Yes."

"But she did not love God. So she's *not* in His house,"

"You don't know that, only God knows that."

The boy's voice began to quaver, "Albion says that I don't get to go to God's house."

"You will, too, be in God's house," Radulphus said.

"You don't know that. You don't know that." William began to cry. "I won't be with Mama again. I won't be with you."

Radulphus lifted himself up on one elbow and looked down upon his son. William's eyes flooded. All of this was too much—such certainty in God's promise and such inability to explain suffering and chaos. William's wants were simple. Radulphus sighed and rubbed the boy's forehead.

"You are right, son, I do not know. No one knows what is beyond—we have only the words and stories of God to help us understand. To help us heal."

William rolled over. A thin line of smoke coiled from the candle wick. Outside, cold stars glittered through a break in the clouds.

All Better

September, 1980
Los Angeles. Helen Craven's Diary

September 27, 1980

Had another dream about a little boy last night. I've lost count of how many I've had—I keep calling the baby Edwin. Albion and I nap with him in the afternoon. I can feel them both—it is so real. It is hard waking up and knowing it was just a dream.

Oh, and the tally—
5 years, 270 days without Albion. He's in England, I guess. God, I miss him. I received a letter from him a few days ago. Cried for hours afterward.

I really do hate it here in LA. I have bad memories. But, that's why I've come, right? And do I feel better about it all? That's the big question, isn't it?

But, I should start with the bad news first. I got a call from Jimmy yesterday and he told me what happened. Bonzo is dead. He got too drunk and didn't wake up. I am crushed and hurting. I loved him. Everyone loved him. He could be an ass—but I loved him. Jimmy says that the band is in shock and not sure what the future holds. I cannot imagine the world without Zeppelin.

Goodbye John—

I'm staying at Tracy's. She hasn't changed too much. She went to see Van Halen at the Forum a couple of nights ago. She said they were good.

*We cried about Bonzo all night, drank screwdrivers—
triples, and smoked. We spun all the records—cranked
Moby Dick over and over. Cried more.*

*Love you, John. I want to call Albion and talk with him
about it, but—he wouldn't want that. Not now. The time
isn't right. He probably knows already, anyway. So sad.*

Wow. A lot of tears over the last few days.

*The good news is I left the envelope at my mom's with the
account instructions. I put more money in—I didn't think
50k was enough, so I doubled it. The letter was simple
enough, I think. I'm sure it will freak her out, but at least
she can move around a little bit—be a little freer now.
Especially now. She'll need it.*

*Because now. . . second piece of good news. . . that
fucking evil bastard of a husband of hers met with an
awful accident yesterday. I shouldn't go into details, but I
can't help it. After all, it's the main reason I came back.*

*Let's just say that he won't pee the same—EVER. In fact,
they just may need to construct a new way for him to do
that. Of course, he'll have to come out of the coma first.
Won't happen. At least, I'm pretty sure my cuts were
correct—according to my research.*

*I was fair, by the way. I let him get the first punch in. And
the second. Pretty good ones, really.*

*Sadistic fuck. He won't hurt anyone again. And for that, I
am glad. But as far as feeling better about this whole
revenge thing that I've been dreaming about? I don't
know yet. It feels good to know he is suffering—that can't
be good for me. . . I don't know. I could have killed him,
but I thought justice would be better served—through a
tube.*

I even put an insurance policy together for him a few months ago—just so that keeping him plugged in won't be a huge cost to Mom. She'll likely want to help him—but after awhile, she'll move on—and she'll have enough money to do so. That's good.

Fuck it. I won't feel sorry for him. And I guess I should put some thought into how I really feel. Maybe I should see a psychologist.

I fly out tomorrow.

The Threshold

November 5, this year
Mel Tiris, France

It is a rendering of Loche Newirth. A portrait in oil. The expression Loche knows. He has seen it on his face many times in mirrors—calm, thoughtful and careful. There is some tragedy in the eyes. The background is a wash of muted orange and grey. The image is loose, painterly, composed of simple, accurate strokes. Loche shakes his head. Then he blinks. He remembers.

A small flicker of light captures him, like a flake of glitter pressed into the portrait's right pupil. The glitter then multiplies and spirals outward. Gold and silver-blue streams of light gather and pulse, forming the rim of a deep abyss. Loche's hands clamp down on his knees as he gazes into a framed chasm. All balance, all reason, all meaning—forgotten. The light spreads beyond the borders of the frame. Then it eclipses, an enormous pitch black circle, unimaginably deep. From the rim fire lines of color, stretching out in all directions, until his periphery fills with the unfathomable gulf.

A hair thin line of silky light—The Silk—shoots from the Center to meet his gaze.

He remembers.

Silence.
Flash.
Gone.

Loche is disembodied.
The abyss pulls him in.
A wide grey blur grows.
Water. A wide, flat body of grey and black water. Mist laces over the waves.

Just as he thinks his vision will plunge into the dark liquid, his senses hover. He is suspended above, nearly eye level to lulling ripples. Silence.

Loche screams. He thinks, What remains? What remains? What remains?

Memory, is the answer.

—What remains? he cries out.

He cannot determine sound as sound, sight as sight. All senses are as one. There is connection. Then an easing, as if there is something to hold.

Stop.

Loche Newirth stands on a nighttime beach. The sand is cold and grey. A single star glints high. Before him is a black ocean. The shore and the muted line dividing two values of black at the horizon are his only points of reference.

The water lulls at his feet.

Nothing.

Quiet.

Shhh. Shhh. Shhh, says the sea.

Then to his right, far down the beach, a figure approaches. Small. The size of a child. A moving shadow in a shadow world. Loche turns toward the visitor and waits.

It stops a few feet away.

—Dad? it says.

Loche's eyes burst with tears.

—Edwin?

—Dad?

Loche kneels down and the boy runs into his arms. But at the first touch, Loche reels backward.

—Dad?

—You're not Edwin.

Loche squints through the gloom at the small face and sees his little boy, but the smiling expression blurs and like a passing cloud over the moon, it changes to a sickly blue—featureless. No eyes or mouth or nose—only the shape of a head, pale and mute. Then Edwin's face again.

    —What are you?

    Loche wonders if he is speaking words. There is no sound of voice—just impressions—thoughts in communication.

    The face morphs from his son to the featureless face.

    —I am a Watcher. And you are the Poet. We have met before. Yes, we have met before.

    Loche remembers. The pale, drowning boy. Loche remembers. In his imagination. Between real and made up.

    —Are these words that we speak? Loche says, or thinks.

    —This is the Elliqui. We commune in thought.

    Loche crimps his eyes and mouth shut. He searches for sanity.

    —But, Edwin. You looked like Edwin.

    —Yes. I did.

    —Why?

    —I reflect your deepest love. And your darkest fear. There has been a crack in the All. Pain and joy, ends and oblivion have come to us. It exists here. It invades. You invade.

    —I do not understand.

    —Your brother's gift. It has opened a fissure into us. We cannot escape. Once we could turn away from you. No longer. And your words have begun the invasion of Heaven. The void fills with questions. The questions that haunt the greatest of all creations. The love of Man.

    It extends a long, thin finger and points into Loche's eyes.

    —And you have written it all, Poet. You have written the end to what was meant to be eternal.

    —I must find my brother, Basil. I must find Basil.

    The pale boy steps back and away.

    —You seek the dead?

    Loche looks around at the empty black landscape and the chilling waste of water and sky. He could not answer. How to answer? Was he, himself, dead? Was Basil, dead? Isn't this the undiscovered country?

—You are not dead, Loche. But your brother exists out there somewhere.

—Can we find him?

—Perhaps. But he is not here.

—Where is, here?

—*Within the borders of his feeling and imagination, Loche. We are visiting what the painting was meant to convey. The emotion surrounding it. The spirit it evokes.*

Loche stares around again at the bleak terror.

—I don't understand. The painting of me evokes a dead world of black seas and dying land?

—Yes, in part. You see and feel a mere sliver of it. There is more, but now, your painting contains augury. Your work has brought chance. It has placed oblivion into creation. Forever is no longer sure.

Loche's mind grapples for something solid. The figure senses it. Its pale blue skin transmutes. Upon the faceless visage appears Edwin's tiny eyes. At the sight of his son, Loche breaks into tears.

—While you remain with me, you will see what your fragile being can withstand. Now you see barren seas and lifeless skies.

The boy draws Loche into an embrace.

—It is only a sliver of the all. Of Thi. The real state of being, look now.

Loche flinches.

A vibration, continuous and jarring rattles through him. Deeper and louder than a bow drawn across a bass string. A tingling high-pitched ring weaves in and through the drone. Orange and red flares of stringing light coil around him and the boy, like ropes suspending them in a cloud of light and stars. The beach is gone. Nothing he sees is familiar save the single star that is still burning above. Loche focuses upon it. He thinks for a moment that it is an eye staring at him.

The boy lets go and his appearance smears to

faceless.

    Darkness. Grey sand. Black sea. Black sky.

    —Allowing you sight much longer would end your life. You would remain here.

    Loche is suddenly thankful for the recognized environment, despite its sinister appearance. He knows sand, water and sky.

    —We now stand within the borders of this window. Just one of Basil's windows. Basil is far from here.

    —How do we find him?

    —You must cross the sea to the edge of this thought. Then we shall see.

    Loche's spirit crushes.

    —I fear the ocean.

    —This is not the ocean. It is the threshold of death.

A Wider View #2

November 5, this year
Venice, Italy

"When I could not die, I laughed." Albion says. He beckons Julia to follow him. She watches as Corey, Marcus and Helen step out. Helen lingers at the threshold and looks back in before the door shuts.

Albion says, "Ah, to be alone with another of Loche Newirth's creations."

Sleet and rain sparkle across the window. Outside a single lamp illuminates the freezing downpour. It crackles on the pane and the balcony floor. Lights along the canals are sparse. The spires atop the basilica domes of Santa Maria della Salute glow like two crystal spikes in the dark. Julia Iris turns from the window to face him.

Albion is standing in the center of the room. A tangle of filigree clamors up the walls into an overhead canopy of vines and sharp leaves, gold and silver. A divinized vineyard. It glints like sun on frost. Though the artisanship astounds her, it makes her uneasy. Many of the paintings upon the walls are familiar, though just beyond her ability to recall why. *Monet maybe? Could that be a Raphael?* Tucked further back are four tall bed posts, and an inviting, soft bed filled with pillows. Crimson bed curtains.

"I was born a slave," Albion says, "though it may sound strange to hear it. During the reign of the great Charlemagne. So long ago." He gestures again for her to follow him and leads her back into the dark. "Of course the moral King Charlemagne spoke out against slavery, but, as it is to be expected with humanity, such abominations take time to fall completely out of fashion."

Ahead a dimly lit hallway appears, then a flash of spark, and Albion, with a flaming match, lights a series of candles. He prattles on. "The fortunate part of the story is merely this: my mother, also a slave, was beautiful and caught the eye of the master of the house, a relatively successful trader in Rome with a great many responsibilities, a large house, two wives, children and several slaves. My mother, like most female slaves, was subject to the master's will—and his carnal appetite."

The room is a smooth polished stone with two windows, comfortable sofa, a chandelier of crystal and gold, and at the room's center is a black grand piano. He sits behind it, raises the keyboard cover and nods at the sofa. "Sit, please."

He plays a chord like a sun shower, delicate and bright. It trembles against the walls—like a lit mist over Lake Pend Oreille—from her house high above the lake in Hope, Idaho.

"This was good because I had a home, you see. I was born into a household and my father was the master of that house—though he would never claim me as his son. I was a slave."

Another series of chords. Sustaining single notes like leaves falling in spirals.

"As early as five summers, I had tasks to perform. Mundane tidying—errands carrying messages, things for a small child—for small fingers. At harvest we would pluck grapes—sneak a few—they burst like sweet August rain on the tongue." The textures of his playing drift into a steady pulse. A single, repeating chord.

"But as the ancient tales tell, a son will rise up against the father. One night, after I had been deprived of food as a punishment for some childish mischief, daydreaming, quite likely, my sweet mother managed to lay hold of a few figs and a small cake. As she watched my grateful face devouring the feast, the master paid a visit to our chamber for some—sport." Albion smashed his left hand onto the keyboard. A booming, hallow bass punctuated the pulsing chord. "Seeing that his punishment was ignored, the master proceeded to beat my mother with his wooden cup." His left hand starts into a circular succession of dissonant bass notes. Loud. Then his other hand, in a flurry, cascades into a dizzying melody. A sudden burst of water over stones.

"And why shouldn't he have done this?" Albion shouts over the loud, circular rhythms. "He is the master of the house, is he not? It is to him that we owe our very lives, yes? He is above us, and we are his slaves. We have no possessions, no name, no family. Nothing but the good fortune to serve him. Such was the law."

The music culminates into a final, satisfying chord. Full and complete. The strings fade to near silence before he raises his fingers from the keys.

"When she was nearly unconscious from the beating, the cup broke into three pieces. Exhausted, he tossed a splinter at me and pulled my mother by the hair down to her knees. He growled at her, 'I said no food for the rat! And what is this I see here?' He pushed her face down to the last fig that dropped from my lap. 'Eat,' he said, 'eat you dog! Eat when I allow, share when I allow, do as I bid! Eat!'"

His hands begin a reprise. The delicate image of shining jewels of sunlit rain.

"As early as five summers, I knew enough to stab a man. The splinter I gouged into his jugular with all the force I could muster. His eyes gaped when it occurred to him what had happened. With one hand clawing the wound, he laid hold of me with the other and snapped my neck like a twig."

He stops playing.

Julia feels her hands knot into fists—her posture tense and upright.

"Sometime later, I woke in my mother's arms. She was bloodied, one eye would never see again. She thought me dead, of course, but she could feel me breathing. The master lay in a pool of his own blood, just a few feet away, in the room of a slave, in his own house—now he had no possessions, no family, no longer any name. I had taken from him what was dearest, his life. And he could not take mine. So, I laughed.

"When I could not die, I laughed, and I laughed because I could not die."

Albion turns to Julia. His face is gentle. A sincerity glassing in his eyes. "From that day forward, I would not be ruled by any man." He stands abruptly and offers his hand to her. She takes it and rises beside him. "Nor by any god.

"As I've asked of you, please be open and consider the future. I will not be ruled, but so, too, I will not rule others. I will merely point the way to the next evolution of human kind. It is the only way. As we spend more time together, consider joining this cause."

Julia says, "I have seen senseless violence, heard of assassinations that you've implemented—a war that you've started. Why would I want to join—"

"My dear," he stops her. "You do not yet understand. I want to survive. *Survive.* I want to live, Julia. We *Itonalya* —have nothing—nothing but the *Now.*"

He drops her hand and turns to the dark window. "Nothing!" he shouts. "Slavery is alive and well. Mortals are slaves to each other, to greed, to ideology, to ignorance. Even to their petty emotions. But *they* are allowed a place beyond.

"Not us! No, Julia, not you and I. Not those that share our blood. We are doomed to oblivion if we are vanquished here. To nothing. The gods in their infinite judiciousness grant us the pain of humanity without the escape. The rest is silence."

Hail clatters against the window. Albion flattens his hand against the glass spreading his fingers wide.

"My vision is simple," he says finally. "Through Basil Fenn's masterpieces we will send the disease of humanity to the abode of the gods, and we shall evolve here into a race of immortal beings no longer shackled to death. We will make the earth our paradise." When he faces her, Julia sees, for a moment only, a quaking, elderly man. Eyes cloven into caverns above the cheeks. A thin, wrinkled translucent skin gathered like pinned fabric. Sallow. Cold. "Simple," he says again. At the word, the old face snaps away. Albion Ravistelle's countenance is sharp and alluring. Distinguished. Not quite the face of a fifty-year-old-man.

He issues a slight laugh, "And if it is, indeed, Loche Newirth that has conjured Julia Iris and Albion Ravistelle to life, perhaps we can persuade him to spin a tale in our favor.

"Those that have joined with me, the *Endale Gen*, we will eliminate those that keep with the old ways. The *Orathom Wis* will be driven from the earth and marshaled to Oblivion. Bridging spirits, we will destroy and cast back to the hell they so desire. Yes, Julia, we are now at war. We fight for our place in existence."

"What about the human race?" Julia asks. A horror filled whisper.

"Fear not," he says. "I will heal them. I will heal them all."

Via Martiri Della Liberta

November 6, this year
Just outside of Venice

"Are we there, yet?" Edwin Newirth asks.

"Not yet," William Greenhame answers from over his shoulder. The windshield is dark.

Leonaie cannot get the street sign out of her head. It read, *Via Martiri Della Liberta*. "Ah. I get it. I'm in Italy," Leonaie says to herself. "That's why I can't read the damn signs. I'm in Italy."

"When we get there, my Mom will be there?" Edwin says.

"We'll see your mom in the morning," William answers.

"I thought you said it was already morning," Edwin says.

"I did," William admits. When the plane landed he had told the boy that it was indeed, past midnight, and now morning. 2:30 am.

"Will there be snacks? I'm hungry."

"Yes lad, there will be snacks. We'll stay tonight with a friend."

Edwin didn't answer. He looks up at Leonaie for a moment. She wraps her arm around him and scoots him close.

"Left lane," Samuel says.

"Hey, who's driving here?" William asks.

"You should have let me drive, mate. I know this country."

"You're an awful driver."

"I am not an awful driver," Samuel protests.

"Need I remind you of—"

"No, William, you don't. And I would appreciate it if you would keep that night to yourself."

"Very well," William smiles. "Anyway, you're missing a hand—best that I've got the wheel."

Edwin, "Are we there, yet?"

Leonaie, "*Martiri Della Liberta.*"

"Not yet, Edwin. We're getting closer all the time," William answers.

"I may be the one missing a hand, my friend. But it seems to me that you're the one missing a plan."

William glances at Samuel and then back to the road ahead. "I will entreat him to a peace," he says. "And while Albion entertains us in his court, you and Leonaie will slip in easily with Corey. But you must be swift. I have informed Corey that the treatment must be immediate. Otherwise, if things go ill for me, you will miss your chance."

What does *Martiri* mean? Leonaie wonders.

"Entreat him to a peace?" Samuel says. "Really? At least I have Corey, a disguise and an appointment for a treatment—also an exit strategy. Peace? With Albion? That's your plan? William, he won't be swayed, you know that."

Traffic is light. Leonaie watches the buildings pass. Sleep is hanging heavy on her.

"We go way back, Albion and I," William says.

"I have a history with him, too. Do not forget, he has betrayed the Order. He threatens Light itself."

"He will listen to me," William says.

Samuel's voice is fierce, "He betrayed you. Because of him, Basil is dead. Now you will bow before him and pray for peace? Peace with the one that has killed your son?"

"I did not say I would bow." William muttered.

"He will try to kill you."

"I hold the root of his aspiration."

Leonaie, "What does *Martiri* mean?"

Samuel turns. She notes a slight flash of incredulity in his eyes.

"The name of this road," she adds. "Vee-ah Martiri Dell-ah Lib-er-ta-something other. Does Martiri mean martini? Like a Vesper or a gin martini?"

Samuel faces forward again. William smiles.

"Martyr, darling. It means martyr."

The Seed of Poison

April, 1338
The House of Albion Ravistelle, London

Before he opened his eyes, William's hand searched for the soft leaves beside his pillow. They were not there. He rose up, frantic. A soft, grey light clung to the window. William tossed the pillows and pushed down the blankets. He did not find his leather pouch, nor did he find his father. His feet hit the cold floor and he rushed around the bed with a quick, thudding run. He put on his clothes. "Papa!" he called, opening the door. "Papa?"

There was no answer.

Some thirty paces through the dark, at the end of the hall was a dim glow and a stair leading down. A menacing gauntlet of tall, closed chamber doors were between him and the light. There was no knowing what might be lurking behind those doors. He took his first step. Both arms he crossed over his chest.

"Papa!" he called. Tears rose.

No answer.

"Mama," he whispered.

"William?" a voice called. It was Alice. "William?" Her shape appeared rising up from the stair. William ran to her with his eyes squeezed nearly shut, and his arms held close in.

Within steps of her, William caught her smile and he stopped.

"Frightful, this hall in the dark. It has always given me the shivers, too. Come down and let's get you some breakfast." She reached a hand to his shoulder and gently guided him.

William paused at the top of the stairs and raised up, "Where are my mama's leaves? Where's my papa?"

"Come, come," she said, gesturing him to descend. "You will see soon enough."

Upon the dining table was a plate of sliced fruit and a small loaf of bread, but most importantly, the leather pouch of leaves. William climbed up into the chair and pulled it to his chest. The leather was moist, "Your father brought it down and bade me water it. I believe it has grown a finger's length since." William's eyes traced the radiant midribs of the leaves.

She gave him a cup of cider. It smelled both spicy and sweet.

"Your father is assisting my lord Albion—preparing for your ride to Strotford," she said, taking a long look at William. This made him nervous. Her appraisal seemed concerned.

"Boy," she said finally, "you know little of what is happening, is that true?"

William let the pointed leaves tickle over his chin and lips.

"Answer me, boy."

"I do not know if I should say," William said. His voice hushed.

The woman sat down beside him. She laid her hand out on the table with her palm up. "May I hold your hand, William?"

Slowly, William placed his hand in hers. She closed her fingers over. They were warm, and calloused, but soft at the same time. The woman stared, still with a face of disquiet and worry.

"I know a thing or two about growing herbs. My lord Albion has taught me much about how to keep a plant green and growing. About how to keep the ones we want alive and how to protect them from other plants that will overshadow them. Harm them. You see, William, some plants are of value to us, the apple tree, the beanstalk, garlic, thistle and mandrake. But they are delicate and hard to come by and if we do not care for them, there are weeds and thorns and tall, leafy plants that will grow beside—and slowly choke out their stems and starve their roots."

William nodded. "Mama grew herbs."

"Yes," Alice smiled, "I've been told. And she knew how to care for them. And how to protect them.

"William, my lord Albion has told me your tale—how your mother died." She squeezed his hand. "I am sorry, lad. And today you ride to the door of the one that took her away. He is a bad man, William."

William fidgeted. "Albion said he is not a man."

Alice agreed, "That is right, he is not a man. He is from a place beyond this life."

William wondered a moment. "Does the Bishop know that he is *not* a man?"

Alice's gaze lowered to the shining leaves brushing at William's chin. "That is a very good question. The answer is no. No, he does not know that his spirit is of the otherworld, that he is a god. He believes he is like us. He is not beyond fear. He is as delicate as any mortal, though he is covered in thorns and bramble—and his great arms block out the sun. He chokes the light from many."

Her expression softened as she studied him. Releasing William's hand she reached for the leather pouch of leaves. William drew back, hesitant to give it over, but he let her take it. Alice raised the leaves to her nose and breathed in their fragrance. William caught a hint of mint, pine and some distant scent he could not place. It brought an image of grey rain over the sea—though, he had never seen the wide ocean before.

"How did your mother kill the weeds that threatened her herbs?" she asked.

William laid a finger along his chin and thought back. He pictured the long wood boxes behind their small house. Rectangular containers of rich, black soil in rows. Lace-like stems and green leaves climbing out of the dark onto ladders his mother had erected, "To help them," she had said. And then the weeds would spring up. She would pull them by the roots. But she would always study them first, he remembered. She would study them, as if there could be some quality that she may have missed. She cared for the plants she knew, but was ever curious about those that seemingly held little or no value. "Perhaps one day," she told William, "I may discover their worth. Everything that lives has some worth."

"Mama tried to heal most everything," William said, finally. "Even weeds."

"I see," Alice smiled. "You know, William, in our monastery gardens, we have discovered a way to keep weeds from growing. We have found a way to poison them before they ever go to seed."

"There is only one seedling," William said, almost unconsciously. "And if it dies, so will its fruits and all of its leaves where ever they are."

"What is meant by that?" the woman asked.

"Mother said that often."

"Perhaps she meant the seed of goodness. If that dies, all else does, too," Alice offered.

William shrugged. "Those are hers," he said. "And she was goodness," William stared at his leaves, still held near to the woman's face. He suddenly did not like the mention of poisoning plants. "Mama didn't make poison." He reached for the pouch. She pressed it gently into his hand.

"I know, dear boy. Your mother would not have such a thing made. But poisons have a purpose—and when something undesirable grows and becomes unmanageable, it is a kinder way to protect the ones you love."

Alice stood, leaned down and kissed the boy on the forehead. William lifted up his eyes. The woman again had worry seated in her stare. She touched his chin, "What must be done, must be done," she muttered. "When you finish your breakfast, join your father and Albion below, through the door there, and down the stair."

Alice stared. William felt uncomfortable.

"If—if something bad happens, William, and you're alone—come back here to me. Say you will."

"I will," the boy said.

She began to turn away when she stopped and leaned down again, almost nose to nose with William. She crossed her eyes and grinned, "But most of all, dear, sweet boy, don't forget to smile when you can. Poisoned or growing, good or ill, fixed or broken, the days carry on —and there's no sense in worrying as you go along. You will do what is best, and all will be well. In the end, all will be well. Everything circles around."

Her broad smiling face filled William with the first gladness since everything had changed. He heard himself giggle. Alice rose up and walked briskly into the next room.

A Letter

November, 1980
Venice, Italy

Helen closed the door behind her and ran to the table beside the window. The very table where she and Albion had their last embrace. As she sat, her fingers tore the envelope open. A letter from Albion. She had received only ten letters over the five year estrangement. Most shared Albion's travels, advice for her training, and disparate pieces of history. But each missive always contained some outpouring of love for her—some shorter than others. The thought of his yearning was the fuel she needed. Desperately, she tore the envelope open.

November 16, 1980

Dearest Helen,

Time has halted. Never has this happened in the millennia that is my life. Without you, days feel as decades. Without you, I feel age. Sweetly am I punished for my ardent discipline. Sweet is this longing I've never known. I have waited for you, Helen.

I have heard of your recent journey to America, and I have been informed of your vengeful motive.

DO NOT DO THAT AGAIN.

Though I recognize a need to punish those that leave scars upon us, I insist that you take some time to consider your anger, pain and suffering now that you have acted upon the one you blame. Tell me, Helen, is the pain still there? As your victim lay in a deadly coma, are you still a victim? If you still feel pain from the past, from your recent revenge, you must acknowledge the pain to be in your own keeping. Cast it away, Helen. It was given to you, but you need not carry it. Your future life reaches forward, centuries ahead. Pack only what you need.

History has taught man nothing with vengeance as a teacher, save what the gods love: our suffering. The less suffering, the less men will need a god.

I return soon.
All my love,
—A

Ocean

Within the portrait of Loche Newirth

—Behold, the ocean.

—I cannot, Loche cried. Is there another way? You're a god. Can't you carry me? You can fly, right?

—Yes, I am a god, at least to your mind. I can fly. No I cannot carry you, for you are human and not yet joined with the Dream.

Loche stares out. What dreamless hours have passed? How long had he been within this forsaken painting? Hours? Weeks? Months? Before him stretched a fear from before memory. A fear of the sea. The size. Its sheer, all encompassing weight and strength. He could sense its might pulsing beneath the surface. Its depth and cavernous ranges of bleak cold. Breakers spraying brine into mist—coral, like needles of glass, spines as fine as fish bones, ladders connecting all life—shell cones and spirals whorling into crowns—countless tubes, bivalves, jelly, tentacles, pulp. And in the deeps, what creatures? What terrors lurk there? And its surface—mountains of water ever in motion—crests and valleys.

—Yes, the boy says. It is vast. This is for you, the threshold of death. Pass beyond it and we may discover your brother in the Dream.

—How? How can I cross it?

—You must take your first step.

The boy strides out and turns. With a blink, Loche sees his son, Edwin, standing upon the water, his arm reaching back.

—Edwin?

—Follow me, the boy says.

A simmering mist tangles over the water. Loche takes his first step. It feels as if he has walked onto a floating *log. Two more paces and he still floats. Unsteady, but buoyant.*

—How is it that we walk upon the water?

—It is not the water that holds you up, Poet.

Loche looks down to his feet. The veil of vapor parts enough for him to see. He is standing upon a surface of bobbing, human heads.

The shock of the sight reels him into an unsteady struggle for balance. The boy reaches out and braces him until the terror eases.

—I can't! I can't!

—Be at ease. Be at ease. These are the heads of gods, the heads of immortals that once lived and breathed upon the earth. Walk now upon them. They live no longer, and they are your path to the far shore.

The Poet raises his eyes and traces the bridge from his feet to the bleak horizon, to the faint star beckoning from the inky black. He is reminded of the single Eye—the abyss that he still has not managed to escape from.

With his focus upon his son, he climbs to heaven.

The Single Star

November 6, this year
Venice, Italy

"I can't believe Albion would let me see this place," Julia says.

Corey Thomas closes the door behind them. "You're immortal, Julia. He wants nothing more than your empathy. He has everything to gain by sharing all he has with you."

In the air is a hint of pot and oil. Shelves along the far wall are packed with records overflowing onto the floor. Easels, draping black fabric, containers of long-stem paint brushes, tables crowded with sketches, pencils—a couple of full ashtrays. On the walls are constellations of paint splatters. Even the ceilings trail long-tailed, crimson comets and distant yellow suns. A half finished bottle of The Macallan sits in the center of a round dining table with three chairs. And so much more. The entire room is a collage of color, photographs, sketches, random items linking into a single art piece.

"Basil's studio," Julia says. "I read of this place. I know this place. It looks just like I imagined."

Corey laughs, "Yes. Or as Loche Newirth imagined."

She nods, squinting. "Yes."

"You look like you could use a drink."

"It's early morning," Julia says.

Corey pours two glasses anyway. She takes the booze into her mouth.

"Loche's journal said there were no cameras or microphones in here. Is that true?"

Corey nods. "One important reason for bringing you here. Are you okay?"

"I still do not know what I am."

"Well, if I might help you into the present, you are ransom. You are immortal. You are being courted to become a part of the *Endale Gen.* If Helen's son is not returned to her, or you refuse to join, Albion will have your limbs removed from your body. He will have them burned—and like the old customs, your head will be tossed into the sea."

Julia feels her eyes widen.

"Oh, and you will cease to exist."

She dumps the remaining scotch into her mouth.

"And if I join with him?" she quavers.

Corey sighs. "You must go to war with the *Orathom Wis.* You go to war against the gods. You will do battle with the whirling tide of the Universe—a course that has been steady since Light appeared."

Julia holds her glass out. He refills it.

"And you are a spy? You are *Orathom Wis*?"

"I am," he says. His chin rising slightly.

"But you fought against Albion at the Uffizi. I don't understand how he doesn't know your secret."

"Albion believes that I spy for *him.* He was under the impression that if I fought at his side at the Uffizi, my cover would be blown with the *Orathom Wis.* Over the years I've managed to master the vocation of double agent. Things are not always as they seem."

"What about oblivion? What about Albion's rebellion against the gods?"

"It is true we face oblivion, or so it is said. But the Order believes Loche and Basil—Poet and Painter, are our salvation. They will bring an end to all that was and a beginning to all that will be." He chuckles. "Though we do not know how. They are not gods—they possess something beyond divinity."

"Did you ever see one of Basil's works?" she asks.

Corey looks away. "No." He reaches for the bottle. "No. But I have talked with some that have."

"Is Albion still showing Basil's work to those with extreme mental disorders?"

He nods. "As we speak."

Julia lifts her gaze to the paint splattered ceiling. Tiny ultramarine meteors race on a trajectory to the corners. A high spray of cool alizarin fumes from a thousand aureolin suns. She reads there versions of Cassiopeia, Andromeda, Cygnus—her eyes follow Diana's arrow from the starry string to a flaring penumbra down into the room again. The horizon is made of leaning canvases, easels, shelves of records, collages of photos, hand scrawled notes and partial works, coffee maker and an unmade bed.

"God, I miss him," Julia says. The booze stings her lips.

"Though I did not know him well, I, too, miss him."

She gazes back up into the spattered paint above. She can imagine his brush's swinging arc.

Then she sees it.

Julia drops her glass and it shatters at her feet.

"Oh my God. . ." she says. Her eyes are trained on a splashed paint cluster on a far wall. She rushes toward it. Corey follows.

"What is it? What is it, Julia?"

"It's—it's—" she falters.

"What do you see?"

Her hand rises to her lips as she stares. She feels a smile at her fingertips. She looks at Corey and says:

Find the single star
And watch it blink.
Until the mountains fade,
And we to sleep."

Circles

November 6, this year
Just outside of Venice, Italy

Leonaie falls silent for a moment. *How long have I been talking? Does it matter? No. More than likely, no. Samuel is here. The little Edwin is here. William is here.*

But, who is this woman I'm telling all of this to? What was her name again? Never mind. Did I mention how we spent our evenings? I had best do that. . . She'd like that.

"My sister Margaret learned how to tap dance from a friend of hers, a girl named Lavern. And I taught my dad how to tap dance when he was about fifty. He would whistle and sing and we girls would dance around. Mom would sit and sew while we all did that. She liked it. She got a kick out of it. And I was the littlest of my sisters, so I always slept in the middle."

"Did you listen to the radio?"

"Oh yes," Leonaie says. "Maybe I was in the fifth grade when we got our first radio. Dad would listen to *Amos and Andy*—and *One Man's Family*—a big show at the time."

"I remember *One Man's Family*," the woman smiles.

Leonaie loves the sight of this woman. Late fifties, maybe. Grey hair, dazzling eyes like blue ocean. She looks as if they could be friends. Old friends. Leonaie reaches out her hand and touches the woman's knee. "Dear, I am so sorry. I get so forgetful. What was your name again?

"Alice, dear. Alice Bath."

"Alice, of course. You see, I sometimes forget things. William and Samuel told me your name on the way here.

"I forget things all the time," Alice says. "But you must be exhausted—traveling all through the night into the morning—and without a warm, fuzzy blanket. And most importantly, without wine." She fires a glare at William Greenhame. "When will you learn, William."

Alice then turns to Edwin. His eyes are swaying like heavy doors in the wind. "When did this little one last get to sleep?"

"Alice, I—" William stammers.

"Don't *Alice* me," she waves her hand at him and stands. "A granddad should know when to lay his grandson down for a snooze."

"I love that word snooze," Leonaie says. "I use that word."

Alice nods, "I love that word, too. And I love snoozing."

Leonaie reaches her hand to Alice and pulls her close. "How old did you say you were, dear?"

Alice leans down and answers. "Older than the hills, sweetheart. Older than the hills and twice as dusty."

"Alice," William says. "I want you to come with us."

She shakes her head and begins wringing her hands. "I don't think so, William. I've not spoken to Mr. Albion Ravistelle for at least a century—and I'm not about to change that now. He's of a different mind—has taken a dangerous, selfish course. He's forgotten the order of things—carving for himself, he is."

Samuel says, "He has changed."

"Nevertheless," Greenhame says. "I need you to help me look after this beautiful little boy while Albion and I reason together."

"Perilous, William. Going to his door. . ."

"I know. But it must be done."

Alice's eyes drop down to Edwin. He is teetering on the edge of sleep. "He looks like you," she smiles. "He looks like my little William. Like the day you were brought to me."

"Circles," William says, placing his hand upon her shoulder. "We drift in circles, do we not?"

The Healers

April, 1338,
On the road to Strotford Manor, north of London

Far above black birds whirled against a bruised sky. William traced their paths. There was the clop-clop of the two horses. The air had sweetened at the last bridge crossing. High pines, oaks and spruce trees were now beginning to thicken, hiding the sky. Hiding the light.

There had been very little talk. Albion spoke every now and then about the road ahead. It was past mid-day, though there was no visible sun. William watched the crows flutter like flecks of black ash blowing from tree to tree. He wondered if they were following the wagon. The turning wheels creaked.

William cradled the leather pouch now sprouting another leaf, viridescent and luminous. "Take good care of your leaves, William," Alice told him as she kissed his cheek goodbye. "And remember that you are a gardener. Protect your garden."

Along with the three travelers, the wagon also carried several boxes of rich soil and newly burgeoning herbs. Albion suggested that such a gift to Gravesend's house would be well received. Dill and ginger for the stomach, mint and coriander for cough, juniper for pain, elm and aloe for cuts and burns, and sage for all and everything else. There was another box, small and black that Albion had separated from the others. It contained an ample amount of dried cowbane. *Gravesend's Bane*, Albion called it when he placed it behind his seat.

William had been told about the herb, and it had been explained how it was to be used. Both Albion and his father showed him the plant. Albion had said, simply,

"Enough placed into his cup or dashed upon his food, and Gravesend will be no more."

His father added, "If Gravesend is indeed a player in the miracles I've seen with both you and Albion, I believe it must be done. His murderous ways must come to an end."

The poison was crowned with delicate, white flowers, like tiny puffs of cotton. William wondered how the plant managed to live—itself, being poisonous.

William looked up. The woods were now clawing at the sky. The crows followed.

"Halt your wagon, Father. Where might you be going?"

William was roused by the voice, harsh and cruel. When he opened his eyes he was startled by a bright torch held before the horses. Night had come on while he had slept.

The smell of acrid excrement on the air made him wrinkle his nose. In the gloaming, surrounding them on all sides were twenty or more red sashed followers of Gravesend. William did not know where they came from, but in the failing light he could see makeshift shelters cluttered in the trees and several campfires, and he assumed that they must have rolled directly into one of their encampments.

"Well, Father?" the sentry said to Radulphus. "The night is coming on. Where are you going?"

William thought he looked vaguely familiar as if he'd seen him on the abbey grounds near his village. *One of the raiders—perhaps they all would look the same*, he thought.

Albion answered, "We make for the monastery at Waltham tonight. Tomorrow we ride to Stortford. We have been sent for by his Excellency, Bishop Gravesend. Here is our summons." Albion produced the note he had opened at the dinning table the night before.

At the mention of Gravesend, the sentry's eyes lit up. He grabbed the note with one hand, shook it open and held it up to his nose. "I see." A moment later he said, "So you are the apothecary? Mr. Aloysius Stell, is it?" He then leaned closer. He sniffed at Albion. "I've seen you before," he said.

"I doubt it," Albion replied.

"No, no," he said, holding the torch higher, "you were on the road near Ascott, a few days ago." He called out, "Jakes! Jakes! Come here, Jakes."

A tall, wiry framed man trotted up. His red sash was torn and stained. Another awful smell joined in the air. William scanned the unkempt group—the felled trees at the road side—the entrails of some creature they had obviously gutted and hauled off to roast.

"Jakes, remember this fellow? Didn't we see this fellow on the road near Ascott?"

Jakes tilted his head at Albion. The man's pupils were slightly maligned. "P`haps, p`haps, John. Was he the one with the white horse?"

The sentry, apparently named John, said, "No, no. This one here, he rode through, not four nights back. A black horse, just like one of these here, pulling this wagon."

"P`haps, John. P`haps. The horse I seen before."

"Not the horse, Jakes, this man, here."

Albion's eyes narrowed.

"This man, here. This man, here." Jakes appraised the three, one eye darting out and away. "Don't know, John." He said. "P`haps he did, p`haps he didn't."

Albion scowled, straining for patience, "You may have seen me traveling to one of my gardens near Kindlington or Oxford."

"Yes, yes, that could be," said John. "We were just out that way. A tidy way from here."

"A tidy way," Jakes echoed.

"And now you ride to Strotford?" John asked.

Jakes, "Strotford?"

Albion held out his hand gesturing to have the Bishop's letter returned. "As you have read," he said.

"Well, if you've an invitation from his Excellency, we will send you on your way. We shan't keep you any longer." He handed the note. "God save you, Father," he said to Radulphus, bowing and crossing himself.

The priest nodded his head in acknowledgement and raised his hand to bless the man. A gleam of fire kindled in his father's eye. Though his expression was not without its wonted gentleness and caring, there was fury lurking behind it. Seeing the subtle glare, William, too, felt his own heat rise. These were the very men that descended upon their abbey—upon his family. The leather pouch felt heavy.

"What have you in these boxes?" He moved the torch to get a better view.

"Nothing that concerns you," Albion said sharply.

The sentry caught the tone and returned in kind, "I lead this very company for His Excellency, and what travels on the road to his door is indeed my concern. Show me and we shan't keep you—"

"No, I daresay you won't keep us any longer," Albion said through his teeth, unable to weather more. "You beef-witted, churlish knave. Move your shite-buggering rout from our path. Aye, me, the stench!"

"Say again," John the sentry said—eyes widening and taking a step back. He gripped the hilt of his sword, "Why, you don't know who you're speaking to—"

"Forsooth! Would thou match wits with me you pox-marked codpiece? Hold your tongue. Speak no more to me, or the Bishop will know of our delay here. Did you not read his summons? He is ill and requires our remedies. *P'haps* you cannot read, you fear driven, bum-sniffing pawn."

The boy sat up at these insults and looked around at the company that was now taking an interest—grimaces and frowns. Many began to gather toward the wagon.

Albion's voice raised ever louder, "And all of you that bear the red sash, you dim-witted hedge-pigs—know now that three travelers—three healers—upon a wagon carrying medicine to his Excellency has been delayed by this rump-fed bag of bile." He spat, "I would gladly step off of this cart and challenge each of you in turn, to pay the theft of my time, and his lengthened suffering. I doubt any here have the courage to face me without his fellows. Poor wretches, I know you work as one, fearful concoction of menace and fear. Individual thought is scarce in this brood of rump-feeders."

A sudden terror tingled through William watching their dangerous guide's rant. He recalled Albion's words, "We are not to be trifled with. . ."

"Be it known, we do not condone your crusade. You are all out of God's favor! Now, we are in haste. Open the way. Open the way ahead, or by God, each of you will feel the Bishop's wrath."

At Albion's last threat, and to William's amazement, several of the rioters stood aside and backed away to their shelters and fires. John and Jakes still remained at the wagon's side.

William could see that Albion's tirade had astonished Jakes. His mouth was agape and his face drew thinner with each insult—one eye on Albion, the other was trained somewhere unknown.

John the sentry was not as shocked, though some incredulity and faint admiration was in his face. There was also a disquieting confidence. He thought to offer one last challenge. "You do not condone our banner of Christ?" he hissed.

Albion leaned toward him with a glare of flame, and issued a harsh, breathy whisper, "I do not, slave. You are nothing but pain and murder. I am the remedy. I am the healer. Step away."

The words smashed into John's thoughts. Albion waited and watched him. The sentry visibly clutched for some response. For Albion, it was enough. He snapped the reign and held John's eyes as the horses started forward. When Albion released the man and turned, William saw him crimp a smile back.

Angry faces tracked them. Albion muttered breathy Italian insults as they rode on, "Mortacci tua. Faccia a

culo. Pezzo di merda."   Early evening had deepened.
Campfires flickered in the trees. Long angled shadows
loomed across the road. William turned and looked back.

John the sentry was standing where they left him. He
seemed dazed. Then, as if waking from a dream, he called
after them, "We are the ones doing the healing,
apothecary! You'll soon see that we are the hand of God.
You will soon see!"

Sleeping In Thunder

September, 1982

Venice, Italy

It was unusual for her to doubt. But lately, at night, before sleep, or just as she woke, she was trembling. *Is what I do, murder? What of the ancient tales that justify my actions? Is what I've done, wrong? Will I be forgiven?* For Helen Craven, guilt had always been easy to handle. It was like an old friend. She didn't know a life without it. But this new calling. The dictums. The discipline. The killing. Every few days the same tremors returned. Rest was getting more and more difficult. Now she was waking in the middle of the night to a whispering voice in her room. A thunder in her dreams.

Arrived. I have arrived.

But what place is this?

From glittered eyelids and her tight wrap of a skirt—the yearning for Jimmy Page—the look in his eyes as she tumbled back into the night to the street below—the look in his eyes when he learned that she could not die—her memory hurtles through seasons, to now, a trained assassin living in Italy, sheltered beneath the roof of Albion Ravistelle, and steeped in a culture that has maintained its identity since the dawn of mankind.

She learned quickly. How to maintain. To overcome. To arrive within her new life. She pictured a future with Albion and their child. In the end, he would reign and she would be at his side. She would be Queen.

It had been two years since Albion's last letter—its closing words, *I will return soon.* She convinced herself as seasons repeated in his absence that two years wasn't long. *In the grand scheme*, she thought, *even half a century is a blink.*

Helen spent most of her time now studying. Three times a week a professor named Dr. Bonin would visit and guide her through math and science courses—through Albion's library of ancient history, literature and poetry. Philosophy and mythology. Corey Thomas would check in—often discovering her wearing the bejeweled mask, lying in the middle of Albion's bedchamber surrounded by open volumes of books. A Zeppelin record pounding out in the background—a chrome coffee pot, and delicate cup and saucer. "Stay and have a listen to this, Corey," she would say to him, then pronounce, "*Ye mock me—but the power which brought ye here / Hath made you mine. Slaves, scoff not at my will! / The mind, the spirit, the Promethean spark*—It's one of Albion's favorites, *Manfred*, by Lord Byron. Ever read that?" The following day it was Dante, then Homer, Cicero, Shelly, Petrarch—the list grew as the months marched by. Most of the time, Corey would nod. Occasionally, he would say, "Yes, I read it the year it came out."

The large leather bound book that Albion left for her she had read cover to cover several times over. She turned its pages usually late at night when the storms in her dreams kept her awake.

The book, *The Toele*, contained the tales and histories of the *Itonalya* on Earth. The earliest forms of language from its telepathic beginnings to the creation of oral *Elliqui*. Of the ancient realm of *Wyn Avuqua*, the first war between the *Itonalya* and the Divine Host, and the plight and sorrow of the immortals and their banishment from the Hereafter. With each perusal she found more of herself. She was a part of all of this. A soldier. A guardian.

She couldn't help but imagine flights of angels, their numbers choking out the sunlight—the gods in battle rage on high, and the *Itonalya* below, the Guardians of the Dream, their eyes skyward, spears raised, defying the impossible powers that bore down. A battle fought before there was memory.

But this war was to be rekindled, and she would be at its center. It would happen again. She would stand amid the ranks of immortals, her voice raising a challenge. She would slash and stab the god and the goddess. And at the host's front—upon the mount, was her Albion. His sword raised and shouting into the thunder clap of God: "Back, ye baffled fiends! The hand of death is on me—but not yours!"

The Stepping

Within the portrait of Loche Newirth

The muses whisper with each wavering step.

Loche has now adjusted. At least, as far as one can mentally adjust to balancing on a bridge of severed floating heads on the ocean of death.

He wonders what Basil would think of such a predicament. He would probably shrug, offer a joint and say something about the big deep heavy. *But to make matters even stranger, Loche had never met Basil. He had written him, but never met him. He considers that meeting Basil might feel akin to meeting Julia for the first time, another of his creations. Though, of course, he met Julia on Earth, whatever that means. Will it be different meeting one's brother (a character in a story that one has written) in the Hereafter? Loche's foot sloshes down into the face of a god. It holds him up.*

—You will know him when you see him, Loche, the boy says.

He staggers again. There is the physical sensation of wet, cold feet, a biting sea air clamoring down his collar, the pangs of hunger and thirst. But most of all, the shaky and anxious tremors of fear. Doubt and madness lurking in the corners of his thought.

—You're not listening, the boy says.

What does he mean, this guide, leading him into kingdom come?

—Listen, you will hear. . .

Still he is able to walk, tottering from face to face, skull to skull. Who were these poor beings? What did they want? Why would they choose a fate that ends here?

Then, it is apparent. Stark and unforgiving. Loche stops, balances and lets the buoyancy hold him.

The muses whisper with each wavering step.

A series of visions come.

He sees what they've seen, feels what they have felt. A swirling vortex of hope and longing. Crushed moonlight upon broken brick and rubble—a bombed out village. War torn countryside and human forms bent and coughing, seeking refuge. Smoke choking the air. Corpses frozen at the roadside.

Loche wobbles to another stop—bodies piled for burning, blisters from long handled shovels, trenches harrowed for mass graves, the pop of firing squads over the bluff. We're next.

Stagger and stop—Cancer. The hospital's ventilation system hushes the room with an even breeze of synthetic cool. The weird, recycled air scent. Hanging tubes, stacked boxes of latex gloves, glass cylinders full of cotton swabs, locked drawers, metal trays with sharp stainless instruments—a woman beside the bed in tears. Tiny frightened eyes staring up from the pillow.

Tumble forward, stop—crystal and lace. The flavor of champagne and skin. Orgasm and vertigo. Flight and love.

Stumble backward, stop—the numbing pressure of the sky's weight falls away. The quiet moment when the voices halt and the questions don't matter. When thought is not measured in distance but in grins. When the only mystery of the night's sky is lodged in the hope of seeing it again, and again.

What are these memories?

A pale light is rising. The boy ahead wears Edwin's expression of wonder—as if his father had just pulled a coin from his ear.

—A thousand poems with each step, the boy says. That is why we come. That is why we die.

It's In The Stars

November 6, this year
Venice, Italy

Corey Thomas squints at the cluster of splashed paint where the ceiling and the wall meet. "I don't understand," he says.

Julia's mouth is agape, eyes wide with amazement. "How could he have known?"

"Known what, Julia? Please, we haven't much time here. Explain."

"You don't see it?" Julia asks. Then she shakes her head. "No, of course you don't. Of course not." She points up to the direct center of the misted dots—as if directing Corey to follow her finger along a trail of mythic stars.

"There." Her voice is bright. Confident. Filled with hope. "Right there. *The single star.* My father taught me all about the constellations—especially when I could not sleep at night. There was one star he would point to— always—a single star tucked within a pattern of other points. It blinks, ever so slightly—when I would find it, looking out of my window, I would drift off to sleep."

Corey looks up. "All I see is paint, Julia."

"Yes," she agrees. "Paint. Random paint splashes coming from Basil's work down here on the easels."

"And you're saying there's a familiar pattern?"

Julia holds both hands over her mouth. She speaks through her fingers. "Not only a pattern—but *my* pattern. My constellation. My dad named it," she laughs, "it's silly, I know. He called it the Julia Constellation. I know those stars. I know that pattern." She steps closer to the wall, her face tilted up. "And there is the one single star."

She bows her forehead against the cool wall, and adds, "And it is blinking."

"I don't see a blinking star," Corey says.

Julia doesn't respond. Instead, she backs away from the wall and studies the area surrounding the cluster. "How could he have done this? Spatters from his brush? It is unbelievable."

Corey watches her. "All of Basil's work carries an unbelievable trait, you know."

She now sees The Big Dipper, the constellations of Scorpius, Gemini, Leo. There are systems. Spiraled galaxies. She notes a curious curve in their array, as if they are arcing toward a point, like a trajectory to a target. A line connecting dots. As her eyes lower she processes the half finished sketches, the photographs and hand scrawled notes. At the top, where the constellations seem to point, is a half finished sketch—a woman in a flowing robe carrying flowers.

"What do you make of this drawing?" Julia asks.

Corey steps forward. "Elpis. I immediately think of Elpis."

"Elpis?"

"Yes. Do you recall the jar of Pandora? Pandora's Box?"

Julia nods, "Of course."

"When Pandora opened the jar, all the spirits of evil escaped and spread across the earth. When she realized what was happening she rushed to close the lid and found that everything had fled the jar save Elpis. Elpis is the spirit of Hope." He leans closer and scrutinizes the rough sketch. "Strangely, she looks a little like you." Julia sees the resemblance. He tilts his head. "Didn't you live in Hope? Hope, Idaho?"

"Yes."

Just below Elpis the shower of paint droplets, like a cosmic path, leads to a photo—a page ripped from a magazine. It shows the pyramids at Giza Egypt at night. A canopy of stars is draped over the ancient structures. She follows the seemingly accidental paint spray as it falls into the photograph. It appears to point directly at the smallest of the pyramids. Tacked just below the pyramid is another image, that of another robed woman carrying a pitcher on her shoulder. Julia points at it and glances at Corey.

"That would be Hebe," he tells her. "Greek goddess of youth."

"And the pyramid?"

"Pyramid of Menkaure," he says. "What are you seeing, Julia? This room is filled with a thousand photos of world mysteries and myths and, well, rock bands. Why do you linger here?"

"I am sure Albion and his advisors have studied everything in here—looking to learn anything they could —"

"Completely. Many times," he agrees.

"Corey," she says, pointing up to the cluster. "There is no way they could decipher *this*. Only I, or we, could— this must be a message for—for me. This can't be a coincidence."

"Tell me."

"That's *my* constellation." She lowers her finger to the sketch of the woman. "Elpis, goddess of Hope? I am from Hope. Hope, Idaho. And Hebe, the goddess of youth? That's what my name means."

"Your name?"

"Yes," she says. "The name *Julia*. It means youth."

"And the pyramid?" His cell phone vibrates. He lifts it to his eyes and nods.

Julia shrugs. "Something must be there."

"I don't know, my dear. It sounds a little far fetched to me," he says as he types a message.

"Tell me that when we get to the Giza Plateau," she says.

The Note

November 6, this year
Venice, Italy

"I fucking hate that mustache," Leonaie says.

"Dear, please," Samuel says as they cross the wood slatted bridge. "You must keep your voice down. There are ears all around us."

"Okay," Leonaie nods, "But why are we here?" Her legs ache. Each step is an effort.

Samuel sighs. His eyes dart from the canal, to the walkway ahead, to the doors beyond. It is late afternoon. The buzzing from the waterway is noisy. His wrist aches.

"And the glasses, my, my, my. Sexy, that's what I say. Whoa!"

"Miss Leonaie," Samuel grins. "Enough. Enough."

"Well, I love them. You look like someone else. Tell me, when I become immortal, will you still dress up for me? I do hope so. It will keep things interesting. Will I tire of the simple things? Truly, will I?" She turns to learn if there's an answer. Samuel stops on the bridge. His hand grips the rail.

"I cannot answer that," he says, his eyes wet, far away and distant. "I hope you will remember me. Remember that we have forever before us."

"Tears?" she says. "Really, dear? You are sweet. Such a delicate soul. I'm sorry. I will always love you, my Samuel. Always."

Samuel Lifeson, with his one hand, and prosthetic hand, turns her toward him. "Soon, Leonaie, the ladder will reach. The ladder will join us."

"Good," she says.

Samuel's cell phone vibrates. He lifts it. A text from Corey Thomas.

West entrance. Angelo Catena will meet you. I will be there ASAP.

Samuel taps a quick response:

We are at the door. Remember, we're in a hurry.

Samuel pulls Leonaie into his arms. He waits. His eyes drift to the doors just feet away.

"I wrote a note. Now, where is it?" Her hand rummages in the bag slung at her side. When she raises it, she holds a yellow Post It note up before Samuel's eyes.

"You see?" she says, "I'm right here with you."

The door opens. Dr. Catena motions for them to come. Samuel's eyes scan Leonaie's note.

Venice today.
Kiss Samuel.
Become immortal.
   And William says, be quick about it.
Kiss Samuel.

Old Friends

November 6, this year
Venice, Italy

"Truly," Albion says, "it never feels as you expect."

"Truly," William Greenhame agrees.

They stare at one another. Julia sees the two *Itonalya* search the past, the long, long years, the moments that only two estranged friends can know. Impossible to fathom the sinews of memory that link them—the countless years that bind them. Julia smiles at the word Greenhame chose to echo. *Truly.*

"And here you are, alone. Unarmed. You bring some message from George Eversman, I suppose? Perhaps you bring my wife's son, Edwin? Tell me, William, why have you come?" Albion laughs, unable to contain his wonted demeanor. "Why have you come?"

William scans his audience. Julia holds her hand to her heart when his eyes fall upon her. He smiles. His eyes drift to Marcus Rearden, his mouth muttering nonsense in whisper, to Helen Newirth, her hand upon Albion's shoulder. Julia notes nine armed *Endale Gen* in the corner shadows.

"Where is my son?" Helen asks glaring at Julia.

"Nearby," William says.

"Not near enough," she says. "Have you come to watch Julia buried alive?"

William closes his eyes and draws a deep breath. He smiles at Albion. "Irksome, Helen. Always irksome. Why is it taking you so long to think like an *Itonalya?*"

"Oh sweet William," Helen says. "It wasn't me that started this war. The love for your children seems to have hurled existence to the edge of ruin." She lays an open palm atop her bosom, and with her best Italian accent says, "We're both part of the same hypocrisy."

Albion's eyes narrow. "Why are you here, William?"

"I am here to stop you."

"I see."

"I am also here to reunite mother to son, bring lover to lover, and friend to friend. I am here to offer you respite."

"How auspicious. I applaud your intentions. Now, what do you want?"

William drops to a knee. He bows his head. "Give me Julia. Give me Edwin and release Helen with them. In return I vow that the *Orathom Wis* will no longer heed their ancient summons. Nor will they stand in your way. Your will on earth," he paused and raised a glare at his old friend, "as it is in Heaven."

Albion laced two fingers over his lips. "Is that all? You take from me my love, her son, and Julia, one that could become great, in exchange for the standing down of a decrepit Order that has outlasted its worth. An Order that is already on the verge of extinction. Slaves? William, even as we speak, I lay siege to *Mel Tiris*. Tomorrow, the *Orathom Wis* will be destroyed. Loche Newirth's journal and the last collection of Basil Fenn's work will be in my possession. Tell me again, how is this respite? Truly, my old friend, is that all you offer?"

Greenhame stood, "No," he said. "I've not mentioned the threat."

Albion laughs. "Threat? By all means, give me your worst."

"If you refuse me, I shall be forced to destroy you and all that you hold dear. You have taken from me one son. I seek no revenge. If you were to take from me my other son, still I would stay my vengeance. For they have waiting a place in the *Orathom*. But refuse my simple requests, here, now, and I will cast both your ambition and you, into oblivion."

Protectors

April, 1338
On the road to Strotford Manor, north of London

Two bright torches lit the road ahead. For the next mile, the only sound was the steady march of the horse's hooves and the creaking wagon. Once they had passed the last of the campfires, William thought he could hear Albion muttering to himself—more curses and name calling.

Radulphus was the first to speak, "Bum sniffing pawn?" The priest wore a faint smile.

Albion laughed. "The bastards smelled to high heaven."

William mouthed the words, *bum sniffing pawn*, but with no voice for he knew that his father would not approve. But he grinned at the insult.

Albion said, "I thought he was going to lose his head. I have no patience for such fellows—ignorant, fearful, power hungry—the worst of all humanity. Like rats in the dark."

William smelled smoke.

"Dangerous," the priest said.

"This is true," agreed Albion. "As a group, such folk will sour the world. Foul the thoughts and hopes of many. Though they might be redeemed, I admit, I am not their teacher—but they are too far gone—so rapt in Gravesend's spell that they've lost themselves. And the horrors they've committed—"

Albion's voice faltered as the horses led them around a bend. Radulphus crossed himself. William lifted the pouch of leaves to his nose. He imagined his mother's touch steadying him.

In the torchlight, five men hung by their necks. Flapping and clawing at the shoulder of the nearest, a black crow stabbed at the gray flesh. Just beyond the makeshift gallows were three conical piles of ash, like the ones William had seen in the village square. They glowed with a muted orange and crimson. Feathers of flame waved in silence. The standard of Gravesend towered over the hateful sight—the branch hewn cross—its arms swathed with a long rag of scarlet.

Albion pulled the horses to a stop. A sign had been posted upon the forward post of the gibbet.

It read:

maleficum ne patiaris vivere eris
neque vindicum
--Cyrus

"And here we see the healing that John spoke of. They believe they heal the woes of this world. . ." Albion hissed. "*Ithic veli agtig.*"

"What does it say?" William asked, quietly.

Radulphus placed his arm around him, "It says, thou shalt not suffer a witch to live—nor those that protect her. It is by order of the leader of Gravesend's sentinels, Cyrus."

The dead eyes were frozen and distant. An expression that seemed to see beyond this life. Their faces reminded William of the statue he had seen when they entered London. That face peering out of this world.

"They dream," William whispered. His palm felt for the sharp edged leaves.

Albion drove the horses onward.

Won't You Guess My Name?

August, 1987
New York City

The martini glass was empty save the single olive. Helen pinched it out and bit it in half. Salt and gin and the heady buzz. The evening was cooling. The fume of hot asphalt and exhaust. She watched the foot traffic beside her table near Times Square. Both men and women noticed her, lured from her black heels and silk summer dress. Most attempted a connection. She allowed a few the joy of her smile, but for an instant only—not enough for any to stop and speak to her. The rest of her countenance was cautionary.

The waiter set another martini before her. The poor man. He followed the line from her bare shoulders to her earrings glimmering with the table's candle. She unlatched her restraint and lifted her face to him, her lips were wet, and she filled his eyes with her light. "Thank you," she said.

"My pleasure," he said. A slight quaver. He fumbled reaching for the empty glass. It toppled—she saved it just in time.

The gin. The honey-pine vermouth. Her skin radiated heat. Sunlight tucked away behind a building. A slight chill crept through her.

But she knew the chill to come would be nearly unbearable. He would soon arrive and she looked into the busy restaurant trying to spot him.

Then she felt it, the *Rathinalya*. A blanket of tiny needles wrapped her body. Slowly it intensified into a mixture of stinging, chills and rapture. A nail dragged from her breastbone to her navel and down. Torment and pleasure. It was the *Rathinalya*—though it was unlike the others. She braced herself. She crossed her legs and squeezed them together trying to control it. She had a job to do. Again, she leaned and searched. Again, she scanned the restaurant.

"I know who you are," he said. He was behind her.

Helen reached for her martini and brought the full glass to her mouth. She sipped it then returned it to the table. Slow and certain, she craned her neck and looked up and over her left shoulder.

A middle aged man stood behind Helen studying her. She felt her lips part slightly at the sight of him. His hair was black. From his eyes gyred flecks of gold and green —or was that the intensity of the *Rathinalya?* Words ticked through her mind as she tried to describe him— exquisite and hateful—beautiful and terrible—glorious horror.

"I know who you are," he said again. He smiled.

She turned back to her drink, "I doubt it," she said.

"This is the third time you've been in my path. Three days in a row you've been here. Seems to me, we should have a drink together."

"I'm waiting for someone," she said.

"You've been waiting for me."

True, she thought, suppressing a compulsion to say it. She wondered suddenly if she had replied or not. *True, I've been waiting for you, to slice you limb from limb and toss your head into the sea*. She could do it here, or in private at a nearby apartment. At a word, he would go with her. *Here or there?* Helen's eyes slid to a nearby sidewalk garbage can where a short sword was buried, hilt up and ready. The scenarios appeared like blue prints in her head: the two police officers two blocks away, one man inside the restaurant, possibly carrying a firearm, the escape route and change of clothes at the flower shop on 8th, her driver waiting for her on 9th. *Or, in private?*

The *Rathinalya* was beyond anything she'd felt before. Thrilling and addictive. Painful. Prolonging it might be unwise. Stop his heart, stop this torturous chill. *Here. Now.*

"True. I've been waiting for you," she said, her hair coiling down over her naked shoulder as she looked back up to him. "Let's have that drink right now." She gestured to the seat across from her. *A short leap to the sword, three steps away.*

She turned back to her martini. As she reached for the stem another man was approaching the table. Raising up she felt both the *Rathinalya* and an explosion of euphoria burst within her.

"Albion!" she cried. "Albion!" she rose in shock.

Albion Ravistelle took hold of her wrist and pulled her to him. Every fiber within her quivered in pain and delight. Tears flooded her eyes.

"My darling, Helen," he whispered in her ear. All of her strength coiled around him.

"Albion," she said, unable to let go. She pressed her mouth to his. She bit his lips. "Oh God! Oh God! Oh God!" She wept between each kiss.

After a few moments, Helen pulled her face away and stared at him. He looked just as he did the day he went away. Keen eyes, elegant and handsome. She could see that he had missed her, too. She was certain of it.

"Helen, I want you to meet someone." His focus was over her shoulder—the man she was sent to assassinate. She turned, still ravished by a million pin pricks and the joy of Albion's return.

"Pleased to meet you," the man said.

"Helen Craven, this is our new friend." Albion's voice then quavered, "Mr. Nicolas Cythe."

The Building Bridge

Within the portrait of Loche Newirth

The star remains. Does that mean that darkness has an end? Does it mean that the black hole does not exist— that this is all a dream—I can wake now—I can wake?

Day is bright blue, though, the boy had informed Loche that it is not really day. *It is what one might call an illusion for, given their particular place in existence, day, night, and time itself is indefinable. Loche, as he tries to unfold the thought, spits. Too much, he thinks. He lurches and leans to another floating face. It carries him.*

—It's day. The sky is blue, he tells the boy.

The boy does not reply.

Ahead, the far shore has revealed itself. The face of Edwin had said, Look, there lies the window's edge. Basil is somewhere out there.

Loche strains his eyes. He sees a sandy and green shore stretching like a cord between the sea and sky.

—Tell me, the boy says. What will you do when you find him?

—I don't know, Loche answers. We must find a way to close the doors—or the windows, as you call them.

—Yes, the boy says.

Loche moves to take another step and notes that the bridge is ending. It is ending well before reaching the shore. He stops and does not move.

—Wait, the boy says.

At that moment, hundreds of heads float to the surface connecting the bridge to the beach. Heads that the acidic brine of sea had not yet tasted by the look of them. The faces still wear shock and pain and fear. Death is new upon them. Loche takes an uneasy step and moves forward. Another and another. He moves faster.

A head turns face up and it halts Loche. He recognizes the eyes. It is the immortal, Justinian Pierce of the Orathom Wis. Two more roll over and glare into the blue. More Guardians from Mel Tiris he had met—when? An hour ago? A week? Ten years?

The boy sees what has captured Loche.

—*The War of the Immortals on earth has begun. The siege of Mel Tiris. It will not be long before the fight will be before your very door, he said.*

Grasshopper

November 7, this year
Venice, Italy

Leonaie, hand in hand with Samuel, follows Dr. Angelo Catena down a long, sterile-white hallway with many doors. White coated personnel with clip boards and rolling stretchers, and vital sign monitors and other gadgetry are busy bustling about. Voices clatter off of the polished floors and shiny walls. Passing a door that is slightly ajar, Leonaie catches a glimpse of a man sitting and rocking back and forth. Something has his arms fastened behind his back.

Now that's strange, she thinks.

"Tell me the myth, again, Samuel," she says. "Tell me how we're not going to let *that* happen to us."

"Tithonus," Samuel says, his voice low, and a little frantic, "was the prince of Troy—and he was loved by the goddess of the morning. She stole him away to love him and be with him forever. But Tithonus was not immortal, so she pleaded with Jupiter to grant the prince immortality, but failed to ask for eternal youth."

"I hate this part of the story," she says as the trio turn a corner into another long, white hall. "Are you listening, Dr. Catena? This is important."

Catena thumbs his glasses. "I am, Miss Eschelle. I know the tale well." He walks fast.

Samuel continues, "After a time, it was clear to the goddess that her lover was aging. He soon wrinkled, then he could not walk, then he could not move at all. She cared for him as long as she could, but eventually she was forced to hide him away within her palace. When she could no longer endure his cries, she turned him into a grasshopper."

"Hear that, Doc?" Leonaie says. "We would like to forgo the grasshopper feature."

Catena stops at a door and slides his ID card into a slot. A red light blinks. The doctor groans. He slides it again. Another red light.

Samuel's voice is straining for control, "You did get the memo that we're in a hurry, yes?"

A green light illuminates upon the panel and the interior lock in the door unbolts.

"Come in," he says.

The three enter into a large, warmly lit chamber. It looks nothing like a hospital room, though it does have the monitors, instruments, and expected medical supplies. The room is wood paneled, the floors are of a deep mahogany and the furniture is rich in golds and greens. A huge copper basin, the size of a bathtub dominates the center of the room. A single, silver light is directed into its center.

"Did I tell you that we had a claw foot tub when I was a little girl?" Leonaie says suddenly. "And at night, my sisters and I would dance to Dad's singing and whistling. We sure got a kick out of that. Then it would be bath time."

Samuel says to the doctor, "Is that it?"

Catena thumbs his wiry glasses again and nods. "The fountain of youth. It is. It is indeed."

Sworn

April, 1338
Waltham Monastery, north of London

"Is he asleep?" Albion asked. His voice was hushed.

"It appears so," William's father said. "Though, I find it hard to believe that the boy will ever sleep well again after such sights. I, myself, must fend off nightmares."

William laid on his side facing away from the two. From the flickering candlelight, faces appeared in the shadowed fissures of the walls. He was wide awake, though he did not want the two men to know it.

Once they had arrived at the Waltham Monastery they were shown to their bedchamber with a plate of fruit and bread, and a pitcher of wine. Without a word, William removed his boots, tottered to the bed and climbed beneath the blanket. Albion and Radulphus sat at a small table near the window.

William listened as they sipped their goblets and took a few morsels of food.

Albion said finally, "I believe I have it, Father. How to remove Gravesend."

"Do tell."

"I must first learn your mind in full. I must know that you are sworn to this bloody deed."

Radulphus paused. William heard him sigh. "I am. It is against my conscience, yet with the miracles that I have seen between you, my son and the graces of my late wife —if what you say is true, and Gravesend is not of this world, I will do what I can to eliminate him. It sickens my heart—" he broke off. Another few moments passed. "A sickness that is not unlike a forbidden pleasure—as if this killing will be justified—as if revenge is allowed. I find it difficult to describe."

"I think I understand, Father. Your vengeance in this matter is justified. And your obligation. I daresay, that when it happens, know the act is truly righteous. And it will be rewarded."

"Then I say to you, I am sworn."

"Very well. Now to the purpose. Your names we must change. William, I believe, can remain, William. It will be easier for him to remember—you however, Father, should go by another name. Father Radulphus Grenehamer is a name too well known. Let me think. . . I have it. In honor of your lovely bride, and in light of your changing view of this world, let us give you an *Elliqui* name."

"*Elliqui?*" the priest asked.

"*Elliqui* is the language of my kind. Older than the Earth itself. One day, I hope I can teach you what I know of it. William, too, for its words will ease his soul as the centuries pass. Now then, your wife had an affinity for leaves, yes?"

"She did."

William's eyes shot to the leaves shining in the candlelight.

"*Falio* in the language of old means *leaf*, though, it means much, much more, as do all utterances in *Elliqui*. Let us call you Father Falio."

"Very well."

"We must instruct William to learn this new title." Albion said. "Now, we must discuss the poisoning."

William shifted in the bed so that he could hear a little clearer. His movement caught his father's attention.

Radulphus rose from his chair and stepped to the bedside. William closed his eyes and let his face relax.

"Still asleep?" Albion asked.

"Yes," Radulphus answered, sitting back down.

Albion said, "In the morning, I will grind the plant into a fine power. I will then combine the powder with a honey mead and water. *Gravesend's Bane* we shall call it. Into a vial I shall pour the mortal distillment and place it among the many remedies we bring to *heal* his Excellency. The vial will have a ribbon of red tied at its throat—a *red sash* to remind us."

William's father said, "Very well."

Albion said, "There is much to chance, Father, but there is one thing on which we can count, we will not be trusted. We will be searched when we arrive tomorrow evening. Our arms will be stowed away. Our cargo of herbs will be taken to the manor's garden, and we will be shown to our chambers. Depending upon the Bishop's condition, we will either be given audience immediately or very early in the morning of the next day. Once we step through their doors, our choices diminish."

Albion's voice halted abruptly. Then he added, "I will give William the vial and instruct him how to deliver the poison."

Radulphus' voice growled, "You shall do no such thing, Albion. You will not place the choice of murder before a child. I will not permit it." There was a subtle boom in his father's voice. A familiar chill scraped up his back.

Albion did not respond immediately. After a moment he said, "Father—"

"No, I tell you. It was agreed that you would kill Gravesend." His whisper rose in anger.

"We will all be suspect, Priest. But least of all, a boy of six springs."

"I cannot allow—"

"He will do no more than hand the poison to Gravesend, pour it upon the Bishop's food, or into a goblet. That is all."

Outside, far away, a dog bayed into the night.

William's father: "Won't they test the food or drink first? The Bishop must have an assayer."

"Aye, that he will. But *Gravesend's Bane* is slow in its potency. If they suspect poison, they will expect a sudden effect. This is not so with our weapon. You could give the Eucharist and dole out bread, and still the poison would hide. But not much longer. We will be on our way to the horses and escape when Gravesend is retching. The plan, as I see it—the innocent boy will deliver the poison, the sweet mead will mask the pestilence, the delay will enable our escape."

"What of the monks? Gravesend's sentinels?"

"I am uncertain," Albion said. "It is likely that they, too, must be eliminated. I doubt very much that we will leave the manor without a fight."

Radulphus sighed. "I am in doubt."

"It will not be the last time, Father."

The two did not speak again. William heard one rise and leave the chamber—he assumed it was Albion. Rolling over, William saw his father with his head in his hands.

"Papa?"

The priest wiped at his eyes and turned to the boy. "You heard us speaking?"

"Yes."

"Everything has changed," Radulphus broke. He hid his face and muttered inaudibly to himself.

"I can do it. I will do it."

The priest looked at his son. William wondered why his father's eyes were tearing.

Sympathy For Nicolas Cythe

August, 1987

New York City

"Helen, I suppose you were expecting something frightful? Something Satanic? Pentagrams? Some Plutonian iconography? Perhaps you would like the classic tale of the fallen angel of light? That is my personal favorite. And by all accounts, true. Or at least, partially. As far as *you* can fathom it.

"I have been here since the beginning—though, in many forms. I have been born as a man and a woman. I have recurred through the centuries. I have been killed by illness, accident, war, old age—by Albion Ravistelle. Many times by George Eversman, leader of the *Orathom Wis.* I am the only *Bridger,* as you're wont to call our kind, fully cognizant of my real purpose and identity. At every crossing, I know what I am very early. Of your myths, I seem to match that darker creature—the devilish sort of fellow. Hades. Set. The bad guy in the stories of every culture. I am represented quite poorly, in my opinion. And I feel, of course, that because I am *me,* my opinion should be considered when we speak of defining *me* as a character. There's always two sides to every story.

"You see, my part in the grand tale of humankind is quite momentous. For after all, what is a story without a conflict? It appears, as does light in the darkness, that I've provided your existence a power beyond all powers. Your very lives, your dramas, your worries, joys, sorrows and fears are what fuels both the *Alya* and the *Orathom.* You are coveted by the gods because you possess what they cannot—fear and doubt. Joy and hope.

"I am misunderstood, Helen. All of the tales about me fall short. I am depicted evilly. But it is because of me that joy exists. Both must exist to feel human. I am both.

"Have some sympathy, won't you? The world is changing. An end is near to the the old ways and the ruling powers beyond. You will see. You will see.

"And your dearest, Albion Ravistelle? He is now my friend. We have met many times. I have fallen beneath his sword twice in centuries passed. But this time, Albion and I have come to a crossroad (forgive the allegorical trappings of that word). And he has given me life. He has built the ladders that connect the gods and man. He has now cultivated the tree of life. He has allowed me to eat of that fruit.

"I am a crossing divinity. I am also an immortal. I am a god on earth that cannot die. I am, Helen, unlike anything in existence.

"Very soon, two doors will be opening between Here and the Hereafter. Two young boys will become men, and discover through their arts the very Center that connects us. It is time to end the slavery of man. Simple evolution. It is time to look behind the veil, and destroy what we find there."

It Will Heal

November 6, this year
Venice, Italy

"William," Albion sighs. "I'm not one for ultimatums. Never have been. You know that about me, since you were young. You must have some memory of that. After all, ultimatums are based on a kind of time element, yes? This or that, right now, is really a bore for our kind, don't you think? I can afford a few years—I could let you all go. Give you what you wish. Let you run free. In time, I would plot a clearer way to get what I want.

"And I assure you, William, I will get what I want. Make no mistake.

"But most importantly, I will not be ruled by you, the *Orathom Wis*, the gods—and certainly not by some ultimatum thrown out in desperation. Now, where is the boy, Edwin?"

William answers, "Edwin is currently residing with one Alice of Bath."

Albion laughs. "Alice, eh?"

Helen cries, "Who is Alice?"

"Alice, my dear, is an old, old friend of ours. She was once my assistant. Part nanny, part housekeeper, part manager. A motherly woman without doubt."

"And she sends word, Albion," William says. "She bade me tell you that you're an idiot."

Albion smiles grimly. "One thing has not changed, Alice is always right."

Helen's voice is now harsh, "William, I want my son. I want him brought here."

William replies, "I think, Helen, even as every part of me says that this is a bad idea, you will be coming with me—and together we shall visit your son. And Julia will join us. . ."

"Nonsense, William. Absurd. You have nothing to bargain with. I am about to allow my dearest Helen to do what she will to sweet Julia to prove to you our resolve." He raises his hand. Two armed men lay hold of Julia. One seizes her arm, the other her hair. They force her to the center of the chamber between Albion and William.

Albion watches William's eyes. "Leg," he says.

Julia feels the sharp cold of a short sword stab through her right thigh. Her eyesight flashes white and red for an instant. Then, searing pain. She cries out as the sword is yanked from the wound. Her fingers fly to the puncture, pressing down. She falls onto her side. Already, an airy white foam is oozing out.

"It'll heal," Helen says.

Julia turns her attention to William. He is staring at her. Concern and sympathy is haunting his eyes. But she lingers on his face for only a moment. His hands are cupped before him. He is holding something delicate. A leather pouch crowned with three luminous green leaves.

Eat Of This Fruit

November 6, this year
Venice, Italy

"You will be the third created immortal, Leonaie. The Third *Melgia*. Your cells will regenerate, your body will reverse to its prime, and you will not die, at least, by natural causes." Catena smiles at her. Leonaie stares blankly back. "You will be a Moonchild."

"I'm not fond of that name," Leonaie says.

The three stand around the copper basin. Bathing in the bright silver light, upon a bed of dark soil, is a coiling plant of thick vines, dark green leaves and four whitish bulbs of fruit. The rising scent is sweet. The musk of turf and rain enter into Leonaie's senses. She inhales deeply.

"The treatment is merely, eating a piece of fruit?" Samuel asks.

Catena nods, but adds, "More or less. Leonaie will ingest as much as she can and we will monitor her progress as the regeneration of telomeres and her DNA chain mutates. It will take a few hours for her system to fully respond to the metabolic change. But yes, eat of this fruit and your eyes shall be opened."

"I expected something very different," Samuel admits.

"The best science, I've found, is natural. Though we have manipulated this plant's genetic structure to cause it to bear fruit. This plant is one of a kind. Something that Albion has guarded for centuries. It has taken us decades to cultivate what you see here. We hope, as you might expect, to produce orchards of the plant. Soon, the earth will be a very different place. And so, too, its people."

"May I?" Samuel says, reaching toward one of the pale spheres no larger than an apricot.

"Please, yes."

Leonaie watches as Samuel's hand breaks the hard stem from the plant and raises the fleshy fruit before her. Citrus and dirt, sweet and sharp. "Here, darling," he says to her, laying it into her palm. "Ladder to the moon?"

Leonaie raises it to her lips and wonders why this all seems familiar. Why was she here? Olivia Langley, her dear ginger-headed, green-eyed nurse from Greenhaven's Retirement Community enters her thought suddenly, as if she were standing right beside her saying, *Ah, to be young once more, with your dear Samuel, tell me the story of Paris again, of how you were picking apples when you met him, you wiggled your cute little bottom, just a tickle, tell me how those memories will never fade, tell me how love can last forever.*

Leonaie bites. The flavor of eternity is honeyed. Its juice is blood red.

Gravesend's House

April, 1338
Strotford Manor, north of London

William's mind repeated Albion's instructions again and again, *Do not touch the potion—I will show you the goblet or the food that you are to taint—when you pour the poison, do it quickly—I will tell you when—I will tell you. Have no pity.*

All that morning and into the early afternoon while Radulphus held the reigns, Albion instructed the boy on how to deliver the poison without it being seen.

A vial, no longer than his index finger, was tied under his wrist. With a simple flick of the stopper with his opposite hand and held over a goblet, the potion spilled almost undetected. The poisoning was to be performed while his hands broke stems—while his wrist hovered over the cup or food and delivered the murdering serum, his fingers would appear to be preparing more ingredients. Albion made the boy practice the action over a hundred times while the wagon rolled toward Gravesend.

Rain muddied the last few miles of their journey. With each splashing clop of the horses hooves, William etched into his memory Albion's words. When they turned onto Parsonage Lane the sun bled out as it was setting, glowering beneath a gloomy canopy of grey. It bathed the approaching Manor of Strotford in red. Torches were lit along the roadside. William could see the day's last light glinting off of the high, black windows. He wondered if eyes were watching from behind the glass.

Albion pulled the horses to a halt. He looked at the boy and the priest. "Bishop Gravesend is a bridging spirit from beyond this life. Mercy is not to be granted. My immortal grace and purpose demands that I retire his spirit back across, to the *Orathom*. Do not come between me and my mandate. Do you both understand?"

The priest took William's hand in his, and both father and son nodded.

"He knows nothing of his own divinity—he knows only his position and power. But he is not above fear. Do not let him into your hearts—do not pity him." With that, he produced the vial of poison and tucked it into William's sleeve at the wrist, tying it with a strip of leather.

The wagon lurched forward. William's mind recited the list again—he added, *do not pity* to it.

There was little or no ceremony upon their arrival. Three of the household servants met them at the doors. Their greetings were kind but abrupt. Albion's sword and dagger were requested. He gave them over without a word. The wagon was led to the stables, their luggage was taken to their chambers. Albion's case of remedies and potions was taken and given to another servant that rushed it inside before all else. They were brought out of the chill of the evening into the great hall. A bright fire snapped at the far end. Two long tables with seating benches ran parallel down the center of the room, and at the opposite end was another table upon a raised platform. It was dressed in a deep plum fabric with gold fringe. Above the table was a wooden crucifix taller than William. A carved Christ hung at its center.

Radulphus led William near to the fire.

A servant entered with a tray of goblets, a pitcher of wine and a basket of bread. Albion thanked him. Then they were left alone. The three did not speak. The fire crackled.

Albion stood and began to pace the room. At first it seemed that the man was merely appreciating the finer decorative elements: a sculpture in the corner of Mary, more embroidered fabrics, stained glass. But William then understood that Albion was making a thorough appraisal of the room and its contents. *Where were the doors? How many paces to an exit? What can be used as a weapon?* William couldn't be sure, but he was suddenly aware that he was making his own list in his head.

Finally, he joined Radulphus and William at a table. "And here we are," he whispered. "We have been invited inside."

They sat for some time in the hall. A servant entered two times during their wait to attend the fire.

"Welcome to the Manor at Strotford," a voice said. The three turned. A man in a long black robe was standing in the doorway, his hands joined together before him. "My apologies for the delay in greeting you, Apothecary Aloyisus, but I am afraid that His Excellency's illness has this household quite out of sorts." He stepped into the room, "I am the Bishop's physician, Robert Peterson."

The doctor's hair was both dark and grey. William liked his face, for in some ways his looked akin to his father, but slightly older.

"How is His Excellency?" Albion asked.

"Ill," he replied. "Quite ill."

"Will we be granted audience this evening?"

"You will, yes. But he is now sleeping. Rest is the best medicine."

"That it is. Let me introduce Father Falio and my ward," the boy stood, "William."

"Welcome to His Excellency's House," Robert said.

Albion's tone then shifted. "Tell me, Robert, if I may be blunt—why is it that His Excellency publicly denounces our herb-lore and its uses—calling the practice witchcraft and demon worship—and he then calls upon me when illness knocks at his very doors? His attacks have been vehement and hurtful. Though I come with my best medicine to ease his suffering, it does not ease the injuries I have sustained from his ideological campaign against me. Does it not seem garishly hypocritical asking his enemy to heal him?"

The physician's response was quick, "It does, and His Excellency will speak to you on this matter, and much more. He is aware that his stance may appear shortsighted, yet, I implore you to proceed with caution," the doctor's voice hushed, "for he is not alone in his convictions."

"I should say he is not," Radulphus' voice boomed. It sent a cold chill through the room. William felt Albion's eyes upon him and he looked up. Only for a moment did the two stare at one another. Albion looked away and placed his hand on Radulphus' shoulder in an attempt to steady him. Radulphus tone sharpened, "For we have met his followers on the road. We have seen the smoke. The piles of ash. The crosses sashed with ribbons of blood. What is this crusade?"

"I beg you," Robert whispered, "lower your voice."

"Why should we provide remedy to one that has raked fear and harm across the countryside?" Radulphus asked.

"Bishop Gravesend's actions are not yours to judge," Robert stated. "It would be wise to hold your tongue and wait to hear His Excellency's thought before you step too far beyond your position."

"As you wish," Albion said, pressing his hand down upon Radulphus' shoulder. "Our charge is firmly set upon healing—and may it please his Excellency, it has nothing to do with magic. Our hope, Robert, is this. Through the use of our remedies and bringing Bishop Gravesend back to health, he will stop his rampage, condone the advancement of our practice."

Radulphus added gruffly, "And beg the forgiveness of the hundreds of families that have had their mothers, wives and daughters torn from them."

"If only it were that simple, Master Aloyisus, Father Falio. I cannot say if his interpretation of scripture will change if your medicine plays a role in his recovery, but God's will is God's will. That cannot be changed by a man."

"That remains to be seen," Albion said.

Robert Peterson held Albion's eyes and replied, "Four of Bishop Gravesend's household wear the simple habit of monks. They are of the Benedictine tradition but they are also studied in arms and warfare. Though their vow of silence helps them to hear God's voice, it also allows them to keenly hear others. Do not besmirch God's word here, I warn. They, like His Excellency, will suffer no evil upon God's earth." The doctor added in a low voice, "Again, I caution you to choose your words carefully when in their presence. I share your disgust at their actions of late, and I share your passion for healing and restoring, but their methods are quite different. They would sooner hack a wounded limb off than heal it. They strike at the root of pestilence, not at its outward flourishes."

A servant entered the room carrying Albion's case of potions. He set it at the feet of Robert and whispered into his ear. He then stepped to the door and opened it, holding it wide.

Robert said, "Your case, Mr. Stell. Our own herb master found three potential poisons in your collection. They have been removed."

Albion raised his hands, "Those poisons, as you call them, are primary elements to many remedies. I do hope you will return them if we require their attributes. To be dangerous, we would need an overwhelming amount—"

"Mr. Stell, they have been removed to assure the Bishop's safety. Now, if you will follow me, His Excellency awaits us."

Albion lifted his case and said, his voice almost laughing, "As you wish. Let the healing begin."

The Final Trial

April, 1988
Coeur d'Alene, Idaho

I have returned.

Helen's lids had been closed for longer than they should. She was daydreaming. She saw crystal goblets glowing red. She could smell the salt chop of the far off sea and the Venetian canals—the musk of Albion's skin against hers. The flaking leather of old books. Her fingers gliding along the spines as she made up her mind which to devour. The hard sparkling rubies around the mask's eyes.

"Helen."

How many times had she felt the *Rathinalya* as she sent gods back across the seraphic gulf? She had lost count. The ravishing chills. A head plummeting to the sea out beyond the Canadian shoreline. The blood smeared leaves on Guam. The time she prowled through the streets of Cairo in search of a *Bridger* responsible for the death of thousands of Jews during World War II. *Evil fuck. Found him.*

Always, always cut them to pieces.

Have no pity.

This was the good fight. And the new war. The silent war that the world would never hear.

"Helen?"

She had proven herself beyond doubt. Albion had said so. She felt a smile. She and Albion would have a child. Her womb ached for a boy. She would call him Edwin.

Albion had promised that they would be together—but not yet. Not until after this final trial. After this, they would be one.

"Helen Craven!"

Florescent lights blurred her vision. She sighed.

Standing just behind her was Mr. Ballard. His voice was angry and sarcastic, "If you're going to sleep in my class, Helen, would you like me to get you a pillow?"

Laughter chattered around her.

I have returned.

Helen Craven sat at her desk in a classroom of twenty-three other sophomore high school students. However, instead of the bell bottomed jeans of her former school years, she was now surrounded by tight, skinny jeans—hair was teased to massive proportions—earrings were the size of plates—bright neon colors were mismatched and worn together—collars were flipped up—denim was acid washed—MTV was god. The first thing she saw when she opened her eyes was the back of a WHAM! tour shirt, proudly worn by the student seated in front of her. She felt pity. Her first thought coming out of her daydream, *What happened to music?*

The world had blended into something unrecognizable since her last experiences in high school in the seventies. The antiquity of her Venetian home over the Atlantic seemed now to be her anchor. It was timeless. Timeless like her blood. Still, it amazed her that she was able to pass for seventeen—hair huge, make up thick, shoulders padded.

"I'm sorry, Mr. Ballard," she said with a layer of practiced shyness, "I was up late studying."

Mr. Ballard made no more of it and continued his lecture.

Helen looked down at her note book. She had drawn the logo for *Led Zeppelin* and just below a rough sketch of the burning Hindenburg airship—the song, *Your Time Is Gonna Come,* echoed in her memory. *How is Jimmy,* she wondered. *I should give him a call.* She pointed her pencil into the drawing and added a last bit of shading. Slowly she leaned her body to the left and nudged the drawing to the right edge of the desk. She waited hoping the boy behind her would see it. She was certain he would, fully aware that he had an eye for artwork of all kinds.

Dark eyes. Long brown hair. His manner was devoid of the neon trend. He said little due to the ever-present headphones strapped around his head—introverted—few friends. She was not expecting him to be as cute as this.

"Very cool," she heard him whisper.

Helen grinned. This would be too easy. Hell, she had not yet even begun to apply herself. She scribbled onto a sheet of paper a question. "What's your name?" She already knew the answer. She passed it back to him beneath her arm.

A moment later, the note was passed back.

It read: Basil Fenn. She then felt the breath of his words in her hair, "Do you like art?"

Sighting

Within the portrait of Loche Newirth

—The far shore. You have come to the far shore, the boy says. His appearance shifts. He becomes Edwin.

Loche's feet feel the heat of fine sand. Or, his brain tells him: sand, heat, fine, loud surf, blue air. He knows that with a single touch from the boy god, the facade would disappear, and he would be surrounded by some impossible chaotic light, hypnotic vibration and maddening vision of infinity. Think sand. Think beach. Think blue sky.

Mixed in the rush of crashing sea, he detects another sound. High on the breeze. A kind of laughter, or singing. He's unsure which. Children's voices perhaps.

Nothing is certain. Nothing can be certain. All we know is what we can perceive. And even that is illusionary. He is reminded of one of his earliest clients. The man had been in a car accident and his forehead had smashed into the steering column. He survived the crash, but he sustained serious damage to his frontal lobe. Many times during sessions the client would claim his soul had disappeared. His soul was taken from him.

It is true that injury to that part of the brain could limit, if not disable, certain emotional and intuitive functions. But the comments, "I have lost my soul. I cannot feel spirit," to this day, haunt Loche. He wonders suddenly if such an injury can eliminate the perception of god, afterlife—soul, do such things exist? It is said that centered just above the eyebrows is the third eye. What if it is damaged. Torn away. Is there still something to see?

Loche stares at the beach and the green trees beyond.

—Do we go that way? he asks.

The sound of children's voices?

He walks away from the sea and into the green.

Not long after he enters the trees he sees a figure standing upon an incline. He wears a black suit and tie.

All goes black.
All air leaves Loche's lungs.

Vault Back

November 6, this year
Mel Tiris, France

"Dr. Newirth! Dr. Newirth!"

Loche's mind flickers like lightning behind shut lids. A crushing pain sears through his temples.

"Doctor!"

Then, he is back. Athelstan is standing over him, attempting to lift his body from the floor.

"An explosion has pulled your eyes from the painting, Doctor. I am sorry that I was not swift enough to brace you."

Loche is on his back. A burst of low percussive thuds. The muffled report of small arms fire. The stone reverberates from beneath the earth to the high tower where hundreds of Basil Fenn's shrouded paintings are waiting. Another clap from below. Dust hisses from the vaulted beams and stone cap.

"They have breached the outer wall," Athelstan says. "But we hold them at the second. There has been minimal blasting, but it is increasing. If they keep it up, they will attract the outer world."

The pain is lessening. Loche rises to his feet and staggers to the slit of a window. Below he sees the inner walls. Flashes and blinks of gunfire. Men upon battlements defend with sword and spear. A high position spits machine gun flak across an open breach. Several bodies are cut to pieces.

Athelstan says, "Did you find what you seek?"

Loche turns, "Not yet. But I feel that I was close. I must go back."

"I will not fail you again. The next time you return from the *Orathom* it will be by your own will, or by my death."

Loche moves his chair and sets its back to the wall. Athelstan positions the shrouded painting before him. "At your command."

"Now."

Silence.
Flash.
Gone.

The One Seed

November 6, this year
Venice, Italy

"You remember my mother, don't you, Albion?" William asks.

Ablion Ravistelle was now standing. His hands are clustered into stone. Julia sees him training his focus on the pouch of leaves. She winces. The puncture wound in her leg is not yet closing, but it is surrounded with white foam.

William speaks again, "My mother, Albion. You do recall her, yes?"

"I do," Albion answers.

"She would often say that there is only one seed, and if it dies, so will all the earth."

Albion shifts uneasily. "I recall."

"The leather pouch? Of course it isn't the same one. I fashioned this just so it might remind you of all those centuries ago when I was a boy." William grazes his palm over the green edges, "I have cared for these three little leaves my entire life."

"William, I—"

"So you understand that if I were to destroy this small plant I hold in my hand—if I were to uproot it—tear it apart, the plant's offshoots, its seeds, where ever they are, will perish."

Albion raises his hands, palms out, fingers spread, "Don't, William."

"If such a thing were to happen, all of your work, your ambition, your revenge against the powers beyond will be dashed. Whatever seeds that you've stolen from this plant, all those years ago will wither. I hold the seedling. There is only one seed."

"Why not kill him!" a voice barks out. "Slice him up, take the plant and be done with this." Julia hates the sound. It is Marcus Rearden.

"Dr. Rearden, please," Albion says without turning from William. "The plant is delicate, as is this situation. I would ask you to refrain from voicing your opinion."

Rearden mumbles something dark to himself.

"Release Julia and Helen to me and we will be on our way," Greenhame says.

Albion finds Helen's eyes and holds them. "No," he says. "I will not be parted from her."

"Albion," she says, "I will go to Edwin, and I will return."

"No," Albion corrects her, "You will not be taken from me."

"Nothing will stop me from coming back—" She tries.

"No! No, I say again." Albion takes his leather gloves from his belt and pulls them on. "Give my friend a sword." From a sheath beside his chair he rings out a long swept hilt rapier. A long, silver blade. "I am willing to place the future I pine for at the tip of a sword. William, let's settle this now. I will not be ruled. I will not allow you to leave, nor will I suffer my love to be taken from my side. No. This time I will err on the side of haste."

Helen protests, "Albion, I will go and bring my son back—"

"Silence!" he growls in command. "Edwin can wait. Patience!"

Julia sees Helen's eyes narrow in anger and she steps away.

A guard offers the hilt of a sword to William Greenhame. He draws it from the scabbard and strides into the center of the room. In one hand, a glinting spike of silver and in the other a supple pouch crowned with three radiant leaves. He assumes a deliberate pose with the sword outstretched and his legs crossed—a kind of ballet posture. Julia thinks of Loche Newirth's journal and the descriptions of William as an effigy upon the psychologist's desk. She glances at Rearden. The two share brief eye contact. A knowing.

"William of the Leaves, son of Geraldine, son of Radulphus, at your service," he says. "Come, sir. Let us, you and I, start anew."

What We Block

November 6, this year
Venice, Italy

Leonaie's feet are dancing. She watches them glide and tap. Her hair dangles and swings down both sides of her cheeks. Beside, her two sisters move in unison. A high whistle is lilting a bright and happy melody. She looks up and sees her dad clapping his hands beside the fireplace. Her mother knits. Bread bakes. Flour dust on the kitchen board.

Then, hundreds of Post It notes cascade like leaves on a breeze. Piles of thousands at her feet.

Here's one:

November 3, Samuel is coming at 3.
Don't forget.
3pm

Leonaie reaches into the whirlwind and plucks another:

Your medication is in the top drawer. Take twice a day

Another:

I love him. I love him. Oh god, I love him.

And another:

Secret courtyard meeting.
It is between us, alone.

Each scribble is a reminder. They are obvious. The memories surrounding each thought, words on paper, memory after memory—experience after experience.

She plucks a handful out of the air. On the first note is a fight between her husband Charles and her. He is furious, violent, out of control. She is cowering, unable to explain her feelings in a way he can understand. She screams that she is leaving. He shouts at her, telling her to go.

She crumples it and scowls.

On the next note is her face in a mirror. Her finger glides along a deep wrinkle across her forehead. Her hair is greying despite her recent salon coloring. Samuel is dressing in the room behind her. He looks as he did the day they met.

The next is death of her mother. She feels truly alone. A bottle of wine is spilled on the kitchen floor. Her son is knocking at the door. She won't answer.

The next note is tears, the following is hate, after that is depression, then there is one with a single word. It reads:

Young.

Leonaie Eschelle opens her eyes. The first thing she sees is Samuel Lifeson. He is leaning over her. His expression is difficult for her to describe. He is smiling but tears have drawn streaks down his face. Awe and confusion are seated there.

"Hello, my beautiful man," she says. "Have I been sleeping long?"

"About an hour," he replies.

"I've got to say, strange dreams. But I feel rested."

"Leonaie?"

"I feel very good. I could eat something, though. I'm very hungry."

"Leonaie?"

She waits. "What?" It is as if her smile causes tears. "Samuel, what is it?"

A mirror rises from the bedside. He angles it so she can see. *"You are the moon. You are the stars."*

Leonaie recognizes the woman staring back, but it takes a few moments to know her—it had been over sixty years, nearly a lifetime since she had seen that face.

The Seed of Poison

April, 1338,
Strotford Manor, England

William could feel the leaves pressing against his skin beneath his tunic. Albion had told him to conceal the plant when they arrived because the servants would insist that it be included with the other herbs that they had brought along. It felt strange to conceal the small pouch. *But there was much that was concealed,* William thought. A deadly poison was hidden within his own sleeve. In his father's soul was an unseen rage quaking for the chance at revenge. Within his own and Albion's blood was a secret power that would fend off death. And in the guise of healers, murderers were in the house.

William thought suddenly that Gravesend's intentions seemed quite similar to their own. *He believes he's doing good. He believes he's healing the world in his own way.*

He shook his head. Too much thinking. The thought of the carved wooden horses came to his mind as they began to climb the stairs to Gravesend's bed chamber. Simpler things. Then a rushing panic and the replaying of Albion's instructions. *Do not touch the potion—I will show you the goblet or the food that you are to taint—when you pour the poison, do it quickly—the vial will have a red ribbon tied at its throat—I will tell you when—I will tell you.* Then the colder directive, *do not pity him.*

As they ascended the stairs, Robert Peterson described the Bishop's condition and symptoms. He was not hopeful for the lesions, the cough and fever all pointed to plague. Albion's voice in William's memory again, *For his life will be taken. Either by illness, or by our hand.* When they arrived at the door, a servant stood just to its right. Robert asked the visitors to wait a moment as he entered. They could hear the doctor speaking quietly, and then louder, he announced them.

"Your Excellency, Apothecary Aloyisus Stell and Father Falio of London."

The servant opened the door and the three were shown into Bishop Gravesend's chamber.

The leaves inside William's tunic seemed to tremble as he entered.

In the wide room, the candles were like stars. They emitted light, but the surrounding walls remained cloaked in darkness. Even the glow of the wood fire in the hearth did not penetrate the corner shadows. An oil lamp was lit upon a table.

The three stood just inside the door. William blinked his eyes as they slowly adjusted. He began to make out the opulent details of the bishop's bed chamber. A four post bed was at the opposite end of the room with what looked to be thick velvet bed curtains. He could not tell a color. A table with a large clay bowl, two pitchers and towels was at the bedside. Rich, gilded picture frames shimmered with the firelight. Upon a wall to his right were two crossed swords over a shield. The device upon it was the Templar's red cross. Heavy tapestries. A musky incense smoldered near the closed window. Despite its fragrance, William could not ignore the stale and sour underlying stench. He immediately thought of the ailing Thatcher and his family near his village, the bloated bodies upon the river, the horrible fumes near the conical piles of ash. The men and children hung by their necks.

When he felt Albion's hand squeeze his shoulder, he became fully aware of another sensation. A sudden and tormenting chill dragged across his shoulders. It pressed outward to the tips of his fingers. He knew, somehow, that Albion felt it, too. Raising his eyes, Albion was looking at him. There was the recognition. There was the *Rathinalya*. William's mouth parched. A fierce thirst—the taste of dust.

Then he saw them, the sentinel monks, and Bishop Gravesend lying in bed. His head was propped up so that he could hold audience. Kneeling at the foot of the bed with palms pressed together in prayer was the largest of the four monks. Standing back against the far wall, with hoods over their heads, were the other three. Robert gestured toward the bishop.

Gravesend began to cough. Gravel in his lungs. "Come nearer," he managed to get out.

With Robert Peterson, the three approached the bedside. William stared at his face—the long nose and proud expression—the pale green eyes. Even in his infirmity, the man exuded a powerful dominance. But he was pale. His long, thin lips were dry and flaking. The *Rathinalya* stung and tingled without a lull.

Albion bowed and said, "Your Excellency." William imagined his mother's raised chin and that flare of defiance in her eye when she faced Gravesend. There was no fear seated in her expression. No vengeance, no anger —but rather a conviction to ease and mend, even when her own life was at an end. *Soil and seed, sun and rain— fire and smoke, laughter, pain,* she said, as she had so many times before. The acceptance of all things and its indomitable circle. He pressed his hand to his chest and the leaves beneath, pining to hear her voice say, "Do not be afraid."

"Mr. Stell," the Bishop's voice rasped. "You must be thrilled to see me lying here—after all that I've done to stop you and your progress in the cultivation of your devilish remedies. You must, too, be surprised, if not insulted, that I would call you to bring your best medicines to liberate me from illness."

Albion smiled. The expression was dry and communicated the dissembling irony. "Your Excellency," he bowed again. Another fit of coughing. The sound was harsh. "Robert has shared with me your condition and symptoms."

Gravesend nodded. "And you know then that my condition is indeed, dire."

"I do," Albion said.

"Is that why you brought your priest with you?" The bishop wheezed a crumbly laugh. "So that he could offer the last rites?"

Albion and William looked at Father Radulphus. The priest's eyes were narrowed and filled with fury. William pressed his hand in his father's closing fist. The *Rathinalya* strengthened.

"I have brought Father Falio to pray for us as we use God's works of leaf and stem to heal you."

Raw and loud, the bishop hacked again. A trace of blood was on his lips when the fit ended. "I'm afraid, Mr. Stell, that it may be too late for me."

"As I've told Peterson, we have come to heal you— and that is what we intend to do. And it is my hope, Excellency, that once you've tasted the effects of my remedies, you will know my true intention—and the Almighty's will."

"Boy," Gravesend said to William. "Boy, come closer. Let me have a look at you."

William obeyed. Radulphus advanced with him and stood just behind. Glancing up he saw his father's face was turned and pointed at the monk kneeling at the foot of the bed. The expression was solemn and quaking with fury.

At the bedside William caught the smell of souring flesh. The lesions were worse than he had ever seen, save the ones upon those that it was too late. But there was a slight pleasure in seeing the cankers devouring this murderous villain. *He is reaping what he's sown*, William thought. Something he was sure his mother might have said, yet, he then wondered if it was just his own view— his own justice. Tears began to weigh below his eyes. *Should one that causes suffering be made to suffer? Is that right? True?* he wondered.

The vial tied to his wrist felt hot. The leaves within his tunic flattened their soft skin to his.

"Boy," Gravesend wheezed. "I see that you are learning the ways of the good earth. Your good master here is teaching you herb lore?"

A heavy tear rolled down William's cheek. He did not answer. He could hear the bishop, but his mind was wrestling.

"Do not fear me, boy. Can you hear me?"

William nodded.

Gravesend's pale green eyes lit for a moment looking at him. Drawing himself up, William met the bishop's gaze. The scuttling chill lessened as he held there. "What is your name, boy?"

"W-william, Excellency," he replied.

"Live in London, do you?"

Albion interrupted, "He does, Excellency. He is of my house."

"I see," Gravesend said. His voice weak and rasping. "William *Stell*, is it?"

The boy nodded.

"Well then, William. William Stell. William Stell that is learning to become a healer. What if I were to tell you that I have been endeavoring to become a healer myself? As God's servant, my words have helped many through these dark days. Praise be to God. Powerful are words. Potent, surely. But they are only words. They will not ease the pains and maladies of the flesh. I am dying, William. And from what I have seen of this illness of mine, I do not think that there is any remedy of your master's that will save me. Slowly it has o'ercrept my poor body—my poor, poor body.

"Oh, I would like to believe that Aloyisus the Apothecary can concoct a drink that will bring me to health. There are many that sing his praises—all of London tell of his miraculous gifts with leaf, berry and stem. Would it not be a wonder if he cured me? Especially now, as these purple sores poise themselves for their final onslaught? The story of my healing would be celebrated. The news would be sung throughout King Edward's realm—Aloyisus Stell brought the Bishop of London a potion, and it healed him." Gravesend laughed—the laugh quickly became another fit of coughing. Pebbles in a box. Recovering, he smiled at William, "People would believe it. Don't you think?"

William didn't respond.

"I would think that Mr. Stell would rather poison me, given the bustlings of a fearful church. Have you ever been out of London, William? Have you ever been east to a little village called Ascott, near Wychwood?"

William felt his eyes widen at the naming of his home.

"Nay," Albion said, stepping closer to the bed. "This is his first time out of London—his first journey—visiting you, Excellency."

"I see." Gravesend bore his focus upon the boy's face. "I traveled through many small villages over the last month, William. There have been whisperings of many remedies—many healers—working their crafts in outlying villages and hamlets. Do you know the kind of healers of which I speak? The kind of craft?"

William could not be sure, but the concealed leaves felt as if they were grasping and reaching—reaching toward Gravesend. William shook his head.

Then he flinched from the shock of his father's booming voice. "He knows the Craft well." The raking thorns along his spine returned. He knew the voice. He had heard his father speak like this at Mass—a voice that was stern, worshipful and filled with both joy and command. But now, it was uncompromising and hard. "We know of the burnings, the killings—all in your name." When William raised his gaze, his father was not looking at Gravesend. The priest was still scowling at the larger, kneeling monk. A challenge was burning there.

Albion attempted, "Excellency, forgive Father Falio. He has had to weather much of the people's suffering over the burnings—"

"Forgive?" Gravesend said, holding back from coughing.

"I should say, forgiveness should be granted to us all, if we could only bear the weight of such love."

The Painter

Orathom

There is a shushing in the air. Leaves rustle. He is certain that the sound is a tree in the wind. But there is more. What is it? Laughter? There are many voices. Small voices. The high, playful sounds of children, some distance from where he is. *Why not open your eyes*? He considers this. But the repose that he has been enjoying, a deep, thick, almost sedated sleep is still heavy upon him, and he is comfortable. Too comfortable. A soft breeze of warm salt air wafts across his face. *Is that the ocean?* He wonders where his face is. The breeze brushes against his feet. He wonders where his shoes are. *Did I fall asleep in the park? Am I stoned?*

Basil Fenn's eyes open. At first, only a twinkling of tiny lights register in his vision. Blurry gaps of sparkling sun through the boughs above. Then shut, open again and struggle to focus. Points begin to take shape, and colors wash in from his periphery—greens and blues—and just as a wind blows a fog aside, Basil sees what he had expected to see—what his ears had told him. He is lying beneath the branches of a broad, reaching tree. Its leaves are fluttering and whispering, and the light glinting through the canopy is gold wrapped within a sheer curtain of blue.

Basil lays still, rummaging through his thoughts—posing open ended questions like, *where did I? What is the? How the hell? Did I really?* Then there's the sound of the leaves, ever-present, hushing his hurried, fragmented musings. He is thankful for the calming effect. *Last question, for now, can I move? Start with fingers.*

The index finger of his right hand responds easily and brushes from side to side. Blades of grass register at the touch. He raises one leg and bends at the knee allowing the bottom of his foot to nestle down into the thick turf—cool and soft. *Movement, check*, he thinks—*now to raise my head and look around.*

Standing is not difficult. In fact, the movement of his limbs nudges the sleepiness aside, and with both feet planted firmly he checks his balance and rubs his eyes. Another wave of half cooked questions, *What the? How the?* The world he can see before him is green and wooded. From his feet there is a long stretch of road, covered with thick grass extending some twenty meters. The path enters under heavy limbs of old cedars and lofty maples. Basil can smell the sea and he can hear the rushing chop mixing with the airy voices of the windy tree tops. He inhales deeply, closes his eyes and breaths out. There is still laughter trailing in the air—the chatter of children.

Basil looks down at his body and sees that he is wearing a jacket and tie, and his feet are bare. Then he slowly raises his hands and reaches to the back of his head, allowing his hand to stop, just inches away, hovering. He shuts his eyes again, squeezes them tight and feels for the jutting bone fragments, the matted hair, the lost piece of his skull, the back half of his brain that should be missing—it must have been torn from his head as the bullet crashed up from his chin and through. But his hand feels nothing but his thick hair and the solid roundness of his intact cranium. He presses his hand against the spot for several moments and breaths intently. He is thankful, he is happy and he is bewildered beyond comprehension.

Vital signs: heart beat, skin is warm, breathing, seeing, smelling, hearing, mouth is dry but he can taste the salt of the ocean air. Check. Now the other vital information—*what the fuck happened?*

He had always had a gift for painting, but the work was dangerous—and he had kept it hidden all of his life—

right up until the end, that is. He met his estranged brother, Loche Newirth, a man that had a similar gift to his. They were in Italy together—abducted by men that wanted to use their works to heal the world and infect Heaven. His and his brother's work was not for men's eyes but for some other entity—gods—beings that were beyond mortal sight—he remembers now. He remembers all of that.

Whatever the fuck.

Basil remembers his only gallery showing—the audience—the faces that had gathered to see the paintings that he had worked his life to complete. Works that he knew would kill many of them if they were unveiled. He raises his hand and touches the stubbly skin below his chin. *The cold barrel rested here—to save them*, he thinks. *I looked at my brother's eyes—I tried to tell him that I understood what he wanted me to do—and I did it. I pulled the trigger.*

A smoke.

Basil pats his breast pocket—both sides, then to the jacket pockets, then stops happily at the right pant pocket. He digs his hand in and pulls out a pack of cigarettes. Latching one into his lips he performs the pat-down dance again, this time producing a Zippo lighter. Click, ring, inhale, hold, burn, blow out—all with a raising of eyebrows and a smooth glance around. *Relax*, he thinks. *Relax.*

Must be dead.

What's the first thing you do in Heaven? Have a smoke would be top on the list.

But this can't be the afterlife, Heaven or, what did Corey call it? The Orathom? I pulled the trigger, I'm certain I pulled the fucking trigger.

The beach is inviting. He wonders if it is truly a beach. There is something synthetic about it. Something artificial. It might be because of the pyramid spiking up through the green land beyond. The pyramids of Giza, Egypt? He doesn't recall an ocean near to the monuments. *Something is terribly strange about all of this*, he thinks.

Basil raises his hand and waves. *Very strange.* Walking toward him from up the beach is Loche Newirth —he looks a little freaked out.

The Kiss Goodbye

November 6, this year
Venice, Italy

Leonaie Echelle thinks of her mother's antique vanity with the two side drawers, the small mahogany table in the center and the gilded frame around the mirror. When she was a little girl she loved to sit and watch as her mother's hands would glide over the vanity's little chrome boxes, fluted glass canisters and bottles. All were filled with instruments as delicate as feathers. Powders and paints that smelled like flowers. Magic happened there. A puff of perfume, sweet lotion and the soft touch of shimmery rose blush, and then she would stand, kiss her daughter and leave for the evening. Leonaie would be left staring into the mirror with a tiny bow of red lipstick upon her forehead.

That was long, long ago.

When her mother passed away, Leonaie brought the Victorian vanity home. Her husband, Charles, helped her to set it up in their bedroom. She crowded the surface with glass jars and bejeweled boxes, as her mother did. She hung her favorite necklaces on the side hooks beside the drawers. She filled the cabinets with delicate things: silk scarves, a velvet box with dried flowers, a bottle of rose water. Once everything was in place, she sat on the cushioned bench and drifted back to that little girl before the mirror. She searched the glass for her mother bustling about behind her, trying this dress, trying that dress. Leonaie was thirty. She lifted a tube of red lipstick and drew a tiny kiss above her brow.

And how did this face return? This must be a thirty something face. Not a wrinkle to be seen. Not a crease near the eyes or a single ridge where millions of smiles had dawned. No rivulets of tears. No years. Leonaie is ninety-four.

"I am ninety-four," she whispers.

"Yes, yes you are," Samuel says.

Memories surge. She is clear. She looks at him. He is glowing.

"You're back," he says.

A light laugh lilts in the air, "So forever is ahead? Forever comes fast."

"Can you sit up?" Samuel asks.

She wonders, *can I?* Her body feels fine. Great, in fact. Samuel says over his shoulder, "Dr. Angelo, can she sit up?"

Dr. Angelo Catena does not answer. Samuel turns. The doctor is nowhere to be seen. "Doctor?" he says again.

Leonaie rolls her head to the right and scans the room. "Doctor!" she calls. "He is there, Samuel." Leonaie rises up onto her elbows.

Catena is sitting on the floor with his back against the far wall. His head is in his hands. Samuel rushes to him and kneels. "Doctor? Are you alright. What has befallen you?"

"Samuel? What's the matter?" Leonaie asks.

"Doctor?" Samuel pursues. "What is—"

Angelo Catena mouths out a kind of drone, "No alone —here. . ."

Leonaie sees Samuel pick from the floor a piece of square cotton, or washcloth. He lifts it to his face and reels. He throws it, stands, and pivots back and away. She can now see Dr. Catena. His head is leaning back and his eyes are swimming in stupor. "Desflurane," Samuel mutters. "He's been drugged."

She sits up. The room whirls.

"What is happening?"

There is a gleam in her periphery. A quick shimmer. Three heavy steps then the sound like a whistle in the air and a subtle snap.

Samuel Lifeson staggers to one side and faces Leonaie. He bangs down to his knees—a scarlet line across his throat. His eyes are wide and his mouth opens as if to speak. As his body falls forward, his head tumbles over his shoulder and rolls to the wall.

Before Leonaie can scream a hand from out of the darkness slaps her face, then the thud of something heavy bounces to her lap. Looking down she sees a severed hand, the skin is white and translucent. She flinches, cries out and flips her legs over the opposite side of the bed and stumbles back. The hand remains on the sheet. It is the hand of Samuel.

Emil Wishfeill with a drawn sword stands just beside Samuel's body. He is watching the blood flow out onto the floor. He takes a nimble step to the side to prevent blood touching his shoes.

"As I have said," Emil says, "I would return the hand. And there you have it. For my father. For my father."

Leonaie is paralyzed with horror. Her mouth opens as if to scream, but there is no voice. Her eyes are glassed and unblinking. Her hand loosens and drops the hand held mirror. It shatters.

"Five years bad luck," Emil says. "Isn't that what you get for breaking a mirror?" Emil moves again to keep his feet from the flooding pool. White foam has formed a collar around Samuel's neck. "Alas," Emil says, "No healing from this one, I'm afraid. Now, what was his famous line to the barkeeper? 'Maria, a bag. Perhaps we should double bag the head?' Something like that." He glares at her, "Leonaie, a bag! A bag! Dear me, I cannot wait to drop his head into the sea."

The room whirls again. A tingle of glass beads chime in her ears. A mist forms in the corners of her eyes.

"I'm afraid you aren't scheduled for termination, yet, my dear," she hears him say as grief overcomes her. "Especially now. You're the third immortal to be made. Albion will want to meet you."

She does not notice him as he moves beside her. Nor does she see the rag rising up to her nose and mouth. Samuel's face lingers like a ghost in a mirror behind her. She reaches out to the bottle of rose water. Her hand brushes over the glass bottles and the filigree boxes of chrome filled with color and powder. She is young again. Forever stretches out. Before he goes to the door, Samuel kisses her forehead.

Test

November 6, this year
Venice, Italy

"I think it would be in our combined interest if you allowed Julia to hold the leaves," Albion Ravistelle says. His sword is raised and pointed at William's throat. "When you fall, they could be damaged."

"Hubris, Albion, hubris," Greenhame says.

"Nay," Albion replies. "It is simply destiny. Out with the old, in with evolution. Remove the gods, remove the greed of man—and you get an earth filled with leaves like the ones you hold. Evergreen and healing. Heaven on earth." He taps William's sword with his, nudging it to the side. "And survival for our kind."

"Such zealotry. You are not seeing."

"On the contrary. It is you that are blind to your bondage." He then raises his voice to the small assembly, "Another thrall is among us. Shall we suffer him to exist?"

"Nay!" the group shouted. Julia recoils from the bursting voices.

As the sound fades away, Albion presses. His sword circles and plinks gently—playfully. William backs up, allowing Albion's advance. Their styles are familiar, almost mirror-like. Their feet shuffle like a dance long rehearsed. Finally, Albion's press becomes a violent attack. His sword extends and his body leans forward into a lunge. Lightening fast, the tip reaches well beyond William's evasive dodge. In turn, William parries the blade, steps forward with his left foot and closes distance. He spins his wrist and slices Albion's left cheek. Blood explodes from the wound as he lurches backward.

"Apologies, Apothecary. I meant to only touch you with the flat of the blade."

Albion does not respond.

Their swords turn and parry in a flurry of moves.

William calls out, "Helen, my dear. Please do consider joining us. Your little boy misses you, and would very much like to be held by his mother." Julia sees Helen's eyes glisten suddenly. "I can take you to him—he is nearby."

Albion hisses and with four bats against Greenhame's blade, at a near run, he finds his target. Albion's blade drags across William's upper sword arm. The hard hit cuts through his sleeve.

"I, too," Albion sneers, "meant the flat."

A door at the far end of the chamber opens. Julia turns to see two more *Endale Gen* guards and a shorter man dressed in grey and black enter. The *Endale Gen* guards push a rolling stretcher in. Upon it is a woman. Silver grey hair, but the face of a young woman. Attractive. Julia's focus ticks to William.

"Ah, Leonaie," he says. "But no Samuel. Distressing."

William moves his position back near to the entrance of the chamber. Julia notices a pair of the *Endale Gen* guards moving slowly around behind him. They draw. As Albion attacks again, pushing William into a retreat, Julia calls out, "Look out behind."

Greenhame twirls his body to the right with his sword outstretched. His sword tip catches the guard across the throat. He falls. William then drops to a knee extending his arm into a stop thrust. The second guard impales himself upon his sword. William does not pause. With a single sweeping motion, he yanks his blade from out of the man's ribcage and circles it through Albion's forward leg. The blow does not separate the limb from his body, but it breaks his ankle. Albion falls to the floor in agony. William rolls his body, shoulder down and rises up behind him, the leaves cradled like a glass of wine. The sharp of the blade finds a resting place at Albion's throat.

"How disappointing, Albion," William whispers. "And it could have been just the two of us. No poetry for you, these days."

With the glimmering blade angled to tear through Albion's throat, William calls out to the audience. His tone is commanding and dramatic, like a stage actor breaking the fourth wall, "So kind of all of you to come, but I would ask now that the house lights be brought up bright, for you have but slumber'd here while these visions did appear. And this weak and idle theme, no more yielding but a dream." He lets out a quiet chuckle. "Aye me, why does my death delay?" He clears his throat, "Friends, drop your weapons, I beg." There is no hesitation in Albion's followers. Swords, daggers, firearms bang to the floor. "Well done. Now then, logistics. Julia, won't you lift from the collection a pistol or some projectile weapon that you can handle?"

Julia finds a small revolver and pulls it into her grip.

"Very good, my dear. Helen, my sweet, won't you step to the stretcher and gently wheel dear Leonaie to the door behind me? Julia, perhaps you might place the barrel of the weapon to the back of her head? I am uncertain if I trust Mrs. Newirth just yet." The two women obey. Helen pushes the stretcher to the chamber entrance with Julia following closely.

He takes a long look around. His eyes stop on Marcus Rearden, "Doctor, do you care to depart with us?"

"Go fuck yourself, William," Marcus growls.

Greenhame is unaffected. He rises. Albion stands with him. The sharp steel nicks his skin. The leaves at the side of his face.

"I thank you all for your cooperation while your master faces the shadow of oblivion." He leans his head to the side and shouts. "Corey, la porta!"

The door behind them opens. Corey Thomas stands with four armed *Orathom Wis*. "Come, William. Quickly."

"Where is Samuel?"

Corey's voice quavers, "He is slain."

"Alack," Greenhame whispers. "Sweet Leonaie."

Corey calls again, "Come away, William. I don't know how much longer we have before *he* comes."

"Then he is here," William says. There is defeat in his voice.

"Come away!"

The far door opens. A figure rushes through.

William, "Julia, have Mrs. Newirth wheel Leonaie into the protection of our friends. Follow Corey."

Running toward William now is Nicolas Cythe. He carries both a rapier and a dagger. He stops just feet away. "Young William," he says, "let poor Albion go, won't you? He and I have made amends. Perhaps it is time for us to do the same. There is much to do between Heaven and Earth."

The man's hair is black. His eyes spiral with green stars. Julia feels a boulder swing inside her chest and pound against her rib cage. A searing rake of spikes crawls over every inch of her body. Everything spins. Tingling needles circling in her vision. Her feet shuffle and she is shaking. The pistol aimed at Helen's head lowers slightly. Corey's hand reaches to her, "The *Rathinalya*. Steady, Julia." She crimps her eyes shut then opens them wide and inhales deeply trying to feel the flat of her feet against the solid wood floor. Leonaie lets out a aching moan from the stretcher. The sound of a nightmare.

Mastering this abnormal sensation, she nods at Corey and pulls Helen back by her shoulder. Helen moves with her.

"Another time, Nicholas," William says. His tone is now solemn. "Another time."

Cythe opens his arms. His head tilts slightly. The points of his weapons are raised like wings. "No time like the present, William."

William presses his blade harder against Albion's throat. Albion's retching forces Cythe a step back. Julia can see drops of blood tapping upon the floor.

"Do not forget, Cythe—I am *Orathom Wis*. Though you might know of me as merciful, I have taken countless heads. Albion is quite aware of the danger he is in—and, I think, you do, too. Drop your weapons."

Helen cries, "William, please—please don't—"

The greenish gold flecks of light in Cythe's eyes flare. Another vicious spasm of chills shudder through Julia.

Cythe's weapons ring as they fall to his feet.

"Back away," William says.

Cythe obeys.

William pulls Albion to the threshold of the chamber. "Follow us and I will destroy the leaves. I will destroy the tree of life."

"Destroy it then, William," Albion chokes. "Destroy it and we will start all over again. I am patient. I can wait. I can wait. I will not be ruled."

"Do not test me." With a heavy shove, Albion is sent rolling to the feet of Nicolas.

Standing in the closing door, William bows with blade in one hand and the leaves in the other. The door slams.

"You have a way out, I pray?" William says as the company moves swiftly down the corridor.

"William, do not test *me*," Corey says. "I aided in the architecture of this stronghold. I knew this day would come."

The Devil Inside

April, 1338
Strotford Manor, England

"William, bring my case to the table and open it, won't you? And Robert, I will need three goblets and a pitcher of clean water." The boy and the bishop stared at each other for a moment longer. Gravesend's eyes pressed him, as if there were words within the gaze.

"William," Albion said.

William pulled away and turned to the case. He hefted the it to the table and raised it up. With the help of Radulphus, he placed it beside the oil lamp. He then clicked the steel latch on the case and opened it. Turning he saw Albion leaning over the bishop. A moment later he came to the table. Looped leather straps held fifty or more glass vials to the lid. The lower compartment was filled with various pouches and envelopes, all organized in rows. William caught the smell of turf and peat. Robert stepped closer to get a look at the collection.

"So many," he said.

"It is unlikely you'll ever see a collection of medicines as thorough as this. Many are proven to ease—some are still in question, but they've shown good results. I do not carry a remedy if it doesn't perform in some way," Albion told him.

Albion's finger brushed along the glass containers, searching. "I've just the thing for that wretched cough, Excellency. I am sure you would love to be free of it." He pinched at a small vial—its serum was blackish. Robert set the pitcher and goblets beside the case.

Albion set to work. With a small blade, he cut the wax stopper from the vial and let fall three drops of the liquid into the goblet. He produced three dried stems from a small envelope. He then moved the goblet to the table's edge.

"William," he said. "Let's give some flavor, shall we?" He gave into William's hand four dried Thyme leaves.

"You know what to do," came Albion's deadly edict.

William took the leaves, and as he reached over the goblet his other hand easily released the stopper from the poison at his wrist. While he crushed the dry herb over a mortar, the scent of lemon bit the air—the poison drooled into the cup. He brushed the last of the thyme flakes from his fingers and pulled his hands away. Albion smiled at him. "Well done, William. Well done." With a stone pestle Albion ground the thyme to a fine dust, poured it into the goblet and then filled it with water. Stirring, he lifted the concoction to his nose and smelled it for potency. "It is perfect," he said. The boy watched the cup in Albion's hands. He felt the cool of the empty glass at his wrist.

But before Albion could deliver the potion, the Sentinel at the foot of the bed rose and stood before the bishop. He was the largest of the four, tall and menacing. His barring gesture was simple to understand, *You will not give this potion without an assayer.*

"Mr. Stell," Robert said, "I'm afraid that we must test your remedies before the bishop receives it. You must understand—"

"Of course," Albion said. "If you would prefer, I will gladly partake of any medicine that His Excellency consumes."

Robert's eyes shifted to the sentinel and back to Albion. "Resistance and antidotes to poisons can be built within the body, Mr. Stell. With all due respect, we believe that one of our own will be a surer trial."

Albion stepped back and bowed, "As you wish." He handed the goblet to the doctor.

"Come, come!" Gravesend said. "Robert Peterson, give me the medicine. I am dead already without his aid. If he poisons me, he poisons me. At least I will be spared a few more days of suffering."

Robert shook his head as he looked to the sentinel. "I am sorry, Excellency. We must test it first."

"Peterson!" the bishop shouted through a series of wheezing, rattling coughs. "You will have Mr. Stell give me the potion, now!"

With another glance at the sentinel, Robert acquiesced. The Sentinel stepped into Albion's path.

"Father Cyrus!" Gravesend commanded. "Bring me the cup." The monk paid no heed. He pulled the goblet from Albion's hand and motioned to William.

Inside the dark hood, William thought he could see a kind of glowing, as if the cleric's eyes were flaring with flecks of gold and green. He held the cup to William's lips, his other hand clasped the back of the boy's head. A menacing shock of a thousand stinging thorns forced the air out of William's lungs. He struggled to keep his eyes from showing the pain. The monk tilted the drink into William's mouth.

The flavor was sour. Abysmal. William thought of crushed insects, twitching legs and larva. Then, death. There was something within him that met the poison. His blood knew the contaminant. A warming rush of adrenaline overwhelmed the lethal drink and within moments the grotesque bite disappeared.

"Cyrus, are you satisfied?" the bishop said. "Now let the boy bring my medicine, won't you?"

The monk remained motionless for a moment only—a slight hesitation, then offered the goblet to William.

As it came into his grasp, William stared into the poison as if it were a deep chasm. Pin pricks of light glinted far down in the abyss—like remote stars. With slow steps, and his eyes peering into the deep, he moved to Gravesend's side. Under his shirt the leaves pressed him back. The surface of the drink now rippled. His hands began to shake.

He saw his mother's eyes. Heard her last words on the grass before the abbey, *"Seek for light in the dark."* Tears trailed in searing lines. The face of this man that killed his mother blurred. Was this vengeance or was it joy? As he drew nearer the *Rathinalya* faded.

William brought the edge of the goblet to Gravesend's lips. The ailing bishop held William's eyes.

But Bishop Stephen Gravesend did not have the chance to taste the potion. William pulled the cup away. He looked into the cup, back to Gravesend, to Albion and then his father.

The bishop, "What are you doing, boy?"

"Give the cup," Albion said.

William's hesitation was like the trigger of a snare. The room around him spun into motion. The assassins' intention was now known.

A shuffling of feet, the sound of drawing steel, a rumbling of heavy steps upon the floor—and then the sudden return of the hissing, crackling hearth. Radulphus had been wrestled to the floor by two of the Sentinels, their swords were drawn and gleaming. Father Cyrus's blade screeched into the light. Its sharp point aimed at Albion, backed against the wall. The final monk was behind William and his blade raised and angled to stab downward through the boy's neck and into his abdomen.

William, with a gentle rotation of his wrist began to tip the cup and spill the poison when Gravesend's hand sprung out, laid hold of the goblet's stem and pulled it away. The bishop pressed the rim to his cracking lips and poured the drink down.

"Excellency, no!" Robert cried.

"I am justly paid," he coughed, tossing the empty cup away. "I am justly paid, for I looked away. I was deceived." A series of deep, concussive bursts from his lungs interrupted. "I will not live to see the dawn. If you have come for vengeance, be at ease. I am paid for my dealings. But learn my cause ere I depart this world. Cyrus! Lower your sword."

The monk did not move. His sword pressed nearer to Albion's throat.

"We will all die here today, William. You. The Apothecary. This priest—the priest I know is your father. Yes, boy, I saw you fall in Ascott before the church. We heard tell that your father was the abbot. I knew your face when you entered my chamber. Do not think the faces of the dead do not visit me in dreams. But you—you live."

Another fit of clotted heaves. "For shouldn't you, young William, be dead? I watched the blood drain from your body. You were left upon the grass. And now, here you are. Alive. I was told that there was but one immortal among your party, but now Cyrus has gained two."

William then felt the *Rathinalya* again. He was now aware that Gravesend was no god.

It was Cyrus. It was Cyrus. He turned.

Father Cyrus pulled his hood back. Long black hair spilled out over his shoulders. He tilted his head slightly at Albion. Albion's face paled.

The monk's voice was low and loathsome. How long had he kept his vow of silence? He said to Albion, "The last time I saw you was just before you gouged my eyes out with your dagger. It was another lifetime. Another life. We meet again. I told you that we would meet again."

"It cannot be," Albion said. "It cannot be. Cythe?"

The monk grinned, "Yes, that was my name then."

Gravesend, "Father Cyrus has sought for you for years, Apothecary. He has held hostage my house, my family, my life—and you are now within the trap he has laid for you." The bishop's eyes began to tear, "God save you. God save us all."

"I shall keep returning, Albion. And it shall be my mission to destroy the *Itonalya* on Earth, now and forever. You, Albion the cruel, will soon face oblivion."

William could not tell if the light in the room had dimmed, or if it was Albion's weakened life force that darkened the chamber. His body shrunk. He was without words. He stared at Cyrus as if he were some phantom from a nightmare. "This cannot be. This cannot be."

"I am beyond the others," Cyrus said.

"Lucifer," Gravesend whispered in terror. "Sweet Lord, protect us."

"Shhh," Cyrus said gently. "Bishop, you know not of what you say. You know only of a picture in a book. A frightful tale told to keep your flock in line. I am vast beyond the shadows of your imagination. Hold your tongue. This is a time for the soldiers of the void to hold counsel."

Begin Again

November 6, this year
Venice, Italy

Leonaie's father is whistling a tune. It sounds strained. She has a fever. She is eight. It is early evening and the sky is the color of a penny. The glass thermometer sticks down jabbing into the soft flesh beneath her tongue. The blankets are heavy but she is still chilled. He removes the thermometer and squints reading it.

She is in his arms. The light bulbs blur passing from her room, into the hall—then the blinding bathroom, white walls with flashing mirrors. The tub is filling with water. It feels as if she is crying, but the tears evaporate as they rise. He lowers her into the ice cold water. She moans.

Above her is fog. Her father's face is disappearing.

Samuel is there.

Samuel's face.

But something is wrong. He is concerned. His mouth is open.

"Darling," Leonaie says. "Darling what's the matter?"

She studies him. His hand is grasping the hair at the top of his head. Tufts are knuckled and shooting straight up.

She screams coming awake. It is not Samuel's hand. The assassin, Emil Wishfeill, dangles Samuel's head over the bathtub.

Leonaie Eschelle sits up. She is moving. Streaks of stone walls blur.

"Samuel?" she cries.

Stop.

William Greenhame is suddenly at her side. He is tucking the pouch of leaves into a small pack hanging over his shoulder.

"Sweet Leonaie. My dear, we are making our way out of this place."

Tears. An ocean wave of grief.

William pulls her into his arms.

A thick coil of gray hair spills down over her shoulder. As her fingers reach to touch it, memories tumble out before her. The skin of her hand is smooth. Soft as moonlight. Beside the cascade of silver hair the hand looks out of place. Her mind rattles between what should be and what is. She has lost all age. Her body does not seem to recall the careworn aches. Her thoughts are not beaded up like drops of mist in the fog. A thumping of steady beats pounds within her chest. Energy and light tugs at the tips of her limbs. There is the quiet sound of water plinking into a basin of stone, far away. The hushed breathing of the woman behind her. The rumble of many running feet a floor above.

The ladder. The moon like fruit in the branches. Below, the courtyard with Samuel. Tea and sweet apples that taste like October sky. *You will be the moon. You will be the stars.*

"We cannot pause here," Corey says through his teeth.

"I can walk," Leonaie says. "Samuel would want me to walk. He would want me to run. To run with him."

"That he would," William agrees. She can somehow see Samuel in William's eyes. They had known each other for years uncounted. "William, I—I do not know how I can—"

"You will heal, I swear it. Come with us, Leonaie. Come with us."

William takes her hand as she steps down off of the rolling stretcher. She looks and sees four men dressed all in black brandishing automatic weapons with swords slung at their sides, Two women, one stunningly beautiful. A pistol is pointed into the back of her head by another woman. She is slightly shorter, dark hair, friendly smile, beautiful, too. Both women study Leonaie with great interest. She suddenly feels self-conscious.

"I am Julia," the shorter woman says. A deep concern in her face, "I am sorry for your loss."

The other woman says, "Welcome to the family."

Poet and Painter

Within the portrait of Loche Newirth

Loche Newirth's feet are wet. He looks down. The bridge. The bridge again. This time, however, he is not far from the shore. Yards only. He takes a step. The floating head of a god holds him above the surface.

Edwin is there—on the beach. No, not Edwin, he remembers—it is the boy god. It is only the boy god.

—I am here, Loche says. I am back.

The boy beckons to him.

Loche takes a last look down. Dead faces in the water. Then, dread overcomes him. Samuel Lifeson's face rolls to the surface.

He leaps over and does not place his foot upon it. Tripping, he rolls onto the beach and looks back. Samuel's face disappears beneath the water.

—That was—that was, Loche stammers.

—Just another immortal, the boy says. Another killer on earth.

—Samuel is gone, Loche says.

Loche backs away from the surf. Along with the crash of waves, the sound of children's laughter is on the air. When he turns inland again, the boy is striding up the sand toward a cluster of green trees. Suddenly, fluttering leaves meet Loche's ears. He follows the boy.

At the top of the slope is the figure he saw before he was shorn away from the portrait. A man in a black suit and tie. His hair is long. Light puffs of smoke drift away from him on the breeze. He is looking around as if he has lost something—turning this way and that—glancing at his smoke—raising his face to the sky—shaking his head. Just behind him rises a massive pyramidal structure. Loche cannot help but think of Egypt's Giza Plateau. Only, the site is pillowed in green land, forest and waterways.

The man notices Loche's approach. He tilts his head slightly and flashes a sardonic smile.

—Hey bro, he says, Looks like I pulled the fucking trigger, eh?

Loche stops, stares and then blinks a few times. It is Basil Pirrip Fenn. He looks like he imagined him to look —or at least close. Maybe the sound of his voice isn't quite right. Or, perhaps, the setting isn't something he could have possibly imagined.

—Hello, Loche manages to say.

—You look a little freaked out, bro.

—Yes, I suppose I am a little freaked out.

Basil looks around.

—Good news is that my mind is not blown. Out from the back of my head, I mean. Otherwise, pretty fucking blown. . .

—Right, Loche says.

—I see that yours is a bit blown. . .

Loche stares.

—You been writing? Basil asks.

—If only I had the time.

—You'll never get a page with that kind of shitty excuse, Basil says. But, I'm a little out of it at the moment. I have a couple of quick questions.

Loche nods. Thoughts are in slow motion.

Basil lets out a kind of sarcastic laugh,

—First, I'm dead, right?

—*Yes.*

—*Thought so. Who's this kid with no face beside you?*

—*It is a Watcher. A god. It sees your paintings.*

—*Far out. He smiles. Not too sure how I feel about the missing eyes. Makes seeing a painting a little tough.*

He takes a long pull from his smoke as he looks the god up and down.

—*I am not sure what is happening.*

—*Yes, Loche agrees.*

—*So, if I'm dead, why are you here?*

—*I am staring at one of your paintings.*

Basil stares blankly.

—*Yes, Loche agrees.*

—*But something tells me that you're here for a reason.*

—*Your paintings are being used to destroy this place, this world, this existence. They are being used to infect the afterlife with the dreads, pains and pleasures of humanity.*

Basil blinks.

—*We must find a way to stop it.*

Basil looks down at his bare feet in the grass.

—*Don't know if you know this, but I'm dead, he says, shrugging.*

—*There must be some way, Basil.*

Basil's voice is sarcastic again,

—*Yeah, last time you said that, you gave me a gun.*

—*I know, Loche says. I know. But you don't understand—I* wrote *that I gave you a gun. I wrote you. I created you. All along we were waiting for my gift of words to arrive. . . and all along, my words were creating reality.*

Loche waits and studies Basil's eyes. His response is unexpectedly astute.

—So, for you, this is the first time we've met? Basil says.

Loche smiles, relieved.

—It is.

Basil reaches his hand out. Loche takes it.

—Nice meeting you. I'm your brother, Basil.

The Two Gods

April, 1338
Strotford Manor, England

Gravesend's lungs heaved again. Blood spattered onto the sheets.

Cyrus' sword tip touched Albion's throat. A tiny cut dribbled blood. "You thought to remove a god from this world—you suspected Gravesend—but I have been at his side, ever. You failed to *feel* the disguise—I wore the church. Now, I daresay, the hunters have become the hunted. Do not move," he hissed. "Watch, now. Kill the boy."

"Nay!" came Radulphus' thundering command. The sentinel's sword that hovered over William did not move. "Nay, you shall not murder my son!" The monk wavered and stepped back as if against his will. His sword lowered and he looked at the hilt in his hands.

Cyrus let out a sigh. "Of course. Of course. Tell me, Albion, when were you going to kill the priest?" Albion's eyes shifted to Radulphus. "Were you planning on gouging his eyes out, too?"

William felt a crushing wave of the *Rathinalya*. It began to make sense. There were *two* gods in the room. One held a sword angled to kill Albion, the other was pinned to the floor: his father, Radulphus Grenehamer.

"Enough!" Bishop Gravesend cried—"Robert! Do something!"

The room, again, swept into a spinning gale. Many things happened at once. Dr. Robert threw his body into the two sentinels that held Radulphus. They were knocked away as one sword clanged down, and Radulphus rose with a bellow of anger. The pummel of the other sentinel's sword smashed into Robert's head sending him to the floor, unconscious.

Cyrus, without hesitation, stabbed his blade into Albion's throat, pulled it back and pounded it into his right eye. Albion sunk to the floor, blood flooding into a black pool on the wood. The air filled with the sound of retching and the smell of metal.

Radulphus now on his feet laid hold of the free sword, and flung it out in a wide circle. The searing edge caught the first monk at the cheek. It crushed the side of his head killing him instantly. As the sword continued its whirl it bore into the side of the other monk. Bones snapped like branches as it entered.

William stood blinking.

From the floor, Albion seized Cyrus' ankles as he turned toward Radulphus. He toppled over onto his chest. Blood splashed up into his face.

The monk behind William shrieked in pain and fell back sending a table of candles down. The cry forced William to flinch and pivot back a step. Bishop Gravesend's arm was extended out from the blankets. In his grip was a dagger. Its blade glistened red from tip to crossbar. "Run!" he wheezed between gravely hacks. He pressed the dagger into William's hand. "Run!"

A lit, rolling candle smoldered at the fringe of a curtain.

A ring of metal against metal spun William around yet again—his father and Cyrus, both with gleaming blades, each were weighing their next move. The monk's blade rose up into an overhead swing. Radulphus' blade met the heavy blow as it fell upon him. The sword glanced away but returned circling to his head. Radulphus stepped back and out of harm.

"Run," Gravesend wheezed, "through there, out into the yard." The bishop pointed to a low, gilded frame. "Pull it open. It is a hidden door. Go! Go now!"

"William," Radulphus shouted, "Do as he says. Run son. I will find you. I will find you."

For a brief instant, William hesitated, frozen at the sight of Albion's bleeding eye and throat, a milky foam leaked from the wounds; at his papa facing what Gravesend called the Devil, and at the horror of *Rathinalya* ripping the skin from his body.

"Son, away, fly!" Radulphus yelled again, this time pressing the boy with his eyes. Flames licked at the curtains. Smoke choked the light.

William reached to the gilded picture frame. It opened on a hinge. Behind it was a black void—a passage leading into the dark. Two more violent rings of metal and he turned once more to see his father's face.

Their eyes met. But in that instant, Cyrus' sword punched through the soft flesh of the priest's midsection. The entire blade flashed scarlet from out of his back. Cyrus twisted his wrist and the blade turned in the wound. He then drew it quickly and turned away. Father Radulphus fell to his knees. "Run, William."

William slipped through the low door and ran into the dark passage. He could feel the sharp leaves flattening to his skin as if trying to encase the bursting heart within his chest. The dagger in his hand was like a spike of ice.

Déjà Vu

November 6, this year
Venice, Italy

Corey Thomas leads the group through a network of dark turns and dizzying rights and lefts. Leonaie is beside William. Julia has lost her sense of direction. Helen jogs ahead of her. Two of the *Orathom Wis* train their weapons at her back. The other two follow at the rear.

"How much further?" William asks.

"Not far. We are well under the canal now."

"Verily, Ravistelle must know of this route."

"Yes," Corey agrees, "but it is one of many hidden escape routes. He will have to make his best guess at which I will choose."

The rock walls are wet. Julia can taste salt in the air. Her hair is matted and dripping from the moisture. In places, small streams of water cross the stone floor.

"I expect resistance once we begin the climb out. *Endale Gen* will certainly be alerted to all exits."

They run forward. At another sharp bend the tunnel floor begins a steep incline. A cool breeze wafts in from the opening ahead. There is little light.

"Hurry now, we'll miss our ride," Corey says. But even before he finishes speaking, his feet slow them all to a stop. Julia knows why, without a word. A sensation of tiny ice crystals, as sharp as broken glass, skitter along her spine. She is certain that William and Helen feel it, too.

Leonaie trembles and sucks air into her lungs as if she is about to plunge into freezing waters. "What is that? What is that?"

William says, "That, my dear, is Nicholas Cythe."

"They are near," Corey says. "Come. Make haste!"

The labyrinth is setting them free. Julia can see a round opening in the darkness. A porthole of sky filled with stars. But it is still far ahead.

Corey pauses and holds his hand up signaling for silence. The group halts. Reverberating through the passage is a host of marching feet coming up behind.

"How far to the boat?" William asked.

"Once we are out, fifty meters," Corey answers.

William lifts the leaves to his face and lets the sharp edges scrape along his jaw line. He peers back into the dark.

"William, come. What's the matter?" Corey says.

Julia touches his shoulder. "William?" There is only the tromp of pursuit. It is gaining, drawing ever closer. Footfalls in the pitch black. "William?" she says again as a thousand pinpricks roll up her legs.

"Lasciate ogne speranza, voi ch'intrate," Greenhame mutters. The sound is sorrowful. "What use? What hope is there?" he says to himself. Julia feels his hand take hers. "But for you, we must. Run!" he says.

The company makes for the exit. Steadily, the round door of sky grows wider. At the edge, Corey pauses. William positions himself across on the opposite wall. The two peer out. There is no sign of resistance. A short path jutting down and to the left leads to a dock. A boat is tied there. Corey pulls a thin penlight from his belt and emits three flashes. A single flash returns.

"Clear," Corey says. "They are ready to receive us."

"Then, let's away," William says.

The company rushes out of the tunnel and charges to the dock. The night is cool. Helen is taken aboard first. "Take her and restrain her," Corey says. Two guards escort her immediately below. The other two take firing positions upon the bow and the stern of the boat. Corey lowers his hand and assists Leonaie onto the deck. He extends his hand to Julia. Before she takes it, she turns to find William. Not seeing him behind her she steps back and turns toward the uphill path. "Where's William?"

He is standing halfway between the boat and the mouth of the tunnel. His unsheathed rapier glimmers by the light of the moon, his other hand cradles the pouch of leaves and his face is upturned toward the hole in the hillside. Words she cannot catch are in the air. He is reciting something. Talking to himself. With each murmur, he paces haltingly back to the tunnel, as if in a daze.

"William? Where are you going?" she whispers.

"Circles," he says to her. "Julia. How we drift in circles. Do we not?"

Above William, Nicholas Cythe steps out of the earth and into the starlight. He looks down and sees William a few yards away. His green helix eyes shine.

"Now," Cythe says, "What does this remind me of?"

Pyramid

Within the portrait of Loche Newirth

Basil Fenn turns his face to the sky. Far off to the East a foreboding shadow has appeared. The blue sky is dimmed by its presence. The boy god points to the pyramid in the distance.

—*What is with the pyramid? Basil asks.*

—*You know already, the god replies.*

—*I do?*

—*You do.*

—*Sorry, I just got here, and I'm not liking the look of the sky. Looks like a storm.*

The god points to the pyramid.

—*It is not a storm. It is hatred. The cloud is hatred. It will devour us if we stay.*

—*Hatred? Basil repeats.*

Loche sees the ghastly cloud. It is enlarging. Black with arms of ragged grey.

—*What do you mean, hatred? Loche asks.*

—*It comes from the many that have come through Basil's work on earth. The paintings have drawn it from their souls like the last breath of the dead. If it reaches us, we will be, hate.*

—*Why do you point to the pyramid? Loche asks.*

—*Basil knows, the god says.*

—*I do? I don't seem to recall. I mean, I dig the pyramids, and all that, but I'm not sure what you mean. Really, I'm still new at this being dead thing.*

—*Let's start toward them, at least. Maybe we'll figure it out along the way, Loche says.*

—*Sure. Sure.*

The three start down the slope toward the shimmering pyramid in the distance. The glowering cloud reaching after them in pursuit.

Roots and Branches

April, 1338
The tunnels beneath Strotford Manor, England

Where was William running to?

The passage before him was pitch black save a single fleck of light far ahead like a guiding star. He ran without heeding the darkness, without fear of obstacles or a broken path—trusting somehow the tunnel was made for an escape such as this. Each whirl of his legs and arms was sure, precise and effortless. Each footfall landed and pressed off with accuracy and speed. The rush of air passing his ears and the brightening flicker dominated his focus. Motion and target.

Far behind him the echo of a voice brought his feet to a sudden halt. "Abandon all hope, ye who enter here! Lasciate ogne speranza, voi ch'intrate!" It was Cyrus. He was in the tunnel.

William sped off again. Faster this time. The *Rathinalya* like pin-sharp cat's teeth gnawing at his throat. The whispered hiss of Gravesend worming its way into William's innermost fears—*Lucifer. Lucifer. Lucifer.*

He knew the name only as evil, as punishment, as fear. He knew the name from the teachings of his father at the abbey, in drawings and pictures he had seen in the village. The malevolent stone face in London staring down at him from a church cornice. The Prince of Darkness. The fallen angel. Was the man racing up behind him the very spirit that his father had warned him of? The ruler of Hell? The center of the inferno?

Fears tangled in William's mind like winding vines reaching for sun—like roots digging in the dark. How similar they both were—the shapes like branches, like labyrinths—mirror images of above and below. Both ever reaching for some life giving force. One toward the light, one delving blind, hidden from our sight. He wanted nothing more than to lay his head upon his mother's breast and breathe in the scent of her skin, lavender and calamus. To visit his father and play with the wooden horses. To accompany his mother as she shared her knowledge of root and berry with those in need. Watch as she would turn a room into a forest glade.

But they were gone. The boy of six springs was now alone and running. The Devil followed.

A cool draft swept across him. The tunnel continued forward, but two more dark openings branched out like a trident. Without hesitation, William wheeled to the right and kept his pace, unyielding and swift. There was no longer a trace of light ahead, but some inner confidence, some inner knowing drove him on without a concern of falling or smashing face first into a wall. It was as if he could see in the dark.

Cyrus would know these tunnels. William reckoned that they were made by Cyrus himself as a security measure for Gravesend—perhaps for himself. If there was a way out, it was known, and troubling that Cyrus probably knew where William was.

His pace slowed. What was the use of running? In the end, he would be found. Eventually, even if he escaped out of reach tonight? How does one outrun the Devil? Go to God? His mother's voice on the abbey green reminds him, "*The Lord is far from this place.*" Even if William concocted some way to injure or even kill the body of Cyrus, *It* would find a way to return. Twenty years or a century from now. He said himself that he had returned for Albion. Now must Albion lie awake at night fearing every footstep out his glass window? Every twig snap? A trap around every corner? What would keep Cyrus from returning for William son of Radulphus?

Young William felt the tunnel curve, and ahead, another glint of light, starlight perhaps. Maybe the moon riding over the wooded ridge toward Ascott.

What use was there in running from gods immovable in their resolve? At least, he might see the sky before the end. He could forget about poisons, graves, bishops, devils and gods. He just might be able to breathe the night air one more time, remember his mother's eyes upon him, his father's booming voice—see the mysterious spheres of fire and ice sprinkled across heaven.

Gain the exit, he thought. *Run.*

What use was there in running from a god? They will track you, they will follow, they will find you and they will run over you. They will trod upon you like feet crushing insects. We are nothing to them. They run us down.

William arrived at the mouth of the tunnel. A moonlit world opened below him. Leafless tree limbs appeared silver beneath the glittered canopy. The moon was brilliant white. The path continued on down a steep hill into the cover of the woods. He could hear Cyrus running up the tunnel. He had discovered the boy's turn.

He glanced down the path. If he was quick, he might escape.

What use?

The boy turned and faced into the tunnel. He then sat down and laid his head back onto the stones, his body half in the hillside, half beneath the stars. An owl, hooted somewhere below in the maze of branches. A gentle wind hurried a single cloud westward. Spring was near. He could smell the dozing green buried just below the soil.

Cyrus' running feet thundered nearer.

He wondered if he would remember this when it was all over. He was told that his kind have nothing beyond. Nothing. It was hard for him to imagine.

The *Rathinalya* flayed his chest and back. The leaves trembled beneath his tunic. They felt like his mother's fingers.

He thought of the steaming bath and the sweet apples on the cart in London. The warm scent of bread and yeast that pulled both he and his father to attention.

"Stop boy!" Cyrus shouted. "Stop!"

Lying flat on his back, William trained his eyes on the bright moon surrounded by the night, and raised his arms like two saplings with the dagger's point aimed into the tunnel.

A moment later, Cyrus passed over the boy and exited the tunnel. He ran a few more paces and stopped, catching his breath. William lowered his empty hands and turned over onto his stomach. He could see Cyrus facing the downward slope to the trees. His sword was white from the moon's glare. His breathing was heavy.

When Cyrus turned around, the dagger was embedded to the hilt through his abdomen. He saw William lying on the stone, only half of him was visible. Cyrus gripped the handle and pulled it from the wound. His shriek of pain shattered the placid silence. He banged to his knees. Both the sword and dagger rattled to the rock beneath him.

Cyrus was silent. He stared at the dagger, dew-dropped with blood. He then inspected the deep breach in his stomach. A stream was flowing steadily out. He raised his green eyes and observed young William. The boy was still lying in the mouth of the cave.

William wanted to ask Cyrus, why? Why, with all of the assumed wisdom, expected benevolence and hoped for sanctity of divine nature, was he a killer? A murderer? A usurper? A defiler? What purpose? What reason? But William was not sure how to ask. He opened his mouth as he rose to his knees and began, "Are you—" but then broke off.

Cyrus stared at him.

William stared back. "Why?" he finally said.

Cyrus did not answer. Instead, the man laid back letting the starlight sparkle upon his swirling green eyes. William crawled to him on his hands and knees. He paused over the wound, flowing heavier now—the blood was black in the moonlight. He swiveled his legs and sat beside Cyrus' upturned, pale face.

The owl called out again in the glade below. A distant crow answered. Cyrus' chest rose and fell in halting rhythm.

William began to cry.

He was not sure of the reason, but he reached into his tunic and pulled out the leather pouch of leaves. Their points turned toward Cyrus like flowers follow the sun. William tore a single leaf from the thick stem. He laid it flat against his palm and then pressed his hand to the sloshing wound. The *Rathinalya* became nearly unbearable. The green of the plant scalded into orange, blood-red, searing to a glowing white. It was like holding a cavern of fire coal.

It was life from flame.

Along the stone beneath them, tendrils reached. Long vines climbed the edges of the tunnel entrance and skirted the descending path. Shoots of leaves and bursting buds of purple and yellow erupted with the scent of sweet flowers and summer rain. William blinked his eyes and wondered at the sight. Wondered if it was real.

Cyrus moaned. The wound was closing. Color was returning to his face. Then, with a scream he sat up. William tumbled backward cradling his blistering hand. The healing vines and flower disappeared, if indeed, they were ever there.

Cyrus rolled over and seized William by the arms. The boy was face to face with Cyrus. His eyes were lightning keen. Twirling flecks of emerald light stabbed into William's pupils.

"And it seems we both share the same question," Cyrus hissed.

There was a sudden trampling of footsteps from the tunnel behind.

"Why. . ." the Devil said.

A sudden jolt and Cyrus' face went blank. The light in his eyes extinguished like a torch in a stream. The grip on William's arms loosened and the man fell over onto his side. Behind him stood Albion Ravistelle, his sword was cleaved into Cyrus' skull.

"Are you all right, boy?" he cried.

Young William of Leaves could only look up. There was no expression the muscles of his face could find. Only the lens of tears. Albion Ravistelle pulled him into a tight embrace.

The Coin

November 7, this year
Venice, Italy

"What, indeed, is a man to do caught amidst Heaven, Earth and the fires that rage below?" Nicholas Cythe asks. He is a shadow against the hillside. "Such a big, deep, heavy question."

The *Rathinalya* tingles. Julia watches William as he takes cautious steps toward Cythe.

"Care to see history repeat itself?" Cythe asks. He looks back into the cave and gestures with two fingers. Out of the dark runs Edwin Newirth. Nicholas pulls the boy to him by the shoulder facing him downhill. In his hand is a small wooden sword. William's rapier drops to the stones. Julia's hand claps over her mouth.

"Who's that down there?" Edwin says.

Cythe answers with excitement in his voice. "Hard to see him in the dark, isn't it. That's what I thought." He then says to William, "I'll ask again, what does this remind you of?"

William does not respond. He takes another step up.

"Now," Cythe says, "*enter—Albion Ravistelle*." Striding out beside Nicholas, a second silhouette appears —with a slight limp and a cane. "We remember what happens next, right? Though, this time, Albion and I have reached an understanding about our positions in existence." He laughs, "Bless my soul, we can play, *This*

Is Your Life. . ." He gestures into the cave again and two men wrestle a heavy set woman out into the night. It is Alice Bath. "Didn't you meet sweet Alice on your journey to Gravesend's house? All those years ago?"

"William," Alice cries, "William, I am sorry. They came just after you departed. There were too many."

"Granddad?" Edwin says.

"Yes," Cythe says. "That is your Granddad hidden down there in the shadows, lad.

"Let me go!" Edwin yells, attempting to pull free.

"In good time, boy. In good time." Edwin freezes. Cythe's grip is now visibly bearing down on the child.

"If only I could bring Geraldine and Radulphus from the earth to complete the game—but, I'm afraid, they are both dead."

"What use?" Julia hears William mutter again. "What use?"

"The leaves, William. The leaves. We will have them. For this time, *I* hold the dagger." He draws his blade and raises it, point up. "And this time, you face another immortal. I have eaten of the fruit of those leaves, William. I am the first *Moonchild*."

Issuing from the tunnel now comes twenty or more *Endale Gen*. The soldiers spread across the upper path taking positions.

Whispers. Again. Whispers. Greenhame's quiet muttering, "What use? *Ithic veli agtig?*"

Julia lowers her hand and steps carefully toward him. "Stay," he whispered to her. "Stay where you are."

Then to Nicholas: "I will as you say. Release Alice and my dear Edwin. Once they are aboard the boat and away, you shall have what you seek, Nicholas. You shall have what you seek. Though, it will not be what you expect." He raises the leaves for a moment.

At the sight of the shimmering green leaves, Cythe unclenches Edwin's shoulder and tousles his hair.

Albion encourages Edwin, "Go. Go to your Granddad, Edwin. Go to your mom." He adds over his shoulder, "Alice. You may go, too. We will meet again."

Alice sighs, "You shouldn't hope for such things."

Edwin runs. His head leaning forward all down the slope. William lowers himself to his knees and catches the boy and lifts him up. "I don't like this place," he says, his head upon William's shoulder, his little arms squeezing tight. "Where's my dad? Where's my mom?"

"Don't you worry my little knight," William says, kissing the boy's cheek. "Go with Alice and Julia. They have a very special surprise for you on the boat." He then whispers to the boy. Julia can catch only pieces. Words from a granddad to grandson. *Love—go fast—magic—see you soon.*

"Hi William," Julia says, now just behind. William peels Edwin from around his neck and places him into Julia's embrace. The boy's arms are crossed at his chest as if cold. As she takes him he leans in and wraps his legs around her. He hides his eyes in her hair.

Alice's face is worried as she approaches. William touches her cheek. "Do not fret, Alice. There was little you could do."

She smiles at him, "Don't you go and do anything rash. Give them the leaves and come along."

William nods. "Get you both aboard." He turns his eyes up the dark hill.

Julia carries Edwin down to the dock. Corey helps her aboard. Alice steps up and faces the shore as the boat pulls out into the waves.

From the deck Julia can see William. He is watching them depart. He waves and turns away as Albion and Nicholas descend to retrieve the leaves.

The three converging men are only shadows now. The sun is rising. A sienna glow touches the distant spires and rooftops of Venice.

The three stand together for a moment. Julia longs to turn away.

Edwin moves his head slightly, "Go fast," he says.

"What?" Julia asks.

"Granddad said go fast. He said, Corey go fast."

Julia looks to Alice. Alice nods. "Corey," she calls, "hit it. Lean on that thing."

Just as the boat lurches forward, Julia peers through the daybreak. William is being forced to his knees. Alice's whispers, "God, no." A sliver of light flashes and swings. Cyrus' sword. A moment later, William Greenhame's head falls and rolls down the slope into the canal. His body slumps over.

Four shots whistle across the deck. They miss.

The wind and the cool ocean air envelop Julia with chills. Cold tears draw lines of ice across her cheeks. Edwin is warm in her arms.

The boy is muttering something. It is hard to hear with the drone of the engines and the wind.

"What? What are you saying?" Julia asks.

"See?" he says, leaning back and looking down to where his arms are crossed. "See?"

Three luminous leaves of green are planted there, as if sprouting from his heart.

"Abracadabra," Edwin says.

Below The Deck

November 7, this year
The Adriatic Sea

Helen Newirth is wringing her restrained hands. The compartment that they have chosen to hold her in has two easy routes out—and a port window—a few well aimed kicks might make a third escape possibility. The two *Orathom Wis* are staring. One has a nervous tick. It could be useful. Certainly, he is the one that will fall first. *I could smile at him. Make pleasant conversation. It would be too simple to gain the advantage.* The zip tie around her wrist might be a problem—at least while they are watching her.

But wait.

Just wait.

She slows her mind.

Why did Albion allow her to be taken? He had said that he would not be parted with her. He made it clear. She is a known enemy to the *Orathom Wis*. If one thing is sure about this conflict, and the wrath of immortals, they do not forget. The nature of the *Itonalya* is resolved, accurate, and they make few mistakes. If they wanted her dead—dead she would be. *But Albion is willing to risk it?* It doesn't make sense. He must have some plan.

Hadn't she done everything that he wanted? Test after test? Hoop after hoop? Years of estrangement? Trial after trial.

She recalls the day she met Basil Fenn in a high school class room in the United States. She was to be his muse. Love him. Get his heart to pulse, his brush to move, his heart to bleed. Get him to fall for her so his art would flow out into the divine.

For a time she thought she had the young artist. But he shut her down. She got too close, too quick. Basil dropped her like a stone into the sea. But she had one more chance —she could still complete the final trial that would bond her and Albion forever—Basil's brother, Loche Newirth.

Becoming his muse was easy. Becoming his frustration, his longing, his desire, his hated addiction— simple. He fell for her, madly. And over a decade, she married him, she massaged poetry from his conservative, psychological mind. He became *The Poet*.

She can hear footsteps above on the deck. More are coming aboard. The rumble of the starting engine vibrates beneath her. She glances at the two guards. They stare at her, expressionless.

She managed to secretly visit Venice and Albion during her relationship with Loche—when Loche traveled to Europe to settle his deceased mother's affairs. Helen lets out a slight laugh. His mother, Diana, was later discovered quite alive and well. But while Loche was in England, Helen was lying in bed with Albion Ravistelle in the very chamber where they had first made love.

The memory stings her. Helen was sent away the following morning. Her final trial was not yet complete. Albion said to her as she stood in the door, "You must make him break. You must bleed the poet's words from him—he must produce work akin to his brother's."

Helen's hands lace over her belly. A child would be the answer, she recalls thinking. An answer to inspire the poet and finally bring her and Albion together.

The boat's engine roars. Her arms push to the wall to steady the jolt of forward motion. The guards also brace themselves. Her head jerks to the port window as four pops of obvious gunfire crack across the stern.

The boat is rushing away toward an escape.

A few minutes pass. The bow has planed out now, and she can feel the steady bounce of chop and speed. They are moving fast.

The cabin door opens. One of the guards steps out for a moment and then lowers his head back inside. He motions to the other guard to follow. The two ascend the stairway.

Helen is alone. She watches the door.

A woman's feet appear first. High leather boots. *Julia,* she thinks.

As Julia ducks into the cabin, Helen notices that her face is flushed pink and streaked with tears. Something unexpected has happened.

Helen restrains a smile. She can see why Loche has fallen for this woman. Julia's face is elegant, framed within long, gentle coils. A key hangs around her long neck. Helen knows the key well. As her eyes drop down the length of her body, she notes the athletic frame and the solid but delicate stance. Her eyes halt on Julia's right hand. In it is a gleaming blade.

Helen's focus darts to Julia's face—wet tears are shining upon her cheeks.

A few short steps forward and Julia kneels down and brings her face close to Helen's. Helen holds her gaze. Julia then looks down. She raises the knife with one hand, and stares at it.

It is Julia's turn, Helen thinks. Her body tenses and prepares for pain. The cold steel hovers in the air between them.

Then, Julia squints and appears to shake off a dark thought. She raises Helen's zip tied wrists. She slides the blade beneath the plastic and cuts the restraint.

Julia stands, walks to the door. With her back to Helen she says: "William Greenhame is gone. I thought you should know."

Helen doesn't respond. *Why did Albion allow them to take me?* she wonders.

Julia opens the cabin door, "His grandson is here to see you."

Edwin Newirth peeks around Julia's legs and sees Helen. "Mommy!"

Helen drops down to the floor with her arms open wide. The boy runs to her. He smells like the sea, like trees, like warm sheets, like candles, like home.

Julia does not turn. She stands there for a moment with her back to the reunion. She then climbs out of the cabin and closes the door behind her.

"Mommy," Edwin says, "Where is Dad?"

"I don't know, baby. I don't know."

The Ancient Realm of Wyn Avuqua

Within the portrait of Loche Newirth

—Behold, do you not see the battle below?

The road to the pyramid opens on an overlook. Loche and Basil discern the shapes of men and streaming blurs of light rising and falling from the sky to the earth. On the ground, men and the luminescent forms clash—all are arrayed with weapons, armor and bright heraldry.

—What is this? Loche asks.

—Do you not know?

Loche looks again and strains to make out details.

Immediately, he sees the banners of the Orathom Wis. The Single Eye on a field of green. He sees the outer walls of Mel Tiris, the high tower housing the paintings—a light within. Smoke rises from a blast point near the main gate. Many bodies lay broken, bleeding and dismembered. George Eversman is there. He rallies a counter attack at the third wall. Upon the ramparts, high ladders have been raised. Soldiers swarm the high battlements. They wear the livery of some strange device—a ladder capped with a moon. A helicopter thrusts upward and riddles the defenses with machine gun flak.

—Albion, Loche says.

Again, he blinks. The helicopter melts away. It is replaced with a flock of black birds exploding from a tree. It is no longer Mel Tiris. It is a conflict far older. The architecture of the stronghold transforms. There is a pyramid at the center. A lake stretches out southward like a ribbon of indigo on green grass. Pulses of light, prismatic and bright, pummel the structures below. Banners of the Eye burn on poles. More godlike forms return and flood through defenses like molten steel.

—Wyn Avuqua, Loche says.

—*Yes,* the boy god agrees. *You know of Wyn Avuqua. You created it with words. It did exist.*

—*Why do I see it now? Why is it burning?*

—*You see it now because strife will always exist in memory. You witness the end of the great realm. The last revolt of the Itonalya against Thi, The One. If the doors do not close, the powers of the Orathom will descend again. They will destroy the earth. Now, behold, Wyn Avuqua as it once was.*

The battle fades. The pyramid is silver in the sunlight. Its high tip sharp against the sky. Woodland and expanses of deep green enfold the structures below. A great wall encircles the citadel—low buildings of all sizes, and high castle-like towers of white stone. Glowing banners with the Single Eye fly high in the wind.

—*The Orathom Wis adopted many traditions for their city. The influence of the pyramids of Giza, for example, found a place in the ancient realm.*

—*Julia,* Basil says, suddenly.

—*What?*

The mention of her drops a stone into Loche's chest.

Basil turns to Loche.

—*She will meet us there. She will meet us there.*

—*What do you mean?*

—*I'm not sure. The pyramid—like the ones in Egypt. The smaller one. . .*

—*What are you saying?*

The boy god interrupted.

—*Pyramids were once used to bridge the gap between here and there,* he said. *Painter, you must return.*

—*Return? I just got here.*

—*I was sent to find you,* Loche says. *To find a way to close the doors.*

—*I thought I already did my part,* Basil says.

With his hand in the shape of a gun, he holds his index finger to his temple and pulls the trigger.

—*Wasn't that the point?* he asks.

Loche looks away to the massive structure in the trees. The dark sky on the horizon is moving.

—I do not know, he says.

—I've got an idea, Basil replies. Why don't you just sit down and rewrite the fucking thing? If all of this comes from your pen, and not my brush after all?

—It is not that simple, Loche says.

—Yeah? Try putting a gun under your chin. . .

The boy god again:

—You cannot truly return, Basil. Your place in existence is here. But your essence can cross over. You can bridge.

—What good can that do?

—You shall become what is called a muse.

—A muse? Basil asks. Ah, I get it. The whole resurrection bit. Don't I get three days here, at least?

—The clouds gather, the boy says. They multiply. Basil, you could not close the Centers of your paintings while you lived. If you return as a Muse, you can assist Loche in closing them, forever.

—How am I supposed to do that?

Thunder booms.

—Loche, you are being called, the boy god says.

His face transforms into Edwin.

—They call you. They call you.

—Basil, go to the pyramid, Loche says. Go to the pyramid.

Loche struggles against a current at his feet. Something pulls him.

The boy god, the pyramid, the grim sky to the east, his brother, Basil—disappear.

All is black.

The Water's Eye #2

November 9, this year
Terciera Island, Azores, Portugal

Green divided by stone and ocean mist. Loche Newirth stares out the window. He has been awake for only a few minutes. It has not occurred to him to question where he is just yet. A fire still burns behind his eyes. With every blink to wet his dry corneas, come flashes of Basil Fenn—in a black suit, smoking a cigarette, and dead —a gleaming silver pyramid—a faceless, translucent blue god hovering just inches off the ground. Rotting heads in the surf. The green view through the window is like cool and delicious water. His eyes drink it in.

He is afraid to look at the ceiling above him. He imagines an eye is painted there. Streaked and slathered in red paint. He is relieved that there are no Post-It notes stuck to the glass. Hazarding a look to the walls he detects no evidence of another of his mental breaks—if, indeed, that is what happened to him a few days ago.

Moving his fingers, he realizes that his hand is interlaced with another. It is Julia's. She stirs and lifts her bowed head.

"We have to stop meeting like this," Loche says.

She rises and lays her body across his and kisses him. "Thank God," she says.

"That was what I was going to say," he replies. "I like the look of the world outside." She kisses him again. "But, where are we?"

"The Azores, in the middle of the Atlantic."

"How did we get here?"

Julia sits up and places her hand upon his chest. "That will take some explaining," she says. Her voice is low, pained. "We lost *Mel Tiris*. You were unconscious when

Athelstan and George pulled you out of the painting. There are only a few of *Orathom Wis* left."

"What of the paintings?"

"Captured by Albion." She pauses and squeezes his hand. "He has the journal, too."

Loche sits up. His back is stiff. "Are you all right? Edwin? Is Edwin safe? Where is—where is my father?"

"Edwin is fine. He is asleep in the next room with Helen."

"Helen is here?"

Julia nods. "And is she a piece of work. . ."

Loche feels his shoulders tense. Lines of stress gather at the corners of his eyes.

"She's been fine. But Corey does not trust her, so they have people watching her closely."

"I want to see William," Loche says as he pulls the covers back. "He did it. He really did it. He brought all three of you back."

Loche can not help but notice Julia's eyes flood. She looks away.

"No," Loche whispers. "No."

Behind his closed lids the bridge bubbles to the surface of that inky sea. He refuses to look down. He refuses to take another step.

"He is gone, Loche. But there is more," Julia says.

Loche opens his eyes. Julia raises a closed notebook from her lap. The cover is red—slightly worn. A crease across the center.

"When they got you out of *Mel Tiris*, they took you to a safe house before flying here. Athelstan witnessed you rise from your bed and—" she breaks off and pushes the notebook into Loche's hands.

"And, what?" Loche asks.

"Seems you've been writing," she says.

Moons and Ladders

November 9, this year
Terciera Island, Azores, Portugal

Leonaie Echelle is looking out over the stone fences, hundreds of squared green pastures and the ice blue Atlantic beside.

The symmetry of the grid-like partitions netted over Terciera remind her of the Tuscan vineyards she saw on the flight away from Italy.

That memory reminds her of wine.

Wine reminds her to look at her cell phone to press that single button that shows the time—it could be time for Olivia to bring wine to the courtyard for her secret meeting.

The secret meeting, of course, reminds her of her Samuel.

Then she recalls Shakespeare's *All's Well that Ends Well,* and Samuel's poem tucked in at page 713. Though Samuel may have been a mediocre poet, the words are to Leonaie, a prayer. She whispers:

> *How did we raise this ladder*
> *From under that heavy husk*
> *Of water, waves and still, empty space?*
> *And where are we off to now,*
> *Climbing together*
> *Out of the grave deep,*
> *Upon this wooden, swaying ladder?*
> *Up and up.*

Now it all connects. Maybe that is what memory is— just a ladder, rung after rung, connecting thought to thought, feeling to feeling. Lifetime to lifetime.

Eventually you circle back to the place you started. It occurs to her that the grid-like landscape looks like a ladder—a ladder beside the sea. And she is now an *Itonalya* as Samuel once was. She has reached the moon.

> *I will be the moon.*
> *I will be the stars.*
> *I am no longer an empty shell,*
> *Come from the sea filled with the sound of the*

void.

Immortality, it was thought, could only be achieved through memory. Through what one leaves behind in words or deeds. Names kept alive through the centuries. We can choose the stories we wish to remember. Sometimes it is hard to forget the darker rungs on our ladders.

Leonaie can see her transparent reflection in the window. Her mischievous smile curls slightly in the corners of her eyes. In the last couple of days her hair has lost much of its silver sheen, returning to her former light brown. Her body has tightened, tummy flattened, and her breasts have climbed back up and taken their rightful place at the center of her chest. Her bottom, too, has firmed. How Samuel would melt if she were to wiggle it just a tickle for him now. He would melt right here.

She bows her head.

What now?

What now?

The sneering face of Emil Wishfeill enters her mind. Her hands compress into fists at her sides. She inhales and struggles to calm her rage. To deaden the sudden thunder of hate. Memory. Emil will be the disease to break from the ladder. A rung to be removed. A rung serving no purpose. She will replace his memory with a foothold painted with his blood.

She presses her hand against the glass. She waits through the afternoon and into the evening until the moon rises. When it climbs up over the ocean, drifting high above the cross-hatched land below, Leonaie says goodnight to Samuel Lifeson. She steps down that imagined ladder, turns from the window and closes the curtain. She removes her clothes, slips into bed and prays for him to visit her dreams.

Action Figures

November 10, this year
Terciera Island, Azores, Portugal

Loche peels Edwin out of his underpants and adjusts the faucet on the tub. The boy stands with his hands on the edge waiting for the go ahead to climb in. Loche drizzles bubble bath into the water. A white mountain of suds froths up on the surface.

"Now?" Edwin says.

"Now," Loche replies.

"But I want Luke and Han and Spiderman and the monsters."

"Where are they?" Loche asks.

Julia, in the next room, calls out, "I've got them."

A moment later, a handful of plastic action figures fly from the doorway and plunge into the water.

Loche sits on the marble floor. Julia enters and sits beside him.

"He was starting to smell," he tells her.

"How was the meeting?" she asks.

He does not reply. He looks at Edwin, and then his eyes move to her. Then back to the drama unfolding between monsters and men.

"What?" she asks.

"It is set. We leave for Cairo in two days."

"All of us?"

"You and I, Corey, George and Leonaie."

She nods to Edwin, "What about. . . stinker, here?"

"Edwin will stay here with Helen, Alice and the few remaining *Orathom Wis*."

"Will she try to run?"

"If she does, George assures me that she'll fail."

"Do you think Basil will be at Giza?" she asks.

"I don't know."

He sees it crash in on her, again—death, afterlife, immortality—the unstable walk in between. Her hands rise to her weary eyes and she covers them. "My God," she says. "So crazy. All of this. In the painting, what—what was the first thing Basil said to you when you met him?" She lowers her hands.

Loche smiles. "He asked if I had been writing."

Julia laughs. "Really? What did you say?"

"I told him that there hadn't been much time for it."

She grins.

Edwin interrupts, "Dad, are you done with your book yet?"

"Not quite," Loche answers. He looks at Julia, "The notebook—the red note book—you're certain no one has looked at it? No one has read it?"

Julia nods, "Yes, I am sure. George thought it would be dangerous. Have you?"

"No. Not yet. I must wait. I—I must—" he broke off.

With one hand, Edwin dives Luke Skywalker from the tub edge into the bath, apparently in pursuit of some monster from the depths. "Are we still writing the good stories?" he says with the splash.

"That's all we can do."

Loche's eyes freeze on the surface of the water as Edwin lifts Luke and walks him along the floating bodies of action figures.

"That's all we can do."

Horses

August, 1350
London, England

"It takes near to a month, sometimes longer, for a leaf to grow from the stem once one is taken," William of the Leaves said.

Dr. Robert Peterson lowered one of the leaves into a steaming cup of water. The scent of warm earth and citrus rose into the air. He lifted the cup to his lips and sipped at it.

"My lord, Albion the Apothecary, has taken the only seed the plant has produced over these twelve years to see what can be cultivated. Our hopes are for healing herbs. Alas, there has been nothing yet. How I wish for more. Once I leave you, I journey to Italy to meet him."

The Great Plague had come ashore and ravaged England. The Great Mortality. Countless had been infected. Countless had died. Blackened skin, lesions, convulsions, pain—death.

William had seen it before.

William had seen death in many forms over his short life. But never quite like this.

William was now eighteen.

"You have grown tall," Robert Peterson said. The doctor's wrinkled hand stirred the tea. Lying in a soft bed beside the window was his wife of twenty-three years. The plague was devouring her. Sable caps of skin tipped her fingers. Blood stained the sheets near her sleeping face.

The doctor leaned down bringing the rim to her mouth. "Drink, my sweet," he said, gently. "All will be well. All will be well." He began to cry.

The woman opened her mouth and the drink fell in. She swallowed. A moment later, she opened her eyes.

"Something is happening, Robert. Robert! Robert! I can feel the sun seeking me. The winter is passing."

Robert sat beside her and wept.

She fell back to sleep shortly after another sip. The blood red lesions were already fading to pink.

William stepped out of the room and into the summer morning sunshine.

Healing the vast numbers of sick was impossible with only three leaves, but he could do his best to give a few doctors a kind of immunity so that they could at least ease those that suffer. The leaves did not grow with the same speed as the pestilence. And there were only three. William did what he could. When Robert Peterson's letter came, telling of his wife's coming demise, he rode in haste.

The doctor looked much older than the last time he had seen him. His hair had washed to a silver-white. There was still a raw scar across his forehead from that horrible night, long ago.

William recalls being carried by Albion back into Gravesend's chamber and seeing the doctor sitting with his back against the wall and a servant pressing a cloth to a wound upon his brow. It was Robert Peterson that set William's escape into motion by sacrificing himself and attacking the monks that restrained his father.

"Thank heaven, the boy lives!" William remembers the doctor saying, when they returned. "Apothecary, well done."

Bishop Gravesend coughed quietly to the cleric at his side, "The boy. There is the boy!"

William pulled against Albion to be set down.

He ran to his father lying on the floor. It was too late.

He stood looking down upon his half-open eyes. Radulphus was statue-like—peering into some vision beyond the room.

William had seen death before.

In tears, William spun and went to Gravesend's side. *Healing is all there is*, he remembered thinking. His fingers felt for another leaf from the pouch.

Before he pulled if from the stem, Gravesend said, "No, William. I am paid. The Devil has paid." Then, with failing breath, to all in the chamber, he whispered, "The boy, the Priest and the Apothecary defended me against Cyrus. See them safely back to London. Cyrus and his followers made an attempt on my life. I go to the Lord. Praise be to God." The Bishop of London spoke no more.

William tucked the remaining two growing leaves beneath his tunic.

There is something about the slant of light as autumn approaches, the William of eighteen summers thought. As if the sun, in its circle around the earth, shifts its glorious, brilliant attention to something other than us. While it looks away, our shadows grow longer. Our days shorten.

William pulled his boots off and set them beside the door. He stepped onto a clay path that was still moist from morning rain. The high sun warmed it beneath his feet. Above the sky was dark blue. Not the midsummer bright sky of June and July. It was hazed with an angled light. A few dingy weeds, a delicate whitish-green, grasped for life beside the road. Eight to ten corpses were piled a few feet away. Their arms and hands were black and smeared crimson. Clouds of flies. A small fire smoldered just beyond the neighboring hovel. The air was curdled and acidic.

William wondered why the seasons circle around us. Why, over and over, we were forced to witness spring into summer, fall into winter—birth into life, aging into death? Year after year. Why would the divinities in their spheres have any interest at all in these horrors we endure?

Treetops rustled. A few poplars arced in a welcome breeze—a breath of distant flowers. William inhaled it. His horse neighed at the scent.

It was time to go.

Across the road, three young, stick-thin children watched him through a low hedge. Dr. Robert said that he had taken them in when their parents had died. With a glance at the pile of bodies beside the road, William hoped the parents were long buried or burned.

The children stared at him. Their little dark eyes were wide and curious.

William pulled his boots back onto his feet. He reached into his saddle bag and produced four wood-carved horses—one black, one grey, one green and one blue. He held them up so the children could see. The oldest, probably seven-years-old, grinned at the shining toys. Slowly he stood up, took hold of his brother's hand. His brother in turn took hold of his little sister's hand, and the three circled around the hedge.

William set three toys on the clay path. Their noble frames carved in the shapes of swift galloping steeds— furies of motion. As the children began to play, William climbed onto his saddle and turned toward the road leading out of London. He held the blue toy horse up and examined the leg—still wrapped with a leathery tendril from a sorceress.

Here ends Part Two of The Newirth Mythology

Acknowledgments

Thank you to my grandparents, Ralph and Gerry Koep, and Bud and Leona Weiser, and my parents, Kenneth and Diana Koep. For unwavering support and creative influence, my deepest gratitude to Stan and Jo Lynn Koep, Bob, Bobbi and the Bean, Eric and Laurie Wilson, Scott Clarkson (*caw minle*), Dani Clarkson, Mark Rakes, Cristopher Lucas, Cary Beare (*Belzaare*), Geri and Walter Perkins, Michael Herzog, Mary Starkey, Dan Spaulding, Tom Brunner, David and Lisa VanHersett, Steve Gibbs, Karolyne Rogers, Randy Palmer (Vlad), Andrea Brockmeyer, Margaret Hurlocker, Terry and Deon Borchard, Anthony Nelson, Jeff Hagman, Adam Graves, Elizabeth Stokes, Blair Williams, Paul and Shannon Erwin, Toby Renolds, Kevin Jester, The Bread, The Rubbish, all at the 315 Greenbriar Inn, The Iron Horse, and The Cd'A Arts and Cultural Alliance. To *The Core*, Mark Lax, Greg and Sara White (the minglers of dreams and making), thank you for your belief, and encouragement. Heartfelt thanks to my editor, Allison McCready (*Luminaare*), and Will Dreamly's Andreas John for guidance, scotch, and enthusiasm.

My love to Lisa and Michael.

⟨ᛏᚱᛉᛝ ᛋᛞᚢᛈᚱᛏ ᛁᚱᛪᛁᛋ ᚻᛘ ᛏᚢᚠᛁᛏᚱᚻᛝⱶ

thia alyoth thave ni tunefore

the final installment,
Part Three of the Newirth Mythology,
The Shape of Rain

2018